CW01213862

Drought

A. J. WILKINSON

Merry Christmas

Copyright © 2023 A.J. Wilkinson
All rights reserved.
ISBN: 9798865349112

To Cheese and Bean.

ACKNOWLEDGMENTS

October 2017, Zanzibar. Pencil hit paper. It felt right to use pencil. And paper. Handwritten. Old school; like Austen, Conan Doyle, Chaucer and Dahl.

Several years prior, my eldest son had playfully asked me what would happen if all the water in the world disappeared. The following 500 pages are what happens when a father with no literary heritage or affinity for books, writes a novel to answer that question. The inspiration behind our leading man was a Maasai dude who sold us jewellery on the beach. It would be poetic licence to say he was a warrior or called Peter. I suspect he wasn't a professor either. But he carved a mean keyring.

There have been multiple locations along the way besides Zanzibar: (Mauritius, Greece, Bali, The Alpes [more than one and more than once}, The Lake District, Gomshall, Coughton, Bradford-on-Avon and Wales.

Ongoing inspiration came (and still comes) from my sons, who feature heavily in all their guises throughout the book, who unfailingly remained positive through the years, at least to my face, about the unfolding storyline and character development. I think my wife will just be glad it's done and hoping the talk of a second novel doesn't come to fruition. Although it does feel a good nugget of an idea…

For editing support and accompanying relentless pressure to finish the book, I am so grateful to Dusty Book (thank you Scarlet) for her persistence and motivation to complete. And finally, thanks to Ellie for her meticulous proofreading and inspiration for the cover.

Prologue

Berlin, Germany

In Berlin, Professor Peter Masai was driving to work, locked on to the radio, listening to so-called experts discuss climate change, making him more and more animated as what he was hearing was making his blood boil.
"Rubbish," he said to his steering wheel, "they know nothing." He had a theory that he suspected no one would take seriously, but he was convinced.

Johor Bahru, Malaysia

Malaysia was always hot, and it was hard to tell if it was hotter and drier than usual or hotter and wetter: there was just constant heat. Elaine Shreeves, née Brennan, felt like she'd lived in every city of the world, without having lived a life in them. She was always on Facebook these days, a bored expat housewife, overeducated and understimulated. This month's craze was the rather unfortunately named hole-tag. Gotta find news and images about sinkholes and tag them, forget the previous ice bucket challenge - that had cost her her dignity and $100. At least sinkhole tag was free, and she didn't have to get wet or cold. So far, she had 32 holes tagged, Margot only had 18. That was important. She had a bunch of expat ladies in her social network and there is an unspoken competitiveness amongst expat spouses about materialistic one-upmanship; whose kids are doing the best, whose house is the biggest, that kind of trivial thing, so having more than Margot means Margot can't gloat about that at least. Plus, Elaine had the knowledge to understand what a sinkhole actually was, she'd just not been using that knowledge for years now.

Same as Peter Masai, she was an alumnus of Manchester University but had chosen a married, admittedly jet-set, lifestyle over a career. She literally chose geography over geology. Regret? Yes, but too late for that now. She'd married a meteorologist called Mark, ten years her senior, kindred spirits at the time, but now he wasn't even a weatherman. He taught weathermen about being weathermen. You almost couldn't make it up, but he'd found a niche - a brilliant, inquisitive scientist now gave TV lessons to shiny wannabe stars. Sold out but boy did the world need great weathermen (and women), according to Mark at least. Also, it kept Elaine in Gucci. But that wasn't enough for her anymore.

Washington DC, USA

After graduating from Manchester University, Jeff Williamson went to New York to do a four-year PhD in climatology, then landed a plum job in the US State Department's Environmental Bureau - advising on trends and ultimately policy. There was a big difference between working on a PhD and working in government. For a start, the government tells you what to think and you have to find the research to back it up. Against his better judgement and that of almost all his scientific colleagues, Jeff spent his time interpreting data to rebuke commonly held beliefs on climate change. It made him a bit sick, but he was quite proud of his achievements - very little evidence supported the evolving government position but like all his workmates, he knew maybe one day in three, perhaps eight, years, the president would change and so would policy. It was just a waiting game, but one that compromised his integrity. He drank a lot and smoked too much. But he had no one in his life to impress so what the heck, you're only young once. Jeff's problem, and well he knew it, was that he wasn't young anymore. He desperately wanted life to begin at forty, so fingers crossed for three months' time.

DROUGHT

1

Washington DC

The one thing Jeff had almost unique access to was global data, reams and reams of the stuff. He knew when every tide was high, at least he could find out, if it was normal, what proportion of the globe was covered in the sea at any time of day, the temperature in every city on every continent and, as he occasionally thought of *her* in Malaysia (or wherever she is now) he knew where every damn sinkhole was on the planet.

Sinkholes. The talk of the Bureau. As it was with 'lady falling into the pavement' on YouTube all those years ago, but now they were getting a little too frequent to be put down solely to bad road construction or leaking pipes. Jeff was pretty sure there were not a lot of pipes in the desert and some parts of the Sahara were starting to look like a colander made of sand.

The official US Government position, and therefore by default the official global position, was that sinkholes come around a bit like Halley's comet - a natural phenomenon that a few hundred years ago would have signalled an apocalypse, now it's just something you were likely to see twice in a lifetime if you got old enough. The critical difference here, and Jeff had admiration for the nerve of the Bureau, is that it was bollocks. No one had ever heard of, or had proof of, such a proliferation of holes just appearing in the ground like this.

Jeff was no psychologist; he was far from it. He was a

'spade's a spade' kind of old-school guy, but he was impressed by how a fabrication of the truth could be used so convincingly to keep the public calm. Any scientist who spoke out against the 'accepted' theory was hastily put on the US government payroll, in whatever country they happened to live in.

The list of global geological experts who now worked for the US, or for that matter any G20 power, was growing weekly, a fact duly celebrated by the president, who made a point at his latest press conference to say: "We've the finest minds from all over the globe working for us, researching for us, for you, to protect the US and global population from natural disaster."

Oh yeah, thought Jeff, sometimes out loud, *it was always natural.* Each time he heard this phrase he'd mutter 'man-made' under his breath.

Amusingly, depending on your standpoint, it nearly cost him his job a few months back. Jeff was hosting a climate conference (although 'hosting' was a stretch, he had a small presenting role in part of the team who were technically hosting the conference). Either way, Jeff had totally forgotten he was miked up at the time, and during the keynote speech, the Environment Secretary cleared his throat for the big crescendo about protect and serve, or some throwaway buzz words about avoiding natural disaster, for the media hacks in the room, and clear as crystal over the speakers came an echo. Although echoes usually repeat what was said, this echo very clearly turned the word 'natural' into 'man-made'.

Jeff was as lucky as he was stupid. He was stupid to forget he was wearing a microphone two inches from his big mouth and three meters away from his boss' boss, and he was lucky that a couple of student protestors had made their way into the hall carrying the usual placards with 'manmade is not natural' written on them. In his wildest dreams, Jeff could not have come up with a better escape plan than this. Clearly, those two bearded lefties had somehow hacked into the audio system and drowned out the unsuspecting Secretary. He was even luckier that everyone else bought it, assuming there was a third accomplice behind the scenes.

Jane Henderson, one of the few of his colleagues he respected wasn't quite so gullible, a rare trait for an American, mused Jeff. As she brushed past him on her way to congratulate the Secretary on his great speech (she knew how to play the game), she leant in and whispered in his ear: "You got away with that one," and tapped his microphone, which was now properly switched off, winked a smiley wink, and carried on her way. She was right. He did get away with it and now a couple of passionate environmentalists were having their faces rearranged on his misdemeanour. On the bright side, Jeff thought it would at least make their stories better when they got back to campus in a few weeks.

Jane, unflustered Jane, like a bright bubble she always appeared to breeze through life, rising to the top. She was rated higher than Jeff and they both knew it. Not that it particularly bothered Jeff, he admired Jane's almost total commitment to saying and doing the right things for her career. The two of them would drink long into the night together, him smoking, her telling him to stop, then taking a drag, then a full cigarette, talking passionately about their work, about the environment and most deeply, about what they knew but wasn't to be known.

They were both geologists by degree, obtained either side of the Atlantic, and her PhD had been analysing sea levels and the causes of variation over time. She'd never been published though, snapped up on a government fast-track training scheme before she'd even realised why. Her knowledge and insight, she was told, would be invaluable to the Environment Bureau and she'd been promised access to more data than she'd ever get at the University of Colorado. Data, she was promised, would allow her more time to draw her conclusions.

"I wasn't born yesterday," she repeated almost every drinking occasion. "I know what they were doing, and I went along with it…. but I can do more from the inside than I ever would on the outside. Remember those students you did up like kippers, they've got no real voice. I've got a voice……"

Jeff nodded but they both knew that wasn't the real reason she'd joined. Like scores of scientists with the 'wrong opinions', she'd been duped into joining the Agency and she was doing her best to cover it. With her guard down she was vulnerable, not that Jeff really noticed, he just saw her as a bit drunk and human, but Jane would often snap herself out of her beery melancholy and get right back on message.

"When we all have the right evidence, at the right time, the Government will act. It will act. I know it."

Jane was either naive or hopeful, perhaps both, but once she had her suit on and was not in the bar, she was unstoppable. She nodded at all the right points, swallowed hard when she wanted to contravene policy out loud, and most of all, she backed every senior member of the Bureau, finding the evidence of data point they needed to suit whatever argument or policy decision they happened to be making at the time, whether she believed in it or not. She was essentially an office-savvy version of Jeff, both had suppressed their principles to work at the higher echelons of government but from the outside, it was only Jeff who showed it.

"Is your microphone turned off?" Jane smiled as she put two beers down on the table in front of Jeff. It was Thursday already, most of the week had gone by in a blur of meetings and policy advice conference calls and both looked forward to some downtime and off-the-record gossip.

"No, I'm wearing a wire," Jeff mockingly tapped his breastbone, "one-two one-two…." he grinned, "Russian secret service think I can trap you into telling me what's really going on with all those emergency meetings."

"Turn it off and I might just tell you," she grinned back, "keep it going and I'll have to kill you….and steal your beer."

"What if I finish it first?"

"Good point, then it will hurt slightly less when I do

kill you, I suppose!"

"Ok I'm clean," Jeff pulled out his phone pretending it was a wiretap and placed it deliberately on the table and slid it across. "Now talk...."

The grin soon left Jane's face, he could tell something was bothering her, even though he wasn't that emotionally stunted. "What's up Jane? POTUS want you to justify why it doesn't rain on Mondays anymore, or that global warming is caused by Mexicans not recycling enough?"

"Not quite Jeff, it's a bit more sinister than that."

"Oh Jesus, don't tell me it's stopped raining on Tuesdays now too?"

"Jeff, behave," Jane replied sternly. "I might need your help on this."

"I'm all ears."

2

Berlin

Peter Masai hated radio phone-in shows and, given he'd lived in Berlin for the past five years, was annoyed at himself for now being able to understand them in German, so they were no longer just a background noise, he actually knew what they were saying.

"Why do you phone in? Idiot!" he shouted, in English. "Why do they even let you on? Idiot!"

If his Bluetooth would stay connected, he was half-tempted to call in. Today's subject was the environment. Again. Those Germans do like a good debate about the planet. In fairness, it was usually recycling which was difficult to be critical about. But the people, God the people, it's as if they gave phones to the least educated section of society then told them they were Nobel prize-winning scientists who needed to teach the world their knowledge.

His colleagues at the Technical University told him that there were music stations he could listen to, or he could even just turn it off, but he was addicted. They were his Facebook or Snapchatter, or whatever it's called. *#phoneinaddiction*, he called it, a syndrome. Peter had called into it once. But his learned two-sided approach didn't float anyone's boat and he was just thanked for his balanced view and allowed to hang up, like a patronising bum tap or hair ruffle.

"There, there clever little science man, we don't need to know the truth, or facts, we much prefer making it up...."

Phone-in loathing aside, he loved Berlin, and it was hardly the city's fault for having tedious radio programmes. A life in academia doesn't always lead to travel, most of the time you end up in a dusty corner of a university science block, wearing browner and browner clothes and with hair that knots itself. But Peter had more life in him and had made a conscious effort to wear brighter clothes and keep his hair at least manageable and clean. A free-spirited attitude mixed with a fierce passion for science was an absorbing and unique proposition in most universities, never mind a German one.

Most Germans, even the students, were pretty straight and understood the traits of sense of humour and free-spiritedness in others, even if they couldn't experience it themselves. They definitely had an admiration for the British sense of humour, it felt like Monty Python was on the curriculum under some kind of 'learning about funny' part of the syllabus.

"You English are so funny, Germans, we are not. Also, the Dutch are quite funny, but not like the British. And the Irish, are they British too? Less funny."

But the Germans had an air of superiority when it came to serious stuff, like science. Or cars. Or taking penalties. They did serious really well, almost amusingly, it was ironic. But they of course, much like Alanis Morrissette, did not understand irony.

The German students at the University had all the same groups and stereotypes as any other. There were the cool kids, who didn't appear to study yet somehow got top grades, and the cool kids who actually didn't study and failed. There were also the music ones, the druggie ones, the bookworms and the sports ones. But there seemed to be a common innocence to the masses, a feeling of reserve. They were all so well controlled and organised, and best of all for Peter, he'd never known anywhere that YMCA coming on in a campus nightclub could clear the bar of students. *Not the dance floor, but the bar.*

"Best way to get to the front of a crowded bar in Berlin," he'd say, "get the DJ to put YMCA on." It was certainly as refreshing as it was hilarious, the lack of pretence in kids who haven't learned to be self-conscious or self-aware, who just dance when they want, listening to whatever music they like.

Peter wasn't a dancer. That intersection of the well-known Venn diagram depicting scientists on one side and dancers on the other, wasn't a large expanse. In fact, in all Peter's years of study and teaching sciences, he could count on one hand those scientists who had the rarest of traits - rhythm. It was the holy grail for a university-based scientist. Ricky Melia, marine biology student back in the 90s: wow, that kid could move. If his PhD had been as slick as his dancing, he'd have been on the board of the Marine Biology Association, which was the aqua-equivalent of NASA. As it transpired, his PhD was a bit wooden-legged legged and, as far as Peter knew, Ricky ended up in the food industry making preservatives or something like that. The glamourous nature of real life.

It wasn't just that Peter had spent the majority of the

past five years in Berlin that meant his lack of dancing skills hadn't caught up with him, he was a well-respected, and indeed well-liked professor. Since he graduated all those moons ago from Manchester, with a first degree in geology, he'd written a number of well-received papers and had become one of the world's leading experts in the physical make-up of the Earth.

"Anything you can't see is what I study," he'd often summarise his work as. "The deeper the better!"

Public fame as a scientist comes from the big stuff - black holes with Hadron were probably the most recent thing to get airtime globally, or you might get rolled out if you're a seismologist with an ability to string sentences together on TV if a volcano happens to go off near you. When the national broadcaster needs a talking science head, they'll send a memo to a few big universities for comment. Geological science only really got attention when something actually happened, you can't blame the public for that.

"Earthquakes and volcanoes are pretty cool…" surmised Peter in a speech once. "If you discount the deaths, broken lives, fear and ongoing financial and emotional damage." It wasn't always easy to tell if Professor Masai was trying to make a joke, but you always knew you'd get a good line or two if you attended one of his speeches.

And in seven days' time he was due to have another audience at the International Geology Association (IGA) Gala Dinner being held in Tokyo. Peter was going to present his most recent works around the 'gravitational pull of the Earth and its effect on mantle integrity'.

"Catchy title," his mother had ribbed him when he told her about his trip to Tokyo and plans to speak. Given his previous thesis had been titled: 'A complex analysis of rock formations in Yucatan', he felt this one might even get a couple of column inches in some higher-brow newspapers and online titles. He'd be guaranteed some coverage in New Scientist, his global following in the scientific community was pretty strong and he had all-important credibility in his field, which he didn't take lightly.

Although, he had mentally sketched out his perfect NS front cover. He'd be standing with his back to a towering volcanic mountain, Merapi ideally, but he'd accept Kilimanjaro or Fuji could work just as well if it came to a creative standoff with the publishers. In one hand he is holding a football sized model of the Earth with a segment cut out, showing the layers down to the core. In the other hand he's holding a handwritten sign *"one day it's gonna happen"*. He'd toyed with "going to happen" but it's his sign so he'd go informal. The heading in Hollywood blockbuster style capital letters carved from stone would read *"ROCK STAR"*.

His main barrier to success on this front cover in Peter's opinion lay not in the quality of the theory but that the current editorial style and feeling in the scientific community appeared to be moving towards more positive breakthroughs, like Alzheimer's cures or miracle irrigation systems in sub-Saharan Africa, rather than apocalyptic theories about the planet imploding in on itself at some point in the next million years.

"That's a bit dark isn't it, Peter?" said his mother again. "Can't you make it have more of a happy ending instead?"

"Sorry mother," he'd replied. "I don't make the rules here. Mother Nature doesn't always hand out sweets and balloons like in the Disney films."

"I know dear. It would just be nice to see you in those fancy science magazines like that nice chap who brought water to Africa."

"It was a little different to that mum."

But in a nutshell, she echoed popular culture, taking an incredibly complex issue and breaking it down into one media-friendly soundbite, regardless of whether the soundbite summarises the complexity of the issue.

Peter's mother followed her son's career avidly and was immensely proud, despite her slightly wayward approach to support and the fact her mind wasn't quite what it once was.

For Peter Masai, the IGA convention was going to unlock further funding to continue researching his theory. He was treating it exactly as it was, a pitch to scientific benefactors and academic institutions…. maybe even governments, although he felt state money was increasingly hard to get these days if it wasn't 'on topic'. The words of his mother echoed through his head constantly, she may not be quite as eloquent as she was, but she was right on the money (so to speak) that the majority of investment was going towards cures and positive impact projects. Or environmental research, the US Government was the exception in recent years. They seemed to be investing heavily in people, word on the street was climate change scientists were in great demand, so much so that one of Peter's former teaching colleagues/students in Mexico City, Marco Hernandez, had changed the title of his last thesis to make it sound more focused on climate change than it was, and it worked! What started out as a paper on erosion of the Amazon Basin, ended up as a call to action to save our planet from destruction. He knew full well Marco didn't believe in it, but he was now on the US Government payroll and Peter was travelling economy class to Japan via Qatar to essentially ask for money to fund his 'end of the world' project. A Dragon's Den for academic funding. Or it might have been, had Professor Masai even made it to the lectern in Tokyo.

3

Johor Bahru

Between yoga classes and iced coffee mornings, as an expat housewife (although she preferred the contemporary version 'homemaker'), Elaine really found it difficult to fill her time meaningfully. She and Mark hadn't gotten around to having children and every expat in the district had a live-in maid so there wasn't even a house to clean or meals to prepare. They'd lived in Durban, LA, Paris and Mexico City and Elaine had been genuinely excited about living in Singapore, Cosmopolitan jewel of Southeast Asia. Shopping on Orchard Road, Chinatown for dinner, membership at a fancy country club, cripes maybe she'd even try golf. After all those years of globetrotting, they'd decided to commit five years to Southeast Asia and put some roots of sorts down, talk of children didn't quite surface but Elaine felt it might bubble up in time. She was knocking on the wrong side of the forty door and didn't need a doctor, her mother or social media to tell her about her ticking clock.

So, when Mark sprung the surprise on where they were going to live, it took a while to sink in. To be honest it was still sinking in, at least she still had a perpetual sinking feeling.

"Let's get this straight Mark, so I'm totally clear," Elaine had said when he returned to Mexico after his assimilation tour of Singapore. "You've got a great job in Singapore, one of the most amazing cities in the world. Somewhere I could possibly find some research work in one of the many amazing universities or scientific academies. God, I could even pop to Java and study Krakatoa, Bromo or Merapi and you decide, for both of us I might add, without consultation, for us not to live in Singapore."

"I won't lie to you Elaine; it surprised me too."

Elaine rolled her eyes.

"But Malaysia is an amazing country, a tiger economy, rich in culture and history, it'll be awesome, and I can just pop over the bridge to work. Plus, it's dead cheap in comparison to Singapore."

"That's because it isn't Singapore Mark!" Elaine hadn't even heard of Johor Bahru; in fact, she couldn't find anyone who had heard of it.

"It's Malaysia's second city," Mark had triumphed, "it's going to be the new Singapore."

"Mark, I've clearly not done the extensive research you have," she could be clinically sarcastic when she wanted, "but I've done a bit and in summary, TripAdvisor says it's a shitpit. Facebook posts seem to mostly be about people saying they're moving to Singapore, and, if you Google 'live in Johor Bahru' it asks, 'do you mean live in Singapore?'"

"Does it really?" Mark immediately regretted opening his mouth, poking an already angry bear with an increasingly sharp stick.

"No, you moron, of course it doesn't but it might as well."

He may have made a fairly impulsive decision to move he and his wife to Malaysia and not to Singapore, but he decided now wasn't really the best time to say he'd only arranged for her to have a domestic residence visa, not a working visa, so she'd be prohibited from all forms of employment.

Even though it was always her husband's job which took them places, Elaine had always managed to find work at a university or college with her scientific background, coupled with a willingness to work for very little money, sometimes simply as a volunteer. It was mostly research but occasionally she'd support teaching.

One of the great things about being a geologist is that you're studying something that's a billion years old, so an extra 20 years doesn't make much of a difference. And it kept her eye in, or so she kept telling herself, it kept her feeling useful. Needed. Wanted. Something she wasn't getting from Mark.

So, they'd moved, and Elaine had gone with an open mind, but she knew in her heart of hearts that this wasn't going to end well for her and Mark. He was away a lot as he'd always been, the demand for improved weather forecasts was as strong as it had been in Latin America, Southern Africa and Europe for that matter.

But all the time she had to think was not good for Elaine. In Durban, she'd been doing some voluntary work for the SA Environment Agency monitoring sea levels, grunt work really but an excuse to get down to the beach every morning to check her marks.

"Bigger picture stuff," she'd tell Mark, "it may just be little old me with a stick and a clipboard but when CNN talks about global sea levels, that info is partly down to me."

"That's nice dear, I'm proud of you." Mark would reply, he could be dismissive without even trying. She used to ignore his jibes and put it down to him being very busy with his own career, which to be fair to him was their agreed number one priority.

However, Elaine was more than just a measuring bod, she not only looked deeper at the long-term levels in Durban but also at various other global locations. She almost made herself a mini project to keep her mind active. Accepted theories of rising sea levels had led to more and more data points for her to study but what started to intrigue Elaine was the lack of building evidence that sea levels were actually rising. Of course, some days they'd be up, some days down, you can thank the man in the moon for that, but the more data she combed through, the more it puzzled her. If anything, the trend was at best levelling but one of her projections suggested a long-term dip and if she extrapolated it a thousand years out then it would mean record lows. And by record lows, she was thinking you'd be able to see the dorsal fins of ground feeding sharks.

'Just being dramatic,' she told herself and didn't think much more of it as not long after she and Mark upped sticks again and moved to Mexico. This time she worked alongside a PhD student and teaching assistant writing a thesis on Amazon Basin erosion, which amazingly turned out to be one of the colleagues of one of the few alumni of her Geology degree course back in Manchester that she actually liked, Peter Masai.

Their crossover in Mexico had only lasted a couple of weeks and it was the first time they'd seen each other in the fourteen years since they'd thrown their mortar boards into the grey Manchester sky. Mark had been offered an eighteen-month placement to work with a number of Latin American TV networks and they had a fantastic apartment in one of the less smoggy suburban zones of Mexico City. They'd only been married a couple of years and, although the honeymoon period had slowed, she thought they were still better together than apart, to the extent that he seemed to be really supportive and appeared genuinely interested when she said she was going to try and get some work down at one of the universities. As she soon realised, or at least surmised, his keenness for her to get work was so she was settled, thus not disruptive, so he could get on and do whatever he did with all those weather presenters.

Elaine didn't even tell Mark that she ran into Peter Masai at the imaginatively named University of Mexico. Although she hadn't quite realised, or admitted to herself, they were starting to live separate lives, despite the smiles and fringe physical benefits that came from his return visits from across the continent.

When she had contacted the university, she had been put in touch with the Geology Department. *Bingo!*, thought Elaine, it sounded like they needed some help. Paid help too. It wasn't a lot, just a couple of hundred dollars a week to support the department. Apparently, the previous research assistant had left suddenly. Later Elaine was to find out this had as much to do with an incident in a lap dancing club and some drug dealers than the quality of their work. Elaine was neither into drugs nor lap-dancing, although both were on the edges of her bucket list.

Getting anywhere in Mexico City takes time, and for the uninitiated, usually costs at least an hour. And for Elaine, this meant arriving late for her first day at the Department. As she ran up the main steps, gulping in thirty-degree thick air, a trickle of sweat forming between her shoulder blades, a total car crash of a first day, the last person she expected to be standing at the front door was Peter Masai.

"Peter," she gasped, "Masai. What, where, when, who...are you doing here?" she stammered, half delighted to see a friendly face, half-aggrieved because she felt like a sweaty mess of fug.

"Elaine Shreeves, or should I say Elaine Brennant?" exclaimed Peter, a massive grin on his face, "You're a long way from Manchester, but at least it's not raining. Although, it looks like it's been raining on you. Mexico City does that to us Northern Europeans."

Elaine was having one of those awkward catching-up moments, trying to piece together what was happening, why was Peter Masai, whom she'd not seen or heard from since college, standing in front of her knowing she'd changed her name? But on the other hand, Peter Masai, someone she had genuinely liked all those years ago, the Mancunian Warrior as he'd been known as, was here, *that's brilliant*, shame she was sweating like a racing camel.

It could have been worse, she thought, *at least it's not Jeff.*

As if he could read her mind, not that it would take David Copperfield, Peter spoke.

"The head of the Geology Department, Lucca, told me there was a new researcher starting and that they'd studied in Manchester so maybe I knew them, as if I'd know every graduate who ever went there. As it turns out he was right, I did know them. The info you'd given him on when you were there and the fact you were the only Elaine on our course narrowed it down. And I'm pretty sure you weren't married when we were living in Manchester, unless you and Jeff did tie the knot, but you chose a different surname....so by an amazing piece of deduction, and some stalking on Facebook, I realised it was you."

Elaine nodded, "Yep. It's me. And you, you're in Mexico. You hated Mexican food."

"I'm finally growing up," replied Peter with a big grin on his face, "and anyhow, I'm not going to be here for that much longer, not that's it's the food's fault. I'll be in Berlin, but all that can wait. I'd better get you to some air conditioning, then to meet Marco who you'll be working for. You'll like him but I think he's sold out; you must tell me what you think."

Elaine nodded but too many things were going on and she was struggling to focus. Aside from being uncomfortably sweaty and feeling particularly unpresentable for a new job, she'd also reeled totally unexpectedly at the mention of Jeff's name. She'd put his memory in that deep and dark place at the back of a married girl's mind labelled *'what might have been'*.

Elaine and Jeff had spent their final year at university almost inseparably in a haze of passion and study, soul mates on a journey to understand the world, literally from the core out. They had drifted apart not long before graduation, no epic fallout, more that she grew away from Jeff. She felt he was destined for a life in academia, pig-headed but always questioning. Elaine could feel herself accepting that she needed to escape from theories and projections and get stuck into the real world, a pang of regret at the thought of it. So many vivid memories flooded back, giving Elaine a chill. A refreshing chill, as it turned out, as she and Peter entered the relative cool of the entrance, accompanied by the blaring hum of the air conditioning, wafting a satisfying breeze over them as they walked.

4

Mexico City

"Marco's in the café." Peter's voice snapped Elaine out of her memory trance and back into the university hall and the 'real life' she'd craved. Ironic didn't do justice to the fact that her version of real-life had led her back into study again.

"I'll see you later, there are loads of questions I should be asking you I'm sure, I'm not good at keeping in touch with people you realise," said Peter as he indicated where Marco was waiting for Elaine in the far corner of the café.

"No shit Sherlock!" retorted Elaine with a wry smile, "I've not exactly been stalking you either, but it really is brilliant to see you again Peter. I could do with some wine and reminiscing." She felt herself flinch a little, unconsciously her mind wandering back to her days in Manchester, free, happy, the world being one huge problem they all thought they could solve. Three very promising scientists, Peter referred to them as geologists, but Jeff and Elaine went with scientists.

"Bigger," Jeff would say, "more scope for genius."

"And I don't want a beard," joked Elaine, "there hasn't been a beard-free geologist in living memory, although it would be nice to be able to stop shaving every day…."

Elaine had barely thought about college, at least Peter and Jeff, for seven years and she'd had more flashbacks in the last five minutes than in all the years prior. Happy memories, but that tinge of regret started to seep into her, luckily Marco's outstretched arm snapped her out of it.

"Ola, I'm Marco, Peter speaks very highly of you Elaine. And trust me, he doesn't say that about many people. Says you stopped being a scientist to become a wife."

A cutting, remarkable candid for an introduction but directionally correct, thought Elaine, deciding not to take offence but smile almost in agreement.

"If you're still as smart as Peter says you were at college, I worry you'll find this work boring. It's quite, how do you say, admin heavy."

"That's no problem, Marco, I like the detail and you only ever get detail when there's a lot of data to look through."

"I like you a lot already," grinned Marco. "Right, I'll talk you through what I'm writing," then his grin changed to almost a smirk, "And if we're still getting on, I'll talk to you about what I think is really happening."

Elaine was a dream research assistant; she had all the experience of being through a tough scientific degree course and a few extra years of maturity than the average assistant. Plus, she didn't seem to be looking to take any glory, she just did her job and that was that. Her husband was away so much this assignment that their paths would only cross every few days, which meant Elaine and Peter had plenty of opportunity to catch up. She thought it might have been awkward not having spoken, never mind a Facebook poke or whatever is used to be, but she and Peter slipped back into their old friendship again just with less alcohol, much fewer drugs (although Peter did have access to some mild weed discretely) and no Jeff.

Peter had been teaching in Mexico for the past couple of years and was winding down to move to Germany, where he'd been offered a pretty senior posting at the Technical University of Berlin. Unlike Elaine, he was neither married, nor was he even close to it.

"Maybe my fraulein awaits me in Berlin," he mused.

"Maybe? I hope so," replied Elaine supportively. "My husband is somewhere in South America, at least you can pin yours down to a city!"

"Yeah, what is it Mark does again, he's a meteorologist right?"

"Yes, by degree he is, and a very good one at that, just he did a bit of presenting not long after graduating when he realised there was very little formal training available for upcoming weather presenters, so he became one. And now he, and we, are travelling the globe so he can teach the world how to present the weather. You couldn't make it up!"

"Good for him I guess," said Peter. "He's found himself a niche and sounds like it's working out for the both of you." Peter was about to ask more about this bizarre career choice when he noticed Elaine had glazed over.

"Yeah, I guess so." she replied unconvincingly. Suddenly, a wave of jealousy coursed through her veins. Yes, she was seeing the world, yes, she was married (*was she happily married, she wasn't sure*) and yes, she managed to keep her eye in with some scientific projects. But Peter was also seeing the world and was being carried from place to place by his love of Geology, a scientific quest, his own quest. Elaine was a bit part, helping Marco to collect data points on the Amazon basin, a role she understood and would honour but it started to make her think. Really think.

Then she unexpectedly blurted out loud, "What happened to Jeff?"

She felt herself blush and a different wave of jealousy jolted her, like a feeling of guilt or betrayal, just for mentioning his name.

"Last I heard he was in the US, New York I think, some Climatology course. But you guessed it, I haven't been in touch, you neither I suspect."

"Nope," Elaine shook her head. "Graduation Day was the last time I saw him, I think we both realised it was time to move on." Elaine did her best to make that sound convincing. What was happening to her? A few days without Mark, a couple of beers with an old uni mate and she was starting to wallow in self-pity. *Grow up*, she told herself, *get back on form again*. And, with a huge swig from her really rather tasty beer, she swiftly moved the conversation on to more appropriate topics for a married lady working at a university.

"I was thinking about what you said when I first arrived last week, about Marco and that he's sold out, why did you say that? Then I'll tell you something I found that he doesn't think I've found in his data."

"Well," Peter was rather pleased to get back onto more comfortable conversation territory, he didn't want or need to open an emotional Pandora's box full of Jeffs! "I was helping Marco frame his thesis, you know, providing some structure and guidance so it flowed, rather than just be a monotonous set of data after data. But I always felt he was holding back something. He appeared to have fundamental evidence to demonstrate, if not prove, the man-made impact on erosion around the Amazon basin, partly deforestation and partly pollution from our ever-growing industry in pockets of the basin. He then stopped coming to me for advice, said he was clear on his approach, but he knew I didn't believe him. However, my role is to allow the students space to learn, make their own mistakes. There's usually an opportunity to course- correct before it goes too far down the road to PhD submission. Then one day I overheard him speaking to one of the other students about a letter he'd received from the US embassy saying the data he'd sent them made him a prime candidate for a government researcher position. I said nothing to him about it, I couldn't exactly come clean that I was earwigging his private conversations but the next day he came to my office to let me know that he was almost complete, and, with some extra support, he would be able to finish. He went on to say he was tweaking this thesis due to a lightbulb moment, one which he didn't offer to share with me, and said as soon as he submits, he'll be off to work on climate change projects for the US Government, here in Mexico.

"'Climate change?' I challenged him, 'But your whole

thesis is about something else, what qualifies you for that position?' I was a bit direct with him to see what the reaction would be. 'I know,' Marco had laughed back, he was pretty arrogant, 'Amazing what a few data points can be interpreted as.' 'Go on,' I poked to see if he'd share more."

"Let me guess what he said," interrupted Elaine. "I bet it was something to do with the river levels at the mouth not rising anymore, sea levels levelling, that kind of thing."

"Bingo." said Peter emphatically.

"That's what I was referring to. He'd buried some additional data in a few tables in his appendices, nominally detailing tidal flows and pollution levels but you didn't call me Data Daisy for nothing at university, I could sense he was trying to find an angle on something other than his topic which, to be honest, he wasn't very good at explaining either."

"But," interjected Peter, "That doesn't explain why the government would want him. Aside from the obvious that they'd want to dispel the theory of climate change, but that's fantasy surely."

"Peter," Elaine suddenly felt super-smart again and she remembered how much she enjoyed that feeling that knowledge gives you, "I imagine the US Government science division, it probably has a better name than that, employs two types of scientists. One, the very top of their field or those who display an aptitude for brilliance and two, those who can be moulded to create evidence-based stories that can be used in politics. And we both suspect which one our friend Marco might be."

"Cheers to that," Peter raised his new full beer, "I can at least say one of my students got a job with the US government, doesn't sound too bad, does it?

"That's more like it Peter, you are the godfather to future scientific policy"

"Cheers to that again!"

"Indeed Professor." saluted Elaine, chinking glasses and exchanging wide toothy grins with him.

Peter beckoned over one of the waiters and ordered them both another beer, it wasn't often he got to go out with someone he actually knew, let alone liked.

"Talking of theories," Elaine started up again, "Mark, my Mark, has this idea that global rainfall is going to increase exponentially in the next 10 years. That's his thing. Says the polar ice caps melting, creating more surface water to evaporate in higher temperatures, means one thing: more rain. So much so that he's invested in a clothing startup, one that specialises in rain gear. No word of a lie."

"'Nano-technology Elaine,'" he tells me. "Repels water, like those clothes that are supposed to clean themselves. A whole range, in fact business, set up to supply globally via an e-store online. He's convinced. 'I've seen the future' he says, 'And it's wet, very very wet.' He's a positive chap my husband."

"But he probably does see quite a few weather forecasts," interjected Peter, "and in danger of sounding patronising, which by the way is a specialist talent of mine, it's not unfamiliar for people to take a few pieces of evidence and data points and come to pretty substantial conclusions."

"I think you might be right on both counts and I can never quite square it in my head whether the people he trains are bad at predicting the weather or just bad at presenting. So does he do two jobs in one?" The beer was getting to Elaine now.

"Judging by the district you guys are living in I'd say he gets paid for both!" Peter was also feeling a little bit bleary, which was not an unpleasant feeling. Living in a foreign country was great, a real experience, but sometimes there's no substitute for someone who speaks your language, literally and figuratively, with whom you feel you can just talk.

"So, Mr. Mexico, what are you doing here aside from teaching some kids about the origins of the earth and why volcanoes are important and not just big hot hills?"

"You're right Elaine, good memory. I do rather have a soft spot for volcanoes, and they do creep into the odd lecture or two...But yes, I have been working on something, well I am working on something." Peter switched back into serious mode. "Remember in our second year I did that essay on the Earth's core? Probably not, anyway it had been nagging away at me for quite a while because that was the worst essay I think I've ever written. You know when you draw conclusions because you've already hit a word count?" Peter wasn't really asking, and Elaine knew not to answer, even he didn't realise he'd been bottling this up so much, but finally he had someone to share it with.

"So, a couple of years ago I got it back out again as I'd been looking at force impact on the Earth's crust and upper mantle and recalled I'd touched on a theory of core expansion altering Earth's central gravity."

He continued, "it's probably nothing and I know we've just been talking about people who make conclusions from the loosest of data, but I wonder if I've stumbled across something. Sea levels are supposed to be rising right yeah? That's the medium-term trend and a quarter of the world's major cities are going to be underwater 30 years from now. Look at the evidence, it's pretty compelling. Greenhouse gases, global average temperatures up, up, up, the hottest 5 years on record all in the past 10 years, more volatile weather, maybe Mark's onto something?" he said with a wink, "Polar ice at its lowest level, until tomorrow. But you've measured it yourself in South Africa. Marco's making a new career out of sharing data, our data, with the US Government but he's got no real idea what he's dealing with."

Elaine was transported back to Manchester, it felt like Peter was always one to get totally absorbed in his work and could convince himself black was white and light was dark, so this was not a new experience for her - he'd convinced himself on a few things. Once he'd played out a future scenario where tectonic activity in the Himalayas got so out of control that Mount Everest got so high that it became physically unstable due to its height and lack of atmosphere supporting it to keep the structure intact.

"Anyway," Peter sensed he was losing his audience

of one, "it doesn't stack up. Yes, when there are long term trends, there are inevitable ups and downs and the ups win vs the downs, or vice versa depending on what you're measuring. But on this there aren't many plausible explanations why sea levels aren't steadily increasing, at least none I'm convinced by."

Peter leant in, beer in hand for the big reveal, Elaine guessed and mentally braced herself.

"The Earth's core is pulling so much against itself that it's holding water levels even. I'm going to prove it, but I bet you our next beer that sea and ocean density is increasing, that's why sea levels have stayed put these past twenty-four months.

"Or it could just be a period of stagnation...." Elaine felt she might have just popped Peter's balloon, but he took it well.

"Yep," he took a huge swig of beer, almost in resignation. "I do admit it may be a blip in the data but I'm going to follow this one up. And when we bump into each other again in seven years' time, you'll be one of the few people who isn't surprised they can walk on water. It's gonna be that dense!" Peter realised he was a bit drunk so may have condensed 300 or 3000 million years of Mother Nature into seven short years, "Or the mantle will have collapsed on itself and there'll be no water left at all - that's the other end game."

"Cheers Peter," Elaine beamed a beer-fuelled but genuine smile, "loving the passion. Glad it's still keeping you up at night all these years later, I suspected something would be gnawing away at you, some amazing theory or nugget of geological doubt."

5

Washington DC

"Hey scientist, your second favourite geologist here!!" Jeff was reading the email out to Jane direct from his phone, "I assume just like me and most other kids of Hotmail, you've not changed your email address in the past fifteen years."

"Oh my God," exclaimed Jane, "who is this guy, your grandfather?"

With a big smile on her face, she loved teasing Jeff, but deep down she admired how he'd not been changed so much by modern technology. It was much more likely to see his head in a book (non-fiction probably) than a screen. In fact, she was quite impressed with the version of iPhone he had, maybe his Nokia 8210 had finally given up the ghost.

"Not quite, it's an old college mate of mine from Manchester. Bit of a bolt from the blue really. We were pretty inseparable back then, the three of us. Me, Pete and...." he hesitated, realising he'd barely thought of Elaine for several years, but it was a memory that burned bright once he pictured her again, "...and another student."

Jane wasn't stupid, she could clearly see Jeff squirming in turmoil at the thought of this, most likely female, third student. Anyway, she'd park that question for their third beer, maybe even later. She had a feeling it might need something stronger to prise that morsel out of Jeff.

"Go on," she said instead, "what does the rest say? Sounds intriguing."

"That it most certainly is." Jeff took a long, dramatic swig of his beer and read the whole message out.

"Hey scientist, your second favourite geologist here!!" Jeff was reading the email out to Jane direct from his phone, "I assume just like me and most other kids of Hotmail, you've not changed your email address in the past fifteen years. Small talk: not married, no kids, lousy at keeping in touch, living in Berlin, working at Technical University teaching geology, sorry science LOL, No beard. Also taught/researched/worked in Mexico (hot) and China (weird food but seriously dart)."

"Are you actually reading it out or are you paraphrasing?" interrupted Jane.

"Oh no, this is how he's written it. And he's still trying to get people to use the word dart, thought he might have given up on that one"

"Wowsers." exclaimed Jane, although not wholly surprised. She loved how men could go years without contact and be perfectly happy with a summary like this, no emotion, just facts. Like those frogs that go into catatonic in dried riverbeds for years then just spark back to life when it rains again. Jeff seemed very much at ease with this information from someone who was clearly once a dear friend and who'd appeared from nowhere.

Jeff replied with an enthusiastic smirk. "I'll carry on."

"...Generally pretty good, Germans are better than I thought. And the city is nice. The point: I need a second opinion. Remember that project we discounted in our final year because Professor Dickface…"

"He wasn't really called that," Jeff interrupted himself, as if it needed to be said,

"...claimed it was geologically unsound, so we did the tectonic extremism piece around Everest toppling and Pangea reforming. Well, if I knew then what I know now then we'd both have been on the cover of NS by now. You need to see this. I need you to see this. Oh, and I saw E in Mexico City about five years ago. Married, though maybe not anymore, husband sounded a bit of a dick. Cheers, Warrior."

"I'm going to get another beer and you are going to have to decipher that for me."

"I will." grinned Jeff. "But don't be too quick to judge until we've at least finished our third beer."

"And you'll tell me who E is?" Jane left it hanging and Jeff blinked first as his face started to colour just a touch.

"Might need a fourth for that one. And a fifth." His mind drifted back to the email, *he saw Elaine five years ago and she was married, although maybe not still....no it's nothing to do with me....*

"Thought so." smiled Jane as sympathetically as she could, feeling that this wasn't the time for a quip. There was clearly more to it than a college project.

"So" Jane landed the beers with a positive thud full of intent in front of Jeff, the froth jumping a thousand silver bubbles, tumbling down the side of the glass like an avalanche.

"Appropriate metaphor." started Jeff, nodding to the

still-sloshing beers. "Peter Masai and I were college roomies and the three of us, Elaine included, spent most of our final two years of university together in study or pubs, generally both." He was concentrating now so even the mention of Elaine passed by without a stutter this time.

"Pete was less conformist, let's say, than your average geology student, or even professor for that matter. He was big on theory as he would call it. Fantasy was how the university teaching fraternity often described it. Thus, he became a 'fantastical theorist' - self-titled of course. 'A Geological Warrior' he then started calling himself, which is where the name comes from. If you saw him 15 years ago, he wasn't exactly a dead ringer for a Tanzanian tribesman. But Peter Masel became Peter Masai and it stuck until the end of uni. I assumed he'd revert back as he turned into a bone fide grown up but a quick scan on the TU Berlin academic staff web page tells me Peter Masai is the incumbent Head of Geological Studies.

"Pete, Elaine and I were all pretty committed students, believe it or not before you say anything. And in a rare show of maturity, we realised that three heads were better than one when it came to our dissertations. Not quite as straightforward as this but, in essence, Pete was the big thinker, he'd propose wild ideas and see if he could find the evidence to prove them."

Jane interrupted; she couldn't keep it in. "Like the Everest thing and that Pangea idea, pretty ridiculous, no? He didn't really do that as a dissertation did he?"

Jeff grinned. "Everest yes, incredibly enough, you'd

be surprised what evidence you can find out there! But Pangea no. That's what makes the email so intriguing, but I'll come on to that." Another long, pensive, almost dramatic glug of beer.

"Elaine was the data guy, sorry gal, she just had a really processy mind, she could get through acres of data and see patterns, links, and most importantly, merge and improve data others wouldn't have linked together at all."

"What about you Jeff, what was your role in all this? Bartender?" Jane realised that was a bit patronising and offered an apologetic head tilt, neither action seemed to register with Jeff.

"Well, believe it or not, I was the glue, it kind of fell to me to bridge the gap between the big ideas guy and the data processing machine. Although at the time we probably just thought we were doing our own thing and it was a convenient excuse to go to the pub more often.

"So, we all did our projects, Elaine's was brilliant of course but not very memorable, mine was pretty functional around erosion blah blah blah. Pete's Everest dissertation was a masterpiece of science babble, I think he only did it to prove a point after several of his other ideas were rejected by Professor Richards (hence Dickface)."

Jane wasn't sure why the link was so obvious but hey-ho, uni life made sense of stuff that makes little sense in the outside world.

"His obsession in the final year of study, when he was actually writing his Everest topping story, sorry I mean paper, was about geological Armageddon. I think it was as much as how he was positioning it rather than the thing itself, although it sure had a few sizeable holes in it too. He argued, a lot, that all the other science disciplines had some kind of end of the world scenario at its extreme, so why should geology be any different. Biology has its superbugs killing all living organisms in a huge global pandemic, the computer science guys had AI taking over the world, the physics dudes had loads - black holes swallowing the solar system, solar expansion burning up the Earth, in fact the physics students pretty much claimed everything to be about physics, which wound up the poor maths department no end!

"Geology, at least in Manchester, appeared to Pete to be about the past not the future, which of course it really is, but he was relentless about it. Guess that's why he stayed in academia - he'd be a great inspiration to budding geologists I imagine, challenging them on their theories but I bet he winds them up something chronic when they try and prove something."

"Just saying..." Jane piped up, "he might have changed in the past fifteen years, I'm sure you have." Jeff then suddenly realised he hadn't so why would his mate Peter Masai? "Carry on..."

"He has this idea brewing in his head about the finite nature of water on Earth and that one day it would all disappear. At least he hypothesised that there would be a chain of geological events that would lead to total climatic apocalypse. No water, no climate, no life. Boom."

"And the reason it was rejected?" asked Jane, her ears

had really picked up now.

"Just that," Jeff replied flatly, "it was about climate not geology. Pete couldn't quite come up with a strong enough argument at the time anchored in geological data points that convinced the professor to sanction it. So, he did his Everest thing as a largely futile protest. Futile as he did such a good job of it that he got a first so kind of proved the professor right in a roundabout sort of way."

"And the Pangea bit?" Jane asked.

"Well, that's what he was calling his theory. I'm not sure of the logic as it had nothing to do with Pangea at all, but it was something along the lines of the size of the idea and that it would change how we looked at the world. I'd suggested 'Project Drought', but Pete had given me one of his 'leave this shit up to me' looks." Jeff smiled warmly; he was enjoying recounting tales of his uni days. It never feels like it at the time but looking back he realised the freedom they had to study and challenge and interpret when now he felt trapped in someone else's way of thinking, knowing full well how Jane had adapted to that environment and why Peter had stayed in academia. If your teacher won't let you study it, just become the teacher. Simple really.

"Jeff," Jane was warm with beer now so was feeling brave enough to challenge, "There are all sorts of disaster movie plotlines echoing through the corridors of our own department about floods, fireballs, volcanic destruction - you name it. You're working in it every day; I don't get why you're so animated by this email from a guy you haven't seen nor heard from in fifteen years. The Bureau has been hiring scientists like this across the globe for years now, maybe he just wants a job?"

"An outside chance of that yes but he might not even know what I do or where I'm working. There was a little more to Pangea than I've said so far."

"I guessed that," smiled Jane, "and I assume you're going to share that with me now, so I don't just think you're a fantasist too…."

"Maybe a little." shrugged Jeff, the beer had totally relaxed him now. "We both know we're working against our principles, you're just better at hiding it. There's clearly all this evidence being spouted that climate change has been halted but neither of us truly believe in it do we?" He left a pause, long enough for Jane to acknowledge he was right, imperceptibly almost, but definitely there.

"So maybe, just maybe, Pete's been working on Pangea for fifteen years, gathering evidence and data points and he's ready to share with someone. But someone he trusts."

"Yeah? Like a man he's not spoken to in fifteen years."

"Exactly." Jeff ignored the sarcasm. "He knows I'll believe him, so he doesn't have to start from scratch again. Plus, in a week's time he seems to be presenting to the IGA in Tokyo a paper on mantle integrity and gravity's pull - that was one of his original theories - so he's about to go public anyway."

"I read a paper once," interjected Jane, "about the Earth's core expanding to such a degree that it got so dense that it was self-contained in the outer core. It affected gravity so much that the moon started to be dragged closer to the Earth. Tides went crazy and basically the whole world flooded every twelve hours."

"Yep, read that too." retorted Jeff. "It was such a single-minded theory it forgot about the impact on all living things. We'd be twice as heavy; planes would use double the fuel yadda yadda yadda." Suddenly Jeff felt like he was back in Manchester, defending his mate's honour and fighting his academic corner. #

"But what if gravity was only impacted by a tiny margin, say 1% or less, would we really notice day to day? I'm not up on my sport but I'm pretty sure the world high jump and long jump world records haven't been broken for twenty years."

"Are you serious?" Jane was almost incredulous. "What about Usain Bolt, didn't he smash every world record available?"

"Yes, you're right, but he's the tallest man ever to break 10 seconds at 100m, his size counters the effect."

This felt good, Jeff was starting to sound like Pete used to. A quick answer for everything, however trivial or lacking in empirical evidence. He recalled a particularly memorable late-night exchange they had in one of the many pubs they'd frequented in Manchester.

"If you say it convincingly, you'll convince people." Pete had said. "People just want to believe what people say, it's much easier that way."

"Not sure it works as easily in our field though, lots

of smart thinkers and knowers." Jeff had challenged.

"Clever maybe, smart probably not - scientists are still people, most of them want to be told what to believe, why things are as they are. Christ, it takes a lot of hard hours to prove shit so let's spend less time grafting and more time convincing."

"You mean lie to people?"

"No Jeff, just because you can't immediately prove something to be true, doesn't make it a lie."

Jeff did enjoy his debates with Peter, even if he was a bit sceptical about the basis for those discussions.

"Ok!" Jane snapped Jeff out of his boozy flashback. "I could probably buy the gravity bit if I have a few more swigs of beer…even if the human impact is low given our mass, the impact on oceans would be immense and weaker areas of the crust, even mantle would be under more strain. But I have to leave behind twenty years of experience to genuinely believe this horse shit, sorry."

Jeff got on the defensive.

"Look Jane, I'm just replaying stuff from fifteen years ago that wasn't even my work. I shared the email as I thought it might intrigue you like it did me, and in this godforsaken Bureau you're pretty much the only person I trust." Jeff realised he'd gone heavy but why not, he'd had a few beers and it dawned on him how little effort he'd made to keep in touch with Peter, a former kindred spirit from whom he'd just drifted, as he had from Elaine.

"Ok I get it, I'll ease off." said Jane. "Tell me more about the Warrior's theories, then I'll get a final beer."

"No, no you're right." a sudden wave of sobriety hit Jeff. "I'm living in the past and I know it all sounds a bit implausible, I'll go back to Peter in the morning. Christ it may be that he's found a couple of photos from graduation or something, guess I'm just looking and hoping perhaps, for something more." He slumped back into his chair and rained the last dregs of his beer. It never tasted as good as the first swig he mused.

Noting Jeff's sudden darkening of spirits, Jane thought she might have missed the most interesting part of the conversation, at least for her. "Guess now's a bad time to ask about Elaine then?" she offered hopefully.

"Jeez, we'd need a bottle of scotch for that now, I think I've dredged enough of the past up for one evening."

"Ok let's call it a night then." Jane was ever impressed by men's, not just Jeff's, ability to avoid certain topics of conversation. She paid the bill and watched Jeff walk slowly out of the bar, clearly heavy thoughts weighing him down. Maybe it was the end of the world, maybe it was a lost love he'd tried to forget or maybe he was just tired. Likely, it was all three, she surmised to herself and exited swiftly after.

If the previous evening's email piqued Jeff's interest, then the one he woke up to almost had him reboot his laptop to check it was still connected. It was the original email from Pete but with a new message on top which simply read: 'Elaine's on a flight to Berlin, clock is ticking, triumvirate is no good with just two of us.' This time there was a Skype link in the email and Jeff hovered his cursor over it for at least a minute, his mind awash with thoughts. What's Elaine doing flying to Berlin to see Pete, where's she flying from, does she know Pete's been in contact? Of course she does. And she's still gone. How long have they been in contact? Pete said he saw her five years ago in Mexico, maybe she's still there. What's Pete up to that Elaine needs to see him so much? Almost involuntarily he clicked, and his Skype app opened as it dialled into Pete's account. It was 7am in Washington so it must have been about one in the afternoon in Berlin. A familiar voice boomed through his laptop speakers.

6

Berlin

"Elaine!" exclaimed Peter as he saw her in the crowd of people and luggage spilling from the arrivals entrance in Schoenfeld International Airport. He was holding a huge sign with the Manchester University logo stuck on it with large letters saying, 'Geology Alumni Party' and was wearing a black flat cap as he beckoned Elaine towards him.

"Nice look," grinned Elaine, "and nice sign, quite the limousine service."

"All true except the limousine, unless you count the U-Bahn as luxury? Great to see you again Elaine, glad you decided to come, and so quickly." The two friends embraced a long platonic hug, a classic airport reunion that meant so little to everyone else but so much to Pete and Elaine.

"Well, it was a toss-up to be honest Peter. Come to Berlin to try to work out if the world is on a slow journey to its death or stay in Malaysia and chat to expat women about the humidity and that we all wished we'd done something with our lives."

The grin hadn't left Peter's face, but he sensed not a huge amount had changed for Elaine since their chance meeting in Mexico City all those years ago.

"So crucial question - how long do I have you for? When's your return flight?" Pete wanted to establish timeframes early.

"Return flight? You didn't mention anything about

having to go back. One way fare for me so you kick me off the team when you're finished with me." A little smirk crept onto her face as she said it.

"What about your husband? Mark, isn't it?"

Life was pouring back into Elaine as if she'd woken up from a coma but even she was surprised by her response.

"Soon to be ex-husband I'd say."

"OK." Peter stopped, thought he'd better sense check that one. "Anything I need to know, all OK with you guys?"

"Nothing that 6000 miles apart won't cure. Crucial question for me, when can I shower, drink coffee and go sightseeing? I've always wanted to see the Brandenburg Gate and where the wall was, can you still see some? Then we can get cracking on Pangea."

"Sounds like a plan, we've got thirty-six hours until Jeff lands." He noticed a definite flicker in Elaine's face at the mention of his name. When she'd taken off, she hadn't known whether Jeff had agreed to come.

"Well, that won't be awkward, will it? Has he got the data you asked for?"

"I don't know, he told me he'd try. I'm kind of working on the basis he won't fly halfway across the globe without it though. Said he'd take a couple of weeks' leave he was owed. Which, with the Tokyo conference being delayed by three weeks due to the cyclones out there, should give us enough time."

"Time for what Pete? What's the real reason you got us both to come to Germany?"

"I told you Elaine, we're going to work out how long

the planet's got left before it dries up completely, that's all."

"Oh, Jesus Christ Pete, you were serious, I thought you just wanted some help on your Tokyo conference speech in your quest to become a famous science guru."

The grin was back on Peter's face, "Yep that too. Just the content of that presentation might be a bit heavier with your input. Let's get you back to town and sort that coffee out, the jet lag will be after you soon enough."

With that, he turned and picked up Elaine's cases. She's definitely packed for a one-way trip, he mused to himself as he strained to get them even onto a luggage trolley, marvelling at how she'd managed to get them through customs on her own.

"I've got a set of dumbbells in the flat, should've mentioned that before you packed yours!"

"Maybe if you'd been using them, my case wouldn't be quite so heavy for you."

"Touche." conceded Pete. "Ausgang." He pointed to the exit sign and led them out of the terminal down to the U-Bahn station.

There was a comfortable silence between them on the 40-minute trip underground to the closest station to Pete's apartment. And 40 minutes was plenty of time for Elaine to contemplate her situation. *Had she finally left Mark?* It felt like it, that's for sure. *Was she going to help confirm or not the end of the world?* Knowing Pete that wasn't out of the question...*what would it be like seeing Jeff again?* It's best not to try to answer that one, just let it happen and try to focus on the job at hand. *What would living in Berlin be like?* Elaine had always wanted one of Mark's assignments to be a glamorous European capital...Paris, Budapest, Berlin, Prague but turns out the Europeans are pretty switched on when it comes to weather presenting. *Ridiculous job she thought, ridiculous man too!* That resolved it in her mind, she was single again. And it felt good. It would be better with a hot shower and coffee...

"Hansaplatz," declared Peter, "that's us."

Like a lot of expats coming to Berlin, Peter Masai was initially drawn to the Eastern half of the city. Unrecognisable from the Soviet, pre-wall toppling days, it still had some of its character (if you can call 40 years of oppression character building, literally), in the form of funky bars and cafés and imposing architecture. So much had been rebuilt, Potsdamer Platz had been totally reimagined. It was no longer just a bleak communist hangout and virtually all remains of the wall had gone – rightly so – and now remained as a distant reminder of the incredible and hard to imagine divisions which split this huge city. Thankfully, the days of spotting bullet holes on buildings were gone and have been replaced by modern office spaces and lush housing complexes. It wasn't all roses, twenty-five years since the fall of the wall and all the pain it had caused didn't mean there weren't the select few who mourned for the great times of right-wing supremacy Germany, as so many of its other neighbours, still struggled to keep the neo-Nazis from occupying the political and social landscape.

Peter had been caught up a couple of times in the

ever more frequent right-wing marches and protests, never really sure what they were trying to achieve, but politics was never his strong suit. He sensed if he ever tried to get into politics, he'd get so wound up by the short-term nature of the decision making he'd go crazy. Governing to stay in government was what it seemed like to him, but he was savvy enough to realise you can't please all the people all the time so maybe pleasing just about enough people for some of the time was the right call to make. Pete thought politics should be run like how he viewed the world, with a long-term view, like the Japanese and their 300-year business plans. Focus on legacy, the next generation.

Pete and Elaine managed to get the bags from the platform, down the stairs and across the road to the entrance of Pete's mid-rise apartment block.

"We're right on the edge of Tiergarten."

Pete sensed Elaine would need to know where they were, why he chose to live there and that he wouldn't have to repeat it when Jeff arrived. Call it sexist or just awareness but Pete had a view that women expect to be told things like this. They had to know why you do stuff, whereas men are much more content with the what, as if to implicitly understand there must have been a good reason why you did something, and therefore it doesn't require an explanation.

"Oh yes I wondered what all those trees were."

Mind reader, thought Pete to himself smugly.

"Tiergarten, one of the world's great city parks, alongside Central...and probably some others..." Pete realised he knew very little about the great city parks of the world but was pretty confident that if there were better parks out there then they would deserve the title 'great'.

"Berlin Zoo at one end, Brandenburg Gate at the other, and the Siegessaule in the middle, that's Berlin's version of Nelson's column." he said, pre-empting Elaine's likely question. "I moved here from the Eastern area of the city a couple of years back, a little bit for the park – it's great to have all that space on your doorstep – and a lot because it means I can walk to work. Amazing in the summer, less so when it's minus double figures in the depths of winter."

Even through the blur of a sleep-depriving night flight, Elaine felt another buzz of life that Peter's flat gave her. All that independence, not stuck in the bubble of a plastic, expat lifestyle. Plus, it wasn't 28 degrees and 100% humidity all the bloody time.

"Great apartment." muttered Elaine as they entered the flat.

"Helps when you've only got yourself to spend money on, so I went for space and location, a double hit of urban luxury!"

The entrance hall opened into a large open plan living room, immaculately tidy. *He's definitely got a cleaner,* thought Elaine correctly. The lounge led on to a compact kitchen area adjacent to a large round dining table to the rear of the flat with floor to ceiling windows overlooking the park. A scientist's flat, the giveaway of several bookshelves full of textbooks and encyclopaedias or compendiums of facts. Plus, a selection of framed covers of

New Scientist.

"Where's your front cover going to go?" joked Elaine as she surveyed the room.

"Pride of place in the bathroom of course. Although if what we're going to prove is correct then there won't be much of a need for bathrooms or magazines." Pete wasn't sure himself if this was supposed to be funny or not, but Elaine took it in good spirits.

"You've got between three and three million years given my quick scan of what you sent me." she replied.

"Maybe we can narrow that window a touch with what Jeff can get his hands on."

"Indeed." A wave of fatigue rolled through Elaine as the thought of dealing with Jeff's arrival was one thing too much on top of the journey and seemingly life-changing decisions.

"Ok Elaine, I've got some loose ends to tie up down at the university so I'm going to pop out for a few hours. I'm sure a shower, some coffee and maybe some shuteye will help."

"All of the above." smiled Elaine, relaxing again.

"Sure, what else would a friend do who you've only seen once in 15 years and invites you out of the blue to fly across the globe, leaving your husband in an attempt to decode the geological secrets of the end of the world." And with that, Peter Masai stepped out of his apartment and strolled off through the park towards the Technical University with a spring in his step.

7

Washington DC

Jeff closed his laptop screen down and took a moment to process what he'd just agreed to do with his long-lost university buddy. Peter had always been convincing in whatever he tried to convince you of and maybe Jeff just wanted to be convinced of something, anything, to get away from his current job. Can a 30-minute Skype call really give him such purpose? It was like two TED talks interspersed with chit chat about Manchester, growing old (if not up) and girl talk.

Fair play to Peter, he'd pitched it to Jeff pretty much on the nose, got right on his sweet spot.

"You're working to someone else's agenda Jeff; you must be in that Bureau…." and then silence. No better way of making a point than leaving it hanging in the air like a ripe apple just waiting to be picked. "They're hoovering up any nay-saying scientists, climatologists, physicists - heck even geologists. You're no conformist Jeff, they're just using you."

Classic Peter, classic Jeff. No detail of who 'they' are supposed to be and Jeff, clearly being told what he has already been moaning about for years and not challenging him on it.

"It's time to break free Jeff, Elaine's got some cracking data from Africa and Latin America, we need the stuff only you can get access to." Jeff's brain started to churn.

"You want me to steal US Government data on climate?"

"Nope, not steal, that suggests you're removing it. We just need you to widen the circulation by two." What started off as a singular, Peter, was now a 'we', this was transatlantic NLP at work here, maybe Peter was a Scientologist now, sucking him into a cult. The Cult of Geological Fantasy. Peter's voice interrupted Jeff's distracted imagination. "No Jeff, not just climate data. We also need sea level data on a global scale, tectonic plate movements for the past one hundred years, anomalies in crust formations like those sinkholes in the Sahara and the landslides in Brazil."

"Oh ok, nothing else then, perhaps the JFK files or Area 51 access codes?" Jeff's tones were off the sarcastic scale. Peter didn't bite.

"If you can get those too why not but as you ask why not add ocean water density data if it exists. Oh, and bring me some of that Hershey's over too. And a Jets baseball cap."

"And the moon on a stick?" Jeff muttered as much to himself as to Peter. But they both already knew Jeff was on board.

"I'll need help getting access to all this Pete."

"I thought you might but select someone you can trust with your life, when this gets out, we'll be hunted down like animals."

"That's a little dramatic isn't it, Peter? I get the implications of what you're saying but it's not exactly mass international terrorism or an assassination attempt we're talking about here, it's some out there theory on planetary evolution and, in layman's terms, some pretty shit weather."

"Earth drying out is a little more than pretty shit weather and you know it." Pete wasn't put off by Jeff's challenge, it was logical and that's why he thought Jeff was great, he would act as the mirror for Pete, a real-life pragmatist to bounce ideas off.

"The truth of it Jeff is this is precisely the type of scaremongering that makes governments go crazy. Give people a gun or some chemical weapons and yes, they'll go kill people but that's quite linear. Put the fear of God into them and normally sane people turn into a collective bunch of idiots. They won't know whether to stockpile sunscreen or bottled water when this hits. We're in Millennium Bug territory here, mass hysteria on a global scale."

It was at that moment that the lightbulb flickered in Jeff's mind then shone out like a lighthouse. Jeff did have all the data Pete asked for – or at least could get pretty easily with Jane's help – and it wouldn't exactly be hard to get. All he'd have to say is that he'd been reading about some tinpot science chap on YouTube spouting rubbish, so he just wanted to release a government paper containing it. That was half of what the Bureau used all the scientists for since it had given jobs to disproving social media theorists. Only Pete hadn't spouted his online and, as far as Jeff was concerned, he actually might have a point. Jeff had been seeing all the things Pete was talking about and more in the past few years but had been too myopic to have pieced together the kind of impact Pete was picturing. Unprecedented global temperature rises, all kinds of disintegration on the Earth's surface and he had heard about some very unusual plate movements in the Indonesian zone but the one thing that stuck out as a total anomaly was the sea level data.

Climatic changes can influence medium term global temperatures, but sea levels were a straightforward equation. More water equals higher seas. And it seemed indisputable, if you'd read almost every scientific or multimedia news feed, that with the melting ice caps there was more water in the oceans. But not according to the recent data that Jeff had seen, and he wondered who else.

"Where's the water going Pete?" blurted Jeff almost as if it were against government policy to actually ask that question.

"Well Jeff it's either going up or out, as I sure don't see enough clouds in the sky to say it's still in our atmosphere, or it's going down."

"Impossible." said Jeff, folding back on more comfortable ground.

"Not impossible Jeff: unproven. Or it's still out there and there is some kind of gravitational pull from the core holding it all in, but even I'm less convinced by that now. I may have put on a few pounds but I'm pretty sure that's the schnitzels and steins not 10% more gravity. Although it would explain the global obesity crisis a little less harshly than telling people they're lazy and eat too much."

"And on that conversation, you're travelling halfway round the world?" was the first thing Jane said when Jeff called her to share his plans and see if she was 'in'.

"Yep," replied Jeff, "I'm overdue a load of holiday anyway and I think Pete might be on to something, we've got a couple of weeks until he presents to the IGA in Tokyo to get our, or at least his, facts straight."

"Ok Jeff, I'm doing this because I think you need this, and a little because the whole proposition is quite intriguing, I won't lie. But we're going to need someone with a much higher ranking than our lowly positions if this thing's going to fly." The use of the word 'we' was not lost on either of them. Jane was part of this too, she also needed a little excitement and was genuinely keen to give Jeff a boost he so badly needed.

"And I don't think it's too arrogant of me to say I might be better connected if you need some extra funding on an internal sponsor. I've heard there are a couple of Senators who are quite damning of the current US policy of climate change reversal. Problem being that telling 25 million voters the world is going to end isn't quite as successful as saying you've saved Mother Earth...funny how pathetic that sounds heh?" Jane took a deep breath as if running through in her mind a quickly assembling plan of action. "Give me twenty-four hours Jeff and I'll access all the info you're after, it's pretty low-level clearance stuff as it'll all be data and no IP with it so hope your brain is switched on, didn't think this kind of analysis was your forte Jeff."

"It isn't." Jeff replied. "Elaine's coming too."

"Wow ok, how's that working for you Jeff?" Jane's question was so simple, but it made Jeff instantly realise that he'd not got round to thinking what that reunion would be like. Seeing Pete again, no worries. A couple of beers and a backslap or two and they would get back in the swing of things he was sure but Elaine, that could be awkward, and Jeff could do awkward.

"Sod it," he succinctly said back to Jane, "according to Pete we're all going to die anyway so what the heck!"

"Awesome Jeff, definitely the best way to look at it, bravo to your maturity and sensitivity." She was heavy on the sarcasm again and with a scornful look to boot. "Guess you're working on the short-term Armageddon theory rather than the 300 million year one then? Not sure there's a massive plughole in the middle of the Pacific Ocean that all the water is draining out through Jeff."

"Well, we'll all know once we've had a proper look at the data with that theory in mind as well. Let's not close any options at this stage." Jeff was happier with the banter than admitting he was terrified about seeing Elaine again.

By ten o'clock the next morning, Jeff's plan was in place. He'd had his two weeks signed off without any real questions from his boss, booked an open return flight to Berlin, who knew what date he'd need or want to come back, and Jane had burned all the data, and more, onto a disc. He was set.

8

Berlin

One of the benefits of working for the Bureau was it was a truly Pan-American, very global role, which meant dealing with colleagues in every state and in multiple countries. Jeff had dreamt of cashing in all those frequent flyer miles, in one luxurious upgrade to first-class on a long-haul flight. He'd always had Bali in mind, but Berlin would do. And, cramped as he was in the middle seat of three in economy Lufthansa, he cursed the invention of Skype and video conferencing which meant he didn't have any frequent flyer miles to cash in and closed his eyes to dream of what might be if he were twenty years older.

Oh God, he thought, *I'd be in my late fifties and confined to economy class.* He glugged down the rest of his mini-Merlot, not his first and definitely not his last of the journey and reset his mind on what life would have been like in the Bureau 20 years ago. Pre-internet, pre-mobile, pre-laptops. When the working day is done, no one can get hold of you until you rock up at the office next morning. He'd have been jet-setting off all over the place, the king of face-to-face meetings, *kerching* as the frequent flyer points racked up.

He now had a Morton's Fork of choosing between leaning left on the enormous German lady with the cold meat snack selection or the right on a 50-year-old architect or whatever he was with all his work strewn across that tiny seatback table, every movement threatening to knock over his thimble of wine. Although that did give him an excuse to drink it all the faster. Instead, in his fantasy world of yesteryear he'd be rocking back in his open-neck Hawaiian, tipping his hat over his eyes and stretching out in his first-class cabin.

Those thimbles of Merlot were doing the trick for him as Jeff became lost in those weird, light moments of pure dozing, not really awake but not quite asleep, senses heightened and dulled at the same time. He pictured Bali coming into view, palm trees defining the shoreline of the island, leading on to the lush volcanic forests and paddy fields tiered up and down across the land. But something was different. The plane was too low, almost at tree level, no it was lower, he was looking out of the window onto a dusty, vacant landscape with the palm-lined island jutting out ahead. Carcasses of whales and thousands of perfectly formed fish skeletons lay across the floor as far as he could see.

Jeff's dream was feeling so real, sleep had taken over him, his eyes flickering, mouth loosely open, inevitable drool to come. It wasn't a plane he was in at all: it was a car. He was in a car that looked like the inside of a plane, and he was in the window seat, looking out over an endless sea of death as far as the eye could see. The car turned again and he could see where they were heading, was a gap in the palm trees up ahead with a well-used gravel track leading up to a huge building, on the side of it a Hollywood sized sign saying, 'Welcome to Bali - no rain since 2017 - a true paradise'.

As the car pulled closer, he saw that the palm trees

were rigid, not just like they'd be without wind but solid, as if they were made with concrete. Then it dawned on Jeff and a wave of desperate fear ran through his entire body…this is what the world will be like when all the water has gone. Dry seabed, no plant life. But how will humans survive? He could feel himself starting to panic. He looked around the plane/car thing he was in, and it was empty, hundreds and hundreds of empty seats. He moved towards the door and could hear a message coming over some kind of speaker system, 'Welcome to Bali, where it never rains.' The door opened and Jeff was engulfed by an intense, dry suffocating heat. He tried to step back into the air-conditioned vehicle, but it had vanished, as had the sign, the building, in fact everything had gone. It was just Jeff, standing alone, gasping for air, tongue hanging out desperate for moisture, in an ocean of desolation under a searing blue sky yet not a whimper of life. And then the shaking began.

"Entschuldigung, entschuldigung." spoke a lady's voice, a word he'd not heard before. And yet more shaking.

"Water there's no water. Need water." he could hear himself saying.

"Sir, excuse me sir." Jeff opened his eyes and was startled back to reality. "This gentleman called the bell to get you some water, he says you've been calling out for it in your sleep."

"Oh, thank you." Jeff composed himself again, the images of the sea-less Bali flickering away from his mind and smiled a slightly embarrassed smile, casually wiping away a drop of drool from the corner of his mouth. "Yes, I am rather thirsty." and took the bottle from the stewardess.

"Maybe one more of those fine Merlots would help too." Jeff figured his dreams weren't going to get much crazier than that one, although he noted there were another six hours of flying time to go. Jeff hoped his vision wasn't some kind of apocalyptic premonition but given he was pretty adept at compartmentalising stuff, he packed that particularly bad one way into a tiny, back corner of his mind, unscrewed the cap of his new wine, drained it into his ever so high quality plastic cup and sipped his way into a much better dream about being able to both fly and transport himself through time. Much better thought and his snoozy adventures got him all the way to Berlin.

The bear hug between Peter and Jeff in the arrivals zone of Berlin Tegel Airport was more one of two brothers who are only able to see each other at Christmas. It was strong, intense and full of all the emotion men hugs can convey to avoid the use of words. There it was, almost twenty years of catching up in one hug. Now the relationship had been reset they could pick up again.

"You've ruined my dreams man." Jeff smiled the most genuine smile. "You know how your theories mess with my head when I lose control of it."

"Sure do," Peter replied, "and I still have that recurring one about losing my dissertation at the top of Everest, which of course stretches all the way to the moon…"

Jeff took over. "… and you fall just out of reach from it…."

"That's the one. Anyway, no time for sleeping now so that'll help us both. *'Du kannst schlafen wenn du tot bist'* as the locals tell me, usually in the early hours when I've had a few too many steins. We've got proper work to do."

Jeff's face contorted trying to recall the tiny amount of German he'd picked up.

"You can sleep when you're dead Jeff - let's crack on."

Pete's face changed, now deadly serious, so much so it took Jeff by surprise, he was still a bit fuzzy from the plane and wine.

"Er, er yeah I guess so."

Peter couldn't hold it in anymore and blurted out with laughter. "Christ Jeff I'm taking the piss mate, thought I'd better try serious on you now we're all grown up and you work for the US president."

"Oh, thank God Pete, you had me worried there for a minute. And the president works for me, he's my bitch!"

"I can see that, Jeff, you guys are clearly on the same page about a lot of stuff! And there's a bin over there," Pete pointed across the concourse, Jeff again looked a little confused, "for that American twang you've developed Jeff - gee whizz you're sure gonna have a swell time in Berlin, Germany." his best US accent he could mock up.

"Pete, I've missed you, but it will take some adjusting to you again, especially after my 135-hour flight in cattle class. Shower, coffee, breakfast, coffee, that order. Then we can start."

"Deal. although I've one issue with that." Pete looked

quizzically at Jeff.

Jeff said, "go on…." expecting the worst.

"I've got you a coffee already." said Peter and handed over a steaming take-away cup to Jeff. "My rules - I get to change them." He smiled.

"Good coffee thank you." Jeff savoured the aroma and hot liquid life as it passed his lips. "Right, where's the subway?"

"Don't call it a subway Jeff."

Elaine had been pleasantly surprised by the lack of jet lag she'd felt since landing forty-eight hours ago from Singapore. She'd always preferred flying West, 'chasing daybreak' as she called it. So, she put her alertness to good use and got to know the city a bit more and spent a day as a tourist. A few serious minutes of chat with Peter made her realise that there might not be a great deal of time for 'pure fun' as he'd called it. To be fair that was the reason she'd flown halfway round the world and away from her husband, so she was clear with Pete that once she'd seen the stuff she had on her Berlin to do list, it would be wall to wall geology from there on.

Therefore, camera round the neck, guidebook in hand, she confidently strode out of Pete's flat into the majestic Tiergarten to start a day of exploration, enjoying the gentle hummering of the beech and oak trees whispering uniquely personal messages to those who strode beneath them. Pete had mapped out a basic How to Guide for Elaine to see the big-ticket items - Victory column, Brandenburg Gate, Reichstag, Alexanderplatz and the Wall

Museum at Checkpoint Charlie. Elaine was a bit concerned that Peter had told her to take 100 buses but on closer inspection of his plan, and the double-decker just passing her on the street as she entered the park, she realised it was the number 100 bus she needed. 'Best bus route in the world' according to Pete's note. It was the first route between East and West Berlin after reunification and as such, acts as a vehicular join the dots for so many of the city's landmarks.

    Elaine revelled in having a luxurious day of culture in a climate she didn't constantly sweat in, without having to share it with anyone. God, she felt so free, not just to be 8000 miles away from Mark as they were often separated by distance, but it was the sense of independence again. And a chance to get stuck into geological fun and games. She knew this might be her last, albeit her first in years, day to just be and she sure would make the most of it. Berlin was hers and she was fuelled by kebabs, schnitzels and coffee as she lapped up the history of the German capital. Given the seismic hypothesis Pete had invited her over to prove (or disprove as she'd almost said back) only added to the detachment she felt amongst other like-minded tourists and the good people of Berlin. There were scant signs of the apocalypse to come but she figured that it was hardly surprising given their location. Even the dinosaurs probably thought they were having a nice day, even after the meteorite, which ultimately destroyed their ecosystem, landed with a bump.

9

For the second time in three days, Pete was bringing an old friend back into his life and up the elevator and more literally, into his flat. He sensed that Jeff was starting to show his apprehension about who he was about to see for the first time in almost two decades and decided to attack it head on.

"It'll be fine Jeff, you're both grown up."

"I know Pete, just all feels a bit odd." Jeff opened up a little. "It's been a weird last week or so with you popping up from nowhere with your end of the world email and me just upping and leaving with half the US Government info on climate change in my backpack, all with the added benefit of Elaine being the other side of that door."

"Yeah, it's pretty cool, isn't it?" Pete was matter of fact, sensing correctly that Jeff wasn't asking for a deep and meaningful heart-to-heart on this. "Just come in and say, 'Hi Elaine how's it going' and I'm sure you two will be fine."

Elaine had been up for a few hours by the time Pete and Jeff got back from the airport and was already buzzing from Pete's very, very good coffee and the set of data Pete had left her to look over to kick off with. She was so absorbed in the files that she hadn't quite noticed that the two chaps were through the front door and had dropped their cases with an almighty boom on the hardwood floor. Before Pete even got the chance to nudge Jeff into action, Elaine popped her head up from the table and smiled a huge spontaneous smile.

"Hi Jeff, how's it going?"

"Yeah, good thanks Elaine, you?"

"Hell yeah." came her response. "I've got a terabyte of geological data to sift through and my boys back with me with zero plan of what the rest of my life has in store for me." She surprised herself, never mind Jeff and Peter, with that rather honest outburst but it was as succinct as it was true.

"It's actually two terabytes you'll be pleased to know." Jeff immediately felt relaxed, which surprised him a little, given the intensity of his relationship with Elaine and the way it had fizzled out in such a short space of time.

"Well, I won't lie," interrupted Peter, "I thought this moment had the potential to be a total fucking car crash." It was a comment which made both Jeff and Elaine's faces turn into tomatoes with eyes.

"Delicately done." said Elaine, her red face contorted in sarcasm.

"Yep, really subtle." followed up Jeff.

"My pleasure." beamed Peter. "I only had one thing on my to do list after picking Jeff up and you guys' sim cards, which was to bludgeon the inevitable elephant in the room that wandered in with Jeff and his years of emotional baggage." Pete was enjoying this but sensed he'd best not push it, the last thing he wanted was to upset them. On two levels really, one because he had no desire to upset them and two, he didn't want either of them to go straight back home again. He needed them both. So, he decided there had been enough of the emotion and going functional was the best plan of action.

"Jeff, your room is in there." He said, pointing to a door at the far side of the flat. "I suggest you drop your things, have a shower and join us for a project meeting in about half an hour, I'll get some food ready in that time." Toast. He thought, *that used to keep them going for days on end*, it seemed.

With Pete out of earshot in the kitchenette, Elaine looked over at Jeff as he carried his bags passed towards his room.

"Jeff, it really is good to see you again."

"You too Elaine, you too. You've travelled the world I hear?"

"Says you Captain America, and yes." Elaine confirmed. "My life story is pretty straightforward as Pete may have mentioned." Jeff was going to say Pete hadn't mentioned much at all but thought better of it. "Left uni, got married, followed him around the world, liked some, not so much other bits, got bored in Asia, Peter contacted me, now I'm starting again."

"Wow that's some shortcut life review! But mine's even easier...left uni, PhD, New York. Job with the US Environment Bureau sold out but not totally, that's why I'm here. Bit like you but without the marriage bit." Jeff let that hang in the air to see if Elaine would react, but she didn't so he carried on to his room.

Twenty-five minutes later, Jeff reappeared from his room looking, feeling and definitely smelling much fresher with a baseball cap in one hand and a massive Hershey's branded plastic carrier in the other.

"You didn't say how much chocolate you wanted Pete, so I thought I'd cover all bases." he said as he emptied the bounty on to the kitchen work surface, bars and bags spraying everywhere, cascading on top of each other and on to the floor and in the sink.

"I always wanted to know what became of the Milky Bar Kid." joked Elaine.

Peter joined in. "And at what point Elaine did you ever picture the Milky Bar Kid looking like that great beast of a man?"

Jeff wasn't holding back. "Come on, everyone knows the Milky Bar Kid doesn't age, he's the Bart Simpson of the chocolate world. Don't go round telling people I'm him, I clearly have issues already with people thinking I'm a famous film star."

"I'm sure they do Jeff, I'm sure they do…" chirped Pete. "Right," he then exclaimed decisively, "to business."

Both Jeff and Elaine were aware Peter had done a lot of thinking about the whole geological end of days scenarios and had a shared scepticism for all the positive noises coming out of global government offices about climate change reversal, but the next hour really crystallised it for both of them. Pete went into overdrive. He closed the blinds with a nifty app on his phone, fired up a mini projector and shared his IGA presentation with them.

"The gravitational pull at the Earth's core and its effect on mantle integrity." Pete brought Elaine and Jeff up to speed with his research and initial conclusions. "I got a bit wrapped up in the idea of the ever-expanding core with nowhere to go and the ultimate disintegration of the mantle and thus catastrophic misshaping, to put it mildly, of the Earth's surface. The premise that the Earth would kind of fall in on itself felt believable, we've seen planets and stars explode and implode: why not Earth? But then I applied the Elaine and Jeff roles to it, and, by that, I mean I projected what I reckoned you'd both have told me, and it was brutal so thank you for that."

At which Elaine and Jeff glanced over at each other with the same expression of *we didn't speak to him at all* on their faces. Anyway, despite the years apart they both sensed this wasn't a good time to say anything as Peter got into a flow, thinking, processing out loud and it was patently obvious he needed to get this out there.

"Geologically speaking, I appreciate the likelihood of my implosion theory manifesting itself is limited." Nods all round. Not dismissively, more encouraging from Elaine and Jeff to see what he'd say next. "...but most of the diagnostics I used to feed the theory made me wake up to a more grounded but potentially equally threatening outcome. And believe it or not, not everything I do has to end with dramatic consequences, although I appreciate they often do. And actually in this case too. Again.

"In the past eight years there has been a noticeable shift in government literature pointing at climate change reversal. Even through the Obama presidency and Paris Accord there were undercurrents of official statistics counter-evidencing popular theory on global warming and such like. Jeff, I think your ears will have really picked up now, you'll have seen this first hand, if not even been involved in it." Interesting, Jeff thought, immediately picturing him and Jane on one of their late-night benders talking exactly about this. He simply nodded in agreement, as if imperceptibly giving Pete's story credibility and the green light to continue.

"The reason the Tokyo IGA conference was postponed wasn't due to the cyclones in the South China Sea, they weren't even predicted to hit land, it was a cover."

Then there was a great 'Pete Pause'. They'd seen him use them impactfully so many times at uni in most of his presentations. "Go with me on this…..I've had a few of my most trusted students keep an eye on chatrooms, message boards and social media for the past few months, and it seems like the US Government are looking to use the IGA to start sending a message that there's enough evidence to prove climate change is a myth. Jeff, I appreciate what you must be thinking right now, given you work there."

Like a mind-reader, Pete had nailed it, Jeff immediately felt exposed. Was he idly just letting this happen under his nose? Pete was about to rescue him back. "The very reason you're here now is that something like this is happening and we all know you can sometimes be too close to something to see the bigger picture, you have all the pieces, and Jeff you've hopefully got those on that drive, but it can be impossible to step back and see something which seems so ludicrous it can't be true." And then a final butter-up for Jeff. "This is partly your doing, Jeff. You were always my mirror, helping me guide my wayward hypotheses back into some semblance of reality. So, I applied the Jeff rule to my scepticism and delusions of grandeur."

Wow! thought Elaine and Jeff, clearly at the same time as they both met each other's glances across the table, Pete had admitted his fantasy behaviour, it was real progress. But as he went on, they both equally realised this wasn't dampening his appetite for dramatic consequences to his theories too much.

"Elaine."

Oh, crikey, here goes, was her immediate internal reaction as she realised it was her turn in the spotlight. "You remember that student you worked with in Mexico?"

"Marco?" she recalled instantly, instinctively knowing where this was going. "The quirks in his data?"

"That's right." Peter nodded.

Jeff was a bit lost now, he knew Elaine and Pete had crossed paths about five years ago but clearly there was more to it. "He left us to go work for the US Government. Jeff, this will be yours to follow up on."

Pete was comfortable handing out tasks. Jeff smiled to himself, it wasn't a new thing since he'd become a professor, it was ever thus. Elaine suddenly came to life and Pete's eyes lit up as he could see the penny had dropped. It was Elaine's turn to pick up the story now.

"I was supporting Marco on his Amazon basin erosion project, doing what I do best," she mimicked a courtesy despite her seated position, unspoken that she was referring to her affinity with data mining, "...and all of a sudden one day it seemed he was done and snapped up by the US Government." Jeff interjected involuntarily.

"But that isn't anything strange Elaine, we've all sorts and everyone coming under the US Governmental Payroll, or other governments globally for that matter - all to work towards confirming this climate change myth, pretty much everyone knows that."

As soon as he said it, he regretted it. Statements like his were nearly always followed by someone saying in a mildly patronising manner: "Yes but what everyone doesn't realise is…." or something similar. So, he pre-empted the inevitable place putting.

"But you're going to tell me there's more to it aren't you?" Big smiles from Elaine and Pete, who appeared more aligned than Jeff could yet fathom.

As if reading his mind again, Elaine added, "I've had a bit of a head start on this Jeff, it's not as secret as you might think. Marco's work, as much as we know from our own research and knowledge, had revealed what he thought was some climate change reversal info. He thought he'd stumbled across the holy grail and hastily sent it across to the Environmental Agency. But we all know there is a spectacular conflict in evidence, hotter Earth, less ice thus more water in the oceans. So, when Marco, like so many others, see the third measure is static at best, they get all excited and basically forget however much they knew about science in the first place because of the magnitude of 'their' discovery." She hated doing it but felt an inescapable urge to perform two-finger air quotes, "And a nice Government salary and pension is a good earner and reward for some 'breakthrough' thesis."

Oh lord, she thought to herself, *that's two air quotes in less than thirty seconds.* What had she become?

"So," interjected Jeff, trying frantically to keep up, "are you saying this isn't about climate change?"

"That's exactly what we're saying Jeff, yes." Elaine took a nervous glance at Peter to check she was on the right path and Pete took that as permission to carry on.

"Yes and no Jeff." Peter re-opened his monologue. "Yes, the fact that sea levels aren't rising in line with widely accepted scientific theories is astonishing and, on some levels, it's magical - it would lead to the protection of over a billion people living in and off low-lying land or islands."

"And no?" Jeff teed him up deliciously.

"No, because it goes against everything Elaine just talked about. And no because climate change must be a lever for something much bigger. So, I've said no but perhaps I mean yes. Take a step back again for a minute. Who does climate change reversal benefit? Obvious answer. Everyone... Yadda yadda yadda. Yes, it's a wonderful world with no climate impact, we are passing on environmental stability to our children and our children's children after all and all that sentimental horseshit."

"Interesting take on it Peter." laughed Jeff.

"Thanks Jeff, I always was a Greenpeace kind of guy. Okay, let me put this another way, what does climate change stop?"

"Global industrial revolution." blurted out Jeff, he

was firmly on the same page now, pennies dropping everywhere.

"Millennials think the Tech Giants rule the world in their sanitized, anti-social, screen-led worlds. Who needs actual human interaction when you can tell the world you're having a happy day or taking a dump or buying a pizza from your sofa. They can sign up to their online petitions and boycott the bad guys, little do they realise that there's a whole new area of the Earth's surface that's being raped for all the precious metals that make their smartphones, electric cars and sexbots." Pete could feel that comforting yet immature rage that radio phone-ins gave him and snapped back into the real world and got back on topic, much to the disappointment of both Elaine and Jeff, who were clearly looking forward to a massive rant and exhaled deliberately aggressively to show their displeasure of Pete's control over his emotions.

"Climate change as it was, had made it a political crime in the West to carry on raiding the Earth for its fossil fuels and sending all that crap into the atmosphere. Oil, coal and gas. The automotive industry. The behemoths of Western shareholder value, the sure bets. Where there's economic prosperity you can bet your bottom dollar there's a need for fuel. To be fair there have been some good attempts to curb pollution and the like. CFCs have gone, river-side factories taking water from downstream and send their waste upstream, so they have to use their own wastewater instead of just pumping any old rubbish out. Also, recycling rates in Europe are high.

"But, and it's a big but, they're only scratching the surface when it comes to the systematic decline in our ecosystem, solely in the hands of less than one percent of the global population. And now the Western goose is fat, having eaten all the food it can see and it's looking East or South, telling everyone else they need to go on a diet, even before they've had a chance to gorge on the feast of economic progress. Because that appears to be the universal measure of progress of GDP. I'm no socialist but three percent growth every year, sorry I should say just three percent GDP growth every year, means a doubling pretty much every twenty years. Doubling the needs of seven billion people with a planet whose resources are becoming ever more finite, a planet which is raising a white flag in one hand and holding a pollutant mask over its mouth with the other, a planet which, in layman's terms, will be fucked by the end of the century. If not before."

"Point being," Elaine jumped back in, "you throw all that in the mix and climate change stops progress as you define it. The handbrake goes on shareholder portfolios and a straitjacket for developed and developing nations' politicians whose currency is GDP. The mantra of sustainable growth is nearly always about sustaining economically sensible growth year in year out, not growing sustainably or even better, or worse, depending on how you see it, living sustainably. I get it. A billion people in China riding bikes. China progresses and what do you get? A billion cars. What does that mean? Car manufacturers with drool on the chins, petroleum companies frothing at the mouth and an exponential growth in drive-thru McDonald's."

"So, it's not all bad then?" Jeff then immediately realised this wasn't the time for flippancy. "Okay sorry." He held his hands up apologetically. "But throwing something out there, yes there's still a lot of mining and drilling for fossil fuels but the world is definitely moving to renewable, with hybrid and electric cars, wind farms and all that jazz - the Germans are mad for it aren't they!? So even if there is evidence that climate change isn't happening, won't industry and Governments just carry on down that path anyway, given the investments they've made already?"

"Jeff thank you for offering an alternative point of view and I'm sure you've very little conviction behind it, but let's play out a scenario. You like beer, yes? Bottled beer, cold, nice and easy, refreshing, makes you feel good, handsome even." Pete smiled: they all knew this was going to be entertaining if nothing else. "Then everyone, friends, scientists, governments even, tells you that beer is bad, real bad, so you buy yourself an expensive smoothie maker or a NutriBullet, other brands are available I'm sure, probably more than one and you start buying fresh veg and fruit and make yourself really lovely, tasty, refreshing drinks which also make you feel good, again handsome because that beer belly starts going down a touch. Then people start telling you that they got it wrong, that beer is actually fine. What are you going to do Jeff?"

"Beer please Pete." replied Jeff without hesitation.

"So, it doesn't take a genius to realise that climate

change not happening is big business. Really big business. Vote winning business."

10

Washington DC

The idea of Jeff flying off to Europe with a suitcase full of US Government data to save the world with his university friends felt to Jane a little like the script to some lame made-for-TV film she could imagine watching, unable to channel hop. Sharknado, but with climate change. She knew she had crossed a line accessing all that information, at least she'd flirted with a line. Her level at the Bureau gave her full access to base data points and approved reports, but not all reports as she was very aware. She'd not left the country with it; she'd only passed it to a colleague, but intent comes into every scenario like this. She wrestled with the rights and wrongs of feeding Jeff all that information, strictly it shouldn't be leaving on a jet plane to Berlin, she was fully aware of that. But on the other hand, she was only assisting a trusted colleague. The fact that it didn't affect her sleep that night told her that her conscience was clear if nothing else.

Jane was a conformist by nature, or more likely nurture, the only child of two teachers, born and raised in Durango, a small town in southwest Colorado. She'd had a structured, disciplined, but not unhappy childhood. At school she'd gone under the radar to a certain degree, a constant yet quiet achiever. She topped the class in most subjects in a reliable, diligent fashion. Never one to get in trouble with teachers, she'd almost go into meltdown at the thought of being disciplined or even told off in class. Once in tenth grade she'd been caught doing Emily Rogers' geography homework, whilst Emily was out on a date with one of the school football team. Emily had begged her and, not being great at saying no, Jane reluctantly agreed. They both ended up in detention, not Emily's first time but definitely Jane's.

"I'm not angry with you Jane," Mrs Withers had told her, "I'm just disappointed." They'd been caught out, not because of the handwriting – Emily had copied it out – not even because of the similarity of both of their submissions, it was the exact opposite. Emily had been awarded the top mark in the class and Jane not even in the top five. Emily wasn't stupid, but she'd win a popularity contest before winning an intelligence test, so they got found out. Jane had made the mistake of doing Emily's homework first and used up all the good answers before doing her own. It was ironic really that the topic for that work was all about the impact of rising sea levels over time on low lying population hubs.

Even more ironic was after the detention, Mrs Withers effectively became a mentor and pseudo-private tutor for Jane to get into college to study geology at the University of Colorado in Boulder. Same state as home but seven hours on a good day and effectively a world away from her folks. She threw herself into university, and like a lot of students it acted as a fresh start for Jane, leaving behind all the stigmas and social chaos of high school. Everyone starts equal at college and Jane thrived, she found a good balance of study, alcohol and boys, often mixing two, sometimes all three. Such was Jane's affinity for all things geology and all things Boulder, she stayed on for her PhD. Trend analyses were all the rage back then, the internet had opened up so much shareable information that students in Colorado, or anywhere for that matter, could suddenly benefit from the work of someone thousands of miles away and vice versa. Jane had considered at one point that she'd stay in academia ad infinitum - she had the brain for it, mixed with a deep passion for geology and a very eloquent and masterful approach to communicating about it. All of which led her to being fished out of the university and onto the national payroll.

The lady from the Environmental Bureau was so enthusiastic and positive, if Jane were to meet her again now she'd call her out immediately as a fraud. Although if she did see her again, she'd struggle to recognise her, certainly no idea what her name was. It was like she was there for one day then disappeared from view. Jane was due to have one of her last tutor meetings before submitting the final version of her doctorate paper on global sea levels. The Bureau lady was already in the room when she arrived with a copy of one of her early drafts in her hand and a smile that would not have looked out of place on a teleshopping channel, believable yet hollow.

A great deal of compliments and congratulations later and Jane was facing a decision. Stay and complete her PhD and go further into debt or 'bring all your knowledge and undoubted passion to the Bureau and leave all that debt behind you. Continue your work in the best-funded geological research programme available anywhere on the planet and be paid for it'. She signed there and then, it sounded too good to be true and to be fair to the generic smiley lady, she also knew it came across as a bit sudden and put no pressure on Jane to fully commit.

"How about you look over the contract agreement and let the HR department know when you're ready." She had said and amazingly, she'd never put a date on it as a deadline, which, looking back on it, made Jane a bit confused. However, she discussed the offer with her tutors and even the dean - predictably she was delighted one her students had been 'handpicked', her words, by the Government and gave her full blessing to go. Her father had the contract looked at by one of his friends, Mack. "He's one of the finest lawyers in the state", although Jane doubted that one hundred percent, but she trusted her father's judgement and, four weeks later, walked through the doors of the US Environmental State Department building in Washington DC.

If Jane and Jeff had crossed paths in those early months of her time at the Bureau, there was little doubt in Jane's mind that they'd have not gotten off on the right foot. Although not particularly unprofessional, Jeff reeked of cynicism, there was an air about him which didn't sit quite right. Jane, on the other hand, went into full Jane-mode from day one. Yes is the answer, what's the question. A willing and honest worker, she was a doddle to manage but wasn't a pushover, although even she wondered if that had more to do with her boss than her self-control.

Michelle Grant had been at the Bureau for getting on

twenty years and had progressed steadily in her first few years, moving from the same researcher role that Jane was in now, through senior analyst to analyst team leader to her current position of Non-US North American Special Projects Head. This most incredible of job titles essentially meant that if stuff was happening that might impact the US but originated outside of the US then it fell under Michelle Grant's remit. "Earthquakes, tidal waves, landslides (really big ones), hurricanes, that kind of stuff." was Michelle's answer to Jane's eagerness to grasp what might fill her time up being in her team. But what she wanted most in her professional career was to join the Bee-Team, a recently formed group of researchers which had been allocated a multimillion-dollar budget to identify solutions to the global crisis impacting bee populations and thus potentially restricting global food supply.

Michelle had spent eighteen months for work experience at the British Bee Association in North Yorkshire, UK before she joined the Bureau so had carried a personal and professional affection for bees for many years. Jane took it upon herself to ensure the NUSNASP Team had the most successes and best research documentation, one because she was a bit of a nerd or a perfectionist (she felt both were a decent description) and two, because she knew what it might mean for her manager to be selected for the role she craved.

As had been the way at both school and college, a motivated and directed Jane was an academic juggernaut and she processed data like a super-computer and handed some high-level summaries to Michelle, who in turn, took them to the powers that be. Jane wasn't really sure who that was but one summer afternoon, Michelle came bounding down the corridor and gave Jane an enormous hug. "Guess the meeting went well then? But I'm sensing this isn't about the hurricane season in Mexico getting later each year, is it?" A grin was building on Jane's face too now, Michelle's excitement was infectious.

"I got it Jane, I got it. They've asked me to head up the Bee-Squad. And I start on Monday. And you're going to be okay too Jane." A slight nervousness washed over her as she braced herself for some troubling news.

"How so? Am I not okay now?"

"Oh yes Jane, you've been fabulous, I really lucked out getting you in my team... but no, they're shutting NUSNASP down, so you'll be getting a new project, I'd take you with me but there's already a full team of researchers there and you're already earmarked for a special project." Jane's ears pricked up as she tried to process all this information at the same time. Firstly, she was out of a job, or not, and someone whom she didn't know wanted her to work for them.

"Worry not my dear, you helped me no end getting me my new job, so I put in a good word for you at the researcher buffet."

Jane had heard about the researcher buffet from some of her junior peers and everyone called it a slightly different name. In essence it was a resource allocation meeting where junior researchers were selected for certain projects in a kind of bidding process by the heads of departments, project leads and sometimes very senior Government officials.

"Sounds like you've got yourself quite the reputation in the Bureau already Jane. I do wish you all the very best for what I know will be a sparkling career be it here or elsewhere." It stuck with Jane at the time as that was an interesting thing for a departing boss to have said; she tried to unpick it for many years following. It was clear that Michelle Grant had been her silent sponsor in her progression within the Bureau and the fact that she'd been seemingly hand-picked by Senator Gordon to run the climate research project was down to her but also the comment about where her career could lie gnawed away at her. That clarity had come during one of her many boozy sessions with Jeff as they challenged each other about their purpose. Perhaps Michelle had already spotted that total conformity wasn't actually Jane's greatest strength, she was just very good at it. If Jane knew what her greatest strength was, she wouldn't be the Jane she was today.

11

A few months into her time working for Senator Gordon led to a rather impactful introduction to Jeff. Gordon only ever needed top level summaries and he liked them in a certain way. One single paragraph stating the outcome, effectively a newspaper subheading after the big headline. Then a maximum of three sentences with some justification of the event or outcome or policy then no more than five bullet points of data or evidence. This was all to fit on the top half of a page of A4. Two charts were permitted on the bottom half, one of which could be a photo, but only if the resolution was 'more than acceptable'.

The Senator was a man of few words, but he was respectful and appreciative of Jane's work and her ethic. Jane had heard stories about Gordon being a bit of an ogre, but they appeared to have a good working relationship, the few times they interacted. He didn't say much when he got what he wanted, just a curt but not overly impolite, 'thank you, that'll do'. And when he didn't like something, he was direct, too direct clearly for some of the junior researchers who had walked in Jane's shoes previously, but for her, she could see past the directness and interpreted it as clarity. He was a Senator and, as such, she felt he had probably earned the right to expect work to be correctly presented and accurate the first time of asking.

Gordon sat on the Central Government Board for the Environment, nobody could explain to her exactly what it actually did, and it didn't feel right to just ask him directly, so Jane just went about her work with gusto, gathering data, mixing it up and getting it all onto a single sheet, same format every time. She loved the challenge of it and made damn sure she never once contravened the specifics Gordon demanded. She'd written papers on such a variety of topics from seismic tremors, wind speeds in Texas, Canadian winter temperatures, even one on bee populations which delighted Michelle Grant no end to be contacted by Jane for some excellent advice and information. All the papers were relatively straightforward in that they were self-contained ideas with limited conjecture needed. The day she met Jeff was the first multi-dimensional task she'd been set, it felt like a test, or more accurately, one of those dreams where your boss gives you a virtually impossible assignment and with an almost impossible deadline.

"Jane I've an unscheduled meeting with the Board at 9am tomorrow and I need something on why climate change isn't happening."

Jane was momentarily speechless, processing the Senator's words, then speechless for the next few moments too. It was immediately and likely deliberately, obvious to both of them that writing a paper demonstrating climate change would be much more straightforward, albeit not without challenge in twenty-four hours. It was the first time she had seen Senator Gordon let his guard down as a small, almost imperceptible grin appeared on his face.

"I look forward to receiving it by 8am tomorrow. And it needs to be tight as we'll have no time to change it."

"Your paper or the climate?" Jane was still a little

shocked by the enormity of her next twenty-four hours, but she was sure he winked at her, maybe not an actual wink but she definitely got the impression he realised this was a little out of the ordinary for a junior researcher. Perhaps he believed in her, perhaps he didn't actually need it and really it was just a test, or even worse, a wind-up, a bullying tactic to see how far he could push her. Or worse still, it was a sign that policy was genuinely shifting towards climate change denial in Washington. That idea terrified her.

    Jane wasn't normally prone to panicking but this wasn't normal, not for her anyway. Perhaps she'd been given an easy ride so far at the Bureau and for everyone else this was just like the day job. She grabbed the laptop and notepad from the hot desk and scampered across the office in the direction of the records room. She wasn't entirely sure what she wanted to pull but figured by the time she did, she'd wish she was in the records room. The one thing she hadn't factored in, which seemed odd really in a building of over three thousand employees, was other people getting in her way. When panic strikes, the mind becomes dangerously self-obsessed and the concept of sharing space becomes secondary, as if moving somewhere else will help solve any crisis, as long as you're moving, you might be moving closer to the solution.

    But from Jeff Williamson's point of view, what he saw in the corridor on the eighth floor of the Bureau building was a blur of long brown hair framing a chuntering face and the feeling of a laptop digging into his ribs, followed by the juvenile sensation of warm liquid, in this case coffee, running down his trouser leg.

"Wow hello." smiled Jeff as he helped to pick a rather forlorn Jane up from the floor having bounced off Jeff's sizeable frame. "Rugby training is 6 o'clock on the front pitch if you're looking for that perhaps?" Jane was already confused enough; she hadn't even seen Jeff standing in the corridor minding his own business drinking his coffee.

"Oh, you're English." as if that helped put some order back on proceedings. "What's rugby?" she asked involuntarily, as if it really mattered now. "Oh, right it's one of your funny games no one else plays, isn't it? Like soccer."

In equal measure, Jeff hated how Americans were so dismissive about the stuff they don't do but also craved on behalf of the Brits, if not the rest of the world, to have that level of self-confidence as a nation that it can only be a thing if you do it.

"Yes, you're right, I am English. I say aluminium, pavement and nappy (although not very often), but I do work here and feel obliged to offer help - it's what the English do well in theory. Chivalry and getting people cups of tea in times of crisis. My bet is you're not too late for something yet, because you're still here, but you're still in a mad rush to do something?" Jane had gathered herself, flicked her hair back into place in a common decency kind of way – not a flirty kind of way – then smiled back at Jeff.

"What's a nappy? No scrap that, not top priority to know that." Jeff sensed she was probably talking to herself so let it slide.

"Seriously is there anything I can do to help, my boss

is away, and I don't really do much anyway, at least let me fix you a cup of tea."

"Look I don't want to sound rude of anything and I'm truly sorry and embarrassed I ran into you the way I did, and the fact you've spilled coffee down your suit pants, but unless you've some pretty salient points around the reversal of climate change, then I'll have to pass on that cup of tea I'm afraid Mr.....!?"

"Jeff," He finished off her sentence. "I'll put the kettle on then."

Jane looked surprised, mainly because she was surprised, as if he'd ignored everything she'd just said.

"Jeff Williamson, Climate Division, I think you and I are going to get along just swell." Jeff enjoyed trying some Americanisms now and again.

Jeff and Jane bonded over that first drink together, vended tea that bore little resemblance to Jeff's view of a decent cuppa, and their friendship progressed from tea to beer in no time at all.

"Assume this paper of yours is needed for Board tomorrow?" mused Jeff.

"Yes. How did you know that?" Jane was again surprised but this time a little impressed at the insight, although she had no real reason to be either.

Maybe Jeff's on the board itself? she thought, *no that's not it...*

Jeff stopped her thoughts in their tracks. "Whenever there's a climate agenda item at Board, our response levels go up and the chatter is noisier than normal in our team.

And you've written it in big letters on the top of your notepad, guess we've got until 8am tomorrow, haven't we? We won't need that; you'll be done by the time the drones have left their desks this evening."

"We?" Jane's voice raised an octave. "Surely you've better things to do than get bogged down with me on this?"

"Anything that gets discussed at any level about climate makes it day-job for me Jane, and the fact that this is going to Board via Senator Gordon I assume…." Jane nodded, "…means there's some serious consideration going into this whole climate denial agenda and I'm not comfortable with it." Jane could already see that there was more to Jeff than him playing the English stereotype, an underlying passion for what he was working on, a passion she could identify with.

"I've been working on climate variation since I left university and, sure, I can find you a thousand evidenced examples where you could argue there's a sustained, or at least impact, on climate. But equally, I could spend the rest of my working days evidencing that something is happening and it's big, really, *really* big. And bad. Scary bad. My concern is you're pushing against an open door here Jane, so to a certain degree what you'll go back with is largely irrelevant."

Jane looked a little crestfallen, she still carried a refreshing naivety that scientific evidence would drive Government policy 'for the good of the people' she hoped, but this chance meeting with this intelligent, curious, articulate yet slightly oafish Englishman had imparted a tidal wave of work experience on her saving five to ten years of waiting to find out for herself that there wasn't a great deal of altruism at the higher echelons of the State.

"Basically, if you don't do it, they'll only find someone else to do it, so my view is better to be on the inside than be excluded entirely. We must work on the basis that one day the smog will clear and someone more important than us decides to do something material or we'll all be royally f......."

"Atishoo!!!" Jane sneezed in an almost comedy show drama that drowned out Jeff's profanity.

"Bless you Jane." the deep baritone of Senator Gordon as he'd chosen that exact moment to walk past the kitchenette cubby hole. "How are you getting on with that one-pager?"

"Oh yes Senator, we'll have it for you later this afternoon." she was surprised that she said 'we', so at least that made it clear to both Jeff and Jane that this would indeed be a joint effort.

"Very good." replied Senator Gordon, glancing between Jeff and Jane like they were a couple of kids caught with their hands in the biscuit tin, and set off again with a smirk on his face muttering, "teamwork makes the dream work."

Jeff looked at Jane and mouthed the words 'thank you'. "Guess that makes up for the coffee spillage now, you saved my bacon. Although not quite like criticising the Führer in front of the Gestapo, dropping an f-bomb in full earshot of a Senator wasn't Bureau policy on how to get ahead in life. Did he just say teamwork makes the dream work as he walked away?" Jeff couldn't be sure he wasn't making it up as it seemed so far-fetched.

"I think he just might have done." grinned Jane back. "I do wonder if he's not all the type of person which he comes across as, there's something deeper about Senator Gordon that I don't pick up from any of the other senior officials I've come into contact with, there's a human side to him." Jane was looking for Jeff's opinion.

"Well Jane there have been rumours for a while that a secret committee has formed to enable an alternative Government policy to be pursued at a point in time, and Gordon's name has been linked to it more than once."

"Interesting." Jane's brain was firing up again. "So maybe this paper he's asked me to write is a double bluff?"

"Indeed Jane, or maybe not, and we can't just ask the chap, too much risk involved there. It's a right hornets' nest and I'm not willing to make my job insecure by following up, so either way you need to get him a credible paper."

"Okay, you're right," Jane was back on task again, "let's get this thing done."

"Deal, I'll give my tuppence worth Jane, then I imagine you can work out how to build on it and make it Senator friendly - you must be good at it, or you'd not be in Gordon's team. Climate change is all about emotion." started Jeff much to Jane's confusion and, noting the crumpled look on Jane's face, he clarified.

"Climate change narrative is all about emotion, if it's happening that means you have to stop using air conditioning in the sticky summer months and the newspapers carry stories of Pacific islands disappearing under the sea, and even parts of GB too, although for a number of reasons, East Anglia underwater isn't necessarily a bad thing." Jane enjoyed Jeff's little sidetrack anecdotes and how he was able to make light of such a significant global issue, but he was English after all. How she wished her country folk could use such subtleties.

"But" he concluded, "if there is no climate change then we can all live guilt free, safe in the knowledge that Earth can cope with whatever we throw at it, clever Earth, clever people (aka Governments). And the most bandied about case for climate stability are, in no particular order: oxygen creation by all the new trees being planted; infant mortality reducing exponentially in Africa; sea levels holding at current levels; extremes of weather being a natural occurrence over the length of Earth's history and the global obesity crisis. If climate change is killing crops, how and why is everyone getting so fat?"

A sharp intake of breath from Jane but Jeff cut her off before she had a chance to say anything. "I know, remember I'm not telling you what I think of what prevailing good scientific practice is telling us, I'm simply telling you what's already being used, all you have to do is get into that mindset to be able to use them as policy backup arguments."

That afternoon with Jeff was a critical part of Jane's professional development where she learned the art of working to someone else's agenda even if she didn't believe in it herself. The world, she conceded, was full of people disagreeing over the same piece of information, she was just being paid for her part of it.

"I know you know this Jane but it's human nature, you offer two people identical evidence, and it is very possible they will draw opposite conclusions. Our desire for completeness and storytelling fills in blanks where more evidence is essential. Pretty much all sports work on this basis, you and I could watch the same game, regardless of the sport and come up with a thousand different opinions on what happened and more importantly why it happened. He wasn't trying, he tried to miss, he doesn't care about the club because I heard he wants to move away. Blah blah blah.

"Anyway, I'm off on one so will drag myself back in again, but you know for yourself when it comes to climate change and we get a few days of sustained rainfall, half the population thinks that means everything is okay because the manufactured story of climate disaster is deserts and withered trees, so rain must mean it's okay. It's scary really how simple we are."

Jane emailed the paper to Senator Gordon at 5pm as promised and she could see from his email icon that he was still logged on so would be able to look at it immediately. As was a ritual in the coming months and years, Jeff and Jane shared a beer that very evening, Jane's treat to thank Jeff for being so helpful and successfully so it seemed.

"Within five minutes he'd emailed back," Jane recounted, "and I had to re-read it a few times, you know when you suddenly think you've attached the wrong document and whoever you've sent it to replies with a bit of a piss-take comment in jest. Well, I checked, and I definitely sent the right paper, our paper, and only that."

"Go on, what did he say then?" Jeff was intrigued now.

"Well, he thanked me for it and said it was exactly what he needed and expected."

"Expected!" interjected Jeff, "That's a word laden with so many possible interpretations, isn't it?"

"Exactly," Jane agreed, "but the second sentence was the real clincher if you want to be even more intrigued. He said, and I quote exactly the words on the email, 'I especially liked the photo of the islanders fishing, right where I'm at with this too Jane, regards Edward.'"

"Oh Christ, he's on our side Jane, I don't think I've ever known a Senator or anyone of that rank to sign off so personally unless there's something more going on you've not mentioned….is there Jane, maybe a little love affair with Senator Gordon?" Jane wasn't offended, she could clearly see Jeff was teasing her.

"No, clearly not, but I haven't quite finished saying what he wrote, he added a winking emoji after his name. He's definitely on our side Jeff, I can't believe we got away with that photo in the first place."

"I did tell you this whole thing is about emotion, especially the deniers, they love a photo. Smiling people don't have problems, how can they, they're smiling. And people who are trying to convince others about climate change always use graphs, pie charts and stats - very dry (excuse the pun) very hard evidence coupled with an apocalyptic withering plant or tree desert image. It's not the world we're dealing with here."

And so, for beer after beer, Jane and Jeff bonded over their common beliefs about politics, science fiction films, how cold beer should optimally be to be drunk and quite often about climate change. They became a great support for each other, and Jeff never got jealous when Jane got the plum assignments. She learned, partly from Jeff ironically, how to play the game better and Jane in turn never forgot how Jeff had helped her that day when it could have been so much harder.

Despite the years that had passed, when Jeff got the email from Peter Masai and needed some data to be collated, Jane didn't hesitate. She admired his impulsions, she wasn't sure she had that in her and thought she could live a little vicariously in his endeavours, her data and his action. She was well known and respected in the Bureau as a manager of expansive knowledge and dedication. She'd been given a number of dedicated researchers to look after (nurture she felt) and they always left her with a level-headed ambition and unsurpassed passion for doing the best they could so when it came to calling in a favour or two to get the wealth of data Jeff and his friend Peter needed, there wasn't a single recipient of the request who even considered not dropping everything to help her. She was known for wanting to know her stuff, not just be told, but to actually have the evidence so her demands, although far-reaching, weren't going to raise any eyebrows. And the fact that she even thought there might be suspicions raised, said a lot for where the prevailing Government were taking things.

Jane struggled with the parallels because they were too abhorrent to genuinely compare, but there was a way of thinking one was encouraged to have in late 1930s Germany and having opposing views just weren't the views to have. Jane had enough trouble with Creationism finding its way on the school curriculum, but she was aghast when she heard the rumours, from quite a reliable source, that climate stability was going to be taught to the nations' children.

The more she thought about it, the angrier Jane was becoming. Jeff had flown all the way to Germany to at least do something about what was going on. Not long after Jane would have landed in Berlin, Jane got her chance, albeit not by request, to vent her views. Just before 6pm, she was still in the office of course, her mobile phone rang. Withheld number, probably some cowboy insurance form asking her about a recent accident that wasn't her fault. That would have been straightforward, what she got was anything but.

"Hello Jane?"

"Yes?" replied Jane, already sensing this wasn't an insurance call centre agent at all and a feeling of familiarity to the voice she couldn't quite pinpoint.

"It's Edward Gordon here." Senator Edward Gordon calling Jane, her life almost flashed in front of her eyes as she nervously held the phone to her ear. "We'd appreciate a few minutes of your time if you're available please?"

12

Marco Hernandez was born in the US to Mexican parents and was the only one of their five children to make it to a university. They were immensely proud of their third born as were his two older brothers and two younger sisters. Like many Mexicans, Marco Snr and Paulina Hernandez had sacrificed themselves for their children so they could grow up with a more prosperous lifestyle than they had experienced in the poorer neighbourhoods of Guadalajara.

Lack of university education hadn't held Marco's siblings back, his elder brothers had both become mechanics in the town they were born in, Fremantle on the southside of Houston, and both had married local American girls and were living a version of the American dream their parents had slogged so hard to provide for them. They'd never be millionaires, but they were secure and happy with dual-passports and an inevitable family to come.

Marco's sisters had also made the most of the opportunities presented to those who applied themselves. Angelina, a year younger than Marco, had been a good but not excellent student and had chosen to leave high school and go straight into work. A new company had opened a call centre in the Northern suburbs of Houston and Angelina took a gamble that they'd make good on their promises to new starters. As it turned out, Amazon had done pretty well and those who were there from the early days prospered the most. She was now running the day shift in the call centre, with responsibility for several hundred employees and looking after millions of dollars' worth of transactions and was terrifically happy with her lot.

The youngest Hernandez child, as is often the way in large families, had to find her own independence, so was a very confident, outgoing and creative girl called Madeleine. Having performed in any part of any concert, play or musical she was eligible for at High School, it was no surprise to anyone who knew her that she would end up in some kind of theatre. Which she did. Houston's leading playhouse in fact, that was great on a couple of levels. One, she got to follow her dream up on the stage and two, it meant Marco Snr and Paulina got free tickets to the theatre almost at will, something they'd scant be able to afford themselves, and more often than not they'd get to see their youngest child perform her heart out in front of them.

Marco had always been the academic member of the family, and for sure none of his siblings felt any resentment that more of their parents' hard-earned money had been directed his way to support his progress to university. However, for Marco himself, he felt it put an unspoken pressure on him which he would carry through his life, influencing his decisions good or bad. It even led to him cheating in one of his high school exams, only once and it barely had any impact on his overall results but the guilt he carried of taking that tiny scrap of paper into his maths exam with a set of microscopically written equations on them stayed with him. He'd never done anything like that again but deep down he didn't think he was quite as bright as his family thought he was, or indeed as his high school results graded him.

He knew from the age of fourteen he was on course for being the first Hernandez to attend university. It was clear that his brothers were better with their hands than their minds and he also knew that his attending university would be that badge of honour for his poor parents that would show to the world that they belonged in the United States, that a Mexican could compete academically with home-grown talents. His strong scientific brain took him to Flagstaff Arizona, where he earned a decent and wholly cheat-free degree in Geology and Physical Geography. Even at that point, he wasn't sure if he was doing it for himself or his parents, and he was terrified by a lack of self-confidence as his graduation date got closer and closer and he couldn't decide what to do next.

His parents unwittingly fuelled this internal crisis by asking all the right questions he didn't want to be asked: "What job have you got lined up Marco?... where will you move too next?... have you got a girlfriend?... what does she study?... is she a law student Marco?... or maybe a medical undergraduate?"

He could sense they were a little disappointed when he told them of his plans to further his studies as a researcher, a senior one at that mind, although he didn't know what it meant to be 'senior' at the University of Mexico. He had responded to a posting on the departmental intranet about 'making the world better understood' under the guidance of Professor Peter Masai, Manchester University alumni and preeminent Geologist and all-round science aficionado (Peter had written the advert himself with gusto). Marco didn't tell his parents, but it really was the first thing he'd actually looked at, and he felt it might delay the bigger decision of what to do with his life now he was the first Hernandez with a degree under his belt, and the family weight of expectation firmly planted on his narrow shoulders.

Marco knew his parents' disappointment was less about the role at the university, they thought it was a great use of his talents, it was just the location that was the issue. It could only feel like a backward step for them, having sweated blood and tears to wrench themselves out of Mexico only for their most gifted child (academically at least) to head back there; it was a difficult story to tell.

Although unstated, it was to everyone's relief when Marco got plucked from the relative obscurity of the University of Mexico to a high-profile role in a major Government department in Washington. It allowed Marco Snr and Paulina some long overdue boasting about their academic prodigy and for Marco Jnr himself this justified his decision to head for a career in research. He was about to go big time and he was damn sure he'd be taking his chance.

13

Washington DC

Senator Nick Johnson and Director of the USEA Nancy Rastik had been meticulously planning the unveiling of their climate change U-turn for the past three years. Both were privately long-term sceptics, unfailing in their belief that the activists were, at best, morons and the naysayers were again in fact misguided. Their commitment to the cause gave them an audience at the Oval Office on many occasions, assisting the president and his closest advisors on the 'real' impact of fossil fuels and carbon emissions. They weren't party to the outcome of those plans or policies but from the number of times they saw senior figures from Chrysler, Nissan, Chinese Energy giants and such like, it didn't take much guesswork to show that they were paving the way for some multi-million, probably billion-dollar deals.

Johnson and Rastik had no problem with that, they too were very well-paid cogs in the American dream machine and if they could do their bit to allow fellow American citizens to make a dollar or two then that was a job well done.

After meeting at the Harvard Speech and Parliamentary Debate Society, Johnson and Rastik had similar trajectories in their fields whilst remaining, if not close friends, then in a productive and warm relationship. Nick Johnson had spent a few years in the Automotive industry, appropriately enough, on a fast-track system, then cashed in his shares and followed his first love – politics – with equal vigour and success, rising swiftly through the ranks to become one of the youngest Senators in Eastern US history. He was charismatic and decisive, the two key attributes of the most successful leaders. He carried himself as if he was handsome, which indeed he was, confident body language with his well-kept physique and exploiting his piercing blue eyes contrasting his short dark hair to act like mind-altering laser beams, hypnotising voters beyond his policies. He roared to power on the back of a high-energy campaign around the American Dream, nothing unique in that but after the lean years of the global financial crisis, a genuinely dynamic, self-assured figure promising housing, jobs and cars to those who work hard was irresistible to voters and he cruised in with a landslide victory.

"Always be one step ahead of the national mood." he'd been known to say about his success. "In times of crisis, be the light at the end of the tunnel, in times of prosperity when everyone is waiting for the bubble to burst, you get to be the guy who they believe can keep it going because if they believe that, they'll be damn sure to believe you'll be the better choice when it all does go tits up." Johnson exuded that very familiar and politically formidable confidence of someone with wealth – 'I'm alright so you can believe in me because you all wanna be me' kind of attitude.

He had a core support from what he called 'aspiring Americans' but what others might refer to as 'trash America' – myopic, nationalistic bordering on xenophobic and significantly less likely to own a passport than other voter types.

Harvard background aside, Nancy Rastik was almost the exact opposite of Johnson. Daughter of Polish immigrants from the late 1960s, she had had to work harder to get to Harvard, as opposed to having almost been born into the alumni. She boasted a ferociously smart mind, as did most members of the Harvard debating team but, unlike Johnson, she would never be classed as a people person. She was very matter of fact, – if she could say it in five words, not twenty, then so be it – to the point and ruthlessly efficient. And this efficiency had led her right to the very top of the Environment Bureau but, unbeknownst to the vast majority of the thousands of employees at the Bureau, she had some views pretty much diametrically opposed to that same majority.

Her alliance with Nick Johnson had begun in the early nineties at the Annual Harvard Debate Shout Off. Members of the team were pitted against each other to attack different subjects but instead of taking opposite views, the debaters had to decide between them which stance to take then both defend them vehemently. It had been a surprise not only to themselves but the audience members and organising committee when Johnson and Rastik chose to defend the use of Earth's natural resources whatever the consequences. The common view was that they'd selected this point of view because it was clearly against popular opinion therefore would be a more challenging stance, however they both put forward such beguiling and convincing cases, most of those present that day would still, twenty years on, swear that they believed in every word they spoke that afternoon.

Through the many lavish Harvard alumni networking dinners and seminars, Johnson and Rastik grew closer and closer in terms of their thinking on climate change, plotting without really knowing it at the time, for a chance to turn their infrequently held views into national policy.

Their big chance had come, like so many breakthroughs for business and political leaders, from a spontaneous conversation out of nowhere - only this one was with the president of the United States, Nelson Franks, no less. They'd both been invited to a high-profile charity dinner, of which the First Lady was patron, and in the pre-dinner drinks mingle, Johnson and Rastik had found themselves alone with the president himself. President Franks, being the president, was exceptional with names and recognised both of them from previous dealings on policy. He made some light-hearted quip about always being left on his own at these functions to fend for himself and that he always worried he'd forgotten to bring his wallet and be the only one in the room unable to donate. They both assumed he had people for that but obviously didn't say it aloud.

The charity itself was centred around protecting the US indigenous wildlife from human habitation, industrial expansion, and the ever-growing threat of 'so-called' climate change. It was this reference to so-called climate change that pricked the ears of the Senator and Bureau Director. Johnson was brave, maybe astute, enough to challenge POTUS.

"When you say so-called…?" Johnson thought he managed to say it without sounding accusatory, if anything it was supportively curious.

"Yeah, this would be a damn fine time for all this climate change nonsense to go away."

Neither Johnson nor Rastik were expecting a fireball answer like that bombshell and even the president himself seemed surprised at his candidness, but he'd had a couple of whisky sodas and even in the seconds following his minor outburst he had processed his response if challenged, that he was merely wishing for climate change to be a thing of the past and they could all move on with other matters. But there was no danger that Johnson or Rastik would be pulling their president up on this occasion, this was their way in. And they took it. The president wasn't at all surprised that Senator Johnson held the views he did, most senior politicians would go whale hunting if it meant a couple of extra votes. The one he was really taken aback by was Nancy Rastik. It seemed highly incongruous to him that the leading position in the leading organisation defending environmental damage would be filled by such a climate change sceptic.

In the months that followed that whisky-inspired chat at the charity dinner, both Rastik and Johnson were frequent visitors to the White House and all parties stood to gain. The president wanted Rastik to be able to demonstrate with concrete evidence that climate change was not actually a thing, that the finest minds in science could collaborate globally to disprove it. Also, he needed Johnson to champion it to confirm it was a vote winner. He realised this would be going against prevailing popular scientific theory so it could be a huge risk to gamble his second term in office on a climate change reversal platform without having stress tested it first. Equally, Johnson needed the president, which was unequivocal, because if you have the world's foremost political behemoth in your corner, you stand a bit more of a chance, not a lot of political rocket science in that. But the science he needed would have to come from Rastik. Similarly, she was well aware that her deep held beliefs were at total odds from the organisation she was paid handsomely to lead, so she needed a mouthpiece to get the message out there. Even more of a delicate balance was she and the president; both knew too well that if Johnson squealed, this would end badly for both of them.

    The investment plan the president signed off for the Environment Bureau was unprecedented and instantly drew praise from the watching world and more importantly, from eligible American voters.

    "We will invest millions to support and fund the world's greatest minds to overcome this climate change challenge that faces us all." He was always conscious to use words concisely but without publicly committing to a stance for or against climate change. He was a skilled and wily politician as all presidents are, Senator Johnson was allocated pride of place as some kind of general to oversee the programme, which allowed Nancy Rastik to take more of a passive role in the elaborate plan to reject commonly held beliefs.

Power is a significant factor in generating and sustaining compliance in an organisation and Rastik made it clear to her direct reports that anything which could be construed as a quirk in data, a blip or anomaly should be shared with her immediately. Being an artist in behavioural science meant she knew the interpretation would be that she was keen to stamp out anything which could be deemed as wrong or controversial against prevailing science. However, she knew, and told both POTUS and Johnson outright, that by telling her team, and by definition the entire organisation, and then, by association, much of the global scientific community that she was in essence briefing climatologists, geologists, meteorologists, all kinds of - ologists around the world to search for and highlight anomalies in patterns of data that could help build a case for climate change reversal.

The most passive of the three of them she may be, but both the president and Johnson were in awe of her skills – the ability to influence a global community to do something she wants but almost the exact opposite of what they think they're being asked for.

"As any great detective novel will tell you," she said to them both, "the most willing accomplice in any case as the one who doesn't think they're an accomplice." Although she was at pains to reiterate that this was only a metaphor, and no one was committing any crimes here.

"Don't worry," she smiled. "Science will prove us right and you'll reach your goals."

"And your goals Nancy." Johnson had retorted.

Nancy kept her smile, "I told you, science will prove us right, that'll be enough for me, I'll leave you two to be the politicians in this one."

When Marco Hernandez's email made its way to Rastik, she immediately called Nick Johnson and told him that this researcher in Mexico had some compelling water level data from the Amazon basin, one of the emotional epicentres of climate change, and the way he'd written his submission told her he'd be perfect for a special project.

"Let's bring this Mexican American home shall we Nancy?" Johnson suggested.

"Indeed." was Rastik's simple and commanding response. They did a little more research and agreed Marco Hernandez would be the perfect addition to their circle, a low-ranking but ultimately smart scientist with sky-high aspirations and those with everything to gain were exactly the type of person Johnson and Rastik were looking for if they were to go public on this.

They arranged for Marco to join a climate research team based in Chicago as a kind of apprenticeship allowing Johnson and Rastik to keep an eye on him to ensure he was indeed suited to the role they had in mind for him. And after a couple of years observing the Mexican's diligence and most importantly, compliance, they felt it was time to step things up and brought him in,

Marco couldn't believe his luck, although with some

justification, he felt that maybe he'd earned some fortune. Not only had he secured a place in a Code 15 project team, the name allocated to Government projects where information only flows in not out, but he was met on arrival in Washington by a very smart young Mexican, ironically, who picked up his luggage and took him directly to the door of his fully furnished, fully expensed apartment overlooking the majestic Potomac.

"That must have been some research you've been doing for them son." his mother was almost in tears when Marco told her what was happening, gushing with pride and desperate to find out as much as she could, mainly so she could tell everyone else about it.

"Mom, I can't share anything, it's against protocol and the work I'm doing is very sensitive in its nature."

"Good boy Marco." Nancy Rastik said quietly to herself as she listened to the Hernandez family chat via the wiretap installed in the apartment. They also had his phone tapped and tracked, it was vital they could trust in their team and so far, Marco had lived up to their expectations.

"All I can tell you mom," Marco wanted to make sure his mother had something to go on or she'd make stuff up for herself which might be just as damaging, "is that my work in both Mexico and Chicago was really important stuff and through some connections I've made in my career, I was headhunted to carry on my research centrally."

Nancy smiled: she loved the bullshit some of her team came up with to explain their dramatic rise to prominence in scientific circles.

"It's nothing to worry about Mom, the challenge with the type of research I deal in, and research in general, is that half-baked research is misleading, so we try to keep projects under wraps until we've a consensus to share."

"I guess that does make sense honey, although I thought you were measuring erosion levels in the Amazon, doesn't strike me as being that secretive, but what do I know, you're the science hotshot aren't you baby?"

"Thanks Mom." Marco didn't really sound it, but he loved all this attention, finally feeling recognised by his family for achieving professionally.

"Now Marco, tell me all about Washington DC and this flat of yours." And with that, Nancy stopped tuning in, she'd heard plenty and had zero interest in Marco's view on the nation's capital.

14

Berlin

"So that gives us approximately seventy-two hours then folks." Peter was clearly excited by the news that Jane had been invited, he felt this was less threatening than summoned by Senator Gordon. "We have to assume that Gordon knows we, at least Jane and Jeff, have all that data so to make things simpler I think we'd best assume he's on our side, or at least we're on his side, even if he doesn't know that yet."

"Agreed." piped up Jeff. "My suggestion is we revisit everything we think we know and be clear what we can prove and what gaps we have then we need to put it in a Gordon friendly format."

Elaine blurted out helplessly, "A Gordon friendly format, what the hell does that mean Jeff?"

Jeff briefly explained Gordon's usual requirements that Jane had to follow all that time ago and assumed the same now.

"My vote," he continued, "is we do two summaries. One that mirrors what Jane and I sent to him previously, a precis of the evidence behind climate change reversal, a classic piece of myth busting, should be fun. And the other, well the other one needs to be about what we really think is going on and that's where I wonder if we're struggling."

"Correct." Peter was getting more animated as he often did when there was a lack of clarity. Most scientists struggle to cope with uncertainty, for Pete this was his oxygen. Don't let the facts get in the way of a global geological theory, he would have said had he not realised himself it wasn't the time nor place for it. "We are struggling because it's so big, this is not a binary conundrum, something seismic is happening to our planet and it's not just about one vote winning policy versus the opposite. We are the greatest minds in geological science…"

"Really Peter?" Elaine rolled her eyes as Peter threatened to embark on another monologue masterpiece.

"Ok Elaine, I understand that's a grand statement, but we are on the verge of uncovering the most significant change to Planet Earth since the Ice Age, possibly even the meteorite that wiped out the dinosaurs."

"Yes Peter," Jeff interjected, "or maybe it's nothing and in seventy million years this will be looked back on as a low volatility part of Earth's history."

"Perhaps Jeff yes, let's all agree it's somewhere between nothing and life changing, so we can get on with preparing your mate Jane for our, I mean, her meeting with Senator Gordon."

Peter, Elaine and Jeff spent the next two hours trying to condense all their views into three areas eloquently described by Jeff as "stuff we know is happening, stuff we think is happening and stuff we just don't know but think we need to know." It was Jeff's time to lead.

"We need to give ourselves as much time as we can to use Jane's data to build a hypothesis for her to share with Gordon."

"Before we crack on Jeff, can I just circle us back so

we're clear on why we're now appearing to focus all our efforts around preparing for a meeting we'll not be at with a US Senator we've never met, Jeff aside once or twice, instead of forging our own path?" Elaine needed them all to be aligned before committing themselves, even if just for her own sanity.

"Excellent question Elaine." Pete inevitably took the reins on this one. "I agree it feels like this has come out of the blue and we've now got a hook but if you think about it, the reason we're so focused on this chap is because he seems to be focused on us, with Jeff having smuggled all that data out of the country – it clearly set some kind of alarm off over there. And if this Senator is who we think he is, we might have a significantly influential and not to say deep-pocketed ally in this project. We'd be doing what we're planning to do anyway, all this for us is an unexpected output for it, earlier than we would have predicted. For me it's a great sign we're onto something here - you with me?"

"Oh yes." chimed Elaine and Jeff together, happy Pete had summarised how they were both feeling so concisely.

A couple of hours and several cups of coffee later the three of them downed tools and gathered their thoughts. Pete's spacious living area in his park view flat had one nice clean white wall and despite Jeff's suggestion that they write straight on it, Pete struck up a load of flip chart paper which allowed them each to add a couple of words or a line of thought. Jeff then handed each of them a different coloured Sharpie and laid out how this was going to work.

"So, team, we've got a fair few thoughts up on the wall haven't we, some are clearly overlapping, and some are pretty leftfield… looks like your writing Peter." he smiled accusingly.

"Hey, don't point the finger at me, I saw Elaine put down some pretty far out stuff, like the biblical flood one about never-ending rain. That's not even yours Elaine, you've nicked that off your husband."

"Haha very funny Pete, maybe you'll want to invest in his nanotechnology clothing line too." responded Elaine, who had tried to be as open minded as she could, but she was fairly set in her view and also fairly set they'd all end up in the same place on this.

A few minutes later it was apparent that there were several clusters of coloured tiles on the charts. And an equal number of coloured crosses.

"So here goes." Jeff took a big swig of coffee. "I, we, are quite unanimous that the concept of climate change reversal is a non-starter, that's probably a good one to get right out on the table. Two, sea levels not rising, getting lower, and water disappearing is a big one. Three, Peter - your geological Armageddon has fared well here, a few variations of core expansion, crust instability, sinkhole proliferation. Four, a lot of likes for 'something out of human control' - guess that's for the 'stuff we don't know yet' list."

"It's a useful list," Elaine sounded surprised, "but it only summarised what we all expected hasn't it?"

"Guess that's the point Elaine." Pete added. "You

guys have more of a handle on the evidence around sea levels decreasing or holding, from a variety of sources, and you add that to my ongoing theory of mantle and crust disintegration with all these sinkholes, there might just be a connection."

"Look let's cut to the chase on this." Jeff was becoming determined. "Jane and I have had many beer-filled late nights discussing some of this stuff." Elaine raised her head noticeably quickly at this and she herself was surprised at her reaction to the idea of Jeff and this Jane lady in the US sharing late night drinks, just like she did with Jeff all those years ago. It was like a pinch of jealousy, as soon as it hit her then it vanished again just as quickly, but it had definitely touched something buried deep down in her soul.

"There has been a load of reports of sea levels contravening their expected values and most scientists are dismissing it as tidal or just the natural swings of the Earth's gravity and our distance from the moon. Christ, some guys have put it down to the increase in desalination plants across the globe. But, although it makes no sense at all, I'd wager a few Deutschmarks on the fact that sea water, the water in the oceans, is disappearing. And if that is true, then climate change really is going to be catastrophic, and not in a degree or two warmer kind of way."

"I'm with you Jeff." Elaine had found a new confidence now Jeff had said what she felt she couldn't as it sounded so preposterous. "I'll gladly spend the next twenty-four hours sifting through that data to find some more evidence for this Jeff, Pete. I measured levels myself in

Durban and the project team there gave me access to some other global measurements, and it struck me at the time that there are always ebbs and flows in climatic data but, with all the extra water filling the oceans from the ice caps, it didn't ring as true. It's almost certainly what got Marco airlifted from Mexico."

"And lord knows how many others have been recruited on this recalibration of scientific mission," added Jeff, "it feels like there's a global brainwashing on the horizon."

"And back we are again folks." beamed Peter almost triumphantly. "All we need to do now is get our capes on, put our pants over our trousers and find a way to save the world."

"Brilliant Pete." an obvious tone of sarcasm to Jeff's voice. "But just a couple of pointers on that one maybe…."

"Oh, you're such a realist and a spoilsport Jeff!"

"Yep, I may be that, but let's go to you again Pete, we can save the world in two ways. Firstly, we need to establish what the hell is going on under our feet that is making the water disappear and secondly, we need to find someone who has influence to listen to us."

"Senator Gordon." chimed Pete and Elaine together.

"Indeed. Thirdly, we need to make him believe us. And finally, we need to work out how to stop it happening. Partly because it might just save humanity and all nature from total extinction, and partly because I really want to cruise around the Caribbean and this lack of ocean debacle is going to put a real spanner in that retirement plan."

Pete was excited now and, unlike the other two, he wasn't grappling as much with the enormity of it all, so found it easier to make light of the situation.

"Dear Mr Gordon, sorry dear Senator Gordon, Edward, no Eddie, if we may be so bold, our good friend Jeffrey would like to go on a Caribbean cruise in about fifteen years' time (that about right Jeff?) ..." Jeff nods as Pete carries on pretending to type the letter, "...but we're ever so worried that all the world's water is disappearing somewhere. Not totes sure where it's going or how but we've a few hair-brained ideas you might choose to believe and, if you do, please can we have unlimited funds to find out what's causing this whole kerfuffle and come up with a plan to make it go away so we can get back to allowing mankind to destroy the planet instead? Oh, and an extra ten thousand dollars for Jeff's cruise. Please."

Elaine stood up, she needed some fresh air and to stretch her legs.

"Yes Peter, give or take, that's what we're looking at. Confidence levels boys?"

"No issue there," said Jeff confidently, "when you know Gordon like I do, it'll be a doddle." Both Peter and Elaine knew full well he didn't know Senator Gordon at all.

15

Washington DC

Six thousand miles away from Berlin, Jane awoke with a sense of renewed purpose for a Monday morning, far from the usual effort to get out of bed. She virtually jumped out with a feeling of vigour, inspired by Jeff and his mates, her impending meeting with Senator Gordon on Wednesday, plus the bit of espionage that Jeff asked her to do. She lived in the southwest of the city, away from the main office blocks and almost in suburbia. She'd chosen the district about ten years ago as it was a classic 'up and coming' neighbourhood, which as it turned out meant quite a few nice coffee shops and street markets and a bit of redevelopment of apartment blocks. Jane's was definitely one that she'd never had chosen were it not for the redevelopments, a classic child of the sixty's architecture, the ten-storey building had looked like it might have been on some kind of exchange programme from Warsaw. Grey and blocky were the best words to describe it when she laid down the deposit for the apartment on the seventh floor, although they weren't the exact words in the brochure. They were something akin to spaciously modern, or maybe it was modernly spacious, or some other vaguely ludicrous marketing spiel Jane couldn't quite remember. But fair play to the landlords, or whoever took charge of the renovations because by the time she and scores of others moved into their modern and spacious new accommodation the place had been transformed. Gone was the bleak monochrome, now the walls were vibrant with deep blues and bright yellows, more tasteful than the way she'd described it to her mother, who said it sounded like she'd moved into some kind of animation. There were plants and trees in all conceivable places, even a vertical garden going up one wall, well ahead of its time architecturally. Out front a half-sized basketball court which she'd never used but enjoyed the energy it brought to the neighbourhood when the youths played in the evenings until winter hit.

 Above all for Jane, it was home and felt a world away from the intensity of the Bureau, which in recent months had begun to grind her down a bit, her boundless enthusiasm for governmental service were certainly nowhere near Jeff's almost grounded levels but it wasn't giving her as much fulfilment as it once did. She'd noticed that on recycling day she was carrying more bottles down than she used to which didn't sit well for her.

 However, it was time for a fresh beginning she told herself. Jeff upping and flying to Berlin was the catalyst she needed to throw herself into a new phase of activity. It felt now was the time to rise up and quash the ever-growing sense of political storytelling in the face of hard evidence that went against her core beliefs. It even went as far as kick starting an exercise regime, and by Jane's normal levels of aerobic activity, it was fair to call it a regime. Jog on Sunday afternoon and another before breakfast on Monday morning. Not long, raking runs but mind clearing and brain focusing on the local park and down along the river. It wasn't perfect but enough to get her ready for the next forty-eight hours, which she figured might get quite intense, but this time she felt more in control. She had a couple of very clear objectives for the day ahead. Firstly, it was to try and find out what Marco Hernandez was up to, what was his remit, why him and who was in charge? Jane had enough connections in and around the Bureau that she felt she'd be able to unearth something that might help in their own plan, whatever that was shaping up to be. The second would have to wait until midday.

Jane had arranged a breakfast meeting with one of her University of Colorado friends, Harpinder Tarkowski, although back then she was Harpinder Singh, a super bright product of India's excellent STEM investment in girls. Famous for providing healthcare professionals for the world, India was now producing some of the world's foremost scientists and Harpinder was on track to be one of those fine experts. However, it was words as much as science that brought fulfilment to Harpinder, and she followed her degree course with a post-grad in journalism. It was on that course she met and ultimately married and subsequently took the surname of Jakub Tarkowski, a Polish citizen, who'd grown up in East Berlin. They proudly, but certainly not boastfully, claimed to be the perfect example of globalisation in its most positive form, a coming together of widely different cultures – and indeed religions – but able to bring those cultures together in unity.

Jane and Harpinder had not been close friends as such, theirs had been a relationship built on mutual respect for hard work and application of knowledge and they'd often vied for top spot and in the occasional class that spanned both their courses, something which spurred them on to higher grades rather than distract them.

    Whilst Jane had gone fast track at the Environment Bureau, Harpinder had taken a circuitous route to become the Environment correspondent for the Washington Post, a freelance role which allowed her flexibility to dabble in other areas as took her fancy. So, her name would appear in some heavy hitting titles like Time Magazine or New Scientist, but she'd also written a few pieces for more mainstream media like Vogue or Cosmopolitan, often around her own triumph against the odds, female empowerment in the face of adversity but also some more whimsical material on being a married Asian in Washington.

    Not in a creepy or jealous way, Jane had followed Harpinder's career through her writing as she always found it enlightening stuff, but they were cut from the same cloth, so it was hardly surprising. What had surprised Jane though, was a recent piece Harpinder had put her name to in the Post around the increasing evidence bubbling to the surface of scientists, not only in the US, but globally putting their weight behind climate change not being manmade but part of the cycle of global weather patterns and in a few years, temperatures would settle again, just like sea levels had been. It was a quarter page piece hidden deep in the heart of the paper but had attracted quite a few comments online, mostly calling her a puppet of the State and some a great deal less delicate.

However, what was more surprising were the more thought-out comments that were actually tending to support her piece, commending her and the Post's editors of being brave enough, as one 'professor' put it: 'to stand up to these hemp wearing, bearded enviro-Nazis.'

You've got to have some kind of belief system to be defending your ideals with that kind of language and comparison, thought Jane. Although she found it incredibly depressing, there was ubiquity to the torrents of abuse that people would write under the anonymity of the online forums. As Harpinder would tell Jane later, she got more abuse for one of her articles in Cosmopolitan about the challenge of finding make-up in Washington for her skin type than anything else she'd ever written. Contrary to what Jane expected her to say, Harpinder told her she actually found it quite motivating that there were so many people out there with narrow minds, that it meant choosing a career in journalism was never going to be one to run into a cul-de-sac.

"If those attitudes still pervade society today then I've got a job to do educating them for years to come." *Admirable,* thought Jane, who hadn't quite seen death threats or 'go back to your own country taunts' as a reason to carry on doing something. However, Jane wasn't meeting Harpinder to put the world to rights on racism and sexism, she needed to have a good old fashioned 'off the record chat' about the goings on around climate change narrative coming out of Government offices.

They had arranged to meet in one of the many coffee

shops in the area around Jane's flat as Harpinder's request. She hadn't challenged the reasons why. Maybe it was suitably far away from the Washington Post's offices or perhaps she lived in a neighbouring borough. Either way, it was convenient for Jane, plus she got to choose a place where she knew the coffee would be good.

16

Sam's Café opened almost the same week the blue and yellow paint job was completed on Jane's apartment block, and Sam was still there making coffee and blending smoothies. Given it wasn't quite nine-thirty, trade was still brisk, but most drinks were to go, for the last few commuters who hadn't set their alarms or stayed up late watching the football, Jane surmised.

After exchanging pleasantries with Sam and explaining she'd be drinking in today, which seemed to delight Sam, Jane took a seat at a table towards the back of the café and waited for Harpinder to arrive.

"Damn, this coffee's good." thought Jane as she took her mobile out of her bag.

"Thanks Janey." Sam was clearing the next table and Jane realised she must have said it out loud.

"Oh, I'm in a world of my own" smiled Jane.

"We aim to please." came the reply and he took the dirty dishes back to the kitchen.

Jane took a long, pleasurable gulp of her coffee and reflected on her current situation. She wanted to feel part of the team, even though a) she'd never met two of them and b) she was six thousand miles away, so she messaged Jeff to update on her plans.

Guten Tag Jeff and team. Gonna be doing my detective work today and tomorrow, hope you guys are making sense of those terabytes. Will update end of day if relevant news to share. Best Jane. She knew as soon as she sent it that Jeff would be aching to tell her she didn't need to sign off with her name on a WhatsApp message, but she was old-school and liked the formality and personalisation of ending messages with her name.

She was pleased to see the two blue ticks appear almost immediately next to her message, meaning Jeff had got it. Then, it said he was typing. *Here it comes,* she thought, but no. A photo appeared on her screen: trust Jeff to send a selfie.

Berlin is ace, came the message, *we are taking a break in the park.*

Next message: *Tiergarten, near Pete's flat.*

Next message: *Regards.*

Next message: *Jeff.*

Then, there was a winking emoji.

And there it is, sighed Jane to herself.

There was even more typing from Jeff: *We're working up 2 scenarios for you to polish for SG 1 devil's advocate against cc, the other about Pete's theory and everlasting drought.*

Next message: *good luck in your mission,* followed by an emoji of an explorer or detective, Jane wasn't sure what it was supposed to be.

She replied with a classic thumbs up emoji and just to make Jeff smile she added 'from Jane'. As the ticks went blue, a familiar voice called her name, and she looked up to see a beaming Harpinder almost at her table. Jane rose and gave her a warm embrace.

"Really great to see you Harpinder, how's Jakub?"

"Jakub's great thank you Jane, we're both really well.

And you Jane, you look well."

That'll be the jogs, mused Jane to herself, and replied with "thank you." She decided against bringing her running up. Pleasantries over, Jane was about to offer Harpinder a drink when Sam came over to take their order.

"So, Jane," Harpinder kicked off, "this is all very intriguing." She was half driven by her journalistic nature and half driven because she was genuinely intrigued by what Jane wanted to meet her about. "And to make it clear from the off, I won't take notes or record anything until you give me express permission to do so."

"Great, thanks Harpinder." Jane gave her a thorough run through as much as she could which took a good ten minutes from start to finish, Harpinder didn't interject or ask any questions, just nodded and muttered to show she was processing what she was hearing.

She told Harpinder about Jeff and their late-night rants about the Bureau that paid their salaries, the idea that climate change scientists were being added continuously to that payroll in what seemed like a gravy train cover up silencing them. She spoke about Senator Gordon, the work she'd done for him and crucially about their upcoming meeting on Wednesday. She shared what Jeff had told her about Peter Masai's theories and the whole IGA conference postponement and about Marco Hernandez. She knew it was a risk contacting such a high-profile journalist with all this, it wouldn't be a great career move if this got back to the bosses at the Bureau, but she felt she could trust Harpinder, that they shared a similar trait in honesty and integrity.

Harpinder did nothing to dispel that characterisation either.

"Okay," started Harpinder, "here's how I read it," Jane was a little deflated by Harpinder's low-key reaction, for her this felt like dynamite, but on quick reflection she assumed journalists, at least the better ones, tried not to sensationalise, certainly not before it was time to go to print. Harpinder continued.

"There's a lot of talk in the Post and across the media titles about an impending change in Government policy. I've been party to some of the low-level stuff as you've already read in my piece in the Post, and you saw what reaction that got. Now I know it goes without saying but I'm not telling you any of this just like you haven't told me anything."

A firm nod from Jane. "Of course."

"But it does sound like you guys are flitting around the epicentre of this one. My personal view, and you've only strengthened it, is that there is some kind of multi-layered cover-up on the horizon to brainwash the great American public into believing climate change is indeed a myth. My editor in chief doesn't know but I saw a few mocked up headlines a week or so ago on his desk when I was bringing him a coffee. One of them said 'Prepare for the second Industrial Revolution', another said 'Climate Change Myth Finally Busted.'"

"Oh my god," muttered Jane, "is he part of it too?" She suddenly realised how naive that sounded.

"Oh no," Harpinder closed it down, "that's his job, most editors and media title owners are in the back pockets of Government communications officers, it's their bread and butter, they'll always be exploring options well in advance of news like this 'breaking'," she accentuated to word breaking, "as most breaking news is only breaking for those who it's targeted at. Most media houses, the big ones like ours, have been crafting the stories in advance, especially ones like this.

"Now the bits that make your situation and hypothesis really come to life are the notes that were written under the headlines. Well, I wouldn't be doing my job if I didn't do a little snooping, even if it is my own boss' desk." A little grin appeared on Harpinder's face, which makes Jane feel like they're going to get somewhere with this conversation.

"I've not got a photographic memory and I really couldn't have taken a photo, and to be fair I didn't foresee this situation so didn't feel the need at the time. However, there was a kind of mind map under the Climate Myth headline with some words and names on." Jane leant in, if this were a TV show; they'd definitely cut to an ad break now to build the tension.

"Senator Nick Johnson, know of him?" Jane felt a sense of adrenaline flash through her body.

"Yeah of course, he's being talked about as a potential future presidential candidate and is a well-known climate change sceptic."

"Correct," added Harpinder. "He made his money from pollution, maybe he's working to wind the clock back. He and the president are said to be pretty aligned on stuff like this so…"

Jane took over her sentence. "Maybe this goes right to the top."

"Maybe," Harpinder was calm, "but it's too early for sensationalist headlines at this stage, there were many names and initials besides Johnson." Harpinder concentrated her mind, trying to recreate that moment in her boss' office, hoping that she wasn't about to make up a load of names that weren't on the page. She understood that studies of people's memories showed a distinct lack of truth versus actual events and even that memories could be created by the brain to fit in with a narrative that's already in the person's mind. It baffled her that the proven inconsistencies with so-called eyewitness accounts of crimes were still permitted in court, sometimes months or even years after an event, the premise being that a significant event like a traffic accident or mugging was so out of the ordinary and dramatic that it would stamp a clear footprint on the brain. However, it seemed to discount entirely the seemingly obvious fact that the events leading up to the incident in question were, by definition, normal and entirely unmemorable. It was only in the aftermath that vivid memories started to build; it was common knowledge that people spend most of their lives on autopilot because if one tried to process everything that was happening every second of the day, the brain would pretty much shut down on most people.

She was all too aware of her role as a journalist, and in her and most her colleagues' view, a credible journalist, she'd like to think this was a prerequisite for this particular job, that accuracy of her memory was a non-tradeable asset. The overarching benefit of this situation versus the traffic accidents of this world, was her radar was already on transmit at this distinct moment. Scores of times she'd have either put a coffee on her boss' desk or dropped a paper or draft piece without a second glance at what's around, back to that autopilot behaviour.

But this time, the mock up headlines had alerted her, like a jungle predator whose hunting gene had just kicked in and she was suddenly poised on her mental haunches, alert to the prospect of either food or danger, even in those swift moments, delving deep into her brain. She was conscious of how much she was processing in such a short space of time. The idea of her next thought-provoking editorial could be all around this, how the brain can seemingly form an entire network of memory in an instant and it arrive in the 'real world' brain as an almost fully formed idea, despite the person trying to find another memory instead. Now she just felt her brain was talking to itself and was conscious to get back to Jane, although as she well knew, this whole episode had only lasted a few seconds.

She took a scrap of paper out of her bag and tried to visualise the information she was recalling, almost mumbling to herself as she did so.

"Senator Johnson was near the top, then there was some stuff around sea levels, rainfall and China. Amazon was in a circle on its own, with some scribbles I can't remember." She knew in her heart of hearts that this creation was nowhere near the real thing, but it was helping her. "Some letters under it. MR was it or maybe MH and there was a line from there back to Senator Johnson's name."

"That'll be Marco," Jane thought immediately aloud, with another adrenalin rush: this was proving to be an excellent morning.

"Then on the right-hand side all I can remember were the words 'what if' and there were definitely some other names or initials, but I'll be damned if I can recall those. And there was something about 'must try upon' with a smiley face next to it and IGR, IGD, IG something."

"Could it have been IGA, Harpinder?" interjected Jane, conscious what a leading question that was from someone piecing together a scattered memory, but it sounded to her like a reference to the aborted conference in Tokyo.

"Yes, Jane it could definitely have been IGA, that would make sense, wouldn't it?"

"Okay, let's play this out Harpinder. There is definitely something coming from the Government's central source on climate change information, my employers in fact, and that I need to open my mind, which I expect you'll be telling me to do shortly," Harpinder smiled supportively, "and this maybe isn't a cover up after all, it's simply an 'up', not sure what the opposite of cover up is."

"I think they call it evidence. Or policy." Harpinder's warm smile had turned distinctly wry.

"I know," continued Jane, "because I've seen it for myself and have indeed been part of the processing of information which acts as counter evidence for climate change, however I chose to dismiss it. What if there are some high-ranking officials in the Bureau who aren't dismissing it, Christ does it even go to the Board?"

"Well Jane, I'm nervous about saying it but in amongst the letters and initials, I'm sure I can see NR there but wouldn't put my life on it." Harpinder paused to let this information and the magnitude get digested by Jane, "But I guess it doesn't mean Nancy Rastik is part of this, although her featuring in this would explain quite a bit given her status and access."

Jane could feel her energy dipping. Her default position was always to believe in the better nature of people but as Harpinder looked back across their coffees at her with an imploring look, it started to dawn on her that this wasn't just a few rogue scientists that might fizzle out, this was seriously big, and seriously real.

"Jane, Rastik and Johnson were at Harvard together." Harpinder just left that hanging in the air to sink in for a few moments. "And I bet if I make a few enquiries, it might just unearth where all the scientific evidence is really coming from and why it's getting stronger and stronger."

"Sounds like the beginning of a plan." Jane had automatically assumed that Harpinder would join forces with her on this without the need to really spell that out and she was right.

"You're on." Harpinder's energy picked up again.

"I'm going to have to go full freelance on this for now, given Roger – he's my boss at the Post – is already deep in this mess. I've a few trusted colleagues and associates so I will make a few calls but keep it tight before you say anything."

"Great thanks Harpinder, you see what you can do on Rastik and Johnson and any other angles around this policy change. All roads, or flights, appear to point to Tokyo still. Our theory is the IGA conference was delayed, not due to the weather but because they, and we are a bit clearer on who they might be, are planning to go public on this one. The IGA is the perfect neutral territory for that, geographically positioned away from the US and quite possibly, the start of a scientific shift for public opinion to grasp hold of. And it feels like the Post has first dibs on the headlines."

"You're starting to think like a journalist Jane!"

"Well if I keep thinking like a geologist, I might end up supporting all this rubbish if everyone else is to go by."

"We both know that's never going to happen Jane. Now I guess you're going to dig deeper in the Bureau to get the picture on this Marco chap you're worried about."

"Totally, we've a gut feeling he's being groomed as the frontline speaker for this IGA announcement, but I need some proof."

"Jane," an element of caring caution on Harpinder's voice, "this is what I do for a living so me trying to dig up a story in Washington is total normality, even if it does go as high as a Senator, or cripes even higher. There are dozens of journos trying to get something on these guys 24/7 so with me, it might just be one more to add to the mix. If the source of all this, as you suspect, is coming from the very organisation who should be protecting our planet then yes it is massive and potentially extremely explosive but there's still a large chance that it's not and you poking your nose in, and more I'd wager, will be massively damaging, almost certainly mortal, for your career, not just here but in most high ranking organisations. I respect you so much for this Jane but if you like, you can leave the interrogating to me and I can take the heat on it, remember my boss can't challenge me without revealing what he already knows so I've got a card up my sleeve already. You, I'm afraid to say, have more to lose."

Harpinder, like Jane, knew this was a fruitless exercise suggesting Jane hold back but it made sense to have it out on the table as a matter of course.

"Thank you, Harpinder, but you know I'm all in now and I'm hoping I too have an ace up my sleeve."

"Senator Gordon." they both chimed at the same time.

"Very much so," continued Jane, "unless I've entirely misread the situation, I think Senator Gordon might be in a similar place to us on this, although I do hope it's not just us wishing that to be the case. Maybe it's a trap to try squash us before we can go public on this whole sorry affair."

"Okay Jane, I'll do some quiet checking up on Gordon. I did a piece once on a day in the life of a Senator a few years ago with a chap called Henry Amblestone, Senator Amblestone at the time. I know he's been kind of a mentor to Senator Gordon so he might be able to confirm one way or the other, and we had a really good day together building that piece so I'm sure he'll share." Another grin appeared on Harpinder's face, slightly devious this time noticed Jane. "Oh yes and as part of that day together I learned something about Amblestone which I omitted from the text, and he knows I know and would go to great lengths to avoid it besmirching his legacy, I'm sure."

"Well can he be trusted at all? That doesn't sound very positive at all then, what on Earth was it?"

"I promised him I wouldn't share it with anyone, and I intend to keep it that way, but suffice to say I don't think any less of the man for knowing this so I'm sure he is to be trusted too."

"Okay I'll take your word for it, let me know how you get on."

"Well, I'll tell you what, you order another coffee, I'll pop to the ladies, then I'll go outside and call Ambleside here and now, let's get one off the list."

Jane was feeling inspired now, she felt part detective, part journalist, part geologist and part ecowarrior. Almost her own perfect superhero. She was more determined than ever to give Jeff, Peter and Elaine something to go on from her perspective, in fact she wondered if actually being in Washington was prime spot for them all to sort this out.

She called Sam over to the table and ordered two more coffees, just as Harpinder brushed past her, phone in hand about to verify, or not, whether Senator Gordon was a good guy or not…

From her seat at the back of the café, Jane couldn't glean anything from Harpinder's face or body language as she paced around out front in the sunshine. *Is a long call good? thought Jane, maybe short was all it needed, or would it be quicker for Ambleside to shut her down with a quick no?*

As if perceiving Jane needed something to take her mind off the telephone exchange she could not possibly hear or impact, Sam arrived with the two coffees, the noise of the mugs and deep aroma of the blend were a welcome distraction. She smiled at Sam and engaged in some pleasantries about the neighbourhood and weather. Sam knew she wasn't paying much attention but could sense Jane needed something to occupy her whilst her companion had stepped outside. He was well used to chit chat, his was not to know the issues people had, unless they wanted and chose to share them. His was to politely engage so they'd feel comfortable, ideally comfortable enough to part with some cash. He felt he'd done a good job on this occasion and a couple of minutes into their mindless chatting, Harpinder arrived back and without being rude, she made it absolutely clear that she needed Sam to wander off before she was going to speak to Jane again.

"So?" said Jane urgently, on tenterhooks to know whether her meeting with Gordon would be one of like-mindedness or conflict.

"So." Harpinder knew she was ratcheting up the tension. "Gordon's good." A smile broke across both ladies' faces. "Ambleside said everything and nothing, a former Senator speaks to a journalist, there was never going to be a huge amount of revelation."

"Then what did you talk about for all that time?"

"Oh, this and that Jane, I wasn't just going to just come straight out with it in the first ten seconds."

Jane nodded. "How do you know then?" She was impatient now.

"He simply said Gordon and he were cut from the same cloth, and Jane, that's enough for me. Ambleside is a good man, and you can carry on as you were, I imagine your meeting with Gordon will be a fruitful one. I'll have this coffee to go and start trying to piece the whole Johnson-Rastik relationship together, you can focus on this Marco chap."

Jane was on it, more convinced than ever that the next few days would be the most important in her career. She also took her coffee to go.

17

Washington DC

"Welcome to Project Green Mr Hernandez, may I remind you that this is a Code 15 assignment, and you must only discuss Project Green with the people you see with you in this room." Marco scanned the room, taking in a blur of about twenty-five faces. "The work you will be undertaking is of the utmost confidentiality and has major implications for the future, not only of the Government, not only of the United States of America, but Mr Hernandez, Project Green is quite possibly the cornerstone of life on this planet. Am I making myself clear Mr Hernandez, do you fully comprehend and categorically sign up to the sensitivities of the work you are about to do?"

"Yes ma'am." replied Marco confidently, making sure he was clear and holding eye contact with Director Rastik.

"Excellent." Nancy Rastik offered her hand, which Marco reached out and shook firmly. His confidence was high, he was damn sure he'd take this opportunity by the scruff of the neck and try to say goodbye to the old self-doubting Marco and bring in the new improved Marco Hernandez, critical part of a top-secret Government initiative to save life as we know it.

Rastik moved away from Marco and to the front of the room, next to the giant screen which had the Bureau logo being beamed on it by the ceiling projector. *It's quite a soulless room,* thought Marco to himself as Rastik prepared herself for what he assumed would be some kind of briefing.

The lights had been dimmed, presumably for an upcoming presentation, but there were no windows and on the walls were some fairly banal pictures of trees and landscapes, like someone had been told to decorate it, but to only spend $20 and have access to car boot sales alone. But this wasn't a showroom, this was a place for work, important work: aesthetics were irrelevant.

I'm here, thought Marco, *deep in the heart of a multi-departmental Government Bureau hit squad, mixing with the top brass and here I am assessing the decor.*

Nancy Rastik's firm voice jolted him back to reality.

"Our team is now complete." she began. "May I introduce to you Marco Hernadez?" she motioned him to stand, he duly obliged.

Am I supposed to make some kind of speech, a statement of intent, or is this just so everyone can see what I look like? he thought, *this is not a great time for indecision and stuttering weakness.*

All eyes in the room settled on him as he stood. *Be confident,* he steeled himself, having quickly resolved that some kind of words were expected. He didn't recall who else was at the table but realised this was the moment when he wouldn't win anyone over, but he sure could lose a few. He took a well concealed breath and forced a smile to come over his face which surprisingly helped him to relax.

"Thank you." he started, a good start, solid. "I'm honoured to be invited to be part of this team and I'm really looking forward to working with you all." He did a courteous scan around the room, making a flicker of eye contact with everyone ending with a firm nod, akin to a bow (were he in Japan) to Nancy Rastik. Her almost imperceptible facial response told Marco he had judged this correctly.

He sat down, untensed and felt amazing that he had commanded the room for a few seconds and was now sworn in as part of Project Green.

Next for Marco was to find out what Project Green actually was, who all these people were and what was expected of him whilst being part of this team. All those things aside he was ready. Rastik took the lead again. "For those of you released for this session by your department heads and line managers, it is important you read and digest the training information which is your cover for the time we have together. A copy is available for everyone. For completeness, I require everyone here to have a working knowledge of its contents, it's an open-ended training meaning we have the option to reconvene probably twice in the coming period without raising unnecessary suspicions." Rastik paused, she knew it was human nature for people to now look at whatever document she had referred to and wanted to allow time for the team to process what she'd said. Folders were being passed around and slid across the table until everyone had one in front of them. Marco glanced down at the folder, although his first thought was more about what department he was actually in and who his line manager was than the contents of the document.

'DON'T WASTE IT,' was the headline on the front of the folder, followed by 'How you can lead the fight against waste.'

Nancy Rastik smiled wryly, "I thought we might as well get on board with some key messages at the same time. To be fair, there are some quite good ideas for you to take back so I suggest you do just that, it'll make your absence all the more compelling but please remember your priorities." This acted as a subliminal command as, almost instantly, the whole room set aside the folders and turned directly back onto the Director. "In the coming few minutes you will make no notes, there will be no handouts, and this will be the only time you get to clarify anything that is said here in this room. I hope that is clear." Again, Marco was in awe at the control she had, anyone holding a pen put it down, notebooks were closed and pushed away. She had this room in the palm of her hand.

18

Berlin

"The thing I can't square the circle on," said Elaine, "is how we're sitting here establishing potential causes of the literal end of the world and it feels like we're on our own, this simply cannot be the case."

Pete responded directly, "Precisely, and this is what we've actually been discussing all along, there has been an incredibly successful suppression on the magnitude of this, remember how many so-called environmental scientists have been recruited in the past few years. Greenbacks are quite effective as a silencer. Plus, most scientists are specialists these days so would only be focussing on a narrow area. A bit like medicine, although to be fair that's changing, thankfully.

"As medicinal science progressed, we effectively discovered new ways that bodies, human bodies, go wrong, some down to nature but a lot to nurture. So, this has led not only to specialisms like brain, heart, kidney, leg, you name it, but there will also be a profession available for a doctor to specialise in. However, as we 'progress' there are specialisms within specialisms. Therefore, heart specialists become aorta specialists, or head experts become tongue or ear lobe specialists. As a community, medicine has become too narrow-minded in treating isolated symptoms and investment and training is directed to more and more niche areas. It's a race to ruin as clearly it is unsustainable for the welfare state to provide for all these specialisms and treatments, which is why it's some poor bugger's job to decide where the funding line gets drawn. Where it feels the profession is moving, albeit slowly and painfully, is to a more holistic view of the human body and hopefully with more of a focus on some accountability for the total crap most people put into their bodies and how little care they take of them.

"My point is, so many hospitalised treatments are diagnosed as specific issues and sick people just have money and drugs thrown at them instead of someone standing back and looking at what's causing all these issues. They're told to stop smoking, to stop eating all those takeaways and to get off their fat arse and stop costing this country loads of money - that kind of stuff."

Jeff felt this could continue but also felt he'd got the gist of it enough to step in, "On behalf of unhealthy people globally, I apologise but on a slightly more serious note, although you're right about a lack of personal responsibility when it comes to health, one for another day, what you're saying is there are scientists and departments everywhere who have all this information but no one's piecing it together."

"Exactly." interjected Pete, before Jeff made it clear he was going to continue.

"The teams looking at sinkholes won't be talking to the guys measuring water levels, and they almost certainly won't be talking to anyone about core expansion and its impact on all of the above."

"Or at least we haven't met them yet." it was Elaine's

turn to weigh in. "What I've seen in the data, aside from the sea level stuff, is a slight, I mean marginal, increase in tectonic activity, I think…" she paused to gather her thoughts. The others immediately leant in, instinctively feeling a breakthrough could be on its way. "Since we got all that US data, I've been dipping in and out of some of the really dry geological stuff buried deep in it, I'm clearly no expert so forgive me for this, but as a community of global scientists, we know so much but understand so little about tectonics and their impact other than the obvious stuff like earthquakes and volcanoes. Much like your view of medicine Pete, globally there are billions of dollars thrown at these events because they materially affect people, economics and ultimately Governments. But I'd wager a fancy fifty or two that those billions, I guess it might only be 'millions', don't filter right down to how, what and why. This isn't to begrudge all the grunt work that goes into it but let's be honest, we'd be as prepared for an earthquake if we just tossed a coin or watched whether starlings or earthworms started leaving an area. What I'm saying, or trying to say, is maybe in some dirty corner of a university there's a dude with all this information, but because he's not linked it to something tangible, i.e., economic value, it just stays there."

Jeff knew deep down that his penchant for US disaster movies would one day be useful. "A bit like Armageddon, you know when they send Bruce Willis to drill a hole on an asteroid to save Mother Earth."

"Jeff, I'm sure it's exactly like that, yes!" Elaine

blurted out, not even herself sure if she was being sarcastic.

Jeff leapt to his own defence, "What I mean is, it was only when they found the asteroid was hitting Earth that the world, okay the US Government, threw limitless funds at the issue. Whereas the film would've been pretty shit if it was about a well-funded research programme which led to an undramatic changing of course for the asteroid. A long documentary versus a kick-ass Liv Tyler movie with epic soundtrack."

"Interesting Jeff," Elaine smiled mischievously at him, "I wondered if a 2012 reference would have also been apt as we're boiling this down to a Hollywood script."

"Indeed." replied Jeff, meeting her smile. Pete rolled his eyes as Jeff countered. "There are some specific plot lines which led me to Armageddon instead but it's six of one so yeah good call." Even if they couldn't see it themselves, Pete could tell where this was going to end up, the initial awkwardness between his old uni mates had mellowed in that instant and he didn't want to be a romance killer, but he did want to hear more about Elaine's tectonic research.

"Elaine," he brought focus back to the apartment, "talk to us more about what you've seen in the tectonic data."

"Well," started Elaine, "we all know how the surface of the Earth as we see it physically today is caused by the constant movements of the plates beneath our feet and they move with glacial pace. We also know only too well the destructive nature of when they get a bit feisty, let's say. You will also know, or maybe it's been so long you've forgotten, that plate movement is measured in centimetres per year so we're talking fingernails here but without the ability to trim them and control them. GPS tracking data goes back a couple of decades now and much of the good stuff came on that hard drive, thanks again Jeff and Jane." The two men were engrossed now, wondering where this was going to lead, and both independently realised the need to give Elaine quiet space to articulate what was going on inside her head. "The other information within that particular folder were historical measures which had been translated into best-guess GPS data so what we have, as far as I can see, is a couple of centuries worth of tectonic plate action, which for someone like me, is a dream." Elaine beamed, she was so caught up in the moment she felt so alive, a purpose she'd not felt for years. "So, and I worry I'm being slightly anticlimactic, I found some recent anomalies in the long-term trends. You know when you look at long-term temperature charts and there is a noticeable change following the industrial revolution?" This was rhetorical enough for Elaine not to need to break her flow. "Well, this isn't like this." Jeff and Pete let out a little breath of laughter. "Yeah, yeah, I know, I'm getting to it." Elaine wasn't trying to create suspense; she just wanted to process her thoughts and hadn't had the chance so was effectively emptying her head out loud. "It's more inconsistency in the movements of the plates. Over time each plate does have changes in speed of movement, but they stand out clearly vs the long-term averages. Since around 2001, there has been increasingly erratic behaviour, geologically speaking, it's not as if Everest is bouncing up and down but there does appear to be a statistically significant change in how the Earth's surface is behaving". She paused, silently inviting a response or questions. And the first came from Pete.

"Extraordinary work Elaine, I don't doubt for one second that all you say is true but why deep dive into tectonics and this data in particular when you had access to bucket loads of data in those files?"

"Well Pete, and you're going to love this answer that's for sure, I was inspired by your mantle integrity work and started to wonder if you'd stumbled, please excuse my disrespectful turn of phrase, upon something tangible and credible."

"Go on," Pete encouraged.

"Well, I started out, as you taught us Pete, with a hypothesis and then looked for data, not to back it up as such, but to associate with it. If I'm honest I'd much prefer data to lead me to an idea but we're past that stage on this one, so I worked on the basis you had had that leading data which led you to your theory."

"I'm happy for you to go with that thinking Elaine, it's a plausible suggestion." Pete smiled wryly.

"So, if there is a manifestation of your core expansion theory, or at least mantle disintegration, then plate movements would be a data-rich place to start."

Jeff piped up with a question, "But wouldn't there be loads more earthquakes and volcanic activity if the plates were speeding up like this Elaine?"

Pete threw him a glance which said immediately he'd

missed something and suddenly wished he'd kept his mouth shut.

"A really valid question Jeff, it's not that all the plates are speeding up but that would likely lead to greater instability and geological productivity, yes, I'm sure." She accommodated Jeff's leaping to a conclusion and carried on. "The trick here is that global volcanic activity hasn't changed that much because of this so we haven't got the red flags so to speak. It's almost hidden what's going on beneath the surface from a data perspective and to a certain amount, a topographical degree, potentially no one has had a cause to question this GPS data, because why would they? Yes, the spread of earthquake activity is more pronounced in some regions, but it was ever thus. I think it's hidden like a custard skin hides the lumps."

"Karate man, he bruise on the inside." Pete posed with his chopped hands in fighting fashion in a strangely accurate yet culturally inappropriate follow up to Elaine's custard comparison.

"Indeed Pete, things are going on beneath our feet and my view is that it is this which is causing weaknesses in land mass and, as ludicrous as it sounds, is allowing surface water and probably more importantly, the water table, to drain away deep into the Earth."

"Not ludicrous Elaine," Pete confidently announced, "entirely plausible."

"Agreed." Jeff joined in, "It does put some meat on the bones around our thoughts on what's happening here but clearly there are some big questions like where is it going, why isn't it coming back as steam, when will it stop, will it stop, how do we get it back…?" It was his last question which seemed to hit the three of them hardest. "There's one thing diagnosing the end of the world as we know it but it's an entirely different skill set finding the solution and reversing it."

"Ever the pragmatist Jeff." bellowed Pete with a smile. "Great, great work Elaine, not surprisingly I'm right behind you but it needs to pass the Jeff test before we smarten this thing up and send it across the pond. Why don't you guys get your heads together on this and iron out any creases whilst I go out and get stuff to keep you fed and watered."

"Perfect."

"Yep."

Elaine and Jeff responded in unison. This was a real flashback now, Pete with his big ideas and Jeff and Elaine filling in the gaps. Pete had a spring in his step as he headed out to his favourite deli just down from the Tiergarten S-Bahn station. Back in the apartment, Elaine and Jeff cleared the table and started to work through the plan of attack and bringing all this together for Jane to present to Senator Gordon.

"Let's hope Pete comes back with a lot of supplies, Jeff, because this is two days of hard graft."

"Awesome," replied Jeff, genuinely excited about the prospect of working through the theory and piecing data points together and equally at spending time with Elaine, something he thought would never have happened again.

"And two days is what we have before Jane goes back in with Gordon."

19

Washington DC

Back in Washington, Jane had put Gordon to one side for now, she had to trust Jeff and the gang to provide something useful for her and she had full confidence in Jeff. She probably wouldn't let him look after a pet fish on holiday, but this felt like something he was well able to handle.

It's funny how some people are like that, she fleetingly thought before getting her train of thought back onto Marco Hernandez. Jane had strong working relationships with several analysts in the Bureau, one of the upsides of being professionally conscientious, no one would likely bat an eyelid if she asked for anything so time again to put that to the test. Getting all that data proved to be quite straightforward, all she was doing now was a little digging around the IGA conference in Tokyo and who would be going. She'd dearly love to be attending and this felt like a pretty good cover story if anyone challenged her intentions.

Jane figured the climatologists would be the best port of call and that meant seeking out Dr. Ian Wormly, a man Jane felt was as dour as his name suggested. She had worked on a short project with Ian a few years on something to do with pollution and its impact on large metropolis' micro-climates, if her memory served her correctly. She had found Ian to be punctual, functional and a largely forgettable but decent man.

Jane amused herself on the way across to the Climate

Department by thinking about what the most spontaneous thing he'd had ever done. Maybe wearing a jaunty hat on the weekend or ordering a set of knives on flash sale on Amazon.

"Must ask him if I get the chance," she muttered to herself, enjoying the freedom of thought before getting down to business.

She'd once described the Climate Team as the kind of people who say, 'you don't have to be mad to work here but it helps.' Genuinely harmless but relentlessly annoying, always laughing at themselves or things a normal person wouldn't even smile at. It perked Jane up even more as she approached Ian's cubicle (she'd tell him it was an office if required but it was definitely a cubicle at best) when she laid eyes on the poster beneath Dr. Ian's name plate. It read 'if you don't know the difference between weather and climate, don't bother me'. It looked pristine so she guessed it must be new, or maybe he just had a stack of them he kept replacing, either way this could be her way in with him, although Ian's voice cut through her thoughts and snapped her back to reality.

"Jane Henderson as I live and breathe! What the devil brings you here to the party zone?" She could never really tell if he was serious because this was as much a party room as the file room in basement two. Nevertheless, it was quite sweet that Ian seemed genuinely happy to see Jane and she felt bad how she'd been teasing him, admittedly only in her head, but she'd be mortified if he found out.

"Well Ian. One, it's great to see you too, and will you

take my word that I know the difference between weather and climate?" For a moment Ian looked confused then burst into life again.

"Oh yes the poster," he guffawed a little more, "it's a belter, isn't it? My wife bought it for me for my birthday last week." Jane suppressed a snort and managed to turn it into some version of a laugh to match Ian. *In for a penny*, she thought.

"What a hoot Ian, she must be a real sweetie, and many happy returns too."

"Oh, thank you Jane, 18 again." another guffaw.

For fuck's sake, Jane managed not to say out loud. She ploughed on. "And two, I wanted to pick your brains about the IGA conference in Tokyo, you know the one that got postponed due to the typhoon?"

"Don't I just know about that Jane?" Ian threw his hands into the air. "The one that got away." Curious turn of phrase thought Jane but let Ian continue. "I have, well had, a ticket to go, but my wife booked for us to go to Cancun over the rearranged dates so I can't make it now. Damn shame as the updated agenda is rather intriguing. Jane's ears pricked up even more, Ian might prove useful after all.

"Are you going there too Jane?" Suddenly the idea popped into Jane's head about how she might be able to go in Ian's place but surely he'd nominated someone else in the Bureau already? It became clear to her that this idea must have been pretty clear to Ian, or he was a mind reader, or possibly more simply he was a man with a ticket to an event he could no longer attend as he didn't even wait for a reply, "if you're not, you're more than welcome to take my place. Angela has booked everything for four nights I think it is, great flights too, she'd just need to change the name, or you can pretend to be me." Another guffaw, accompanied by an awkward but ultimately harmless wink.

In her mind, Jane had ripped Ian's outstretched arm clean out of its socket, ticket still clenched in his tiny hands, but she kept her reaction a little more restrained compared to how fast her heart was beating.

"That would be simply amazing Ian!" Loving the fact she didn't have to pretend anymore, she was going now. "I was bitterly disappointed not to get one in the initial office ballot so, assuming I can clear it upstairs, then I'm in." Both Ian and Jane knew instinctively that attending the IGA conference would be a no-brainer for someone in Jane's position, for a fleeting second a tiny, confused look passed over Ian's face, making him have to adjust his glasses. Jane clocked it and, unbeknownst to her, correctly assumed it was down to Ian's slight befuddlement that she wasn't already going. But the confusion passed, and Jane ensured it wouldn't become an issue by taking control of the conversation.

"You had mentioned the updated agenda, is that a biggie or some backroom specialty that caught your eye?" Ian appeared at ease again and was chuffed that someone he respected so much was going on his ticket.

"Ha no!" he exclaimed with a goofy grin. "Although I was quite keen on catching Professor Masai's talk on geo-instability, sounds like he's one of those," he mimicked air quotes, "'big geological thinkers' who can spin a great yarn." Now it was time for Jane to have a flash of uncertainty and suspicion across her face, and Ian noticed it and, as he spoke, she felt herself redden in the cheeks.

"Oh, you know him, do you?" Ian was being so light-hearted and freshly naive that Jane felt comfortable letting her guard back down. Ian was surely not caught up in all this Rastik nonsense, that was a preposterous thought. So much so it made her smile as she replied.

"He's kind of a friend of a friend, I've not met him but am told he's quite the orator so yeah maybe I'll swing by there and let you know what happens." Jane totally forgot all the talks were being live broadcast by the National Geographic YouTube Channel.

"I'll be glued to the laptop in Cancun that's for sure, even though it might make Mrs Wormly a little tetchy, but I'd be keen to know the vibe from the conference." Jane's immediate thought was that Ian was not someone who really should be using the word 'vibe', but she was beginning to feel a bit mean, especially because he'd just given over his coveted ticket to the event which was totally dominating Jane's life right now.

"Of course, Ian, anything for you." This actually was, and sounded, genuine.

"Do you have the updated agenda, Ian? I know those things always have late amendments given travel difficulties or illness, but I heard there were some major movements on the main stage." Jane was fishing now, and Ian was more than happy to nibble on the bait.

"I get the impression the IGA is going to be used as some kind of global platform for a massive announcement about climate change." started Ian as Jane's ears felt they got noticeably bigger, "we've all seen the positive movements in sea levels these past couple of years…"

Leave it! Jane forced herself to stay silent.

"…and the general tone of the agenda seems to be moving towards one of progress against climate change, as a number of the original speakers have been dropped, but the original agenda is eighteen months old so perhaps they've acknowledged the narrative is turning."

"Seems unlikely don't you think, Ian, that decades of destruction have suddenly pivoted and everything's okay now?"

"Look Jane, the official line for us salaried climatologists is one of recovery and we have the data to prove it." Jane could sense Ian's guard lowering.

"Seriously Ian?"

"Let's take a walk Jane."

A blast of fresh air, as fresh as city air gets at least, hit them as they exited the revolving doors of the Climate Building and into the modern plaza out front, offices on three sides but stretching into one of the city's newest parks, and it was into there they headed.

"The headline keynote is being delivered by a chap called Marco Hernandez, you know him?" It felt now Ian was the one fishing but Jane sensed only to check if she was on his side.

"I've heard the name yes, plucked from nowhere

right, and now he's front and centre?"

"Exactly!" Ian confidently carried on. "Something strange is going on, the group he's representing – and remember he's been given top billing at the conference – is called the International Council for Climate Stability."

"Wow!" blurted Jane, genuinely reacting given this was new news to her. "That could mean anything and nothing, but the idea that an entirely new organisation that neither you or I have heard of is fronting the IGA is laughable, and slightly terrifying." They both paused, letting this sink in. They were still silent as they approached a coffee concession nestled beneath two young oak trees, which seemed to be fighting to provide the best canopy for the wooden hut below. Coffees in hand, it was Ian who broke first, picking up the conversation again.

"Look, I don't know what's going to be said and given who you work for and with, I'm being selective with my words."

"Really Ian, you don't need to be cautious, I think this whole thing is total horseshit."

Nice Jane, tell it like it is.

"Oh, wow cool," Ian continued. "I'm all for positivity and would never want to derail efforts to reverse climate change but the past year, maybe longer, it feels new funding is directed away from researching causes of climate irregularities to evidencing normalities. It's only slight, believe me there are plenty of projects continuing as before, but the natural order of things has changed, a cultural shift and that can only come down from the top."

"How far up do you think Ian?"

"I don't know Jane, you tell me." Ian exhaled dispiritingly. "I've worked here for nearly twenty years, never missed a deadline, never over-budget and for what?" Jane could feel Ian's emotions rising so gave him space to vent. "Now, on the biggest stage of all…" Jane was tempted to challenge whether the International Geological Association Conference would be recognised in many places as the biggest stage of all but wisely kept it to herself, "…some unknown dude from a research lab in the depths of the Amazon basin is all of a sudden the Golden Child, it's simply not fair." Jane wondered whether Ian's anger was really more about the fact he was being overlooked in his job rather than a seismic global cover-up threatening the future of humankind but reasoned that was largely irrelevant at this juncture. At least this explained the walk, Ian wanted to get out of potential earshot as couldn't say these things in the confines of his office. A compliant, diligent Government worker breaking rank like this was clearly making Ian feel very uncomfortable with his own views.

"I'll tell you what Ian," Jane tried to pacify him now, "I can see why you were so keen to go to Tokyo, but I'll be there and promise to be on the lookout and soundout for anything untoward, especially about this Marco Hernandez character."

"Well, I'm already one step closer to him!" exclaimed Ian rather darkly. "He's also fronting some kind of Bureau wide - maybe even state-wide - war on waste and tomorrow he's coming into the office in person to launch whatever initiative it's all about. Sounds like a cover to me but we'll see tomorrow."

"You might be right Ian." Jane was delighted she might get the chance to see or even speak to this Marco guy face to face. "So, I'll come by your office again if that's okay and we can check him out together." Ian appeared much happier at the thought of Jane being with him tomorrow and almost had a spring in his step as he headed back towards his office, the sun illuminating his ice white shirt as he disappeared into the throng of similarly dressed people in the plaza, leaving Jane to reflect on what was a very fruitful encounter.

Just as she was considering when, and with what information to go back to Jeff and the team in Berlin, her phone buzzed, and a message popped up on screen. It was from Harpinder: *Free for coffee?*

Perfect, thought Jane, *that's got to be good news, so Jeff can wait.* It was Jane's turn to have a spring in her step as she opted to walk the mile and a half to the coffee house at which Harpinder suggested they meet.

Thankfully the coffee was immeasurably nicer than the kiosk fare she'd had with Ian earlier and Jane cherished rather than tolerated every sip as she updated Harpinder on her meeting with the climatologist.

"Sounds like you've had a productive morning Jane, I suspect I'll be adding to that." Harpinder let a slightly mischievous grin envelope her face, at which Jane involuntarily leaned in expectantly. Two sumptuous coffees later and Jane's head was buzzing, and she knew now was the right time to dial in Berlin.

20

Berlin

Whilst Elaine and Jeff had been working through the back story, front story, one pager for Senator Gordon (they weren't really sure how to describe it), Peter was busy tweaking his own IGA presentation. He was acutely aware that his slot at the conference was currently their platform for counterattacking whatever it was Marco was about to say on behalf of whoever was behind all of this. Despite his best efforts to be seen as a big thinker, he knew, as did any academic of note, that making this stuff up on the hoof wasn't an option, so he was diligent in trying to process his train of thinking, maybe not in the same way as everybody else, but he definitely had to do the grunt work. His overarching challenges as he saw them right now were interleaved and pretty hairy. For starters, he had already submitted his presentation to the conference organising committee a couple of weeks ago. All the 'lesser' names had to in order for them to piece the audio-visual together, so he'd need to resubmit or find a way round somehow. He was also preparing himself and the team to counter-argue whatever Hernandez was going to say and all the authority, data and surface-level credibility he might present when they didn't really know what the Mexican was going to say.

He was compounded also by the timings on the agenda which had Hernandez and Pete timetabled to speak at the same time in different rooms of the same conference building. There was also the risk that Senator Gordon posed, although it could equally swing the other way, but he could totally derail the whole thing. He was the greatest unknown in the entire project aside from one miniscule nagging doubt that Pete was unable to squash completely. He could be wrong. Pete allowed this possibility on the basis he was a bona fide scientist so valued evidence, although maybe not quite as highly as others. But he was also a student of psychology and the concept of a winner's mentality. He marvelled at the almost denial with which sports people talked about their chances in a two-horse race. Heavyweight boxers know they are going to win, tennis players visualise how they'll dismantle their opponent's game, sprinters, who can't realistically do anything physical to slow down a rival, have total faith they will win. Each and every top player, or low level for that matter, knows at varying depths in their psyche that losing is a distinct, if not likely outcome. The putting paradox was Pete's favourite mental tussle, with golfers visualising the ball going into the cup being the only way to win but if it doesn't then it has to be close enough to go in next shot. But if it does miss the hole, then failure is a more likely outcome, at least not winning. The juxtaposition of committing fully emotionally to the fact the ball can either miss closely or go in creates a myriad of conflicting goals in the golfer's mind which makes it near impossible to pull apart from one another.

So, Peter, seeing himself as a top-level geological sportsman had the inner monologues and was a big fan of Mike Tyson's reality check on life - 'everyone has a plan until they're punched in the face.' Therefore he needed to stay cognisant that there were plenty of places these punches could come from in the next couple of weeks so needed more than one plan to cope with them , however he had to have a Plan A. Luckily for Pete, positive mental agility was not something he lacked and failure didn't happen to him, just a chance to go over stuff again from a different viewpoint, maybe changing some goalposts along the way. Not an excuse, just a different approach. And it was this strength which made him the ideal leader for this little 'end of the world' project. All Peter knew right now is that there were gaps in his revised presentation, but until the next few days unravelled, he neither knew exactly what the gaps were, nor how or with what to fill them. Fortunately, dealing with uncertainty didn't faze Pete but this level of ambiguity so close to a big deadline would send most scientists into a tailspin.

As evening drew in, Pete got a shout from Jeff that Jane would be online in thirty minutes for a debrief. This gave them, at Elaine's suggestion, a good opportunity to stretch legs and get some air.

Pete took them towards the S-Bahn station plaza so they could grab some more supplies from the delicatessen to keep them going through what they all assumed was going to be quite an intense period. Which is why Pete and Elaine went in to get the food and not Jeff, there appeared to be a common understanding that Jeff would buy pizza rolls, sausage rolls, in fact any kind of high fat, processed, rollable foodstuff. But if he was presented with healthier alternatives he'd just as happily, well maybe not as happily, but certainly eagerly gobble them up too. Gastronomy wasn't one of Jeff's defining characteristics, however efficiency was so if he needed to trade preparing his own food for consuming others' healthier options, that suited him just fine.

As Pete and Elaine were in the store, Jeff had a nose around the other shops and hawker-style stalls in the immediate vicinity. His knowledge of German wasn't great to put it mildly but the headline at the newsstand for the recently revived Berliner Abend post caught his eye, less for the headline 'Klima: hoffe Endlich' (*Climate: hope at last*)' but for the image. It was a standard issue, stereotypical climate change image of the Earth in the palm of a hand, one side desolate, the other lush and vibrant. He had a five Euro note in his pocket so Jeff bought a couple of copies before realising only Peter would be able to read it so one would've been plenty. A quick scan of the front page didn't help Jeff hugely, although it continued inside and one line caught his attention, mainly as it was in English, and it referenced 'The International Council for Climate Stability'. Instinctively Jeff reached for his phone and unconsciously weighed up the cost of roaming for what he then, consciously, reprimanded himself. He frantically typed in 'International Council for Climate Stability' and was immediately struck by the cited dates on the search page, they were all today's date.

"It's started." Jeff muttered to himself.

"What's started Jeff? Your night school German lessons?" Pete heard Jeff's utterance and clocked him with his two newspapers.

"This," Jeff handed one copy of the paper to Pete and his phone to Elaine. "I think we're getting a sneak preview of what's going to hit us in Tokyo."

"This is brilliant news! So dart!" exclaimed Pete triumphantly, with Jeff and Elaine eyeing him with suspicion on how even he could find positives in the news that this new research group, clearly with some serious backing, had just effectively announced publicly evidence that climate change was being reversed.

"They've played their hand." delighted Pete, although they all knew the three of them weren't likely to be known players in this imaginary combat. The relief for Pete was this helped fill those gaps in his conference and overall strategy, his brain was already piecing threads together. "Send the links over to Jane, will you Jeff?"

"Already done, she says she heard about these guys today too." As if signalling a shift in the severity of the situation, a dark cloud blocked the sun and an imposing shadow cast across Tiergarten and the plaza.

"Let's get back inside to digest this and get Jane online, this is feeling very real now. And I also don't want to get rained on, although it'd be good to know there's still some water left in the atmosphere!" Peter couldn't resist making light of the situation and they all hurried back to the apartment.

He had just finished reading the Abendpost article when Jane called in via WhatsApp on his Mac.

"Hello Jane, lovely to see you. We've all got beer and

our feet up as it turns out everything's going to be okay after all."

"Hi Pete, Jeff's usually got his feet up with a beer so even if the world is ending or being saved that probably won't change." Jeff grunted and mumbled a version of hello to Jane, who spotted Elaine at the back of Pete's apartment making her way to the table.

"And hi there Elaine, lovely to see you too, feels like an odd way to be introducing ourselves."

"Ha, doesn't it just, hello Jane."

Jeff felt this whole interaction could get awkward, especially for him so decided to emcee the situation.

"OK let's get this show on the road, shall we? There's loads to get through and we've the added element of this press release which appears to have been globally coordinated." It was this last point that really focussed them all, the realisation that whoever or whatever this International Council for Climate Stability are they seem to have been able to grab gold standard editorial across the world's media.

"It's not as if every week there isn't some kind of press release or scientific body which talks up or down climate change and for these guys to appear from seemingly nowhere and get front pages with what, on the surface, seems pretty evidence-light is extraordinary."

"You're right Jeff," replied Jane in real time. *The wonder of high-tech fibre connection,* thought Pete to himself, "but I've not had a chance to digest what they've actually presented, other than it says that, and I quote the New York

Times website, 'we're winning the war on rising sea levels.'" Pete took this on.

"Yes, Jane, you've pretty much got it in one there. The interesting thing for me, having read the Berlin piece and I suspect it's reflected across the other media is there is very limited credible evidence behind the headline other than the sea level reading we are all very familiar with already. I've only scanned it but from what I can see there's a reading from the Amazon..."

"Marco!" they all shouted at the same time.

"....and another from the Philippines which are being used as proof that sea levels are back at 1900 levels. Which presents the most intriguing and to be honest disturbing aspect of this rubbish, for it to have made it to the media like this must mean it has been forced upon them, because I reckon this would maybe get column inches in some papers and websites, not blanket coverage, although I do appreciate the world does need some good news on climate change, it's just there's not a lot of it about."

"Well," interjected Jane, "I think I can shed some light on this part of the equation." She brought the team up to speed on her contact and relationship with Harpinder Tarkowski and the green lighting as it were for Senator Gordon's decency and trustworthiness. "I went off to do some digging around Marco Hernandez, whom I'm hoping to bump into tomorrow before seeing Gordon...." The Berlin trio were already impressed with Jane's progress, but nothing compared to what she told them next. "...whilst Harpinder went to try to unearth what's going on at the top of the chain. She and I met up earlier today and I trust her. In a nutshell Nancy Rastik, Bureau Chief, and Senator Nick Johnson are working together to provide evidence, however credible, for the president of the United States to claim he's solved the climate change problem. This is conspiracy theory stuff of movie status. President Franks is being funded by global utility and car giants and apparently sees his legacy as being the world's saviour. It's scary stuff folks but that's not it." The atmosphere in the Berlin apartment was tense and all of them were glued to Pete's Mac screen, trying to process the magnitude of what they were hearing.

"Johnson is grooming himself and being groomed to be in office, succeeding Franks after his second term. Johnson is the link to the media; he comes from a family of media tycoons and sounds like he's been building up favours by all accounts to be able to unleash in the coming weeks and months to change the global narrative on climate change. And he's got some frighteningly big hitters on his side." Team Berlin independently assumed these could be oil giants or car manufacturers or some such kind, but Jane was almost reading their minds.

"It's not business or infrastructure conglomerates. It's nations guys and not just any nations."

"Don't say China, please don't say China." Pete pleaded, knowing how damning this would be.

"Not just China, Peter." Pete closed his eyes, bracing himself for what Jane was about to say.

"Russia too. The Cold War is officially over, they've all found something to bond over and it's taking a collective dump on Mother Earth, pardon my language."

"I don't get it." Elaine blurted out, not with naivety but with a genuine intrigue as she tried frantically to join the dots with all this. "How come Nancy Rastik is in this Jane, from what you say she's of a sounder mind than this?"

"Elaine, for me this is the darkest element of the whole shitstorm. From what I can glean and interpret is that she doesn't gain anything material from this. I abhor what the president and Senator Johnson are doing but at least I can see a tangible outcome that benefits them both with status and no doubt untold riches via backhanders or donations or whatever but Rastik, from where I'm sitting, she loses everything and gains nothing. Harpinder managed to find out quite a bit about Rastik, don't worry she's an excellent journalist so no suspicions, and it sounds like this is a personal quest for her. She's in one of the most responsible jobs in the world when it comes to influencing global policy on climate change and she's a fundamental denier. This is not a play for riches we're trying to unpick, it's the career ambition of an extremely motivated, savvy and ruthless scientist who, not unlike the president, sees her legacy and life purpose as being the reversal of global climate initiatives. She holds the keys here and she's the one we need to fear." A long silence followed as everyone tried to process what they'd just heard. Elaine was the one who broke the impasse.

"This suggests they have more than just the sea level data to reveal, that can't be enough to convince the world, however much it's her life's ambition or destiny or whatever."

"Correct Elaine, in that we should assume they have more." said Jane, nodding in agreement. "We're not certain but it sounds like there's another big global press release going out in five days then some preamble teasers about the IGA conference. It's gonna feel like a G20 summit by the time Tokyo finally arrives."

"That's why they delayed it, to get more nations on side." blurted Jeff. "Jane, do you or Harpinder know who else is backing this theory?"

"Not yet Jeff, all we got to was Russia and China. Oh, and Australia of course, they love a fossil fuel down there. The one question Harpinder insisted I raise with you guys before we go any further on this…"

Pete interrupted, not rudely but partly to show he understood what risks Harpinder was undertaking professionally. "She wants to know if they might be right, and we might be wrong."

"Bingo!" replied Jane. "I know we are all sceptical of the sceptics, but she urged us to be laser focused on our approach as we may only get one shot at undermining and stopping this juggernaut."

Peter spoke again, "Reality check for all of us and despite what you might think I do, I am capable of thinking for both sides, but even if we didn't have our slightly apocalyptic theory, our natural, well scientific instinct, would be to challenge this kind of bolt from the blue claim which goes against prevailing thinking. However, Joe Public loves a good news story, so we've got our hands full here.

What else have you got Jane, before we show you ours? You said you're seeing my good friend Marco tomorrow, do give him my regards."

"I'm hoping to, yes, Peter. We all suspect they're using Marco as some kind of mouthpiece for this International Council for Climate Stability, the ICCS I suspect it'll be referred to as, but from what Harpinder and I could glean, he is just this. You know as you worked with him but, unless he's been on some kind of acceleration course in politics, science and public speaking, he does not present as a likely candidate to have earned this honour, if you can call it that. More like a Rocky style name out of a hat job, a face that fits. He does what he's told because suddenly he's hit the big time, they've put him up in a plush city apartment so he's going to be compliant, plus they've genuinely used some of his own work, sorry Pete, from the Amazon, to help build this leading-edge position." Pete decided not to get involved aside from a massive eye roll, allowing Jane to continue.

"Which reminds me, if I haven't made this clear, there is no obvious link between the ICCS and Rastik, Johnson or the president. Faceless organisations are not so uncommon when it comes to situations like this, so they just become accepted as a think tank or an actual bricks and mortar government or international building. We don't actually know how public they'll go on this."

"My guess is none at all, if they can get it steamrolling across public thinking." Pete interjected again. "Once they get openly involved, they're neck deep in it but from a distance they can literally surf in and pick up on all the things which make them vote worthy. If I were Franks or Johnson, I'd be earmarking Rastik to take any crap that comes from this and vice versa. Rastik will be looking to blame political pressure blah blah blah, so they're tight now, but it's fragile so let's keep our gunpowder dry for now."

"Agreed." they all said in unison.

"So, Marco." Jane carried on. "My bet is they'll need someone with him to answer the really challenging media questions. I can't believe they'll let him stand there on his own in front of the world's media, he might as well have a clown suit on."

"I'd pay to see that." guffawed Jeff.

"Me too," replied Jane, "but I don't have to as I've secured a US Government sponsored ticket to the hot seats, courtesy of a romantic old friend of mine in the Climate Bureau." They all laughed, trying to decipher whether Jane was dropping some juicy hints as to her love life in the past and she second guessed them before, inevitably Jeff, would blurt out something mildly inappropriate. "No, not romantic for me, his wife has double-booked him so he's off to Cancun and I'm heading to Tokyo. On expenses."

"Well good for you Jane, it'll be great to see you in person in Japan, you've really had some great success these past few days." Peter was genuinely impressed with her tenacity and progress, especially considering she didn't know them from Adam. "And good for this chap."

"Ian." Jane helped him out.

"Ian, you say, yes good for Ian. Cancun will be

lovely, and he should make the most of it I guess whilst he still can. Man, this water thing is going to be a bitch to the coastal tourism industry. Anyhow…" Pete realised this wasn't the time or subject on which to dwell, "…see if you can get a sense from Marco how central he is, or likely isn't, to the ICCS. I'm sure you're already in that space so let's turn our attention to our, or rather, your date with our soon to be best buddy Senator Gordon."

Elaine took Jane through her work and theory on tectonic shifting and, with Jeff's help, had managed to sum it all up on one sheet, although there were reams of data to back it up. They spent a good hour or so countering Jane's questions and challenges, and they all acknowledged they had absolutely no idea what Jane was going to walk into the next day in Washington. The one thing they did all agree on was for Jane not to put too much pressure on Marco Hernandez in the morning, they felt he was a potential loose cannon in their whole scenario, purely on the basis he was totally out of his depth and that kind of pressure or status can manifest itself in a variety of ways, unpredictable ways.

"So, unless Marco initiates something specific about Tokyo, the ICCS, even you Peter, I'll try be cute and just get a sense of what's going on."

"However," interjected Pete, "your romantic friend on the other hand Ian, he has every reason in the world to ask questions about Tokyo and Marco's involvement, you might want to get him onside and play that card tomorrow."

"Awesome Peter, the thought had crossed my mind,

I'm sure Ian would love to find out more about Marco anyway so yes, I'll tee him up in the morning."

"Great stuff Jane" Jeff was ready to wrap it up for the night as it was getting close to midnight in Germany. "Do you have everything you need for now? We've transferred the data and one-pager and Pete's sent you his mantle disintegration presentation, at least in its current form, in case you need it for Gordon tomorrow, or something to help you sleep tonight," a comedy glance across at Pete. "So, I reckon you're all set. We'll be online all day in case you need us. Sweet dreams."

"To you all too." replied Jane with her pluckiest grin, she didn't feel four thousand miles away but as she closed the call down, it dawned on her that she was indeed, very much alone in Washington and it was going to be damn hard to get to sleep tonight after all that coffee earlier.

21

Washington DC

By the time Nancy Rastik closed off the meeting for the Project Green team, Marco was almost salivating at the prospect of what lay ahead for him. He, Marco Hernandez, was going to tell the world, yes the whole world, that the war on climate change had been successful and that this would signify a 'new dawn for global prosperity'. Those were the words echoing around Marco's head. Not only was he going to Japan, a country he could only dream about visiting before now, but he would be presenting world changing information and some of it was his own actual work. His subconscious was already creating a narrative that in some respects, Marco Hernandez was responsible, at least partly responsible, for stopping climate change. At night he allowed himself to dream about his legacy, would there be statues? Probably. He'd guess the University of Mexico would likely dedicate a building or maybe a scholarship in his name. Perhaps some kind of global initiative would take his name, like what happened to Alfred Nobel, and he invented dynamite of all things. He imagined the Hernandez Award would go to great, creative young minds in fields of scientific excellence and, whilst alive, Marco himself would present the awards in person, handing the baton of scientific immortality on to future generations.

"I hope it happens in my lifetime; you know when he gives the first award out. We're so proud of him, of course we always knew he'd amount to greatness, he was the first, of many I guess now, Hernadeses to go to university. And look what he's made of himself, Lead Climate Consultant to the president of the United States of America."

"Is that his current job title Mrs Hernandez?" probed freelance journalist Julietta Cornet, former college roommate and, when they're in the same city at the same time, drinking buddy of Harpinder Tarkowski.

You're a legend, Harpinder! Jane had replied to the WhatsApp she received as she woke to the rattling of her alarm.

Sent a friend of mine to see if Mrs Hernandez has heard much from Marco, he's now publicly going to Tokyo so can assume he's spilled some beans, just wanted to find out how many, and what type of beans.

A second message followed: *Worry not J, it'll all be above board and without suspicion*, before a selection of smiley and water based emojis were sent.

"I really do appreciate your time and honesty about Marco, I can see how proud you are just by the way your eyes sparkle when you talk about him. And to clarify, this is not a scientific piece I'm writing so nothing will go out before the IGA conference, you don't have to worry about spoilers, this will just be about the rise of one of our own Mrs Hernandez. An inspirational story about your son's dedication and hard work, supported by his family to become one of the most influential scientists of our time." Harpinder had told Julietta to lay it on thick and she did just that, layer upon layer of gush so poor Mrs Hernandez couldn't help but talk about her son.

"Well, given this is going out after Marco's big speech, I guess it doesn't matter what I tell you that you don't already know or are going to find out in a week or so."

Jackpot, Julietta almost squealed. She, not Harpinder, expected her to know a great deal about the ins and outs of the plan as Nancy Rastik had almost certainly sworn them all the secrecy but usually a loving son with a chip on his shoulder wouldn't be able to resist. And they were right, where Rastik has dangerously misjudged both the size of the chip and Marco's inferiority complex within his own family.

"Well, I'm sure you know about this new global organisation that's stopping climate change, the ICCS I think Marco called it, and I know you're a professional journalist and all but something he said might just make a super headline for your piece on him." Julietta played along, inwardly delighted as to how well this was going.

"Oh yes please, it always helps to get ideas from those close to our subjects."

"Well, when our Marco tells the world he's solved climate change," *Interesting interpretation,* thought Julietta, "he'll announce what he calls a 'new dawn for global prosperity.'" Julietta almost gagged, instinctively knowing what this was a likely reference to and ironically, the dire consequences this would actually have on the planet.

"That, Mrs Hernandez, is a really excellent headline, yes I can see it now, not just in my piece but across newspapers, TV and media sites around the world." And now for some artistic licence, "A new dawn for global prosperity, renowned scientist Dr. Marco Hernandez, pioneering visionary for climate stability is now considered to be the father of the second, but this time green, industrial revolution, paving the way for all nations to enjoy the rich fruits of economic development....I could go on but do you get where I'm going?" Paulina Hernandez was audibly purring now, her face red with pride.

"Dr. Marco Hernandez," she repeated to herself. "And hopefully you have someone who can translate all that into Russian and Chinese as Marco said they were on his team too, it's a widely international setup he's leading up there in Washington."

Another shudder from Julietta. Harpinder had let her in on what was going on so this signal that it wasn't just the USA alone going live with this stuff, that it was indeed Russia and China at least, made her feel she'd got what she came for. As Harpinder had also suggested, Julietta thought she might actually write a piece on Marco Hernandez, as promised to mum after the Tokyo conference, so she stayed with her for quite some time after finding out about their wider family and enjoying some very lovely homemade peach iced tea and muffins. She didn't, however, think her piece would reflect Marco in quite the basking glow that his family might have hoped for.

22

That the alarm woke her was a big surprise to Jane, not only due to its shrill and belly wobbling ring but also that she barely remembered turning off her light. *That makes sense*, she thought as she gathered her senses, noticing her bedside lamp was still on, she must have just passed out. Perhaps the crash after all those coffees outweighed the caffeine. Either way she felt refreshed and ready to start her big day. The messages from Harpinder buoyed her greatly and she immediately shared the news with the guys over in Berlin. Nothing new as such but just as Harpinder alluded, it showed Marco might struggle to keep it together entirely. He was clearly not used to this level of responsibility and if Nancy Rastik were to find out how much he'd blabbed to his own mother, then she suspected Marco might quickly disappear from her team and potentially disappear altogether. Peter was the first to respond, but then Jane realised he was likely replying for them all:

Even more reason to tread carefully with MH and make sure your romantic friend doesn't push his buttons too hard.

Despite the potential enormity of the day ahead of her, Jane still pulled on her joggers and sweatshirt, clambered into her running shoes and headed out into the crisp morning air for a run. It certainly impressed Jeff when her 5.1km route popped up on his Strava notifications. It even made him consider doing the same but chose a mug of coffee and cinnamon bun instead.

Jane arrived back at her apartment by 8am, energised

rather than exhausted as she thought she might have been by these early jogs. She glanced at herself in the mirror as she closed her front door and had a moment of mild elation. She wasn't sure she's lost a lot of actual weight, but she definitely looked fitter, stronger and this in itself gave her a bit of extra physical confidence. She knew she used to carry herself as if she were a bit tired and podgy even though she was never totally out of shape, despite the late-night booze sessions with Jeff. Her shoulders would slope, and her head would be slightly bowed. Now she walked tall, back straight, chest out but not in a 'look at my tits' kind of way, more of a 'look how confident I am' kind of way, which ironically made men look at her tits more than if she had them on gaudy show. She felt good about herself, she was giving life a real go, bursting with so much confidence that she turned the shower dial to full blue. Yes, an invigorating cold shower, that's what powerful women take daily to fire themselves up.

She stepped under the icy blast, ready to revel in the chilling strength it would give her. "Oh, Christ no!" she screamed and yanked the dial back up to scolding and basked in its comfort and warmth. *One step at a time,* she thought.

Ian came down to meet her and they swung by the office café on their way back up to his floor. This gave Jane a chance to discuss the plan she hoped he would deploy on Marco later that morning. She didn't quite divulge everything but made it mysterious enough that Ian clearly felt a little like a spy or maybe detective. Either way, he was very keen to play along, partly for Jane but also for his own sanity. He was still reeling from the idea that this Marco guy had been put in a position, even if Ian didn't agree with the purpose, that Ian felt significantly more qualified to fulfil.

Jealousy, thought Jane, *is a powerful motivation tool.* Their plan was for Ian to have a copy of the IGA agenda and online links printed out with Marco's name on in order to ask him about his upcoming trip to Tokyo and see where that takes them.

As they exited the lift on the eighth, which housed Ian's climate team, colleagues and also a rather sizable conference room that served the entire building, a couple of sports catalogue style models handed them both a four-page glossy flyer. Both Ian and Jane did a double take on the two individuals in front of them, entirely incongruous in an office space seemingly sponsored by the colour grey. She had a blue cheerleader style mini-skirt, and he was wearing a pair of yellow shorts that looked like hand-me-ups from his seven-year-old brother. They had identical pink t-shirts emblazoned on the front with 'WASTE NOT WANT NOT.' Jane resisted the urge to reach out and touch them to see if they were actually really human.

Confirmation came as the multi-coloured duo jumped up, span around and raised their arms over their heads, thumbs pointing down at another logo on their very pink backs. 'IT'S A WN WN FOR EVERYWN'. Jane was pretty sure she'd decoded this, mainly because it wasn't hugely cryptic, but also because the smiling twinset sang out together:

"Waste Not Want Not, It's a Win Win for Everyone." Jane involuntarily sniggered as they pronounced everyone as if it was spelled 'everywin.' The young handsome lad in the tight shorts' grin faltered and his face fell which surprised Jane almost as much as the rhyming effort of win-win.

"Look ma'am, you do your job, and we'll do ours, we're just making money for college so give us a break."

Ian bellowed out, "Good for you guys, we'll be more respectful, sorry." and gave him a hearty and awkwardly paternal slap on the back and linked arms with Jane and semi-forcibly dragged her away from the rather uncomfortable situation she'd created for herself. She tried to mutter some form of apology as they scuttled down the corridor, but Ian cut her off.

"I thought you were supposed to be a little more discreet than that Jane." he ribbed, suddenly in high spirits.

"I just wasn't expecting that, that's all. It threw me a bit." Behind them the elevator dinged once again and they could hear the cheery welcome of 'Waste Not Want Not, it's a win win for everywin'. "Those poor buggers," mused Jane.

Ian and Jane took their seats in the conference room, which was decorated, if it was fair to say decorated, with banners and pull-ups with 'It's a WNWN' and associated headlines.

"You do realise Jane," whispered Ian, "you're the only person here who doesn't officially work in this building I suspect."

"Good point." Jane did acknowledge that it may seem odd for someone to go out of their way to attend this session. "If needed we can just say I arrived early for a meeting."

They sat in silence for about five minutes as people continued to stream in, nearly all of whom had the distinct air of low expectation, as if they'd be corralled into attending yet another Bureau-wide 'hot air' idea. Office-place cynicism was endemic these days, people would routinely complain about their jobs and when they get a chance for an hour off with a free coffee, maybe biscuits, they also moan about that too.

The curse of instant gratification and entitlement borne from social media and the always-on culture, mulled Jane, *millennials, it's always them to blame. They just think everything should be handed to them on a plate without any graft.*

"Oh, stop living in the past Jane." she babbled to herself.

"You OK Jane? You're talking to yourself."

They were cut off by a clear, booming voice at the front of the room.

"Good morning, everyone and a winning welcome to you all." Ian nudged Jane to draw her attention to the very clean, very smartly suited young man addressing them. He'd clearly got the same idea and had sought Jane out in the audience and was seemingly speaking directly to her.

"It's the same guy from the lift and yellow shorts." whispered Ian.

"Do you think I don't realise that?" Jane's cheeks had

noticeably reddened as it dawned on her that the yellow and pink had been replaced by a very well fitting, very smart, very imposing charcoal grey suit cloaking an ice white linen shirt and iridescent purple tie.

Jane responded to him with her best nod and smile which, in her mind, said 'well-done young man, you've really put me in my place, I'm humbled and now stand corrected, please continue, you have my undivided attention and newfound respect, I was wrong to judge you.' Whereas his glance at her simply said 'up yours'.

The girl has also metamorphosed from bubble gum cheerleader into catalogue model for IBM and it was she who led proceedings to get the session started.

"This is Max and I'm Minnie, and we are delighted to be hosting you for today's launch for the Climate Bureau of 'Waste Not Want Not.'"

Max chimed in. "It's a win win for everyone," pronouncing everyone with a very short vowel at the end still trying forcibly to make it rhyme with 'win'.

Minnie continued, "This is an initiative that has been piloted in a few states and will now roll out across all federal and state-run workplaces and be available to any private sector corporations, however big or small. I can report that so far, we have Apple, Chrysler, Google, Pacific Gas and Electric, Shell, Southern California Edison on board, and that list goes on and on. Before we hear from your local project lead, Marco Hernandez, who will let you know how you can get involved, we are super lucky to have the opportunity to hear the global aspiration for Waste Not

Want Not from none other than Bureau Chief and project sponsor and all round amazing inspirational leader…." a pause for effect, giving Jane a chance to process what that meant.

"Rastik is here." she whispered excitedly to Ian just as Minnie introduced her to the room.

"...Nancy Rastik!" A murmur amongst the hundred or so attendees in the conference room as they suddenly realised this might be a bit more significant than they'd thought. A few audible gasps of "Wow this must be serious," and, "Jeepers." Jane, however, was a little more sceptical.

"She's here to check if Marco is up to the job I reckon." she turned to Ian, who gave her a quizzical look back. He seemed truly excited that Nancy Rastik would be attending in person, for him she would be the pinnacle, akin to meeting, or at least being in the same room as, a professional hero so he was now a bit giddy. Jane's brain was in overdrive, but it started to make sense to her. If Marco Hernadez would be presenting to a room of say a thousand global delegates and the world's media under Rastik's tutelage, it did make sense to observe a dry run beforehand.

"Once our presenters are underway, we'd all appreciate it if you'd keep your phones and other recording devices switched off, on silent or simply away please. And thank you." One glance around the room made it very obvious to Jane the need for this message, she reckoned over half the room had a smartphone pointed at the makeshift stage at the front of the room.

In seconds, she was one of them, and in another few seconds a notification popped up on the phones of Elaine, Jeff and Pete in central Berlin with a slightly blurred photo of a smartly dressed woman, dark blue trouser suit and short dark hair walking towards a lectern, laden with three to four microphones, with a slightly lurid background with large letters spelling out 'WASTE NOT WANT NOT, IT'S A......FOR E.......ONE'. The lectern obscured the view of the whole statement but no matter.

"That's Nancy Rastik!" exclaimed Jeff moments before Jane's second notification landed, *Rastik's here. Rastik!!*

"I reckon she's there to check on Marco." Pete calmly said as the third message pinged on their screens from the conference room in Washington.

"Gotta be here to check on MH."

There was an audible hush as the Department Director took the stage, full of purpose and charisma despite her diminutive frame. For most of the room, she would undoubtedly be the highest-ranking Government employee they'd likely ever be in a room with, and she knew how to keep them on her side.

"What a warm and respectful welcome, thank you, you really are the backbone of our common effort to make our world, our beautiful planet, a better place. Which is why I personally chose this session to attend so I could extend my heartfelt thank you to you all personally for your commitment and support."

Wow, thought Jane, *she sounds like a politician at a rally,* but one sideways glance at a transfixed Ian confirmed that Nancy Rastik definitely knows her audience so, to make sure she wouldn't be singled out for sniffing BS, Jane put on her best 'intrigued and amazed' face. Rastik continued but speedily got down to business.

"As you know, we have been facing unprecedented challenges in our fight against climate change." A subtlety Jane picked up on, not 'we are facing' but 'we have been facing', as if it were a thing of the past. *Interesting,* she pondered.

"And one of those cornerstones in our battleplan is the ongoing war on waste. I know that, with the support of everyone in this room, and countless rooms around the US and globally, we will win this battle and one day soon, you will be responsible for restoring Mother Earth's precious balance to foster harmony, happiness and prosperity for humankind." Jane held back the urge to roll her eyes and shout obscenities, but she appeared to be the only person there able to hold in emotions as the room erupted into spontaneous and rapturous applause. Rastik gave a very obvious glance to Marco Hernandez, a look which Jane decided was 'that's how you do it son, now it's your turn'. She half-heartedly made attempts to calm the adulation but was clearly enjoying it. Once the cheering subsided, a number of hands stayed raised in the air to which Rastik spoke.

"I would love to stay up here and answer your questions," she smiled, "but I really am not the main event today." she said with false humility. This time an audible groan.

"Poor Marco, having to follow her." whispered Jane to Ian with genuine sympathy.

"So," Rastik continued, "aside from asking for one hundred percent commitment on this initiative, which I'm sure is no problem at all, my only remaining task is to introduce you to your project lead, responsible for not just this Bureau but all federal departments on the Eastern Seaboard. An esteemed scientist in his own right, who I'm led to believe is presenting on the main stage at the upcoming IGA conference in Tokyo, Japan so we are honoured to have him on board this team. Dr Marco Hernandez ladies and gentlemen."

Perhaps fearful that Marco might not get quite the reception she did herself, Nancy Rastik led the clapping before the delegates joined in supportively and she ushered Marco onto the makeshift stage, shook his hand, clearly whispered something Jane would have paid good money to hear, and stepped to one side, far enough away to allow the audience to transition away from her back to centre stage again, where stood Marco Hernandez.

23

Berlin

"So how was it? Are you a fully signed up member of the Marco Hernandez official fan club?" Jeff teasingly asked Jane as she group-called him and the gang whilst exiting the building following the presentation.

"To a certain degree Jeff yes, the guy did a good job, he actually sounded like he believes in the waste reduction plan he is now poster boy of. In reality, it's another reduce-reuse-recycle initiative that'll make people feel good about themselves, whilst simultaneously creating loads of waste, whilst stripping the planet of its finite natural resources. That aside, I'm two thumbs up for it Jeff, but do you want to know the fun stuff instead?"

"Yes, we do please." interrupted Pete, almost barbed at Jeff for making light of the situation. Pete was acutely aware that Jane had precious little time before walking in with Senator Gordon and God knows who else or what that might entail.

"Well, it's no surprise but Rastik disappeared pretty much as soon as MH had closed off. I think she was happy with him, he was coherent, sounded credible and dealt adequately with the delegate questions, although to be fair I could've answered most of them, they were a bit basic, like about the colour of waste bins and sensors in toilets. Our new best friend Dr Ian collared him once the microphones were off and sounded like Marco's guard was down, not surprising if this was his dress rehearsal in front of Rastik.

For context, Ian doesn't know what we know but he is suspicious and brass tacks simply jealous Marco got a gig he is arguably more qualified to do."

"No shit Sherlock." Pete's turn to ad lib and echo Jane's thoughts, "Hardworking employee gets annoyed when overlooked for promotion shocker."

"Indeed Pete, however," Jane continued, "he did get some titbits from Marco. He told Ian this wasn't the only project he was working on with Rastik and Ian asked him about Tokyo and what it was all about, you know scientist to scientist, and apparently Marco was very tight all of a sudden and said and I quote: 'she won't be happy if I talk about that'. Ian asked if he meant Rastik, which we know he did but Ian probably doesn't, and he fobbed him off with some garbage about a lady called Pearson. I couldn't find anyone by that name in the Bureau database, so he's clearly been sworn to secrecy and is not great at it. The main thing though, and super ironic after presenting about waste to a bunch of climate scientists, is that he left his notes and speech on the lectern. So now we have his speech which, for obvious reasons, I won't bore you with. However, there were a few notes and scribbles on it which seem to be telling our mutual friend Marco what to avoid. Things like, 'This isn't the ICCS, not here to talk about that', 'sea levels off agenda' and 'stay on message', but also 'good luck' and 'you got this, see you in Tokyo.'"

"Rastik." they all chimed together in Berlin.

"Yep," said Jane, "it's got to be, and not wanting to sound like a detective but if nothing else, we've got an example of her handwriting."

"And a pretty strong link between her and Marco when it comes to the ICCS and Tokyo which could be a useful asset with Senator Gordon." added Elaine.

"It sure does." Jane was in high spirits as she said her goodbyes on the WhatsApp call to her teammates in Germany.

"Good luck this afternoon Jane, you know Gordon better than any of us but still be careful not to get yourself into trouble before he shows at least some of his cards."

"Thanks Peter, solid advice and thanks to you, to Elaine and of course Jeff, at least by this evening we'll know if this is going to go anywhere or not. And in preparation, I'm going into the meeting on a full stomach, I could murder a halloumi burrito!"

"Cantina Carnivale?" shouted Jeff.

"Oh yes Jeff. Oh yes."

"Aha enjoy it for me too please, catch you on the other side, wear a napkin, you remember what happened last time?" The others looked at Jeff and without needing prompting he proceeded to tell them. "We went for lunch a few weeks back and Jane spent the rest of the day with a massive salsa stain on her chest."

"Easily done Jane - you got this too!" encouraged Pete. They all closed WhatsApp down with a zing of positive energy that this afternoon would define not only their next few days but their careers and ultimately lives, in fact the lives of every living soul on the planet. And in anybody's book that deserves a massive burrito.

24

Washington DC

Senator Gordon's private office was located in a fairly inauspicious block in Georgetown with very auspicious views over the Potomac River.

"I've always been hypnotised by rivers and their majestic independence," Gordon had personally met Jane in the entrance hall of the building block to escort her up to his office. "I am humbled by the flow of life and the water we see here in DC was once in the sea, fell as rain, watered the high grounds of West Virginia, it has supported more life on this Earth than we could ever comprehend. That water we see here could have fallen as rain on Julius Caesar, run past the Great Pyramids of Giza as part of the Nile, been drunk by Socrates in ancient Greece. It is beyond the comprehension of the small-minded man or woman to consider the true nature of the water cycle and its infinite power. I chose this location, not as you can guess for the beauty of this building, though it's well insulated and supported by excellent public transport access." Gordon smiled, putting Jane at considerable ease. "But so the river could constantly remind me and inspire me of our greater responsibility and place in this world."

Gordon was calmness personified, Jane thought to herself as they stepped into the elevator and headed up to the sixth and top floor of the building. She wondered if this was a tactic he'd developed over the years to appear relaxed and in control, using long silences to draw out his political opponents, whilst all the time underneath he was a nervous wreck. He was definitely a man of experience and, as Harpinder had confirmed, a man of integrity, so Jane decided it was okay to feel comfortable in his presence but was very conscious this did not mean she could let her guard down and slip into unprofessional behaviour. There was no danger in that as Gordon brought the focus right back to the fore. As they walked along the corridor from the elevator towards the double doors at the end with a brass plate to one side reading 'Sen. Gordon Private Office' he slowed to a standstill and looked penetratingly into Jane's eyes and with his deep and controlled voice simply said:

"Tell me why you are here Jane."

They both knew Jane was slightly taken aback by this as her eyes momentarily flickered in confusion, the only part of her body she'd failed to keep from displaying her surprise given her immediate response was to almost blurt out, 'I'm here because you invited me' which she knew was not an appropriate answer. She already knew the Senator was a man of clarity and brevity, so she took a few moments to gather herself before realising this almost certainly wasn't a trick question.

"My friends and I believe the Earth's core is expanding uncontrollably, destabilising tectonic activity causing mantle and ultimately crust disintegration, leading to surface water draining inward, potentially irreversibly which, in turn, guarantees all life on the planet will become extinct." Gordon nodded, and to Jane's significant relief said:

"That's what I thought," accompanied by a small but warm smile.

Bravely, Jane followed up with a question of her own. "Sir, I know why I want to be here, I'm just not clear as to why you want me to be here." There was that smile again.

"Let's go inside, shall we? Feels like it's time for a coffee. I want you to meet some people."

Jane hadn't really expected an explicit answer but felt that she'd passed whatever old school initiation test the Senator had just put her through. As they entered the main doors, Jane could see the size of the place, practical rather than spacious, homely rather than lavish, on the walls hung striking black and white landscape photographic images.

"I'm a big Ansel Adams fan." Gordon read her mind

"Oh amazing, me too." Jane said, trying hard not to sound sycophantic. It looked like there were three separate rooms, a desk office set up with a view out over the river, a smaller meeting space with a single table and four chairs. *It looks like a hiring and firing zone*, thought Jane. The final room was a larger meeting space, not quite a boardroom but definitely where they'd be heading now, predicted Jane, driven mainly by the fact she could hear chatter coming from within. A brief pause from Gordon who turned to Jane on the threshold.

"This is the point of no return Jane, from this point on you will be party to conversations and information which cannot leave our circle and the world you know will change forever. But I sense you know this so let's go meet the guys." Even after this most stern of statements, Gordon had a spring in his step, belying his advanced years, as if Jane was the missing piece in his jigsaw.

Here goes. Jane took a deep breath and entered the room.

26

Shortly after Marco had closed up at the Waste Not Want Not presentation in Ian's office, he had to dash across town to run virtually the same seminar but this one without the razzmatazz of the bubble gum twins and Nancy Rastik. It was an altogether forgetful affair which, without a shadow of a doubt, failed to inspire a single member of the US Postal Service, to whom he was speaking en masse. *However*, Marco thought, *this is not my primary role*, and he was right. Rastik had been suitably impressed by his performance earlier and confirmed this via WhatsApp with a thumbs up and instructions for a follow up meeting that evening with brutal functionality. *1745. Roosevelt Tower. Room 1321. Don't be late.*

    In the foyer of the Roosevelt Tower, a burly suited tank of a man took one look at Marco, tapped his ear as he mouthed something to someone remotely and called out "Mr Hernandez" as much as a statement as a question and Marco instinctively nodded and followed him. He was so commanding and intimidating that if he'd have told Marco to remove his clothes and dance, he probably would have done so. It encapsulated why they had picked Marco; he was reliably compliant. Predictably, Marco hadn't given much thought to who would be in room 1321 this evening, he just assumed it would be Nancy Rastik. He was wrong. There was a similarly muscular henchman at the door of the room who stepped aside and opened the door inwards allowing Marco to pass through.

"Thank you." he said without reply. As he entered the room, he recognised a couple of faces from the original Project Green meeting when Rastik had welcomed him to the team.

"Marco welcome, how the devil are you?" It was a polar opposite welcome to the one he'd received so far, making Marco much happier that he was back with 'his people'.

"I'm great thank you, thanks for asking."

"Hope the WNWN presentations went well, I heard about the first one, it sounded like a royal success, well done Marco." Marco puffed his chest out, which made it job done for Project Green's lead on public relations.

"Chester Rogers," a hand extended to grasp and shake Marco's outstretched palm. "Friends call me 'Cheese'. I'm leading the PR on this revolution and you, Mr Hernandez, are my epicentre."

"Nice to meet you Mr Rogers." Marco wasn't really sure how to deal with this bundle of energy but fortunately for him the situation moved rapidly.

"We, Mr H, will have plenty of time to get to know each other, but first we have a briefing session ahead of your starring role in Tokyo next week. I know you're fully up to speed on the scientific, geological and meteorological background to the project and that's why our colleagues here are not our scientific buddies. We're here today to drill down into the so what?"

"The so what?" Marco asked naively.

"Yeah, we'll need to fill the gaps for people, so they

don't fill them themselves. You can't just stand there, tell them you've sorted climate change, drop the mic, rock a little end-zone dance then moonwalk off stage, although note to self, that's an awesome idea, bank it Cheese." Even Marco was aware enough that if he said nothing, Rogers would fill the void and he was keen to understand what was about to happen. "So, your role is two-fold in Tokyo…." Marco didn't pick up on the fact that Rogers only talked about Tokyo and not a role beyond, "….is one to reveal our, and your own, data to the world signifying Mother's Earth's restoration and sea levels under control, the ultimate 'proof point'…" there were air quotes from Rogers highlighting this would be a key phrase for Marco, "….and secondly, we need to put the global economy on the right path to make the right decisions, as we double down to focus on prosperity for the world. And correct me if I'm wrong Marco, but having checked your résumé, I didn't spot an economics degree hidden away anywhere and the world's media are going to say: 'Mr Hernandez, so what? What's next, what does this mean for the world?' and you're going to tell them."

"I am?" There was a slightly nervous reaction from Marco. Rogers was right, he actually had zero idea how to answer this question.

"You are Marco, yes. And to help you, I would like to introduce you to Senator Nick Johnson, whom we are honoured by and indebted to for his political and economic wisdom to help us navigate this most exciting new chapter in Earth's history. I also think it's only wise to remind you of the absolute and non-negotiable confidential and top-secret nature of this and all Project Green meetings." Suddenly Rogers dialled down the joviality and turned up the seriousness, looking Marco directly in the eyes. He lowered his voice and his tone changed.

"Senator Johnson is not here in an official capacity; he is giving us his time and experience purely altruistically. He is a passionate supporter of the work we are doing and very nobly in my book doesn't want to bring politics into this mix so for all intents and purposes you will be speaking freely with a friend of the Project, special advisor Nick Johnson, however for all our sakes I'd counsel you still refer to him as 'Senator'. You on board with this Marco?"

"I'm all in." Marco knew his place was fragile and Rogers sensed it, just as Rastik had predicted. Marco could not believe his fortune and would do nothing deliberate to compromise it.

"Great to hear Marco and remember if you need to talk to anyone about Project Green…." he pulled his phone out and twirled it in front of their faces, "…talk to me"

"I understand Mr Rogers, loose lips cost lives, right?" Marco had a momentary flash of his mother's face as she congratulated him on his rise to fame. *She needed to know,* he told himself, *she'll be ok*. He just wanted his parents to be proud of him.

"I wouldn't say lives," responded Rogers, "more money, credibility and our ability to control this situation." Although it didn't take a huge leap of faith to think Marco Hernandez might just disappear off the face of the Earth if he were to leak all this, Rogers had suspicions of his own, which he was doing very well to suppress about the darker side to both Nancy Rastik and Senator Johnson.

The suited tank at the door suddenly straightened up and a booming voice called through the office space. "At ease boys," as if a military commander had come into the room.

Senator Nick Johnson was walking, talking charisma, he oozed power and confidence. Marco's immediate impression was that he looked like the kind of chiselled superhero from a film who could stop time just by holding his hand up, palm out. He was everything Marco wanted to be. Handsome. Suave. Impeccably dressed. At the same time, he came across as your best mate but also that he controlled you. All this came from the first few strides Johnson took into the room.

Marco was certainly not alone in experiencing the Senator's intense pressure, his rise to power was built on his innate ability to draw people close to him unwittingly and, coupled with his very shrewd and calculating brain, this made him a political and economic powerhouse. Chester Rogers had learned a few things already from how the Senator dealt with people, a faux humility focused on making other people feel like they were the main event, whereas the whole time he was controlling the situation.

"Oh wow, Marco Hernandez, scientist extraordinaire, soon to be leader of a global economic revolution, what an honour it is to finally meet you." Marco feared his chest might actually explode, he was already putty in the

Senator's hands and everyone in the room could see it. This was the same Marco Hernandez that not ten minutes earlier, Johnson had referred to in conversation with Nancy Rastik as 'that little, white-coated Mexican weasel'.

"You're going to love that weasel Nick, he's loyal, malleable and most importantly, he thinks he's won the fucking lottery with this gig, so just get him in shape to deal with ten minutes of media questions. Then you can skin him and make a pair of gloves out of his coat." They had both laughed at poor Marco's ultimate fate, used as a pawn in a game too big for him to comprehend. They hadn't even discussed what would happen to Marco Hernandez once he stepped off the stage in Tokyo, Rastik wasn't even sure if they'd bought him a return ticket. He will have set Project Green in full motion and his part would be done, like a mayfly, a short but productive lifespan but once the primary task was complete, he would be entirely obsolete. Rastik and Johnson's plan for Marco Hernadez could scarcely be more different than how Marco understood his role. Because for an hour in the company of Senator Nick Johnson, he felt like the most important scientist of his generation and at the end of their time together, he also felt like he'd been studying global economics and business at Harvard.

Rastik's phone pinged with a notification from a contactless number but no doubt who it was from, it simply read, *the weasel is ready.*

27

Across town Senator Edward Gordon ushered Jane into the meeting room having ensured alliance and trust were established. As she entered the room, she was already holding her phone out so it could join a selection of others in a tray on one side of the room.

"Yes, great Jane thank you, we don't take any chances or court any unnecessary distractions here, like the good old days, nothing leaves the room except knowledge if we can avoid it." For a fleeting second, Jane reflected on how different politics and diplomacy must be for the generation like Gordon, who worked across the digital revolution. Handshakes over whiskey replaced by Twitter messages of support were poles apart so it made sense to keep things analogue.

The decor in the room is classy, thought Jane. Nice solid chairs, a hardwood but not ornate table, hanging ceiling lamp and more Ansel Adams adorning the off-white walls.

There were already five people at the table, with Jane and the Senator making it seven. Two were feverishly pouring over some kind of charts at one end, whilst the other three were deep in quiet conversation, yet loud enough for Jane to pick up at least two accents that were not American, one certainly European and the other English maybe. She recognised the third immediately and was unable to control her reaction, one of utter bewilderment but also of delight.

"I know you already know Michelle Grant."

"Well wow yes." Jane hadn't seen her former boss since she left for the UK to work on bee conservation, and it rendered her almost speechless.

"Hello Jane, it's so lovely to see you, although under rather challenging circumstances as I'm sure you'd agree. And yes, I'm still working for the British Bee Association, but I kept ties with the Senator as we had inklings that something was afoot so, although I officially left the Bureau, I kept one foot in the door." The whole episode made the Senator uncharacteristically goofy for a moment.

"Yes, Michelle is part of both the Bee Team and our A Team if you will," which he followed up with a kind of snort, much to the surprised amusement of those in the room. It did seem to break whatever tension there was and allowed him to introduce Jane to his inner circle. "Jane Henderson everyone, expert researcher with a record of supporting both Michelle and I over the years, she and her team, who I think are now in Berlin am I right?" Jane was slightly taken aback by this reference to 'her team' and even more so by the fact Gordon knew they were in Berlin but imagined he had access to all kinds of information if he so called for it.

Jane forced herself to refocus as Gordon presented the other two very well-dressed individuals who'd been in deep conversation with her former boss. She was convinced she knew them both as if they'd met several times before but in the way that when you meet famous people you forget they haven't a bloody clue who you are, but you seemingly know everything about them. She frantically searched her brain for names to go with the faces in front of her and as soon as the Senator introduced them, she was set, and rather taken aback at both the seniority and responsibility they represented.

"UK Ambassador to the United States of America and former Minister for the Environment in her Majesty's Government, Dame Penelope Norton."

"Please just call me Penny, we don't need formalities here and I'm delighted to meet you Jane, the Senator certainly is a big fan of yours so welcome to our little team." Jane was processing the fact she was now mixing with some serious political big-hitters and being told to call them by their first names so she just gave up trying to remember who the other dude might be, although something was telling her he was European.

"And Klaus Jurgensen, Germany's accomplished Minister for the Environment, Nature Conservation, Safety and Consumer Protection".

"Guten Tag Jane, it's certainly a catchy job title, isn't it? You should see the size of my business card." Clearly not the first time he'd told this joke, but he always found it a good icebreaker and it got the customary smile from Jane.

Crikey, Jane managed not to say out loud, but she did manage a coherent enough response, "Herr Jurgensen, Penny," that felt odd, "I'm honoured and humbled to be here in your presence."

"And these two young ladies at the end are the brains and brawn of our operation, I suspect you'll get on like a house on fire, they're our lead analysts although I'm not sure your paths have ever crossed." The Senator noticed both analysts had raised their heads in anticipation of their introduction and took it upon themselves to do that for him.

"Hi, I'm Kelly Chan, great to meet you."

"And I'm Rose Carmichael, also lovely to meet you, big fan of your work."

"Right, that's niceties over with, we have fresh tea and coffee and some pretty amazing Scottish shortbread, thank you again Penny, so let's get cracking, we really need Jane's input and time is no ally."

Jane still wasn't remotely sure why her presence was so sought after but at least, she thought, her five-minute monologue of where Pete, Jeff, Elaine and she had been researching gave all parties in the room a chance to savour Penny Norton's well-hyped shortbread.

As she approached her conclusion, she clocked the awkwardness of the last piece on the plate and, despite the undoubted focus of everyone listening to Jane, no one in the room had any misgivings that the final piece of shortbread needed to belong to Jane.

"We've seen the proliferation of surface disturbances from low level tremors to mass sinkhole generation. But, given so little of the Earth's surface is actually urbanised, it's not been newsworthy enough to generate public questions and the scientific community have their hands full, either of US government dollars, sorry sir I appreciate that's not very patriotic, or with their own projects and theses. There aren't many in the scientific fraternity who are able to freely pick where they focus their time and efforts and we believe very few, if any, perhaps the people in this room aside, are joining the dots. Correction, we know plenty of dots are being joined but our version of this puzzle does not lead us to conclude that climate change is reversing, sea levels have stabilised, and everything is hunky dory for us to further exploit the planet for round two of global self-destruction. Our primary concern is to align the scientific and even political community behind solving a geological crisis of biblical proportion and…" Jane was feeling much more confident and at ease in the room now she'd been able to unload their theory without anyone raising even the slightest query, "…I'm seriously hoping as I finish that final piece of shortbread to remove that unwanted tension in the room…" everyone smiled sheepishly yet warmly at Jane. *She was fitting in well*, thought Johnson without surprise, "…that one of you might just have the back end to this little issue sorted?"

Jane got a clear sense of the trust and team in the room when it wasn't the Senator nor the European political heavyweights who assumed control of the conversation but Kelly Chan and Rose Carmichael. As those in the room turned towards the young analysts, the large screen on the far wall behind them burst into life with a revolving image of the globe on, cut through showing the Earth's layers down to the core.

Chan began. "Much like yourself, Jane, we have been monitoring sea levels forensically for some time now and agree it's scientific fantasy to attribute their lowering to a successful battle against human caused climate change.

Quite the contrary, we've never been more harmful to our home, the past five years have been more destructive than all preceding human existence. Not wanting to drift away too far from facts and evidence but there is a school of psychological thought that once a lie gets so preposterous it almost can't be untrue, that's when it gets the most support. Especially if it's a lie we all want to be true."

She's a smart cookie this one, thought Jane.

"Our data has pinpointed a number of zones around the globe where we have identified what we're calling 'critical water loss portals'. Topographically speaking, and you've already spoken on this Jane, there has been increased instability over the past two decades manifesting in low level occurrences, like tremors, sinkholes and as you eloquently pointed out, tectonic irregularities. Until now we have only been able to prove these are happening and not the cause, mainly because we simply don't know if the Earth's surface has ever been thus, this may be a cyclical event or just the way it's been put together over the millennial. We estimate that in the past three years, these irregularities in the crust have opened up to the extent that the equivalent of the volume of water in the Great Lakes has gone, literally, underground, an almost immeasurable quantity. We're talking millions of cubic kilometres of sea water." Chan wanted this to sink in for everyone, whilst Jane processed the facts that backed up their hypothesis.

"And where is it going?" Rose Carmichael took up the reins by posing her own question. "And can we get it back?"

"Let's just bring Jane back into this before you discuss those two precious questions Rose," interrupted Senator Gordon calmly. "We've all read your paper Jane, but it feels a good time to ponder why this is happening given at least we're all agreed it *is* happening." Gordon's emphasis was a clear shot across the bows, even in their absence, of those who were subconsciously or deliberately ignoring the evidence.

Jane took centre stage again, "I suspect you've all read or had a summary of Professor Masai's theory of core expansion that he is due to present at the IGA Tokyo conference," nods all round, "but I sense his presentation may take on a slightly different perspective, but we can cross that bridge later." Gordon smiled kindly at Jane.

"It's commonly acknowledged that the Earth's inner core is slowly expanding as it cools, about an inch every twenty-five years, nothing that would lead to this kind of instability we're talking about. Peter's viewpoint is that this expansion is happening at a vastly greater pace and potentially always has been and if this is true, then at some point something has to give, either the outer core gets absorbed, that it becomes part of the frozen inner core but that's three thousand kilometres of liquid, at least non-rigid geo-material, or the pressure is felt further up towards the surface.

"So, with the core effectively expanding faster than the Earth can cope, the rigidity of the mantle, a three thousand kilometre solid ceiling barrier if you will, prevents physical expansion and the net effect is density increase, leading to gravitational pull increasing such that even the mantle is impacted, sinking ever so slightly inward, thus pulling the weaker parts of the crust, and by definition, the bit we live on downwards too. In basic terms, way beneath us, cracks are appearing on the ocean bed like drains and there goes our sea water."

Rose Carmichael followed Jane, "I won't lie to you Jane, until we read Professor Masai's piece, we were not connecting sea level reductions with core expansion in the same way it appears he was not connecting them the other way around either. However, we all feel this could be a plausible and potential credible theory, so we have outsourced this as a research project to a team at NASA." Before Jane could protest that this might lead to a leak of both Peter's speech at the IGA and also of their apocalyptic hypothesis, Rose put her mind at ease.

"The special projects team over in Houston are forever investigating the more enthusiastic, let's call them, theories so Professor Masai's will merely be one of many that NASA, and other science-based organisations, will pull apart to prove, disprove or amend in the days, weeks and months preceding and following the IGA conference. Believe me they get sent more outlandish theories than this one, that's for sure." Rose smiled, which took any kind of tension away.

Keen to get back on topic, she quickly continued. "Our research and evidence starts a little closer to home Jane, but not to say core expansion is not a factor, however we've located several zones globally where we are fairly sure there is leakage. We've then correlated that data with fossil fuel extraction regions and also weak spots in the Earth's crust. So, we're talking deep sea oil drilling in the Gulf of Mexico, down the Filipino Plate in Asia and across Southern Eurasia, and then places like the Ring of Fire across the Indonesian archipelago, the coasts of Italy and Japan and even our own San Andreas fault." Rose picked up a sleek black remote control from the table and pointed it at the plasma behind her and a map of the world illuminated the screen. Flashing circles covered the regions Rose has called out but the ones that jumped off the screen were the bright red circles on the Caspian Sea and off the multitude of coast of Indonesia.

"So, what you're saying is," Jane interjected, thinking out loud but considered, not randomly, "that we've made the world's most unstable geological zones even more unstable?"

"That's exactly it Jane, you said it yourself, the tectonic movements you identified, not us, led us further down this path. Given the vastness of the plates, extra speed, however tiny it might seem, has exponential impact on the stability of the topography around it. You add the fact we've been systematically weakening the areas beneath these already unstable zones makes us masters of our own downfall. If we bolt on the professor's theory about the Earth collapsing in on itself, we've got one hell of a problem to solve."

"When do you expect to hear back from NASA?" Jane asked hurriedly.

Before anyone was able to answer, Penny Norton spoke up. "Where I think we have common ground, even if our theories are yet to intertwine…" *such a nice way to say she thinks Peter's work is bullshit*, thought Jane with a hidden smile, although in fairness, she was just trying to move things along so Jane set aside her cynicism, this was not the moment for partisan bias.

Norton continued, "….is that we're thinking big, really big. Scary big. It is widely acknowledged by the scientific community that human activity has led to earthquakes, although I suspect the mining and drilling industry will contest this. The Wenchuan quake in central China which killed about a hundred thousand people has been attributed, outside of China of course, to the construction of nearby dam. Nepal 2015, groundwater extraction is cited as a contributing factor and this one caused an avalanche on Mount Everest no less. Best estimates put earthquake activity levels nine times higher in Oklahoma in the past decade as a direct result of fracking, where the injected wastewater is opening faults way below the surface. Many argue that these incidents are merely topsoil issues and can largely be overcome by defence mechanisms like better architecture making stronger buildings and that earthquake tremors will always be a factor where plates come together - an intense mix of belief and denial. The majority of the outspoken geologists, seismologists and scientific commentators appear in the last couple of years to have softened their stances or in some cases, entirely u-turned on their theses."

Before Jane, who had become instantly animated as she and Jeff had always suspected foul play on a global scale silencing environmental doomsayers, could get a word in, Penny closed her down firmly but fairly. "We don't like to say global conspiracy, yet I may just have done so folks," a wry smile appeared on her face, "but we know there has been exponential growth in the recruitment and comms messaging from some of the world's largest economies - USA, Russia, China, Brazil, Australia seemingly poaching experts from more moderate, from a climate change perspective, nations like Japan, India and across Europe."

Klaus stepped in to support his UK colleague. "In the European Union, and I include the UK in this for simplicity, we estimate that forty eight of the fifty top ranking 'environmental'..." Klaus laboured on the 'environmental' with his hand itching to make air quotes but it was plain to everyone he was desperately trying not to as if it were unbecoming of such a politician, "...scientists are now receiving their salaries from either a different nation state or, we are fairly sure, state sponsored private companies or quangos. Sadly, and rather worryingly," Klaus was clearly a master of the understated, "the direction and spiritual leader of this new movement appears to reside in their very city."

"Nancy Rastik and Senator Johnson, with the unequivocal backing of the president!" exclaimed Jane, "and with a global political alliance made up of the who's who of industrial polluters," she was growing impatient now, "what we need is a plan to derail their agenda because from where I'm sitting, there's one single outcome from what we're talking about, whichever way we dress it up. Either Pete is right to some degree and all the water disappears or he's a million miles away, but sea level falls continue to permit and facilitate the material destruction of our ecosystem and atmospheric stability." "Rose, I think it's important to revisit your questions on where the water is going and how to get it back."

Senator Gordon, who had stepped out of the room to take a phone call, popped back in with a business like look on his face which made everyone stop what they were doing, eyes and ears fixed on Gordon.

"That was Louis Charles from the NASA Special Projects team, a man I trust as if he were one of us in this room. They've completed their simulations from calculations based on Professor Masai's hypothesis." The tension in the room was intense, with everyone holding their breath, metaphorically and literally. "Jane, I think we should get your team piped in ASAP, Louis will be taking us through their conclusions in about thirty minutes."

At this command, Jane rose from her seat and headed to the mobile phone rack, slipped out into the corridor and hastily typed a message to Jeff, Elaine and Peter, whom she imagined were on tenterhooks awaiting news.

NASA ran simulation of Pete's mantle theory, will send secure link to join in 25 mins. Two blue ticks closely followed by a thumbs up emoji.

"OK," announced Jane to the team in Washington from the door of the conference room, "they'll be online and ready, I'll step out and bring them up to speed on who you all are and where we got to, save time later."

"Good plan." There was an efficient response from Senator Gordon, he'd already had a precis from NASA and realised more than ever how important Professor Masai might prove to be.

28

As Marco Hernandez shook hands with Senator Nick Johnson's hand, he felt an almost physical transfer of power as if he were connected to a charisma charging machine in human form. Chester Rogers certainly spotted the change in the Mexican as Johnson made his exit, phone in hand, ironically messaging Nancy Rastik about Marco himself.

"Well," started Rogers, "I'm sensing you're ready for anything now sir." Marco almost blushed at the PR man's formal tone, "That's the back end of your Tokyo presentation sorted, what an honour it was that the Senator chose to give you his own time and wisdom, I won't say I'm not just a little envious. The Project Green team have been busy finalising your audio visual for the IGA. This will be your 'I have a dream' moment, Marco. The spotlight will be on you and you alone, the lead representative for the International Council for Climate Stability, speaking to the world about the world on behalf of the world."

Chester Rogers was playing a little game with himself, mildly unprofessionally but also to check whether Rastik and Johnson had indeed selected the right guy for this job. He intended to inflate every situation, making it as grandiose as he could, feeding the burgeoning narcissist Marco was becoming, whilst remaining within the boundaries of his brief; he still valued his job. He marvelled and slightly despaired about Marco's apparent lack of challenge or questioning about his role, the ICCS, Tokyo, the long-term plan, basically avoiding anything which might burst his bubble. Essentially it was quite a smart self-preservation strategy, don't ask a question if you're not prepared to accept the answer.

So, this perpetuated the dynamic between Rogers building Marco into a global science heavyweight and Marco's uneasy sense of fortune which was making him feel invincible yet with a distinct taste of fragility alongside it. *As long as we get through Tokyo,* thought Rogers, *then my work here is done.* Chester Rogers was an ambitious man too, and having aligned himself to Rastik and Johnson, it was also in his interests to make this work, despite his own misgivings on the content and strategy. This wasn't uncommon in the world of PR, his role to enable the public to believe by creating stories, gossip, clickbait, news, you name it, any tactic to change, enhance or reinforce public perception on whatever he was paid to do.

His early career was in the music industry and some of the artists he had represented and promoted made him look at Marco like some kind of genius, such was the vapid nature of some of his early wannabe clients. The internet had brought the world much but for a PR man in the music industry in the early 2000s, it brought a devastating number of self-interested, pop-up, talentless celebrity hunters, desperately chasing fame on the back of some YouTube clip or appearance on a reality TV show. However, for an equally success-hungry PR executive with flexible morals, this was a rich territory for building the experience needed to move into the grown-up but no less scrupulous world of politics. His nose for creating celebrity out of nothing was the exact résumé Nancy Rastik and Senator Johnson were looking for, so he was thankful to all those naive chancers whose lives he changed beyond all expectations of the talent they possessed. He was good and he intended to keep this good form going with 'Marco Hernandez, Chief Scientific Advisor to Planet Earth'. He was particularly pleased with this one and it felt it would be an ideal way to introduce Hernandez to the world in a few days' time in Tokyo.

However, what he would be introducing Marco to present was the task in hand in front of them right now. The clandestine Project Green Team had given Marco very limited licence to adlib or even put his own views or words into the presentation to the extent the speed of his delivery was already mapped out by virtue of the subtitles embedded at the bottom of the screen. Marco looked momentarily crestfallen, he had been allowing his brain to work on what he would be saying to the world but even before Rogers could put his mind at ease, he felt an enormous stress-reducing release that it was not his responsibility to script this, just deliver it.

"This is your work," Rogers said positively. "Literally I'm told after nine minutes and eight seconds you'll be referencing your own ground-breaking Amazon basin study, they're going to feel such a connection to you Marco, I can sense it now."

Pre-empting a potentially obvious question that even Marco might ask, Rogers shot it down in advance. "We want the personal touch of a live presenter instead of rolling out some pre-recorded video, once you're done the live vocal will be added to the file for sharing with the global press. We toyed with live subtitles but there are still teething issues with that software that it can't identify nuances in accents and some words which might lead to unintended consequences. Plus, we're comfortable following a tight script aren't we Marco?"

There was a compliant nod from the Mexican, "then it just makes it more impactful to pre-load the subtitles. It'll also help you time your delivery to perfection."

"Like karaoke," blurted Marco.

"Indeed," said Rogers. "You have seventy-two hours to essentially memorise this presentation and I'll be with you at whatever time, for whatever need until you set foot on that stage. The only people who have seen this are you, me and the Project Green members you met last week so let's keep it this way." Chester Rogers decided it was unwise to share the fact that a number of world leaders aligned to Project Green had also been sent a copy on behalf of the president and it didn't take a Political Sciences degree to work out who it was in that loop, given the appearance of the Kremlin, Great Wall, Uluru, Christ the Redeemer statue as well as the Grand Canyon and Statue of Liberty in the opening two minutes.

"Flight leaves 10pm Marco so get your stuff together," before Marco had a chance to ask a question that had been rolling around in his head for a while, Rogers answered it. "We'll give you your presentation outfit when we're in Tokyo so no need to think about that. Your job is to memorise the words and flow of your presentation, we'll worry about what you look like." This was Chester Rogers at his best, he understood people and knew what made them tick. There's no way Rastik nor Johnson would've given a second thought to whether Marco knew what he needed to bring to Tokyo or what he might be wearing. But Rogers could always sense what was going on behind the eyes of his clients, although rarely his employers much to his chagrin, but he could read Marco like a book and he could feel the vulnerability radiating off the Mexican, as if he was in a constant battle with his own self-belief and the lofty position he found himself in.

"Oh, and there's been a slight mix-up in the flights Marco. I appear to be up front and you're at the back. But in the same plane, that's the main thing, right?" A hesitant nod from Marco, who looked momentarily forlorn but really his mind was so focused on the task ahead that he didn't have the mental space for cabin envy. Just as Chester Rogers had predicted.

29

Berlin

The atmosphere in Peter's Berlin apartment was electric, even Pete himself was feeling giddy with excitement. Elaine couldn't help but have flashbacks to what felt like a lifetime ago, from bored housewife to international scientist in the blink of an eye. She glanced over at Jeff, who smiled back, acknowledging that their short but intense project was about to take a dramatic turn and the unknown direction of that turn made it all the more exhilarating. Jeff took a deep breath, then another, then another. The calm before the storm, something was going to happen, and he was enjoying the unpredictability of their situation. Too long he realised he'd been coasting unambitiously, directionless. Then Peter Masai arrived back in his world like a bolt from the blue and he wasn't alone, he'd summoned Elaine from halfway round the world and now here they were all, university revisited, waiting to speak with some of the world's most influential politicians, at least in their particular field. One final breath, deep and full of portent, as if inhaling to match the enormity of their situation, exhaling with the hope that somehow, they'd got this horribly wrong, and they weren't about to discuss the end of the world.

Funny how life turns out, he thought to himself as he motioned to Elaine and Pete to get in front of the laptop camera and galvanized them into action with a commanding and confidence-boosting, "We got this." Then he punched in the secure-link code Jane has sent and patched them through to Senator Gordon's meeting room where Gordon, Jane, Penelope Norton, Klaus Jurgensen, Michelle Grant and the analysts Rose Carmichael and Kelly Chan were waiting, equally excited, nervous and intrigued as to what Louis Charles from NASA was going to tell them.

Dr Louis Charles didn't look like a NASA researcher and, by popular convention, didn't look much like a doctor either, a medical one or a PhD one, the latter of which gave him his official title. A title he chose to forgo in the majority of professional and personal situations. His mop of blond hair appeared to defy gravity with its seemingly immaculate yet irregular quiffs and tufts that lesser men would spend hours tousling and gelling, unable to replicate the natural surfer look. Under his hair, Charles sported model good looks and an athletic body that seemed at odds with both his age, forty-five, and his job. Outside of office hours, Louis Charles was a devoted practitioner of yoga and a national standard player of Ultimate Frisbee, although his representation on the US national team was a decade or so behind him now.

"Unconventional and brilliant," was how Senator Gordon introduced Charles to the group in Berlin and Washington. Their relationship spanned twenty years, back to when Gordon, in his pre-Senator days, was Dean of the University of Michigan and effectively mentored the young Astrophysicist. Dean Gordon, and in time, Senator Gordon, was not one to judge books by their covers, he knew his own background ran much deeper than his own appearance, so he was able to look past the unkempt high-school jock who presented himself in his first year at the college. But even in his early days, Louis Charles was the talk of the academic staff, how he defied his beach boy style and offered critical analysis way beyond his peers and a grasp of the subject akin to a professor, not freshman. So, Gordon took Charles under his wing to guide and support - not in a controlling way - his journey through university and beyond. This was not a politician calling in a favour, more a grateful mentee paying back years of kindness and mutual respect.

"The floor is yours Louis, please share with us what you've come up with, bear in mind that there is no one with eyes and ears here you cannot trust." Jane wondered how many times Gordon had mistrusted people in this exact room, given DC life. *It was probably quite a few,* she mused.

"Thank you, Senator, and a warm welcome to you all in all your various locations, Guten Abend I should say." Instantly charming, Louis Charles proceeded to debrief the teams. "Professor Masai, your hypothesis is a once in a generation piece of geological thinking, I am humbled to be addressing you amongst all these other amazing people."

It was genuine from Charles, managing to avoid sounding too ass kissy. "So, to cut a long story short Professor, I'm sorry to say and if I'm honest slightly terrified by this too, that our models show a ninety-five percent probability of your mantle disintegration theory being true and realised within the next hundred years." Louis Charles looked down from the camera, giving everyone watching the chance to let this sit with them a while. What kind of reaction should one have when they are told the world is literally collapsing around them? For the individuals on the call, solemn silence was the universal response. It was Charles himself who broke the silence, although he'd half-expected the Senator to lead given he'd had advance warning of the outcome of the modelling.

"I'm very conscious of the fact you all have the intellect and maturity to cope with this level of information, however, I think context is critical here, and sorry folks, it doesn't get any more palatable. My team's remit encompasses the analysis of unpredictable and unforeseeable events. In other words, we are Doomsday scenario planners by trade so are well-versed and skilled in evaluating what we call 'material threats to humanity'. Over my eleven years here at NASA, the average Armageddon score is nine per cent and the highest we've had across our desk in my experience is twenty-two per cent and that is a scenario where volcanoes set each other off like a set of beacons, starving the world of sunshine for months and this ranks as only twenty-two per cent. Professor Masai, your ninety-five per cent result is only comparable to one event we've ever modelled, given our almost limitless access to high quality data."

"Let me guess," interjected Pete, "the dinosaur extinction?"

"The dinosaur extinction," echoed Charles. "This is the scale we're talking about, irrevocable decimation of the Earth's accessible water source and potentially widespread land collapse as a result of mantle disintegration."

"Who else knows about this Louis? Or who else do you think knows?" Jeff felt calm and sanguine despite the circumstances.

"Well, we always have one ear to the ground on critical events like these, well not quite like this but you get the idea, and so far, not a peep from Russia, China, the EU or even from our own US allies in government or Homeland Security. All we've been registering for the past few weeks is rhetoric around sea levels and how, ironically, the world is saved. That's been coming from all corners of the globe and it's getting louder and louder, I'm even starting to believe it myself." A sarcastic grin made the point even stronger, "It is virtually impossible that the sources of these theories haven't seriously considered that what they're saying is absolute horseshit, excuse my language. But, and it's a big and generous but, the senior leaders involved have become so blinded by the good news that they've subconsciously or even consciously decided to ignore the reality.

"Out lithospheric and topographical data analysis suggests a statistically significant drop in water coverage of the Earth's surface. Commonly we'd say seventy-one per cent of the globe's surface is water, that's on a downward trajectory, currently under seventy-one per cent and likely to be closer to seventy. Even we haven't got the modelling accuracy to say what a critical level would be, but the smart money is on sixty-five per cent to critically damage the Earth's climate and atmosphere. This isn't just oceans though people. The Caspian Sea is metres lower than in 2000, Inle Lake in Myanmar is at a record low, as is Victoria, Tonle Sap in Cambodia, Malawi, Titicaca, Kyrgyzstan's Issyk-Kul, multiple lakes in China including Qinghai and Poyang. Lake Toba and Lake Batur are the most alarming of the high-profile bodies of water. Although the Indonesian government are playing down any suggestions of geological haemorrhaging, both are at fifty, yes fifty per cent of their 2000 capacities. Estimates cite that over seventy per cent of Indonesia's freshwater sources are less than half of where they were twenty years ago."

"And I assume industry and over-use by local agriculture to support a growing and industrialising population is blamed?" Elaine had come across such data in her analyses.

"Bingo," agreed Louis Charles. "Ceteris paribus, all other things being equal, population increase is a plausible and publicly credible explanation for freshwater declines. And from what you told me Senator, the overarching global political message is that this is good news. I'd like to believe there is a joined-up, multi-national, combined global think tank exploring options around this but sadly it appears the opposite is happening, but that's not my area of expertise. We need to be mindful, as I'm sure the professor is, that the surface disturbances leading to water leakage are also happening on dry land so to speak. So, we're facing an equally fatal threat from populated land collapse. It might be a toss-up to determine which will be worse for Planet Earth. I'll send over my report and if still involved, I'll see you all in Tokyo in the next day or so. My guys here are long-term colleagues with the combined brain power of a super-computer so are happy to act as an extension of your team if required, no issues with confidentiality. I've already got them working on scenarios to reverse the disintegration process. But, and it won't be much of a surprise, dealing with man-made climate change is pretty straightforward, we just turn off the power, I appreciate the obvious complications but in reality, it's that simple. Dealing with unmeasurable geological forces is an entirely separate brief so we, and when I say we, I really mean you guys, probably have a decision to make whether and how to go public with this and prepare for the fallout. Good news is," Louis Charles forced a plucky grin, "there's a least forty-eight hours until the stage is yours, Professor."

"Plenty of time Louis." Pete never shirked a cerebral challenge. "As you said yourself, there's a five per cent chance I'm wrong!"

"The thing I didn't tell you Peter, is our modelling software maxes out at ninety-five per cent, acknowledging certainty. So as weird as it sounds, I'm sorry to say you're not wrong." Louis Charles leant forward and closed off the video link and stayed almost motionless, reflecting on what he'd just been discussing.

For a man with a seemingly unlimited positive mindset, even he struggled to process his own impending mortality, or at least that of his future offspring. He knew his job wasn't to solve the problem, he and his team had the task of play-booking the Masai Scenario, as they had termed it, in their hidden away corner of NASA. *What could the world expect to see, feel, experience as the fundamental basis for life on Earth disappeared away beneath their feet?*

Although he knew he was clutching at straws, his human nature overrode all else and he picked up his internal phone, punched a four-digit extension and as the female voice answered, he simply told her, "Tanya, please run the model again."

"But sir…." Tanya was cut off before she could fully protest.

"I know Tanya, I know. But we need to be surer than sure. Thank you." His next phone call was to arrange his and fellow researcher Tanya James' travel to Tokyo.

30

With the link to Berlin still live, Senator Gordon took control of the conversation. "Penny, Klaus, you need dialogue with the very top of your governments and with other political global allies. Michelle, please support Kelly and Rose, your experience and helicopter views will complement their analytical skills perfectly. Jane, I need you to work with your journalist contact Harpinder to establish a potential comms plan based on a variety of scenarios, she seems well placed, trustworthy and well connected to be brought in. Peter, Elaine, Jeff, your thinking and diligence has filled the gaps we had to understand this grave situation, despite the outcome you should be immensely proud of what you've already achieved. I don't want to sway your thinking at all so please use the next twenty-four hours to process and throw some brain cells at the next steps, even a solution, if indeed there is such a thing. I'll try get a handle on what Rastik and Johnson's plan is for Tokyo and beyond, call in a few favours. Eat well, try to keep active and amidst all this, try to get good sleep. We need to be in tiptop condition to fight the jet lag and challenge ahead when we meet in Japan in…" Gordon looked at his watch symbolically, "twenty-seven hours give or take." And with that he closed the secure video link, and the sombre participants began their own preparations for the trip to Japan and the denouement of this geopolitical cliffhanger.

31

"It's so exciting you going to Tokyo Marco, I've always dreamed of going to Asia, and Japan, oh how perfect. Maybe you'll meet a nice local girl, they're all so very pretty aren't they. And they don't get big and fat like us Mexicans, they eat so much fish I guess and not as many chimichangas and churros." Marco was starting to regret calling his mother from Dulles' departure lounge but he knew he just needed to ride out this particular topic, a familiar recurring theme he sensed until he either married or came out, the latter of which was even less on the cards than the former, and that felt pretty remote now, given how absorbed he was in Project Green.

"Mother, it really isn't that kind of trip, I don't think I'm going to have a lot of free time, and it's definitely not my primary focus, even if it is always yours." he felt he'd done enough to close it down for this chat, proved correct when his mother moved the conversation on herself.

"You know I like to follow your work Marco darling, so after that nice journalist lady came round to talk to me all about you, I started looking into your ICCS, or whatever it's called so I can talk about it with my friends when they're bound to ask once they see you in the paper or on the news." Marco was taken aback by the mention of a journalist going to meet his own mother in Mexico. But he had no real reason to be suspicious, in fact he felt the opposite: perhaps this would be a taste of things to come, the distinction of being one of the world's leading scientists.

Before Marco had a chance to probe more, his motherhood once again started up. "So, I went online and did my own research Marco, what you're doing is incredible. I was speaking to Gabriela and we both thought sea levels were supposed to be rising. Gabriela thought she'd read some NASA predictions that said most of our lovely coastline, like Acapulco and Cancun, would be lost underwater within a hundred years or so. Rose said similar stuff."

Wow, thought Marco, his mother's own coffee mornings really had progressed from gossiping about the neighbours or the latest soap plot. "Rosa thought loads of those idyllic tropical islands were about to disappear." Marco guessed she was reading something now as his mother paused and grappled with pronunciation. "The Mall Dives and Too Value," she said, "are going to be totally underwater."

"That's right Mother, The Maldives and Tuvalu are high profile examples that I will be talking about in my speech."

Once again, the unstoppable talking force that was his mother, took over. "So, then we started googling your project, Marco, and we found a lot of different stuff. Your work making the water levels go down really feels like it'll be a lifesaver for those poor island people and hopefully for our own vacation resorts. I asked everyone to get online to see for themselves. Sofia, Camila, Rosa's sisters Maria and Guadalupe, Gabriela got her singing group involved so…"

"Mother" Marco tried interjecting again but needed

more force. "Mother!" he almost shouted which at least got her attention again, as it did a number of other passengers in the departure lounge. "Trawling your way through the internet is going to confuse you even more you know that don't you? It's a sea of conspiracy theories and plain lies." And his next sentence made Marco feel distinctively uncomfortable. "You'll probably end up thinking climate change should be making sea levels rise not fall so something else must be happening."

Marco's mother made sure he didn't get to tease his thoughts out a little more as she took over once again. "Yes, yes, darling, we'll be careful, but we just want to be ready for when you take the stage, your father and I are so proud of you at last."

It is often the brutally honest things people say by accident that have the most impact and Maria Hernandez had no idea how this 'at last' came across to Marco. To her it was merely an expression of joy that their son had made it to the top of the top of something serious and international but to Marco, it cemented his inferiority complex within his own family and made him instantly double down on the task in hand. There was no time for outside influences or doubting thoughts, he could scarcely believe his lofty climb, so he felt there was literally zero upside to letting it go this close to his coronation. Therefore, true to form, he didn't call his own mother out for strengthening his ever-growing imposter syndrome, he simply made his admittedly valid excuses about his impending flight departure and wished his mother and her friends an enjoyable research project and bade farewell.

As he walked to his gate, he began reciting his Tokyo speech, working hard to commit it to memory so he could then start to work on adding some gravitas, power poses and grand hand gestures to deliver some theatre. He'd downloaded a few clips of Steve Jobs to mimic and felt if he could come across even half as passionate and credible then he'd have done himself and the Project Greem Team proud. As he boarded the plane, it did cross his mind that Steve Jobs probably turned left when getting on a plane, like Chester Rogers must have done, assuming he'd had priority boarding. But there was almost certainly a time when a young Steve Jobs boarded a plane with the same determination Marco was feeling that one day, and one day soon, he would be the one reclining back, bubbly in hand, enjoying the fruits of success. Perhaps that's why he'd only been given a one-way ticket, he smiled, and that made him feel much better about sitting between a rather smelly old man and a morbidly obese, wheezing American lady for their seventeen-hour flight to Narita Airport, Tokyo.

31

Washington

"I'm not exactly Rupert Murdoch, Jane. I'm a freelance journalist with a curious nature synonymous with the job that I do." Harpinder clarified to Jane that she'd not suddenly become a multinational media mogul overnight. "I have a tenuous relationship with the editor of the Washington Post, and I've had more than one conversation with a number of feature editors of glossy monthly mags." Jane knew Harpinder was humble, a classic self-deprecator, and whilst she knew her journalist college mate clearly didn't control a media empire, what she was tenacious and hungry and this kind of lead on a story was the stuff of dreams to kick Erin Brockovich into the column ads. Jane's belief was well placed too, once she'd brought Harpinder up to speed with the clandestine goings on in Washington, Harpinder showed why Jane, and by proxy, Senator Gordon, had placed faith in including her in the wider team.

Jane had left Gordon's offices straight after their call to Berlin, as did the others, hastily following up on their own actions before congregating again halfway around the world. She dispensed with the fresh air and hailed a cab to meet Harpinder again at the same coffee house near her apartment they'd met at only a few days before, although it felt like weeks given how much had happened. Harpinder was sitting in the very same seat having ordered for them both, a warm but urgent look on her face. She had always taken this scenario seriously, both due to her own journalistic integrity and probably more because it was Jane Henderson, but with Jane turning up fresh from a meeting with senior domestic and international politicians this had become a career, in fact, life-defining story. Although it wasn't as straightforward as that. It never was.

Like most journalists, Harpinder had to develop multiple personalities to deal with her job and the situations she found herself in. To get a real personal angle she'd dig deep into her already empathetic nature but at the same time raise an invisible barrier between the real world and her own. If nothing else, it was to protect her own mental health from too much real life. She had to stay detached in order to write impartially and selfishly to remind herself that this was her job and that, in the majority of cases where emotions ran high, going public was actually a cathartic release for those involved, a chance to tell their own personal stories. She wasn't a gossip columnist, so this wasn't a matter of suppressing her morality, it was just a mental firewall to keep her sane.

Now, with the biggest scoop of them all, it was near impossible to escape the fact that this was no personal story for an individual or group, this was mankind's future at stake, and she was a bone fide part of that. It also hadn't escaped her critical mind that so far no one had been talking about solutions. It seemed to be a straightforward fight between natural geological apocalypse versus natural geological apocalypse boosted by human-induced climate catastrophe. No good versus evil here, the ship is sinking so maybe just raid the mini bar one last time.

As she sat waiting for Jane to arrive, sipping on the rich dark coffee, this was one scenario that intrigued her. *If you know the world is fucked and out of human control, why not pillage it fully right to the end?* But her train of thought was derailed as the chair opposite her scraped along the floor and in front of her sat down Jane. And so they began, with Jane sharing as she had always done with Harpinder, everything that had developed since they met such a short time ago. Harpinder listened intently, mentally checking off the things she already knew, clarity on water levels, multi-layered geopolitical disagreements, potential conspiracy, Tokyo IGA being likely platform for a new economic era announcement. She wrote down some of the gap-fill elements, partially as a reminder to come back to Jane on them, names of the key players and in particular their national representation, the NASA modelling of Peter Masai's theory really intrigued her, she knew instinctively that on a global communication, or any kind of media communication, it was a damn sight easier to sell evidence than theory, regardless of which scientific body was backing it. She'd covered too many personal stories about the impact on people of this policy or that decision, when politicians and decision-makers relentlessly say everything is tickety-boo and problems won't even or, even worse, 'shouldn't' happen, and how this doesn't wash one jot with a family who've lost everything or a grieving mother. Actual stuff beats intellect, rhetoric or promises every time. And Harpinder gave Jane a cold reality shower of what they might come up against from her media connections.

"I put some feelers out on the premise that this IGA conference was shaping up to be more than a beards in beige convention."

"Harsh but fair," smiled Jane at her friend's turn of phrase.

"I'm part of a freelance journalist chatroom type thing, glad I've been paying my subs. I hoped one day it might pay back, it's a bit of a free-for-all with journos like me across the world sharing experiences, hints, tips, sometimes leads on stories which stretch beyond where they can get to."

Jane broke her off to ask, "Is that why some articles have two, maybe more, contributors sometimes with wildly different sounding names?"

"Exactly Jane, I've never had to outsource geographically until now, so this was a new experience for me. I put a post up about who's going to the IGA and what's the messaging across the world. Didn't share anything that wasn't already in the public domain, just that the ICCS looked like they were going to evidence reversal of climate change. Well, I got some response I can tell you. I started to print it off to show you but thought that the planet had already lost enough trees. The message board went haywire. I think because it's subscription-only and journos speaking to journos no one holds back. Everyone bar none, and this thread spanned every continent, agreed universally that big stuff was coming at the IGA and media coverage would be unprecedented. Lady Diana massive. But the key part for me was the overwhelming feeling that high-profile news journalists and editors were going, not the environment or weather guys. Much like I told you about the NYT front page mock-up, I'm now more convinced than ever on what I definitely saw, the copy has already been written. All they're waiting for is the words to come out of someone's mouth."

"Marco's mouth."

"Indeed Jane, Marco Hernandez's name came up more than once, but very little more about him. As we suspected, he appears to be a potentially disposable mouthpiece for this whole charade. The two names that did pop up, and they popped up across multiple countries, were Nancy Rastik and Senator Nick Johnson." Involuntarily, the very mention of these two made Jane shudder. "To be fair Jane, a lot of names I didn't recognise also popped up but turns out Rastik and Johnson have conducted quite the world tour. Nothing specific about the ICCS or even the IGA but it seems Johnson has been hobnobbing with the global political elite, invariably at energy or oil conferences or policy announcements. Seems a few people just raised it as being a long way from home for a US Senator to be without the premise of official state visiting status."

"So, greasing palms, making promises, that kind of thing?" Jane surmised.

"Absolutely," replied Harpinder, "and I suspect a few bulging paper bags were in his luggage too."

"What about Rastik then? Wouldn't have thought the Big Business circuit was her scene?"

Harpinder shook her head in agreement. "Totally,

piecing together what the journos were saying, it sounds like she was building a network for the International Council for Climate Stability. If Johnson was going after Big Business, then Rastik looked like she'd won the lottery and was beach-hopping around the world. Fiji, Mauritius, Seychelles, Maldives, Bali, Indochina. I hope she took Mr Rastik with her. If Jimmy went on those trips without me, I wouldn't be a Tarkowski for much longer I can tell you!"

It was Jane's turn to tease out her thoughts. "So Rastik has been on a charm offensive to all those headline-grabbing islands and coastlines previously under threat from rising sea levels."

Harpinder raised her eyebrows at this, and Jane immediately realised that for the first time she'd automatically referred to sea levels levelling off as the norm. "Be interested in whether she went anywhere inland to speak to those freshwater locations benefitting from this wonderful climate change reversal?" She was all the more assertive after her pang of guilt for her acceptance of this global scam that was developing and spreading fast.

"So, we're up against a pretty spectacular array of global players, with each one standing to benefit from this whole sorry episode, if we're going to smash, never mind scratch the surface contradicting it then we need some pretty strong arguments and crucially, evidence. As brilliant a geologist, theorist and no doubt orator Peter Masai is, it's what he actually says that matters."

Harpinder openly challenged and Jane responded. "How about who he is saying it with?" referring indubitably to Senator Gordon, Penny Norton and Klaus Jurgensen.

"Yes," Harpinder came back pointedly but not aggressively, "those white western heavyweights are impressive, but they are neither under much threat from sea levels in the same way as let's say the South Pacific is, nor do they stand to gain enormously from the re-emergence of fossil fuel exploitation."

"But London is under threat from sea levels rising Harpinder, and there was talk of most of the Netherlands literally drowning in the next two hundred years."

"I'm not saying there aren't parts of Europe under pressure from our version of climate change, you asked me to come at this through the lens of the media so if you ask me to choose between some fat, rich Dutch people and a family from Tuvalu about to lose their entire culture and civilisation as a result of those very Dutch people getting fat and rich, it doesn't take a genius to see where the sympathy vote will go."

"Yeah, when you put it like that…" Jane trailed off, deep in thought, gathered herself then came back. "So, we need to find an angle that has scientific value but also pulls on the heartstrings?"

"Exactly Jane, if not the hearts, then at least some part of the emotional minds of the public." Harpinder hadn't solved any of Jane's problems, arguably she'd shown how big they were going to be. In her naivety, Jane had kind of thought that a convincing rebuttal of the ICCS with a dazzling geologist, namely Peter, and the backing of some western superpowers, albeit not the US president, would be enough. But Harpinder was right of course, they either had to find something the public would want to believe, which at this stage felt like too steep a mountain, or something which made the ICCS so impossible to be credible that their alternative was simply less awful.

Jane and Harpinder agreed this had been a very useful, if not particularly yielding, meeting and Jane was delighted to hear that Harpinder was also Tokyo bound. "I'm not missing this for love nor money. I kind of want to know from a selfish perspective when the end of the world might be." She surprised herself at her own nonchalance, "and you seem to be a pretty good person to follow to find out." A cheeky smile and wink at Jane, who responded in kind. *Such kinship develops from extremities*, she mused. "And secondly, I need to be the one writing this up when I do find out."

They pushed their chairs back, Jane left the coffee money under her cup, and they headed towards the door, next time they'd be drinking together would be in Japan, so they said their goodbyes and laughed as they simultaneously bowed to each other.

"Get your guys thinking about some good solid counter-evidence Jane, I'll keep my ear to the ground on any other developments." Then she whistled a cab and headed off to say goodbye to her husband and then onwards to Dulles later that night.

32

Jane had a few minutes' walk back to her apartment so used it to catch up with Team Berlin, she figured they'd also be almost in transit to the airport so hoped she'd get them before airplane mode shut them down for a few hours.

"I think the bigger question Jane, is how long should I be packing for?" Jeff, like all of them, really had no idea what the next few days and weeks had in store for them, and he was a lousy packer at the best of times.

"Good to hear you have your priorities straight Jeff. You might want to bring some extra water too if you've got room, I hear there's a bit of a global shortage." Probably not the sort of joke she'd make in earshot of Senator Gordon, but Jeff was an entirely different proposition.

"I did see something about that in the papers here Jane, the International Council of Stupid Twats or Fantastical Dicknobs, I can't recall which neo-geo organisation it was that professes miracles but according to them all our worries are over. I think they might even be paying my taxes this year."

Fearing this conversation, although a good giggle was what they both needed, was leading in the wrong direction when neither of them had the time, Jane closed it off with some very Jane-esque advice. "Basically Jeff, pack everything and more, borrow from Peter if he has your size, I'm not sure Japanese sizes are going to be very good for you guys."

"Good plan, I'll max out on clothes, maybe take out

the inflatable boat to make room." Jeff then switched gears, proving he was very capable of a proper chat about science and real life. "We had a good discussion here about how we could use Pete's platform to take on Rastik, Johnson and their whole evil empire." Jeff stopped short of a Doctor Evil cackle, but it was implied.

The knowledge that Pete, Jeff and Elaine were also sharing this conundrum was a comfort to Jane, who found herself missing Jeff and was strangely jealous that he was with them and not her, not romantically, she just missed his amity. She realised in that moment what a constant Jeff had been in her life and how his presence and calming influence had seen her through some stressful times over the years and now for her greatest challenge, he was across the Atlantic helping others. Reassuringly, she knew they'd be reunited in a day or so and that gave her renewed strength.

She shared with Jeff, so he would pass on to Peter and Elaine, the information Harpinder had discovered about Rastik and Johnson's world schmoozing tour and, against her expectations of Jeff's reactions, she was heartened that he appeared emboldened by these revelations.

"That makes loads of sense Jane, great work and to Harpinder, we're so looking forward to meeting her, she sounds like a right detective."

"Why so pleased Jeff? Doesn't the whole Rastik/Johnson getting the world onside make everything so much harder for us to get our message across?"

"The total opposite, it's far simpler to tell a group of

people something than have to go round each one individually. It's got the touch of emperor's new clothes about it, just we're the ones calling it out, and we're not children standing in the street."

Changing the subject, Jeff posed an open question… "I wonder how your mate Senator Gordon is getting on generating his own global alliance, you reckon POTUS already has his number?"

"I guess we'll find out soon enough Jeff, see you in Tokyo."

"Sayonara Jane, safe flight." Jeff closed their call down and looked up to see Pete and Elaine staring at him, their fully packed cases sitting obediently by the front door. They'd overheard enough of Jane and Jeff's conversation to set their own minds wandering, searching for answers that were not always forthcoming.

Pete was consciously and subconsciously repositioning his own IGA presentation, consciously in that all this new information meant a fundamental pivot in his delivery, from mind-opening theory to evidence-based geopolitics. Subconsciously, his brain was always ticking over in the background, each nugget of data was getting processed somewhere in his mind, churning around, mixing with relevant and often random other scraps of information, and overheard word here, a newspaper headline that catches the eye there. They say the brain has to process as much as seventy gigabytes of data every single day, akin to watching sixteen feature films. Compared to five hundred years ago, this would be the top end for a lifetime of information. Pete wondered whether having a scientific awareness of how much information he, and all of them, had thrown at them directly and indirectly made it easier to process. Did a conscious appreciation of all the subconscious messaging act as a defence mechanism or was it akin to trying to fall asleep? The more you think about it, the more conscious the mind, the harder it is to switch off.

Either way, thought Pete to himself, allowing his brain to converse with itself as he stood there simultaneously thinking Jeff may never actually be ready to leave, he had to trust that all the rich, powerful data he'd been storing in the back of his mind somewhere would soon come out as a fully formed, coherent argument. Or maybe Jeff's inability to pack his cases would mean they'd never make it to Japan, and all this would play out without their intervention.

Oh no, Pete's brain pleaded seemingly aloud, *please don't make me work that scenario through, I've already got so much to do with the actual plan, never mind some sliding doors, alternative universe crap to deal with.*

A voice interrupted all parts of Pete's highly active brain, it was Elaine. "What you thinking, Peter?"

"Just wondering whether the cuisine offered on a long-haul flight is determined by the nationality of the carrier or the departure and/or destination of the journey." He lied; he had been thinking about this way before this moment.

Elaine, who was an experienced flyer looked departure-ready, grey yoga pants, vest top with a light-fitting, long-sleeved top over it. She had her own sleep mask and inflatable neck pillow which would make appearances just after take-off.

Her own train of thought was crystal clear compared to Pete's disconnected brain frenzy and she also didn't believe airline cuisine was what was dominating his mind right now, but it didn't make a difference as she'd just use that as an opening to share her own thinking out loud.

"Given what Harpinder was saying about the apparent alliance of all those island and coastal nations, I've siphoned off all the information I could, in the time I had, on inland water bodies."

Pete snapped back into focus. "Great idea Elaine, I'll be needing that for sure."

Elaine continued, glad to have Pete's attention, she felt she still needed his approval, even though Pete would disagree with this entirely. "I'd already done quite a bit on the Tonle Sap and Caspian Sea, both well down FYI, and a quick scan of Titicaca, which appears unaffected interestingly enough."

"Maybe down to elevation?" Pete responded, eliciting a kind of snort of agreement from Elaine.

"My thoughts exactly Pete, I've also got our very own Great Lakes, plus Bikal, Victoria, Tanganyika, Oinghai China and the very limited information we have on Vostok."

"Antarctica." Pete piped up, impressed with Elaine's thoroughness, he smiled positively at her which almost made her blush with pride, she was relishing this challenge after all these years playing mate.

"That's right Pete, it's so far under the ice, it may yield something but who knows? Maybe the ice cap melting has kept it topped up."

"Or it could be masking one of the Southern Hemisphere's plugholes," surmised Pete. "Tell you what, I'll drill the data and we'll leave conclusions for after we land maybe, there are too many variables here and we don't have time for rabbit holes."

"Agreed," replied Pete decisively.

"What are we agreeing on?" Jeff arrived back in the entrance hall area, bulging suitcase by his side, similarly bulging carry-on over his shoulder.

"That Elaine's amazing, you're late and the cab is here." Pete smiled.

"OK," replied Jeff, "I can agree to that, well done Elaine, tell me on the plane what you've done."

"That's going to be easy, our seats are together Jeff, Pete's on his lonesome a few rows back."

33

Tokyo, Japan

Japan is one of those destinations that brings out the wanderlust in pretty much everyone. Either it's 'I've always wanted to go' or, 'oh my god, it's just so amazing, you have to go'. 'Yeah, it's Ok I guess, quite boring and the food is crap' says no one, ever. It's not quite the sensory overload that India gives you, or the wall of heat Dubai welcomes visitors with, it has more of an ordered chaos about it but the kind of ordered chaos which is very well educated, tidies its bedroom daily and is almost saintly polite. The West and Japan had had a few differences a couple of generations back, but these appeared long forgotten. Much like the British, a rich imperialistic island nation mentality meant Japan had a strong sense of self, which helped them welcome visitors from all over the world be they there for business or pleasure, for most, it would include, at some point at least, the latter.

Tokyo is one of the world's greatest cities, frenetic, densely populated, expansive, tranquil and claustrophobic all at the same time. Within the same area it felt like life was a hundred miles an hour and then around the corner it could be serene, maybe a shrine or temple, or a crowd of ninety-somethings practising tai-chi.

The youth of Japan, like everywhere really, drag their seniors kicking and screaming into the future, ironically a future generated by that very same generation who always seem stuck in the past. A 'vulnerable confidence' was how

Pete had described the Japanese, having spent time there himself mixing scientific business and pleasure. 'They want to be different, just like everybody else' was his favourite summary of the young local population, particularly in Tokyo. A fragility and humility emanated from even the most outwardly gregarious Tokyo-ite. Pete had always thought the world could benefit from being a bit more Japanese in their day-to-day behaviour and outlook on life. Having said that, he was very aware that so much of what one sees in Japan is only surface deep. Japan has one of the highest suicide rates for men anywhere in the world, keeping your feelings suppressed is no good, it turns out. The Salarymen burn out, living so far out of the city, they cram on to the morning subway to the extent some guy with essentially a massive broom pushes them in like sardines, then they work as many hours as they feel they need to and then there's the office paradox, which so tickled Pete. The workers feel they can't leave before the boss and the boss feels they can't leave before the workers, so inevitably everyone stays late, every night. Then the salarymen go out and drink their stress with whisky, fall back onto the subway, trudge back to their tiny apartments, get a few hours poor quality sleep then do it all again. The business culture is certainly evolving but old habits die hard and there are worse traits in the business world than indestructible work ethic.

34

Marco was giddy with excitement as his sleek Mercedes traversed the glass-smooth roads towards his hotel in Shinjuku. Given his Mexico City roots, he was certainly no stranger to sprawling cities, but Tokyo felt like his country's capital after a few years at Swiss finishing school. It was pristine, he didn't see a piece of litter for the whole journey, the taxi driver, and this was just a run of the mill, no-frills driver, wore white gloves and it made Marco feel like a celebrity. Even the taxi's door opened automatically, which is why Japanese businesspeople always get an earful from taxi drivers elsewhere in the world because they just walk off leaving the doors open.

As he gazed out of the window up at the never-ending neon signs, he found himself muttering the opening few lines to his upcoming speech. He had managed to catch a few hours of sleep on the flight over but the rest he put to trying to memorise every word, every nuance of the text Chester Rogers had given him to perfect.

"Great to hear you reciting your performance Marco, sounds great." Rogers was sharing the cab as both were staying in the Hotel Skyline in the heart of bustling and sleepless Shinjuku. The sun was setting and in the warm orange glow, the neon signs were really coming into their own. "Look Marco, why don't we drop our bags and head out for a wander round and grab some food before trying to get at least some sleep before we have our Project Green meeting tomorrow morning?" Marco's eyes lit up, he really wanted to see some of the city but didn't want to come across too much as a tourist when he was crafting his new serious science persona. But given Chester, even Marco wasn't going to call him 'Cheese', had suggested it then it felt perfectly fine to go into sightseeing mode. He could worry about Project Green in the morning, tonight he could send some photos of Tokyo back to his mother in Mexico, that should keep her happy for a while he thought to himself.

35

Across the city the following morning at the Cherry Blossom Hotel in Shibuya, a different yet similarly immaculate Mercedes pulled up and out stepped Elaine, Jeff and Peter, adjusting their eyes to the bright Tokyo sun and they dragged their heavy bags into the lobby of the hotel. Not only were they greeted by all members it seemed of the hotel staff, welcoming them by screaming "Irasshaimase!" – translation: 'welcome'. They were also greeted by the familiar to Jeff-only face of Jane Henderson, who had arrived not thirty minutes prior. A broad Duchenne smile developed on Jeff's unshaven face, belying his tremendous fatigue from a restless night on the plane from Berlin. He dropped his case and carry-on, not for the first time by the looks of them both, and bounded over to Jane and warmly embraced her, which felt like more of a bear hug to Jane, who wasn't expecting it and was surprisingly delighted to have so much affection from her colleague and friend.

"Jane, so good to see you again, how cool is Tokyo?" he didn't wait for a response, "Meet Peter…" Jeff made the introductions, feeling like kingmaker bringing together a transatlantic alliance, whereas the reality was much more akin to him introducing some friends.

Jane, Peter and Elaine exchanged pleasantries and made quiet jokes at Jeff's expense, if required, he was happy to be their social glue for now. Friendship and trust operate in such a myriad of forms. The three estranged university buddies, reunited, pursuing a seemingly personal cause, at least to Pete, that would manifest into an apocalyptic nightmare. And Jane, a total outsider to Pete and Elaine, known only be association with Jeff but had quickly become an essential part of the group remotely. Then, on meeting everyone in person in the hotel lobby, all final connections had been made and cemented. They were a team, a team that Jeff currently pointed out who needed a proper shower and a near-deadly shot of caffeine.

"We're going to need it Jeff," said Jane, a note of urgency in her voice, Senator Gordon is expecting us at two o'clock this afternoon.

"Then let's get a wriggle on; I've got a bit to update you on." answered Elaine.

Jane was still feeling the emotional high of finally meeting everyone, so her guards were well and truly dismantled and she let out an almost silent snort but plenty obvious for Jeff to pick up on.

"What is it, Jane?"

"Just the usual, Jeff, but now there are three of you from British land with all your funny words and phrases. We say get a 'wiggle' on, no r. I like wriggle, it's way cuter." The interchange between Jeff and Jane did not go unnoticed by Pete and Elaine, who looked at each other and nodded in silent agreement, they knew instantly Jane was a good 'un and all four headed up to their very tiny rooms to freshen up and prepare for the day ahead.

36

    Marco had anticipated and mentally prepared for a night, maybe a few, with disjointed sleep so he was surprised and delighted to wake after a full night of undisturbed rest. He pondered if his mind was so overblown by his current situation that his brain's over-activity demanded some time off. He didn't even recall if he had dreamed, which brought up a sudden panic through his body that he'd forgotten his entire presentation overnight. But with a deep breath, he steadied himself and refound his rhythm again, sharp clarity returning once again. He almost skipped down the three flights of stairs to the breakfast area - it would be wrong to call it a room. Marco assumed this corner of the hotel ground floor was put to a variety of uses through the day. A couple of long tables arranged in a V-shape, packed with a selection of glass jars with western cereals on one side, a large steaming vat of chicken noodle broth in the centre, straddling the tables imposingly and to the right, a covered urn of steamed rice surrounded by a few plates with a selection of foods Marco did not feel brave enough to try. However, he did set aside 'cautious Marco' and opted not for the Frosties but a generous bowl of noodle soup.

    He was soon joined at his chessboard-sized table by Chester Rogers, who always looked like he slept well, carrying a plate of rice covered with what looked to Marco like something swept off the floor after a massacre at an aquarium. He had ordered them both a black coffee, for which Marco was grateful. A good night's sleep was always crowned by a large cup of the good stuff. It boosted Marco's already buoyant mood as opposed to dragging him painfully into consciousness as it would need to have done if his predicted jet lag had set in. Hopefully he'd dodged a bullet on that one, he thought happily to himself as he slurped and sucked his way through the simple, savoury masterpiece which was his local breakfast.

"We're meeting some people this morning Marco," Rogers' face tightened, not aggressively but assertively enough to make Marco physically adjust his position upright and focused. "It's game face time Marco Hernandez, your final audition. Absolutely nothing to concern you, this is about rubber stamping the plan and presentation, just in case there are any last-minute tweaks." Marco twitched, unsure what this meant. "I can see your worry Marco, my fault sorry, this is a dress rehearsal so we're all sure we're, and you're, ready for Wednesday. That gives us the best part of two days to stay focused, learn, relearn if necessary. But I know you've got this Marco."

So, thought Marco, *it's just a dress rehearsal, that's' OK, in fact better than OK, a chance to properly practise the presentation.*

"There will be a few heads in the auditorium to give you an audience, make it feel a bit more real."

"That's good Chester, I'd like a dry run, will Senator Johnson or Mrs Rastik be there?"

"Do you know Marco, I'm not sure, I imagine a few of the Project Green team will be there as it's partly their work you're reciting." Rogers lied barefaced, he knew for a fact Johnson and Rastik would be there, not to mention the heads of most of the world's media conglomerates and a number of top global government officials, he almost didn't want to entertain the security detail that must be in place for this. He figured, totally correctly, that knowing even a tiny proportion of his audience might send him into a spin and he needed to protect Marco from over-thinking this, as he would for anyone. The presentation equivalence of dance like no one's watching. Rogers could sink a three-foot put ninety-nine times out of a hundred, but you put him on the 18th green, round four of the masters with that same putt to win the green jacket, the eyes of the world watching, it was a different story. Even at the thought of it he shuddered and got back to the task in hand, babysitting Marco Hernandez in advance of his practice run later that morning. Please Lord, don't let them put the lights on in the auditorium, Marco might actually soil himself.

37

Jane, Elaine, Jeff and Pete emerged from the Cherry Blossom Hotel and into the warmth of the city. It was humid, not quite uncomfortably humid, but enough to make Jeff think any walking of significance would lead to a damp head and beading back. Air-con was his friend. The side street was incongruously calm given its location. Mostly private residences were wide enough that only one car could fit down. Perfectly smooth surface and not a piece of litter in sight, it was like a film set. Across from the hotel was a tiny shop, more of a booth than a stall, but not big enough for a door. A bamboo drape hung from the beam over the front counter, patterned with exotic-looking tigers and dragons.

Elaine looked at the store, uselessly trying to decipher the kanji which she presumed told customers the name or maybe what was being sold, as it was deliciously unclear to her what she might take possession of if she actually bought one of the hundreds of small white pots which covered wooden counter. Peering in she could see shelf upon shelf of more of the little pots, some with gold labels, some silver but mostly white. She recognised a basket full of tiger balm and surmised it was some kind of local apothecary but not the type she was used to in DC, that's for sure. She watched as a tiny old lady shuffled up to the store and began animatedly talking to the similarly old lady whose store it presumably was.

I hope I'm still shopping for myself at that age, thought

Elaine to herself. Some white pots and a handful of yen changed hands and old lady one headed off down the street to continue her day. For a moment Elaine felt such a desire to follow her to see what her life was like, but she was pulled back to the here and now by Jane gently grabbing her arm.

"Jeff tells me you've been living in Malaysia most recently, that must have been interesting." Elaine had quickly warmed to Jane, boosted by the fact she suggested Malaysia was 'interesting' instead of most people just saying how incredible it must have been, just because it's remote and tropical. It made her feel Jane understood things could be good or bad regardless of location.

"That's a spot-on word to describe the place, Jane, yes," she smiled openly. "I suspect Jeff gave you a tad more context than that though, right?" Elaine assumed Jane knew she'd left her husband and essentially her life behind. Jane nodded sympathetically, allowing Elaine space to continue.

"I think it's fair to say my time in Malaysia has come to an end." It didn't feel strange saying that now, "my husband is still there, at least in the region, we had drifted apart, although I'm not sure how close we were to begin with." She certainly found it easy talking to Jane, maybe it was because she was the first independent female she'd talked to in months, maybe years even. "I've just felt so alive since going over to Berlin and working with Pete, you may or may not know our paths crossed in Mexico a few years ago?"

"Yes Elaine, when Marco Hernandez was working

there?"

"That's right" Elaine carried on. "And of course, Jeff coming over from the US was a bit strange at first, you know given our history." Jane knew all about it but stayed silent. "But it's been so much fun, all of us getting back together again, working on this crazy project, I've missed that the most."

"Well, it certainly sounds like you've lost none of your scientific acumen, I know how highly Jeff and Peter rate your input and contribution to the team, I'm pretty sure they can't do what you do."

"And nor me them," responded Elaine characteristically humbly.

"So what next Elaine, have you got that far?" Jane probed, sensing Elaine's comfort with the level of personal disclosure.

"To be honest Jane, all I know is I've got a one-way ticket to Berlin, I'm part of something that truly means something, I'm back in Geology, I'm around people I love, not sure I need much more than that at the moment."

"I'm not sure any of us need much more than that Elaine, sounds like you're in a good place.

"That I am Jane, I just have more than a nagging doubt we're fighting a losing battle on this one."

"Yeah, I know what you mean, I feel it too, I think we all do under the surface."

"If we're right, we're doomed, if we're wrong, we're doomed, unless the Senator has some geological miracles in his locker."

"He's a truly great man; let's wait and see, he's in town so we're all meeting at two this afternoon in Yutenji, a couple of stops on the subway from here."

And the here Jane spoke of was Shibuya Station. "Now this is Tokyo!" exclaimed Jeff with aplomb. "I'm crossing this whether we need to or not. This zebra crossing shits on anything the Beatles tried to make famous."

Interesting comparison, thought Pete, although he shared Jeff's enthusiasm about the crossing. Slipping into tour guide mode he explained about the extremely popular statue of a dog outside one of the station's many exits. "This fella is called Hachiko, and it's a true story of dedication and loyalty. He would walk his owner every day to this station, then be here in the afternoon to walk home with him. Nothing truly remarkable about that I hear you say, but when the owner died, Hachiko kept coming back to Shibuya Station every single day for almost ten years until his own passing. A true Japanese legend, thus the statue. He's a real hero and inspiration for the people of Tokyo. And me too."

"That's so cool Peter," Jane was genuinely moved. "Oh, time to go," she said as the green man lit up and people scrambled onto the roads like a giant had poured them from a bucket.

"The world's busiest crossing," exclaimed Jeff enthusiastically, having done his homework on this one. "Three thousand people at a time. See, it's organised chaos. Brilliant." He was truly enjoying himself simply crossing the road. They all got across unscathed and still together and came face-to-face with a giant, glass-fronted Starbucks.

"I'm happy if you are." Jeff said optimistically to the others, mildly surprised when they all agreed and stepped inside.

"I hear they do all kinds of matcha drinks so I'm game," said Jane. A few minutes later, drinks in hand, Peter climbed to the second floor and located his friends at a table overlooking Shibuya Junction.

That should keep Jeff happy, and probably distracted, mused Pete to himself as he passed everyone's drinks around. "So, let's get down to business," he said emphatically. And with that, the joviality ceased, and the floor was Elaine's, sharing from a layperson's perspective a whole load of jumbled up numbers, coordinates and science jargon, but to the trained ears of her friends, this provided the basis of an evidence-based counter-offensive to rebuke the upcoming Marco-fronted ICCS plan.

38

As the four debated, questioned and stress-tested Elaine's data and worked together, fuelled by espressos and matcha, to rescript and reposition Peter's presentation, across the city Marco was pacing backstage. He was muttering to himself a combination of parts of his speech and just giving himself a pep talk. Chester Rogers, as is frequently his wont, took the calculated approach not to let Marco know in advance where this 'dress rehearsal' as he called it was taking place and very deliberately avoided letting him know who would be in the audience. Once they exited the subway after a half-hour ride eastwards, it became very apparent to Marco that the IGA conference was not going to be a quiet affair.

"I won't lie to you Marco," Rogers felt this was true enough, there was a distinct difference between bare faced lying and not offering the truth, although in this particular scenario, he was actually sharing the truth. "The delay, you know the postponement of this conference," Marco nodded earnestly, "wasn't due to a typhoon, it was so it could be relocated to a venue more befitting for the events you will be part of. The Tokyo Convention Hall is pretty central and would have been perfect but given what you have to say, and how and to whom you're going to say it," Marco's attention piqued again, "they felt the fact their main theatre only holds five hundred people wasn't big enough." Marco suddenly felt like he'd had a sack placed over his head and thrown into a tumble dryer, to the extent his legs buckled a little under the weight of this latest bombshell. He knew this was pretty significant, but this was next-level stuff. Rogers sensed the question he needed to address and was spot-on.

"Tokyo Big Sight," Chester Rogers pointed to a large eight-storey tower up ahead of them, the glass panelling of the inverted pyramid structure glinting in the Tokyo sunlight, "was originally constructed to house events for the Olympics but ended up being essentially a media centre. The major conference tower has a reception hall on the first floor, that's where we will be, that can seat up to eleven hundred people. Although," as if this would help Marco's ever-increasing nerves, "there won't be anywhere near that amount of people today so don't worry." They both knew the unspoken implication was for a full house on the actual day. Marco racked his brain to think of his biggest previous audience for a presentation, maybe ten he recounted and that was over ten years ago.

"Marco," Rogers stopped dead in his tracks, realising he needed to take Marco's heartbeat down a score or two, he could see the Mexican had glazed over, playing scenarios out which could only lead to negative outcomes. "The audience is irrelevant." *OK*, he thought, *that's stretching credibility.* "At least the audience size is irrelevant. You'll be on stage, yes, with the eyes of the world on you," and before Marco could even react to that, "which we already knew about, you knew it, you know it, we've always talked about it, and you knew you'd have an audience, all you've found out now is that it's a big audience, nothing more. When you're up on stage and believe me, I've been there,"

Introducing but certainly not presenting, he thought to himself. That idea put the fear of God into him, but he wasn't going to share that little insight. "Once you're in the glare of the spotlights, you can pick out a few heads on chairs, maybe a face in the front row or two but essentially in a theatre like this, presenting to ten, a hundred or a thousand makes no difference. You just need to do your thing, you've practised and practised so all that's needed now is you go through it today on stage and get used to the place, no TV viewers, just a few guys in the stalls." Again, he omitted to say who would be there for fear of Marco literally running off, "and you'll be in and out in a matter of minutes. Some hired help juniors will throw a few questions at you, but we've got that under control, haven't we?" Rogers could see colour returning to Marco's face.

"I guess so," he replied timidly but as he thought about what Rogers was saying, he looked up again at the hugely imposing conference tower standing before them, steeled himself, puffed out his chest and with a renewed confidence exclaimed, "Let's do this!" *Job done again for now,* thought Rogers with relief. He really was rooting for Marco, this plucky underdog thrust into the global limelight of epic proportions and to be fair he was coping well all things considered.

Inside the cavernous conference building, as Marco paced back and forth, steadying himself for the all-in dry run, Chester Rogers peeled back the deep red velvet curtain, weighty in his hands, and cast his eye over the awaiting audience. Even he needed a double take, there were security guards everywhere and, given the auditorium lights hadn't been dimmed yet, he could clearly make out some very familiar faces. He couldn't stop himself saying out loud, as if he needed to say it to believe it, luckily Marco was so deep in his own thoughts that he didn't hear, which almost certainly saved him an awkward change of trousers. "POTUS is here." Indeed, he was, the leader of the free world was sitting about fifteen rows back, flanked on either side by Nancy Rastik and Senator Johnson.

"Who else is in there then?" he whispered to himself. "Oh, jeez you're kidding me!?!" Some three rows back and to the right, some shuffling across the seats towards the president were a group of security personnel in black combat gear with the iconic red and yellow flag of China on their sleeves. As they approached POTUS they broke apart and a small, but not frail, elderly man with greying black hair and the tiniest pair of glasses Chester Rogers had ever seen, neared the US president. Rogers was under the impression that relations between the US and China were at an all-time low, despite the noises around the ICCS. There was a trade war that seemed to change from manufactured goods to energy import-export tariffs weekly, a huge public kerfuffle over Taiwan and a simmering animosity about drug talking at the 2008 Beijing Olympics. But what he saw now drop-kicked that so far into touch he'd never see that ball again. President Franks rose to his feet, opened his arms, grinned like a groom at the alter and warmly embraced the president of China, a man notorious for his total avoidance of public emotion. Instinctively, he scanned the room, almost joking to himself that there would be a Soviet delegation heading over to get involved in the camaraderie.

"What the fu…?" he trailed off in his own disbelief when, sure enough, from the left of the theatre a group of about eight massive muscular men, dressed almost identically to the Chinese security but about a foot taller and two feet wider were making their way over to the East meets West love-in. Rogers was tempted to get his camera out and video this but as he reached down to grasp his iPhone, he thought better of it. It was suicide he figured, and no one would believe it were real anyway, so he chose to stay hidden, simultaneously realising the rest of the theatre seats were empty. The room housed only the delegations supporting and protecting the three most powerful men on the planet, plus PR man Chester Rogers and a blissfully unaware Marco Hernandez.

Captivated, Rogers watched as President Zarkov appeared from amidst the black-clad Hercules, dressed in a beige pair of slacks and ice-white open-necked Hawaiian-style shirt. *He was a moustache short of being Magnum PI*, mused Chester to himself, still grappling with the union in front of him. He wasn't hugely surprised at the obvious ardour between the Russian president and Chinese Supreme Leader Guo, but it was his own president's relationship with his Russian counterpart that mesmerised him. President Franks seemed to almost tentatively offer Zarkov a fist bump once he'd unwrapped himself from Guo, but tentatively was the converse of what Rogers witnessed next. Zarkov politely reciprocated the fist bump, paused dramatically then opened his upper body wide like a father encouraging his son to leap into his arms, which the president of the United States duly did, figuratively speaking. As the two leaders embraced, President Guo enthusiastically beat his compatriots heartily on their backs. They looked like salesmen who'd just landed the biggest clients of their lives, all smiles and guffaws and belly laughs. This wholly incongruous interaction only lasted around thirty seconds, then as quickly as they'd arrived at the US president's seat, both Supreme Leader Guo and Russian President Zarkov slipped back into their security details' protection and en masse, they scooched back to their allocated positions. In a matter of seconds, it was as if nothing had or ever could have happened, all parties seemingly doing their best to look menacing and hostile. President Guo then gave a signal, which led to a pair of huge double doors opening at the far end of the room and in started to come who Rogers assumed were global media leads and various other international dignitaries, plus some local fillers to ensure the place didn't look too empty. Rogers closed tight the slender gap in the curtain and turned to face Marco.

"Anyone interesting out there Chester?" he asked, fishing for clues and this time Rogers opted to play loose with the truth.

"No one to worry about Marco, you know Nancy and Senator Johnson of course, they're here to support you." Marco felt better knowing they had his back, or at least the belief that they had his back, and steeled himself for his run-through. "As I said, with the lights down in the hall, the AV playing behind you and a couple of spotlights directed at you Marco, you'll be in your own world. Go smash it."

It took both of them by surprise when the speakers boomed out Marco's introduction announcement. For some reason, they'd both assumed Marco would just quietly slip into position and then start but even better, thought Rogers, it was the full works. This meant it was his cue to scamper off-stage but only after he offered Marco his hand to shake firmly with a confidence-boosting power stare.

"Knock it out the park Marco," Rogers told him, who responded with a smile, he was on his own now, breathing deeply, keeping himself calm so he didn't sound out of breath as he spoke. It may only be a dry run, he told himself, but he wanted it to be a gold-standard performance, to prove to himself, if no one else, that he could mix it with the big guys.

"Now, welcoming to the stage our headline presentation at this, the thirteenth International Geological Association conference in Tokyo, Japan, representing the International Council for Climate Stability, please put your hands together as we await the Chief Scientific Advisor to Planet Earth..." *Wow they used it,* grinned Rogers in the wings, "..and renowned globally recognised expert, ladies, gentleman and distinguished guests, let's hear it for Dr Marco Hernandez." The curtains swished open, two white spotlights lasered in on Marco as he stepped forward to the lectern, applause still ringing out, he was too focused to notice it was coming through the speakers not the audience in front of him at this time and behind him, the tennis court sized screen came to life with a majestic view of the Earth from space, a powerful image to complement Marco's opening words in his twenty minute presentation. The speakers toned down the piped-in clapping, leaving the room in an anticipatory hush, all eyes on Marco and the mesmeric image behind him. To the side of the stage, Rogers clenched his fists, even he was tied up in knots, lord knows what the real thing would feel like. On stage, Marco looked up and took a long, deep breath and realised, just as Rogers has told him, that he couldn't pick out the audience even to get a feel for who they were or how many, giving him an extra boost of confidence for him to begin.

39

The private meeting room in Tokyo's Shangri-La Hotel, temporary residence of Senator Gordon, had been arranged conference style. So, the first thing the Senator did on arrival, well before the 2pm start time, was to ask the attending staff to rearrange the tables boardroom style, one big table so everyone had a physical and metaphorical seat there. Rose Carmichael and Kelly Chan had travelled widely for both work and pleasure, but Shangri-La levels of luxury were yet to feature in their accommodation experiences. Senator Gordon had insisted they join him there as much as a reward for their excellent recent service as fact he wanted them close by.

In their downtime, albeit limited, they had taken full advantage of both the location of the hotel, enjoying a walk around the Imperial Palace Gardens and the facilities, entering the meeting room fresh from a quick swim and a thirty-minute massage in the hotel spa. They weren't a couple, romantically speaking, but from an outsider's perspective it would be easy to think that given how much time they spent together. Meeting on the first day of their graduate training programme at the American Institute of Scientific Research, they roomed together, socialised together, even played badminton and became quite a formidable doubles pairing. It hadn't gone unnoticed that their combined brainpower seemed to exceed the sum of the two individuals and, having graduated streets ahead of their peers, they were recommended for a fast-track government sponsored programme for promising scientists. Senator Gordon was one of the programme patrons at the time and kept a close eye on their developing expertise in data mining and use of credible evidence to prove and disprove claims made by individuals, businesses and sometimes nation states or world leaders.

Gordon also valued them for their willingness to stand up to him when others just sided with the politically more powerful man. It was actually Rose Carmichael who connected the Senator to engage further with Jane Henderson and subsequently Pete, Jeff and Elaine. The Senator was against bringing more bodies to the table when the ICCS was in its clandestine infancy. Rose almost demanded they get an outsider's perspective in the scientific community alongside Michelle Grant and his European political allies. Similarly, Grant all but tore strips off the Senator when he told her he was thinking of leaving Jane out of their working group, reminding him in no uncertain terms of the knowledge, thought and scientific acumen that had gone into that original one-pager that anchored their relationship.

"She doesn't believe climate change isn't happening any more than you do Senator." Michelle Grant's words frequently echoed around his head, he wasn't too proud to admit to himself he was fallible, and he knew every great leader, although he would never refer to himself as such, needs a strong, honest and brave team around them, filling in gaps, course correcting and capitalising on momentum when the time is right.

DROUGHT

With Rose and Kelly helping themselves to a jasmine tea, a relaxing cleanser following their massages, Michelle Grant strolled confidently into the meeting room, as much relieved to be in air conditioning after a ten-minute walk from her hotel than anything to do with the actual meeting. Until Jane's team, or the Masai Four, as he was beginning to refer to them, Gordon's 'outsider' brains had come in the form of this former NUSNASP (Non-US North American Special Projects) Head and current Lead of The British Bee Association, a role which was significantly more global than it suggested. The parallels between the US Environmental Bureau public raison d'etre and the BBA founding philosophy were remarkably aligned, making Michelle a key voice around the table. Ensuring Planet Earth remains environmentally viable through a greater understanding of human impact and proposing specific actions and intervention plans to promote balance and harmony between people and nature. Grant was not above using a little squirt of fake news to nail a point, even Chester Rogers would be proud.

"It is reported that Albert Einstein, no less...." she'd often begin with, always kicking off with the get-out-of-jail-free-card by saying 'it is reported', which these days permitted almost any nonsense, although in this case it was just that he didn't actually say what he is reported to have said. However, the scientific value of the quote is painfully accurate. "It is reported that Albert Einstein, no less, said if all the bees disappeared from the world, humans would only survive for four more years." What a headline.

Impossible to fact check and impossibly more impactful that just saying bees are really important. As a rule, Gordon didn't allow or encourage this kind of hyperbole but this one had done the rounds enough that he tolerated it, even enjoyed it. He knew, as they all did, that this wasn't about whose science head was the biggest, it would come down to narrative, and that was why he was glad to have Grant and the Masai Four in his corner.

Five minutes later and the Shangri-La Meeting Space 6 had filled. Jane had spotted Klaus Jurgensen and Penny Norton approaching the elaborate entrance from the opposite direction and they all entered together, exchanging introductory pleasantries and the customary gushing about the crazy but inspirational feel Tokyo imparted on every visiting soul. Louis Charles was the last to arrive, cordially welcomed by one of Senator Gordon's firm handshakes and respectful nods. *Wow*, thought Jane, suddenly distracted as her whole body tingled, *he's quite something*.

"Jane, Jane," Jeff whispered forcefully at her, snapping her out of her teenage gawp. "You're drooling Jane, put your tongue away," he said playfully.

"A girl can look, can't she?" Although her blushes had already made her cheeks noticeably rosier. "I've seen the way you look at Elaine, Jeff."

It was his turn to blush. "OK, we'd better concentrate Jane," he quickly changed the subject, but she had been right, Elaine's presence had stirred a whole viper's nest of unresolved emotions, exacerbated by her falling asleep on his shoulder on the long flight over and his instinctive and unstoppable urge to gently stroke her hair as she slept. Or as it turned out, helped Elaine off to sleep, he wasn't the only one rediscovering feelings after all the years, especially now she felt independent and free from Mark.

"In two days, almost to the minute," Gordon's deep voice commanded attention and duly got it, "Professor Masai will take the stage at the very same time as Marco Hernandez, the ICCS headliner. Our task is to use Peter's excellent work and embellish, tweak, deepen, broaden, whatever we need to do to nullify what's going on next door."

"I'm all in," piped up Peter supportively, which Gordon appreciated, conscious he'd railroaded what was initially supposed to just be Peter sharing wild but interesting theories with his international peer group.

"So, in anticipation of your operational questions," Gordon continued, "much of the world's media will be with the ICCS crowd, we are expecting heads of state to be in there, this is big folks. I have secured, with thanks to Penny and Herr Jurgensen, a large selection of more sceptical, let's say, media houses and in no small measure thanks to Harpinder Tarkowski, who on Jane's request shared the names of some journalists she felt would be sympathetic to and also vocal about our cause. Secondly, Peter, we do not expect you to carry this burden alone up there, although I have no doubt you'd do a fine job." Pete was never against his ego being stroked. "I will be joining you on stage, as will the Prime Minister of the UK, the German Chancellor, the Secretary General of the Commonwealth and the Prime

Minister of New Zealand, but only once you've delivered your, and our, message."

If these names weren't enough to drive home the intensity of the situation, Gordon added, "and Penny is working very hard, and I think is getting somewhere, is that fair to call it out?" A supportive smile towards the UK Ambassador to the US, to which she responded with a confident, albeit slight, nod back in his direction. "Great, we feel we have the support of the African Union so Chairperson Deri Koont should be on stage, plus Prime Minister Ito. Now that would be a real coup for us, not only should Mrs Ito remain neutral as host but also, she is no doubt being courted relentlessly by our friends in the ICCS. Let's park this for a moment as we have some viewing to do." "No way!" or versions of that came from everyone except Louis Charles, Kelly Chan and Rose Carmichael, who had already viewed the footage.

Louis Charles was the one who took over now. "I bet you all thought Senator Gordon was pretty well connected, now you can be sure he's doing some of the heavy lifting too. We received this less than an hour ago and you need to see it too, it probably helped Kelly and Rose that they watched it whilst in the spa to keep them relaxed." Charles grinned at them both which, as seemed to be the norm for him, made the two ladies giggle like teenagers. *This guy has some charm about him*, reflected Jeff, with not an insignificant amount of jealousy. "Watch this, then we'll go through what we all have and make our final plans." With that, Kelly Chan speedily typed into her laptop and up on the giant wall screen appeared crystal clear image of Marco Hernandez standing in front of a huge image of the world from space.

"Enjoy," smiled Chan sardonically. "Just wait until we tell you who was in the audience for this practice session."

40

A little over twenty minutes later, Gordon returned to a stunned set of people in the meeting room, they weren't really sure what to say once they heard about the US, Russia and China love-in, and that was some risk Gordon had asked someone to take.

"So, I bring good news, I expect you'll need it after that home movie." Indeed, they did. "Prime Minister Kapoor and Wahyumi of India and Indonesia respectively are on board and Deri Koont has confirmed. That's representation for another couple of billion citizens." Gordon announced proudly, impressing his team even more than ever. "So, let's give them something that'll keep them standing by us. I've securely shared this footage with some pretty big hitters as I imagine my good friend Senator Johnson has too and it's frankly fascinating who buys it and who doesn't." He was saying this in such a matter-of-fact way that it seemed more like a class president vote at high school rather than deciding which version of global apocalypse you were hedging bets on.

Pete took the lead now, he'd had zero doubt Senator Gordon would drum up support and equally lacked the others' astonishment that the US, China and Russia were secret bedfellows. "I need ten minutes to set up my mantle disintegration theory, Louis, it's got serious teeth now thanks to that report you sent me, it makes me sound less like a geological madman and more like a professor."

Louis Charles laughed, he liked Peter, his aloof

confidence and clear ability to manage the enormity of the situation. "You are a professor, aren't you? And the mad professor look worked well for Einstein, didn't it?"

"True, true," agreed Pete, enjoying the comparison. "Then we need to weave in the lakes, inland seas and water table stuff Elaine has, I think Michelle your BBA analysis on climate and water loss on bee populations will be really important and Senator, now we've seen the competition's hand, I'd say we rip them to shreds at the very same time my old pal Marco is spewing all that propaganda." A resounding chorus of yesses, including the Senator, teed up Elaine to share her analyses into the critical water loss that had been conveniently absent from the ICCS video. Kelly Chan and Rose Carmichael acted almost as verifiers of Elaine's accuracy as she produced a clear and concise, evidence-based synopsis of diminishing water levels at several high-profile global locations.

"And you did all this in twenty-four hours?" Rose asked in wonderment.

"More like thirty-six," Elaine responded with a proud grin.

"Where did you say you'd been researching Elaine?" Rose asked, hoping she'd be told this genius Englishwoman was a colleague of Louis at NASA or maybe she was funded by Elon Musk.

"I've not done any scientific work for five years Rose, since I bumped into Peter in Mexico, just been slowly dying from an expat-wife life, it's good to be back." Instant heroine status for Kelly and Rose.

"Kudos Elaine, serious kudos." Kelly added before Elaine continued.

"I think what's interesting and not wholly unsurprising is the rise in global humidity levels and I suspect Michelle, you'll be no stranger to this trend..." there was a powerful nod from Grant, "...I haven't been able to pinpoint any direct causal link between global rainfall and the disappearance of surface water, but, and it's a big but, I suspect there is a link to find if I had the time."

"You're right Elaine, there is, we can share that later." Chan interrupted supportively. "But we didn't run it for humidity," she suddenly felt inferior, like a chess grandmaster being outplayed by a rank outsider. For her whole academic life, she'd been told she was peerless, aside from her science clone and best mate Rose, and had forgotten what it felt like not to be the one who was proving stuff or correcting things in a group situation. She bore no grudge against Elaine, it just made her question all those late nights, party declines, panic-driven revision sessions chasing top grades when a career-free expat who'd only recently dipped her toe back into research could challenge her mentally.

"Kelly, you've got your over-thinking face on again." Rose had noticed her close friend's change in manner even if no one else would have had a second thought.

"Yep, you're right, thanks Rose, I'm good." This interchange happened so fast it wasn't noticed by the group, which allowed Kelly to gain control of her mind again and encourage Elaine to continue.

"We're talking about almost unquantifiable amounts of water here, from the public's perspective, and this isn't a matter of dumbing down, but millions of cubic kilometres of water are incomprehensible. Just wanted to share that I think we, well you Peter, need to ground this."

"Noted, thanks Elaine, good point," Pete responded, although his modus operandi wasn't very science jargon-heavy, he liked to articulate in ways everyone could relate to. "The water, be it sea or fresh, as it is flowing out of our access and heading subterranean is going in such quantities it's not simply hitting geothermic rock, turning to steam and coming back like a geyser, but that would be something to behold. But it's happening. Average global humidity levels have gone up by between five and ten percentage points in the past thirty-six months alone. Meteorologists would no doubt tell us trend fluctuations are a part of the global climatic cycle, but you layer on what we've done with greenhouse gases, polluting the oxygen-breathing oceans and what Mother Earth appears to be doing to herself, then this rise is anomalous. I'm also concerned about how quickly this impact has materialised which makes me question the timeline on this whole scenario." That thought had also crossed Peter's mind.

"However," Elaine carried on, "given global temperatures are at their highest long-term level for centuries, it's not inconceivable to attribute humidity rises with straightforward evaporation. From my calculations, this will continue to adversely affect weather systems which were already on a downward spiral. Intense rainfall, tropical storms away from the tropics, flash floods, heat waves, drought, will all become more common. I believe this is being accelerated by the unbelievably massive and pervasive release of water vapour as large parts of our escaped surface water heats as it makes its way through the increasingly hot rock beneath our feet."

"I can add to that if you're happy for me to jump in?" Michelle Grant respectfully interjected.

"Yes of course, I was hoping you would Michelle."

"I entirely concur with you Elaine and, permit me to go a bit doomsday on you for a moment, the impact is pretty devastating if you consider where we think the ICCS nations are going to take the world, or parts of it. We have been on a trajectory of poisoning our planet for a while, not only manifesting in bee population decline but widespread extinctions and loss of life-sustaining habitats and environments. You mix together accelerated fossil fuel extraction and usage, I can't even believe I'm saying those words, and the atmospheric humidity concentration we're experiencing from the subterranean water loss, it's hard to know which will destroy life as we know it first. What's your read of the ICCS, as in the leaders of what appears to be the fossil-fuel alliance, it's inconceivable they don't have the same data as us right?" Michelle asked the direct question they had all been wrestling with, the pitiful lack of scientific credibility, despite the very beautifully choreographed, superficially believable video presentation they'd all just watched.

"Data is information," Gordon spoke again.

"Information leads to knowledge, knowledge leads to power but as everyone around this table knows, the same data, especially when there's a virtually infinite amount available, can lead different people to decipher different information, generating different knowledge then wielded in very different powerful ways. The cycle is certainly not that linear. Those with power often believe they already have the knowledge, then they demand information, backed up by evidence and data, to reinforce or strengthen their current powerful position."

"Therefore, you're saying altruism is non-existent?" Penny questioned the Senator.

"Not at all but one might cynically say altruism works when it suits everyone, every action in some way impacts others however slightly but when we're talking about the highest levels of global governments in the US, Russia and China, we're talking about pretty devastating impact."

"So, we're essentially saying the ICCS, presented with the same data, have taken themselves down a fundamentally different path to ours?" Penny continued, seeking clarity for all.

"Indeed," the Senator would now up the ante, despite their continuing bafflement and animosity towards the ICCS and its high-profile sponsors. "We have to weave one final thread into our short time on stage with Peter." Gordon now turned to Louis Charles, who was clearly expecting the nod as he had taken control of the meeting room AV and the three screens across each wall of the room, aside from the entrance doors, came to life with a simple heading: 'Timeline Hypothesis for the Masai Scenario'.

"Give me a clear run through this, probably take five minutes or so then let's deal with your questions." It was Louis' polite way of telling them not to interrupt him, which they respectfully adhered to. "We've run, or allowed the super-computer to run, essentially millions of scenarios based on the data we have, and the end game is all the same. Very few ended with a planet capable of sustaining the global population we have today, never mind the future. The output boiled down to us showing you the two most likely scenarios so keep an open mind, as I'm sure you will."

Louis Charles' charm and charisma did not extend to his presentation design, this set of information slides was dry, bar charts, scatter graphs, geological and topographical map segments, even a mix of fonts. Jane wondered how Gordon felt about this, given his penchant for one-pagers but one glance of the Senator confirmed he was a million miles from worrying about style, he looked pensive and a little worried, much to Jane's chagrin. She had always been optimistic that there would be a long-term and peaceful solution to this whole ordeal with Gordon's presence acting as a security blanket, protecting them and the world from harm. But that face, creased in thought, eyes suddenly looking tired and old shattered this illusion of positivity with every word Charles spoke. As he took the team through a second modelling exercise given the ninety-five per cent confidence level of Pete's mantle disintegration theory, he shared NASA's vision of the likely next steps. He showed their best estimate as an animated timeline, demonstrating where water would disappear from over an unspecified length of time. It showed great bodies of inland water going dry as rivers and water courses were dramatically altered. The oceanic visuals were so impactful that they made a number of those glued to the screens gasp in horror and amazement. The images transitioned, showing a once-blue planet become less and less so as the oceans, all oceans, shrank until there were no oceans at all to speak of, just what looked like a collection of lakes where the seas used to be. Jeff's main observation at the end of the transitions was that you could literally walk from Britain to America, such was the dwindling of the Atlantic. It was pretty much the same for all continents he realised, although it didn't take much of a science brain to realise by this point there'd barely be anyone left to make those journeys anyway.

"Scenario two about to project," Louis called out. "It factors in the lithospheric damage that causes the water to disappear but models its impact on non-water-covered land. We must assume the planet isn't just targeting areas which hold water, that would suggest Mother Nature is a sentient being and I suspect even Professor Masai wouldn't be pushing that theory." He glanced over at Pete to make clear he wasn't mocking him but referring to his innovative mind. The second animation had very few obvious differences from the first, aside from higher water levels remaining at the end, meaning no trans-Atlantic walk for Jeff's posterity. But what this model depicted was the mass degradation of continental land masses. A message flashed up on the screen and stayed at the bottom of the images, 'data not sufficient to directly identify impact locations so damage shown is hypothesised - but expected to be widespread.'

Louis Charles spoke up again. "I know the one thing glaringly missing from these animations is the actual timing, I deliberately didn't want to distract you. But I'm now going to run them again with our best-estimated dates against each image. Live for today folks." an ominous comment as the lights dimmed again and the AV started up on the screens. A funereal hush swept through the room; mouths open aghast. Klaus Jurgensen plunged his head into his hands, tears fell from Penny Norton's reddening eyes.

"So," Charles proceeded sombrely. "The two critical dates. 2060, the planet becomes unable to support the current forecast population, we estimate around ten billion people. Then 2120, assuming a slight reduction in global population, depending on where land destructions occur reference model two, and assuming technology permits humans to cope with the likely traumatic climatic impact of water shortages but it remains our primary source of life, also assuming carbon emissions follow the global plan for neutrality by 2050, the Mother Earth will support in the region of one billion people. By 2200 we need to be living on Mars cos we ain't living down here." Louis Charles paused to allow the team to process but not long enough to think he was finished; this slice of bad news cake was some portion. "Now let's assume these plugholes get blocked, either through our own doing or some geological miracle and play out the timeline with the predicted impact of our favourite pop group, the ICCS. Their drive for a new industrial revolution crucially plays out in a poetically comparable timeline to ours simply taking most of the world's water away. They'll just poison it instead. We have it on good authority that this scenario has been modelled by the ICCS, oddly it didn't make the final cut and it is accepted as acceptable on the basis of technological advancement that does not yet exist. Now, I'm all for positive thinking, and as a student of almost countless end-of-the-world scientific playbooks, I'm a little uncomfortable with this one. There are more two-headed dogs in the world than there are predictions which have stood the test of time of the magnitude we're talking about. This one is a bit more life-changing than hoverboards or smart clothing." Not everyone got the Back to the Future reference, but he could see by Jeff's smirk that he did.

"I'm sure I don't even need to take you through the scenario of which we advise Peter to paint the picture on stage. Even our NASA super-computer asked us if we had a death-wish, not really." Addressing some of the surprised looks around the table, he continued. "Although the infant AI software we are using does actually interact with us scientifically, if not emotionally, or it would probably tell us we were lunatics. Anyway, here's the animation which we feel best plays out where the ICCS plan, as we believe it to be, terminates." His mildly playful and sarcastic style changed in an instant, he was back to a stony-faced reality merchant once again as the images scrolled through

NASA's predicted end of life as we know it scenario.

"By 2080? And this is their actual plan with none of Peter's theory data in?" exclaimed Jane more as a statement than a question, unable to suppress her anguish and she was not alone, chuntering from around the table signalled the grisly end to Louis Charles slot.

Pete was first to speak, "That's next generation stuff, might even be our generation." He glanced over at the youngest members of the team Rose and Kelly. He had always played out his mantle disintegration theory as if it *could* happen in his lifetime, but he had never had access to the amount of data or processing capability like the NASA software to really put a date on it. But, given the Earth's multi-billion-year lifespan so far, in his heart, and in reality, his head, his educated assumptions had placed the endgame at least a couple of million years into the future. Planet Earth and life's ability to survive and adapt both on and below the surface was an epic tale of endurance and legacy. What NASA's projections showed, based on every available shred of geological evidence they could find, was that Pete's initial theory, that the Earth's crust would open up at a consistent rate over time, leading to his much longer-term Armageddon. Louis Charles had just shared a perspective that Pete was comfortable changing course to support, that mantle disintegration was happening now and happening exponentially. And that was a whole different kettle of life-ending fish. There seemed to be an acknowledgment around the table that Peter Masai would have first dibs on a response, which he duly took.

"So, in a nutshell, I originally discounted the accelerated demise of the surface of the world as we see it today but I'm very quickly reappraising that position."

"I'm afraid so Peter," Louis sounded almost sympathetic, partly because Pete had disregarded it, but also because he had considered it at all. Everyone was feeling pretty mixed up right now so were grateful to Pete for giving them time to come to terms with this stark reality.

"It's like a sheet of ice which is cracking and melting at the same time, the cracks keep on going and the melting speeds those up, but also lead to new cracks appearing. Basically, the worst of all worlds, especially when you replace the ice with the Earth's surface."

"Bingo." replied Louis, instantly seeing why the professor was the perfect moniker for the IGA. He had the scientific and mental capacity to process and understand the complexity of the situation but also the rare ability to articulate it in such a way that everyone in the room, whatever level of scientific knowledge they happened to have, could instantly get it. And boy did they need people to get this.

For the next two hours, the team challenged each other's thought processes and further queried both Pete on his theory and Louis Charles on his NASA-generated forecasts. Elaine, Kelly and Rose set their combined analytical power to hyperdrive. Senator Gordon, Penny Norton and Klaus Jurgensen focused on how they could gain further political and media traction whilst Jeff, Jane and Pete virtually restarted Pete's IGA presentation from scratch, supported by Louis Charles, whose hard-hitting animations would play out well to drive home the reality of Pete's theory, and with a tailwind, maybe convince the world to work together to find a solution. Senator Gordon had always been open about the fact he, and by definition they, didn't actually have a viable reversal strategy, neatly summed up by Jeff.

"So essentially we're telling the world it's going to end during potentially their own and certainly their children's lifetime, to ignore and in fact rebel against the three most important powerful leaders on the planet and to believe our version of the apocalypse, even though we offer no solution or hope of one?"

"Where do I sign?" Klaus tried to lighten the mood, instantly regretting his total misread of the room.

Gordon simply ignored the German. "Precisely Jeff, we need global support because to this point we only have access to a tiny, but clearly magnificent..." he gave a nod to Louis Charles and colleagues, "...scientists who believe in this. If the ICCS have been able to hoodwink, essentially buy, the scientific community by appealing to their wallets then we must wrestle back the narrative by chipping away at their collective consciences. And Pete is our sledgehammer and we'll be right there swinging with him. We will meet again, here in twenty-four hours, I am supremely impressed by all of you. You didn't have to come to Tokyo, you certainly didn't have to show as much faith in me as it feels you have, and I'm inspired by your intelligence, grace and commitment."

"Likewise," Penny squeezed in on behalf of the humbled group.

"Now, the brain can't cope with this level of intensity for extended periods of time, our working memory is finite and I, for one, need some downtime or mistakes will happen so, if you'll allow me to pull rank." They looked at Gordon in earnest, he had become an almost father figure to the team in a short space of time, they'd have worked all night if he asked them so there was a bit of surprise when he told them what he wanted. "You need to go let off steam, I'm pretty sure you could use a beer, am I right Jeff?"

"You read my mind," Jeff smiled deliriously.

"I counsel a couple of looseners will work wonders for your clarity of thought, and we're going to need buckets of that and a few of creativity to pull this off. But we can and we will, so go and try the Sapporo and Asahi; we can cross the i's and dot the t's tomorrow afternoon. Pete and all, send me anything, anytime of course but if all I do is see you again tomorrow, that's OK with me. I trust our process and I trust you all."

Rousing and seriously thirst-making, thought Jeff. "Let's do this thing, I've been doing my research on the local izakayas."

"Have you indeed?" Jane asked sarcastically.

"Yes, I have actually. And I concluded I should visit one."

41

Once Marco had delivered his final sentence, the screen behind him dimmed, leaving the ICCS logo seemingly embossed across it, unimaginatively designed, just initials with International Council for Climate Stability in uppercase written below. Fleetingly Marco thought it looked like something the Russians would design, imposing and cold, little did he know how close to the truth that was. He stepped away from the microphone and realised he had not been briefed on what to do next, did he just wait for something to happen? Would Chester Rogers appear and compere the Q&A? He decided to bow, partly as he hoped he'd get a round of applause and partly because he was in Japan, and it just felt right. He was relieved and then overjoyed that a ring of polite but strong applause did indeed erupt from the floor. It dawned on him that the bow signalled the end of his presentation and invited the audience appreciation, which then facilitated the round of questions that he and Rogers has practised. Marco dealt with these with confidence and competence, it was just as they had choreographed, each answer felt like it was embellishing the last, peppered with media-friendly soundbites.

"A new dawn for global prosperity... sea level falls mean economies can rise again... global alliance leads to climate stability... island nations thank the ICCS... it makes no sense to disagree... welcome to all our futures." Marco stayed on script and after his last response which closed the event off and led to Charles gritting his teeth and pumping his fist, they'd done it. He was pretty sure Marco would get the green light for the main event now, although he did wonder who the understudy was, maybe a Johnson/Rastik double-act, he amused himself at the thought of it. He called out to Marco to vacate the stage, who duly complied, high-fiving Rogers once safely back behind the curtain.

"You nailed it Marco, truly well done. Just gotta do it one more time, I've got a couple of slight tweaks for you, working on the emphasis of keywords and phrases and some body language bits and bobs but it's just tinkering around the edges." He hoped Nancy Rastik and Senator Johnson would be equally supportive when he met them later that afternoon to confirm final arrangements for the keynote in less than two days' time. With that in mind, he turned to Marco and as deadpan as he could, he said, "There's just one thing you have to do Marco if you're up for it?"

Marco, ever eager to please, responded obediently, "Yes Chester whatever you need," thinking there might be another high-profile responsibility he was about to be given in Project Green.

Rogers' face broke into a beaming smile, yet a little forced, given his own day was nowhere near finished. "I need you to put your feet up and chill out a bit. Go enjoy the city, take in the sights. Or order room service and watch TV. Keep your phone on but I'm hoping not to need to contact you until we meet tomorrow for lunch over in Ginza. A friend and colleague has recommended a sushi restaurant she's been raving about since I told her I was coming here, and tomorrow is the only free slot I have." Marco's emotional sensitivity wasn't developed enough or at least switched on to work out if he was being invited out of courtesy, friendship or simply necessity. For him, all stress had just evaporated. He had a free evening in an amazing city and a sushi working lunch date to boot.

Life in the fast lane was one he could get used to, he thought to himself before jolting out of it. "Just realised I left my notes out there on the lectern, I'll just grab them then I'll head off if that's OK Chester?"

Rogers nodded, he had his own stuff to worry about now but what he hadn't accounted for was what or who Marco might see when he ventured back out onto the stage. The auditorium emptied in reverse order so, before the lights went back on, all those who came in after the world leaders' union were ushered out, allowing the security teams to manage the exit of their precious cargo. By the time Marco headed back out, both the Chinese and Russian delegations had evacuated, leaving just the US team in the room and this meant Nancy Rastik, Senator Johnson and US President Franks barely fifteen metres from Marco. Initially he ignored them, just assuming they were some media guys in deep conversation having nowhere to go urgently, simply hanging around. But there did seem to be a fair few security guards looking around so as he reached for his notes, he took a closer look. It took a second or two for the penny to drop.

Of course it's Rastik and Johnson, he thought to himself,

just as Rogers had said. He raised his hand, half waving, half as if to grab their attention but they were buried in discussion with a third man, he looked familiar, but Marco couldn't place him. Probably one of the Project Green team he told himself as he turned to head back behind the curtain. That face was nagging at him, making him twist around for a final glance before slipping through the drapes. Then it hit him as he sidled back up to Chester Rogers.

"Chester," he said frantically, "is that President Franks out there? Was he here to watch me? How can that be? Why Chester? How…?" he trailed off, not believing himself. He reached for Rogers' arm and almost forcibly dragged him to the gap in the heavy red curtain he'd just come through. Rogers was caught off guard: 'play dumb or come clean?' The US contingent had upped and moved towards the back left exit, a mass of security guards meant POTUS was barely visible but Johnson and Rastik were clearly walking alongside the group.

"Yes Marco," Rogers gathered himself, "we knew Ms Rastik and Senator Johnson would be here and Marco, we can't pretend this is not a globally significant event." He'd decided to come clean as he needed to avoid spooking the Mexican scientist. "We are expecting several political leaders on Wednesday, just as we discussed, it surprises me that the president would come today but I guess it shows how serious he and the US government are taking this project and your announcement. Let's be honest, if you'd have known the US president was watching before you went out there today, how would that have affected you?"

Wow, thought Marco, *President Franks just watched my presentation, wait 'til Mother hears about this,* was his immediate reaction.

"You're right, best not to think about it." But his heart was pounding, this really was a global stage and Chester Rogers could see Marco processing the magnitude so decided not to tell him Franks' Russian and Chinese counterparts were there too.

"I know it's easy to say Marco but head off to your hotel or wherever and try not to think about it, I'll let you know if anything changes." *Job done again!* Rogers breathed a sigh of relief as Marco exited backstage with a noticeable spring in his step. That relief was short-lived as the thought crossed his mind that his meeting with Rastik and Johnson later that afternoon might also have President Franks in attendance.

42

Rastik and Johnson were staying in a boutique hotel with views towards Tokyo's famous Rainbow Bridge, which meant a short transit from Big Sight, the venue for the IGA conference. With Marco Hernandez effectively on leave until tomorrow, Chester Rogers finally had a couple of hours to himself, so he decided to have a wander, maybe try to clear his head. No meeting with those two ever ended with Rogers having nothing to do. He stopped at a 7-Eleven to get a can of drink of something that was like drinking cold fruit soup, he had no idea what it was, but it was cold and not unpleasant so was proud of his risk taking.

After a few minutes of strolling randomly, Rogers stumbled across the most ironic of tourist attractions, the Tokyo Water Science Museum. Glancing at his watch, Rogers figured he could spend an hour or so in this 'fun, interactive experience of everything water', according to Google translate. The museum was primarily full of pre-teen kids playing on all the exhibits, sometimes getting well and truly soaked. He found the displays on the third floor particularly poignant and, despite the whole thing being in Japanese, any non-linguist could tell this was about climate change and rising sea levels. One illustration showed Tokyo 2100 and the impact of sea level rises, it appeared to say 200km^2 would be impacted, hitting thirty-seven per cent of the population. Rogers wondered how the curators of the museum would react to their announcement in a day or so that would essentially make this model redundant. It was certainly not in his sphere of expertise to doubt the science behind Project Green, but it did niggle that wherever you went in the world, there appeared to be pretty much universal agreement that oceans are rising, and ice caps are melting. But Rogers' job was not a geological science advisor, so he continued to suppress his urge to challenge and moved on through the museum, trying to declutter his mind rather than tie it in knots. He needed clarity of mind to support Marco through the next forty-eight hours and, if it were deemed successful, Rogers would be in high demand.

"Have you been doing some background research Chester?" Senator Nick Johnson drew immediate attention to the visitor sticker Rogers had forgotten to remove following his brief trip to the Water Museum.

"Oh this? Yes sir," Rogers smiled, slightly embarrassed. "Not sure there's a lot in there for you and Ms Rastik if I'm honest though. But it was air-conditioned and served a call of nature if you know what I mean," he lied. Johnson had virtually no interest in what Chester Rogers had been doing for the past two hours so swiftly moved on when Nancy Rastik joined them in the small café on the ground floor of their hotel. All eight tables were in use, mainly it seemed by local workers grabbing a quick bite to eat, there was a real hubbub, complemented by the continual hissing and whirring of the coffee and juicing machines. The perfect backdrop for their conversation, thought Johnson.

Rogers was expecting to receive some pointers on Marco's performance but he soon realised his naivety. That was his job, his responsibility and the fact neither Rastik nor Johnson mentioned Marco until the very end of their meeting told him all he needed to know.

"POTUS has got Russia and China fully on board. You may not be aware that all three leaders, against the Japanese security forces' recommendation I might add, were in the theatre earlier."

Rogers forced a surprised but professionally understanding response. "That's great to hear sir," felt an appropriate response, versus telling him he'd spied them through the curtain.

"Now," continued Johnson, he was definitely the mouthpiece for this unlikely partnership with Nancy Rastik, they were such different personalities. "We're getting intel, some directly, some indirectly, that a number of other world leaders have gotten cold feet and withdrawn their support." Rogers wondered if this was a poetic licence too much to ask if they'd ever actually been on-side. He could see Johnson's face was getting flushed, as if he were withholding some serious stress.

"Most of Western Europe, the African Union and India have refused to sign up. Even the fucking Japs have deserted us. They're our fucking hosts for Christ's sake and half of this fucked-up city will be saved because of us." Johnson had let his guard down and both Rogers and Rastik knew it. Normally ice-cool, the pressure had mounted on Johnson in the past couple of weeks, mainly from his de facto boss, President Franks, and this moment was when it finally bubbled over. Franks had made the point to his wannabe successor that he'd secured the two most powerful nations on the planet, so Johnson needed to deliver more than just Brazil, Australia and a handful of Pacific Island nations. Rastik saw that her political partner needed time to gather himself by giving him a very telling, disappointed look and then taking lead of the conversation.

"Chester, talk to me about Senator Edward Gordon." Rogers suspected there was nothing he could tell her that she didn't already know but he guessed this wasn't the point of her question. Chester Rogers was well-connected and Rastik knew that, he'd played the game for a good few years so if word was out there, he'd know. She was right.

"I know he's a staunch believer in man-made climate change, that's an open secret I guess." Rastik stayed silent, prompting Rogers to continue. "I understand he's hijacked one of the participant's presentation slots on the IGA agenda, and English professor of Geology based in Berlin, goes by the name of Peter Masai although I'm told his actual name is Masel. He's on the programme pretty much at the same time as Marco, the original material was some kind of madcap, boundary-pushing geological apocalypse about the Earth collapsing in on itself."

"Sadly not that madcap," Rastik muttered to herself, loud enough for Rogers to notice and find a little surprising.

"Do carry on, what else?"

"Well," Rogers continued, "I understand Senator Gordon is pushing to use this slot to bang the drum on climate change, he's got some NASA scientist Louis Charles, or Charles Louis, some combination of first names on his books, plus a couple of other lower-level research scientists. I mean it's not totally unlikely that there'd be some lagging support for the previous scientific momentum before Project Green, huh?"

Rastik took that as a rhetorical question and followed it with one of her own. "Do you not think it's quite auspicious timing on his part?" Her face was so serious that the penny dropped for Chester Rogers. He'd send some loose rumours online about a counterattack from a high-profile US Senator, but he wasn't going to share this kind of tattle with his present company.

"Gordon's taken India, Africa and Japan, hasn't he?" blurted Rogers. "Plus, he has the UK and Germans physically on his team here in Tokyo."

Rastik added, deciding talking straight to Rogers would be the best way to secure his full commitment, "Let's be totally clear here Chester." Senator Johnson had gathered himself after his little emotional outburst, "We have to win hearts and minds on Wednesday, not just in the audience, or the global public, but those of the nations who have the influence to derail this plan. Project Green is the only solution to inspire and spark a much-needed economic revival. And shut down this climate change nonsense once and for all." And there it was, laid bare. The power-hungry Senator, whose future rested on the regeneration of global utilities and the Director of the US Environmental Bureau, whose primary role was to protect Mother Nature for future generations, but in reality, she was the biggest climate change denier of them all. Suddenly Chester Rogers felt this meeting was about to turn dark, very dark.

"We need to stop Gordon and Masai's little sideshow by whatever means it takes." Senator Johnson sounded to Rogers like some kind of movie bad guy and Rastik quickly intervened.

"What the Senator means," although there was very little doubt around interpreting his threat, "is that we need to undermine their message and persuade some of their high-profile but sadly misguided supporters to align with us. Ideally the result might be a postponement of their IGA session, you get so colourful with your language Nick." Rastik tried to smile as it gently ribbing the Senator, but it was clearly a scowl. They didn't really know Chester Rogers, other than they knew he appeared to have purchasable morals, but Rastik was the more cautionary of the two. Johnson, on the other hand, had gone past the character evaluation stage as far as he was concerned, and Rogers batted for their side and right now he needed allies who could make things happen. He viewed Rogers in the same way he viewed Marco Hernandez: they were both disposable assets, with a short lifespan of usage, to be discarded when that usefulness turned obsolete. If it came to it, and it wouldn't be the first time, Johnson knew people, bad undocumented people, who could make this kind of disposable asset simply disappear. Although it had crossed his mind that they probably weren't in Tokyo so he macabrely made a mental note to fly them out here and fast - he was desperate - they were so close to securing a global alliance that he'd be damned if another moral high ground grabbing Senator and a scientific fantasist would foil his destiny.

Rogers sensed the tension in the corner of the café, this was not what he was expecting at all. It didn't take a genius to predict that there might be someone presenting at an international geology conference who might be sympathetic to recently, widely, if not pervasively, held views on man-made climate change. Rogers had read up on Peter Masai and was a little disappointed that his and Marco's presentation overlapped. Masai had been originally billed as a bit of a quirky look at Armageddon but with a genuine scientific delivery. He hadn't really given it a second thought when he heard Senator Gordon had moved in on Masai's turf, he just assumed the Senator wanted the slot and maybe a generous contribution to the professor's department might just have persuaded him to give it up. But thinking about the detail of Masai's theory heightened Chester Rogers' feeling the that the clear and slightly worrying ire Senator Johnson was displaying suggested he thought Masai was perhaps still involved. Could his theory not be just crazy modelling, did the Senator think that this was what was making sea levels fall and, more critically, did Johnson also fear that to be the case? Was it that at the very same time Marco would be declaring an end to the climate emergency, that in the very next room, evidence was being presented directly contradicting him? And was this why Johnson had lost so many nations' support? Probably best not ask him this directly he counselled himself.

"Masai not presenting is unlikely to bring them

running back to us Nick." Rastik was clearly trying to placate the Senator and seemed oblivious to, or perhaps was deliberately ignoring, Rogers' presence. *Do they trust me and am I too deep in this?* Rogers' mind was whirring, *or am I disposable like Marco?* He felt himself tense up.

"No," Johnson retorted assertively, "but their message will be significantly weakened without the amplification the conference will generate, ask Rogers, he'll tell you that." Rogers felt this was a good time to side with the Senator so nodded with conviction. "Nancy, I need you to divert all your attention to lobbying Africa and India through whatever channels you see fit, throw POTUS' name in there, that usually gets you an audience. I'll make a few calls myself, work on that conference postponement," he said with sinister casualness.

He then turned to Chester Rogers, who hadn't really known where to look and now feared he was about to be given a new role in this ever-evolving saga. "You, Rogers, need to keep Hernandez locked away for the next thirty-six hours, you have to make that presentation an oratory masterpiece." Rogers nodded again. His immediate thought was wondering where the hell Marco was right now after he told him to take some time and then questioned himself whether that meant cancelling their sushi lunch, the one thing he was genuinely looking forward to on this crazy trip. Surely the Senator was being extreme. If Rogers knew where Marco was that'd be fine, he convinced himself.

He also didn't need much convincing that this was his cue to leave. He stood up, waited a second to check if there were further instructions, then pushed his coffee cup into the centre of the table in a 'I'm leaving' kind of motion and headed to the exit. As he did so he was sure he heard Nancy Rastik almost hiss at the Senator, "You're not killing the professor, Nick." *Was it a question, was it a statement?* Either way, Chester Rogers didn't break stride, he figured his best course of action right now was to keep walking and locate Marco Hernandez as soon as possible.

43

"You look like a man who could do with more than a cup of coffee Chester," a strangely familiar voice that took Rogers a moment to realise was real and not in a figment of his imagination as he waited for the subway back towards where he hoped he'd find Marco. He turned his head toward the voice, half expecting no one to be there but true enough, there was a face he recognised, and not one he was pretty sure Senator Johnson had sent to kill him.

"Oh my god Harpinder, what in Christ's name are you doing here?"

"Bit jumpy aren't we Cheese? Not surprised after meeting those two."

"What the hell Harpinder, are you stalking me?"

"Not you silly, Rastik and Johnson. I'm working a lead so thought I'd hang out near their hotel and see if anything interesting might happen, then you turned up and I figured it'd be easier to ask you about your conversation than them." She beamed an affectionate smile at her old friend; he looked like he needed treating gently.

"OK Harpinder, there's a lot to take in, can we just get out of here so I can gather my thoughts, then you can tell me why you're tailing the Senator and Director."

"Of course, Cheese," she replied warmly, and they both stepped on the train together and sat in total silence for eight stops until Rogers simply said 'here,' and they both alighted the carriage and made their way out into the comparably fresh air of the city.

Harpinder didn't know Chester Rogers was involved in Project Green and she'd only seen him a couple of times in the several years since they both took the same New Media and Technology course at a Washington University offshoot college. Harpinder to sharpen her journalistic techniques, Rogers to learn the dark arts of social media persuasion, or 'manipulation' as Harpinder would describe it, although the course used the term 'positive power' as opposed to 'dark arts'. But no one was fooled. The whole premise of the course was underscored by the fact that the internet had made the world smaller, meaning you could access virtually the whole population from your smart device. Despite this training, Harpinder, and Rogers too, firmly believed in the power of actual human interaction if you really wanted to know something or someone. Which is why she wanted to see with her own eyes what Rastik and Johnson were up to in Tokyo, and this plan had certainly paid off the moment she saw Chester Rogers walk into that café and sit down with them. Now Rogers sat next to her, nursing a cold beer in a little side street izakaya, waiting for Harpinder Tarkowski to explain to him why she was watching him, and what she wanted. Acknowledging it was on her to kick-off, but without giving too much away, her assumption was his allegiances lay with Rastik and Johnson and she was nominally siding with Jane and Senator Gordon, given what she'd discovered to date.

"I'm covering the IGA conference Cheese," she was one of the very few who actually called him this still. "I know the ICCS are going to announce a significant breakthrough in the war against climate change with Marco Hernandez taking that lead. I know Nancy Rastik and Senator Nick Johnson are the driving forces behind the ICCS and Project Green, and that it has backing at the very highest level in the US government and that Russia, China, Brazil and Australia are also on board at an equivalent level. I know Senator Johnson has been lobbying global utility conglomerates and plans to reignite the world economy through a new industrial revolution, putting him in a very strong position to run for the oval office. I know sea level data is at the heart of the ICCS plan, evidenced one assumes by Rastik herself and her motivation appears personal rather than professional. I know Marco Hernadez is way out of his depth, which is where I suspect you come in Chester. Does that strike a chord with you, Cheese?"

Chester Rogers wasn't really sure how to respond, it appeared Harpinder was pretty well-informed and lying was never a good tactic to a journalist, never mind one he'd call a friend. But he didn't know if she could be trusted, what else did she know or was she fishing for more? This was usually his speciality, getting out of tricky questions with artistically constructed answers but he'd been knocked off his game by his threatening meeting with Senator Johnson in particular and he was thankful for the restorative nectar that was calming his nerves and his mind. It was strange how the slight fuzz of alcohol can clear the mind.

"Harpinder you're right," he resolved there'd be no harm confirming her statements. "I have been coaching Marco and to be fair to him, he's come in leaps and bounds and will do a pretty polished job up there. Fair play to the guy, he's not exactly got a résumé packed with public speaking engagements, but he gets it and feels part of it, I'm sure you also know some of his own work is in the presentation."

Harpinder nodded, then demonstrated how much she did know. "Yes, his Amazon basin research, under the stewardship of Professor Masai in Mexico City." She wanted to test how much her old friend had been briefed and given his fairly poor attempt to look like he knew, his face screamed that this was news to him, his eyes flickered as he frantically tried to join the dots.

So Masai knows Hernandez, they were colleagues… his brain mulled this in the milliseconds he had to respond, knowing it was important but not sure what it really meant. "Of course, he's really proud of his work and I think it brings some real ownership to the message if it's delivered by…"

Harpinder finished his sentence with a slightly sarcastic grin on her face, "…the Chief Scientific Advisor to Planet Earth. That one of yours, Cheese?" He went red. What didn't she know? And who else knew and how much? He felt under pressure, but the beer was renewing his confidence.

"Harpinder, you appear to be even more invested in this than I am, my role here is to ensure our mutual Mexican friend Marco delivers a seamless performance the day after tomorrow, answers a few questions, then once he's walked off stage, we shake hands, and my job is complete."

"Are Nancy Rastik and Johnson happy with Marco? They certainly didn't look happy Cheese." Again, she noticed his eyes flickering, he looked uncomfortable.

"What is it that you want Harpinder?" He asked abruptly, her turn to be interrogated. The way Chester Rogers had left the café earlier suggested to Harpinder that he was on the receiving end of the Senator's wrath or at least he wasn't as wrapped up in this saga as she'd initially feared. Given their relationship, she decided to come clean, pretty much, about her role in the hope that Rogers might just do the same. She knew it was a gamble but one worth taking. And she was right.

Harpinder walked Chester Rogers through her own journey from her original meeting with Jane Henderson, her outsourced interview with Marco's mother in Mexico, research into both Senators' motivations and latterly her global media trawl and contact strategy. She let Rogers fill in his own gaps.

"So Gordon's gonna hijack the conference with a counter attack on Rastik and Johnson. Whilst Marco is on stage. They must have the support of Africa, India, Japan and the EU, oh my god, that's why Johnson was raging. Masai's going to counter-evidence the sea level fall with his sinkhole, mantle crushing theory thing." Harpinder could see Rogers piecing it all together. "And Johnson needs more than just Russia and China to get what he wants. Presumably one of them is right and one of them is wrong… they both can't be right, or can they? They can both be wrong, that's for sure. Man this is big. But surely the ICCS have credible evidence, not just because of Marco, but they've got the Director of the US Environmental Agency at the head table. She's literally the Queen Bee when it comes to this stuff surely?" Rogers was challenging his own thinking and Harpinder was with him.

"You'd think so Cheese, and I agree she's the one part of this whole messy situation I can't, to be honest, we can't square off. I still can't quite believe she'll be one of the public faces of this movement, feels to me like she's a cerebral sponsor, which makes her role even more intriguing." Rogers had nothing more to say on Rastik, she was clearly a strong ally of the Senator, but he came across as the driving force behind the whole thing, it was almost as if she'd been involved but left no prints so could just evaporate and plead ignorance.

However, it was Johnson that Rogers was most concerned about, and he found himself processing that out loud, "So that's why Johnson wants to stop the professor's presentation then..." he mumbled but clearly loud enough for Harpinder to jolt into action.

"Say that again Cheese."

44

A couple of hours after Senator Gordon had told them to stand down, Jeff, Pete, Elaine and Jane had been resolutely compliant and had started to order a selection of snacks to accompany their beers. None of them could decipher kanji so they ordered by picture on the menu, not knowing what may arrive, or what part of which animal or vegetable it might be.

"All part of the Tokyo experience, like a buffet lucky dip," smiled Pete. He was happy that the changes he and Louis Charles had made to his presentation did not change the fundamentals of what he'd set out to discuss but the output and conclusion were markedly different. Pete's style was not to work off a script, he preferred to let the words come out in as natural a way as possible, but his brain was working overtime in the background to give him access to the right words at the right time. Louis has added a few videos and animations for which Pete had needed to learn some of the critical data, but he'd promised he'd join him on stage to answer any questions which allowed Pete to focus on delivery and tone, rather than detailed content.

He was enjoying getting to know Jane too, partly because she had a vast and very real-world grasp of environmental issues that complemented Pete's world view perfectly, but also because she was a window on Jeff, who Pete hadn't seen much of for several years, much to his growing frustration. It had been great to have him around again. They flitted between deep and meaningful conversations about the future of Planet Earth and the end of humanity, whilst punctuating them with novelty anecdotes about their mutual friend, who sat just a couple of feet away, himself engrossed in conversation. There had been an obvious tension in the air when Jeff and Elaine first met again after all those years and although it had settled down, a couple of beers, a dark bar, finally some level of privacy and the looming threat of the end of the world, all contributed to them finally addressing their relationship.

"I can't believe you got married Elaine; I can't believe you are married in fact."

"Barely," replied Elaine truthfully. "It kind of just happened, I think we just fell into it really, we fit pretty well together, on paper at least. I wonder if Mark just wanted a companion to go round the world with him, someone to come home to after week-long trips. It wasn't all bad, just didn't have the passion of well, you know…" They both knew she was talking about her and Jeff's intense college relationship. "Have you been with anyone Jeff, you know long-term, are you now?" she probed.

"Not really Elaine, and before you ask, no not Jane, she's just a great friend and much needed supportive colleague in that order." That ticked one thing off Elaine's list anyway. "I mean, don't get me wrong, there have been women over the years but nothing that's stuck."

"I'm sure you're quite the player in Washington DC, they must think you're James Bond over there," she said with a smile.

"Maybe Bond's less active brother Elaine, sadly more

Boris than Bond."

"Whatever works for you Jeff, it didn't hold you back in uni did it?"

Jeff had never been the athlete-type but he'd managed to keep hold of his shape, just, but women found him attractive more with his wit and subtle intelligence than his looks, he wasn't an ugly man but that didn't make him a head-turner. He'd worked out in his teenage years that he'd need to talk girls into sleeping with him because he sure wasn't going to dance or simply smile his way there. He'd always thought Elaine was beautiful and couldn't get his head around why this chap Mark would ever let her slip through his fingers. He'd never really figured out why he himself did the same all those years ago, having gone home after graduating, he broke off contact. Over the years of painful reflection, he'd convinced himself it was for the best but really, he didn't think he was good enough for her and the fact they had drifted apart compounded this insecurity, one that Elaine would entirely disagree with, were it to surface.

For her, at the time she felt young, she was young of course with her whole life ahead of her and it wasn't even as if Jeff was stifling her, holding her back or being possessive, but she thought she should go off into the big wide world alone. But it wasn't long before she realised her mistake, sadly long enough that she felt she couldn't go back to him, assuming incorrectly that he'd moved on. Then Mark appeared in her life, a more serious, stable version of Jeff. She romanticised her relationship and persuaded herself, and indeed Mark, that their future would be a married one. Less of a whirlwind than a gentle breeze of a courtship. She missed the spark, that feeling of life, simply laughing out loud that were all replaced by the practical reliability Mark brought to their liaison. Unlike Jeff, she'd discovered nutrition and had looked after herself in the intervening years, she still fit the same clothes she'd worn at university, much to the jealous annoyance of her age group peers, but years of physical insecurities built from Mark rarely telling her he found her attractive made her wonder what Jeff thought these days. She didn't have long to wonder before Jeff made his views characteristically clear.

"Elaine, you are still the most beautiful girl in the city," and stretched his hand across the table clasping hers.

"Enjoying the beers, are we, Jeff?" she giggled awkwardly and sheepishly, not really knowing how to react. Their situation, holed up in a dark corner of a Tokyo bar, drinking partly to forget, partly to remember, contemplating the end of days, reminded Elaine of those pacts friends make if neither of them has found a partner by the time they're forty then they agree to get married. They hadn't made that pact, and despite their separation all those years, the comforting familiarity they'd rekindled made Elaine think she could see her and Jeff living out however long they had, together.

"The beers and the company, Elaine. I've missed this, truly missed this, missed you. I regret so much the way it ended between us."

Elaine stopped him. "Don't regret Jeff, it was both of

us and if it's one thing I've learned, it's that regret is unhealthy. I spent too long looking back and trying to make the best of a bad situation, wishing it would change by itself, but you must make things happen and take opportunities when it comes along. I'm not trying to live in the past Jeff, or even recreate it, but you have to admit this is pretty close to what we dreamed would happen way back then?"

Jeff smiled in agreement, "You mean us together, not just you and I, but the three of us on a global stage sharing one of Pete's mind-boggling geo-theories with the fate of the world hanging by a thread?" They had indeed prophesied this many times, usually after a few more beers than Jeff had had today, but he had to admit this was an unerring manifestation of those early dreams. "If only it wasn't so apocalyptic," Jeff felt he needed to add, as if he had to clarify the end of the world was a bad thing.

"Yeah true, I always pictured us doing the Everest theory but no, we have to front up the universe's greatest drought instead, boo hiss."

Their conversation was punctured by Jane, who suddenly appeared at their table then involuntarily exclaimed, "Oh wow, you're holding hands, must ask about that later." which made both Jeff and Elaine immediately pull back their arms, neither had clocked they'd been intertwined this whole time.

"But we've got stuff to deal with." Pete had also joined them and both he and Jane squeezed around the table as Jane shared the message she'd just received.

"Harpinder Tarkowski is in Tokyo and had been monitoring Rastik and Johnson when she spotted a PR guy she knows well called Chester Rogers. He's been recruited to manage Marco Hernandez through this whole presenting to the world thing on Wednesday, you know, polish him up, get him ready for press questions." They all nodded, waiting for the inevitable twist. "Sounds like Rogers is pretty neutral in the whole thing, almost deliberately avoiding asking any deep questions, but he did say Senator Johnson is raging about Gordon's involvement and they know about our counter-attack strategy, mainly because some of Johnson's key international partners have deserted him in favour of Gordon."

Pete jumped in, "Presumably Africa, India and Japan are the biggest of those fish?"

"Correct, Pete," Jane continued. "She told me Senator Johnson plans to stop us, stop you Pete, from presenting on Wednesday and this didn't sound like an 'unplugging your microphone' kind of threat, it was pretty sinister. Bear in mind who Johnson is, who he wants to be and crucially, who he's answering to right now. For Marco's dress rehearsal earlier, check out who was in the auditorium."

"POTUS?" queried Pete expectantly.

"And some," Jane replied. "Both Presidents Guo and Zarkov were there too, like some kind of band of brothers according to Rogers."

"No wonder Johnson's feeling the pressure," Jeff almost sounded sympathetic. "Where's this Rogers guy now? Has he officially defected?"

"I don't think he needs to Jeff; I get the feeling his role is just ensuring Marco gets on stage and is able to deliver his speech and then expects to not hear from Rastik or Johnson again, but let's ask Harpinder when she gets here."

"Have you told Gordon?" Elaine asked Jane.

"I messaged him, he said to wait for Harpinder to see if she's got more intel to share then to get ourselves back to the hotel and call him once we're there. Harpinder should be with us in about thirty minutes so let's order some proper food, just in case this turns into a longer night than we'd planned. Sorry Jeff, might make sense to hold off on the beers, maybe you can be in charge of ordering the food."

45

Chester Rogers' mind was whirring, on the one hand he felt a huge weight off his shoulders having talked to Harpinder about Johnson's ranting but equally he felt guilt, like he'd cheated on Rastik and the Senator. He now regretted not just telling Marco to hole up in his hotel room, he didn't want to think about what would happen to him if Johnson wanted to see them both and he didn't know where Marco was. He had visions of Marco, tanked up on sake and whisky, holding court in an expat bar in Roppongi, talking to a selection of the world's media about Project Green and how he was saving the world. What if right now, there's a live Twitter stream of Marco Hernandez drunkenly rambling about the US president watching his practice run and God knows what else? Rogers knew he was spiralling, and he was annoyed at himself for losing control and he also knew finding Marco and babysitting him was the only antidote. He got out his phone and scrolled to Marco's contact, praying he'd answer and be close by. No answer as the trills just rang out. *No message,* thought Rogers, but he didn't want to spook him. *I'll try again, if he's had a few it may take a few buzzes in his pocket for him to realise.*

This time, after three rings, a voice connected them. "Mr Rogers, is everything OK, how can I help?" There was no obvious slurring or background bar sounds.

"Marco where are you?" asked Rogers directly, slightly more directly than he ideally wanted to sound.

"I'm in my hotel room like you suggested. I was tired

after today, so I ordered room service and a movie. Is there a problem, it sounds urgent?" Chester Rogers quietly punched the air in triumph, from worst case scenario to best case in one sentence and he eased up with Marco instantly.

"Oh, sorry Marco, I've had a busy afternoon, so I just wanted to check in with you, but it sounds like you're all sorted."

"Oh yes thank you, although I did go a bit overboard with the room service. I hope that won't be an issue?" As far as Rogers was concerned, Marco could order room service for the whole floor and Senator Johnson wouldn't bat an eyelid.

"Of course, Marco, you deserve it. Rest up and I'll join you for breakfast at 9am, just stay in your hotel on the off chance I do need you, OK?" *Nicely played*, he thought as Marco happily agreed and finished their call. Chester Rogers thought the idea of room service and a movie was just the ticket right now and called a taxi to take him directly back to his hotel.

46

Harpinder Tarkowski arrived true to Jane's prediction half an hour later and declined the offer of food, which had also arrived and was now soaking up some of the Sapporo the team had been enjoying. After brief introductions, Harpinder confirmed in person what she'd commented to Jane about her monitoring Johnson and Rastik, and her subsequent catch up with PR-man Chester Rogers. "I'm pretty sure Chester is just a pawn in this whole thing, as is Marco Hernandez. I strongly suspect Hernandez is a single-use mouthpiece and we'll not see or hear much from him after this."

"Agreed," Pete spoke on behalf of the group.

"Chester was pretty wound up by Johnson and it's not as if it were directed at him even, he'd just misread the situation and the significance of it all. To be fair, he'd been focusing pretty single mindedly on Hernandez rather than the wider geo-political issues at stake here. But the way he said Johnson was talking so coldly and remotely about stopping your presentation Professor, and Rastik's reaction to it, makes me think you, of all of you perhaps, could be in danger. Not meaning to disrespect you all but I imagine for a power-hungry and politically desperate heavyweight like Senator Johnson, you guys are very disposable. Especially if he thinks you've got any kind of momentum to stop his plans."

"Jesus wept," was all Jeff could muster, and even Pete was silent.

Jane spoke up, "Does that mean Senator Gordon is in danger too Harpinder? And the others, I'm thinking of Rose and Kelly, maybe even Louis Charles. Surely he wouldn't go after Penny Norton or Klaus Jurgensen? Oh no, what about Michelle?" Panic was clear in Jane's voice now as it dawned on her that her mentor was involved too.

"Well, you're incredibly selfless as always Jane, thinking of others before yourself." If she were honest, it hadn't really registered that Senator Johnson would even know who she was or what role she had but as she thought about it, she figured he'd have a massive network of people, probably infiltrating The Bureau where she worked, likely via Rastik.

"Right," she said decisively, "I'll call the Senator!"

"Johnson or Gordon?" Jeff joked sarcastically.

"Hilarious Jeff, although Johnson may be listening in to my calls of course," she responded, also joking, but Harpinder cut them back down.

"It's not beyond possibility Jane, have you got a secure connection for Gordon?" Jane realised Harpinder wasn't kidding. "Message him to expect a call from an unknown number and use this burner phone." Harpinder reached into her bag and pulled out a cheap Nokia.

"Cool," whispered Jeff.

"All part of a journalist's toolkit Jeff, I'm no spy."

"Well Harpinder, you're behaving like one and it's pretty awesome," Jane said enthusiastically, temporarily forgetting she was about to speak to one of the most influential politicians in the US about potential threats to life.

As with most of her interactions with the Senator, her call with him was concise, informative and action oriented. He listened respectfully and calmly to Jane, allowing her to explain what she'd learned from Harpinder. Gordon thanked her and gave her a set of clear instructions. She felt this whole threat thing wasn't a surprise to him, but he wasn't the type of character to let emotions derail him, however grave the situation might appear. Within ten minutes, she was back with the group again, all waiting on tenterhooks.

To everyone but Jeff, Jane looked composed and serene as she approached them, but he could tell she was putting a front on and made sure when his eyes met hers, he gave the best, 'I know something's happened and you're trying to protect us' smile. She responded with a miniscule nod and pursing of the lips, it gave her much needed strength, knowing Jeff had her back.

"Senator Gordon has offered us an out. And it's only fair we take a moment to consider the circumstances, and anyone can opt to walk away, no questions asked." No one moved, just as Jane expected, so she continued, "The Senator's view is that we proceed with over-caution." Sometimes Jane decided it was OK to make up a word if it was the best way for her to explain something. "He told me that Johnson has a yet unproven record of making people disappear." If they weren't paying attention before, they certainly were now. "And also, some fairly widely recognised intimidation tactics. His sources corroborate our view that he's out to sabotage or prevent Peter from taking the stage on Wednesday and has arranged for a security detail to accompany us back to the hotel, to collect our stuff and head to a new accommodation. Gordon is the chillest person I've ever met but not this time, he sounded genuinely fearful for us and asked me to ask you, having explained all of this, if you now want to pull out. He doesn't trust Johnson one jot, the guy is inches away from his destiny, inheriting the Oval Office, on the cusp of global economic alliance and along we come and scupper him on the home straight."

"But Jane, surely if not us, then someone else would be the counter for this climate change reversal madness?" Everyone nodded at Elaine's logical question, and continued to nod as Jane closed that one off.

"Indeed Elaine, but that doesn't change the fact that it's us in the middle of this. So, assuming we're all still in," firm nods all round, "let's map out the next thirty-six hours and stay alert for every eventuality. Harpinder, entirely your call but Senator Gordon has offered to include you in our new location under protection."

"I'll take it. I'll go back and get my stuff and meet you there, share with me the location when you have it."

Jane instructed to Jeff and Elaine, "You two are on hotel duty," and with a sly grin followed up with, "which I suspect won't be an issue for you both." She then looked across at the professor, "Peter, we've got a date with Senator Gordon." Pete looked up, alert, sensing there was more to come, and he was right. "The Senator wants us to work with

Louis Charles, Penny Norton and the UK Prime Minister."

"Wow he really does have friends in high places, I guess he can't really go to President Franks can he?" Jeff piped up, confirming everyone's thoughts that this was a deeply political situation.

"Literally," continued Jane, "Gordon and Prime Minister Keeble were at Oxford together so there's clearly a relationship there but that to one side, it seems the Prime Minister is the next best thing to the president, she's a lead vehicle in the alliance against Senator Johnson's proposal, a.k.a. the voice of reason."

"I won't lie," Peter opened up, "I'm getting a strong sense of imposter syndrome here and I think it's worth clarifying as much for myself as anyone else, my working assumption is the governmental and Bureaucratic leaders we are now mixing with have had their views on climate change long before my paper on mantle disintegration. And if anything, and even this might be overplaying it, I am at most a catalyst for action or more probably an excuse for intervention and I happened to have a slot at the IGA. If the world was making decisions based on my theories, we'd have some pretty outlandish policies on managing a ten-mile-high Everest, or reformation of Pangea throwing political bodies into chaos."

Jane was the first to react. "Your humility is refreshing but remember what Louis Charles said, having modelled your theory to the nth degree, you may not be the reason for all the debate, but you have provided the scientific thinking and evidence to establish likely cause and in the process you, and you alone, may have destroyed Senator Johnson's path to ultimate power."

"No wonder he's pissed off with you Pete, I'd want you dead if you did that to me."

"Sensitive as ever, Jeff." Elaine scolded him as if she were his exasperated wife, a reaction that didn't go unnoticed.

"Jeff's right, if indeed I'm in any way responsible for derailing Johnson's power assault, or just using me as someone to blame, either way it's suboptimal. Even if I am finding it hard to detach myself from all the moving parts here, maybe a quiet sit down with a global leader will actually help." He added sarcastically.

"I wonder if you might have a representation from Brazil there too," interjected Harpinder, who had been scrolling through her phone.

"I doubt that Harpinder, Brazil are firmly in Johnson and Rastik's camp." Jane immediately regretted publicly correcting Harpinder as if she was so uninformed and tried to make amends, "Why do you say that? What's happened?"

"Twitter is reporting a massive landslide in the heart of the country." A moment of confusion amongst the group because landslides in Brazil were quite frequent and that was the pervading but unspoken reaction in the bar. "When I say landslide, it seems it's more of a sinkhole, but bear with me, reports are pretty frantic." The group all noticed Harpinder's hands were shaking, as was her voice. "Let me just read this from a Brazilian journalist I follow. Reports are coming in from the outskirts of Manaus - that's pretty central if you're not familiar - that the majority of the city and its two million residents have been swallowed up in the world's biggest ever land collapse. No word yet from the government but local sources say mass panic has hit the surrounding area."

Pete's immediate reaction summed up the thoughts of the other geologists. "Brazil is one of the few massive countries that sits entirely within tectonic boundaries so conventional earthquakes are out of the question, which leads me to believe…" he trailed off as if realising the significance of what he was about to say, to the extent that he didn't actually get to say it because Jeff finished off his sentence.

"The Earth collapsed just like you've been saying Pete. It's been happening under the oceans but now it's hit a major landmass. Christ almighty."

"Are you certain Harpinder?" Jane was clutching at straws, "Twitter can report and misreport all kinds of rubbish."

"There's your answer." Harpinder pointed at the TV in the corner of the Izakaya, above the main bar. There was no actual footage yet but instead a clear image of Brazil with Manaus highlighted and a lot of large Japanese characters saying goodness knows what but for Pete, Harpinder and the rest, it confirmed something major had happened in South America.

"Christ almighty!" Jeff cussed again and a sense of shock and intense reality reverberated through the group.

"I'll keep an eye on developments in Brazil," Harpinder was ice-cool and the first to speak. "You guys need clear heads for your meeting with the Senator and UK PM, I'll update you before you go in, although I'd be amazed if they don't have the intel." And with that, Harpinder grabbed her backpack and scuttled out of the bar into the Tokyo night, leaving the others to contemplate the unfolding disaster in Brazil and wider ramifications.

A message popped up on Jane's phone. "It's from Gordon," she shared, "it looks like the professor's worst-case timeline is underway. Pray for them. My team should be with you imminently, code name Hendo." As Jane finished reading the Senator's brief message to the team, a couple of large, suited bodyguard types entered the izakaya. Without thinking, Jane had expected burly American FBI/bouncer type thick set men but checked herself as the men with local Japanese servicemen, the taller of the two approached them, bowed, and uttered the word "Hendo".

47

Pete, Jane, Jeff and Elaine sat in contemplative silence as the jet-black Lexus smoothly traversed the illuminated streets of downtown Tokyo, past locals going about their business, likely unaware yet of the dramatic events unfolding beneath the feet of their Brazilian cousins. Japan would share their mourning, the two countries had historical links dating back hundreds of years to the first Portuguese explorers. In fact, the largest Japanese community outside Japan is in Brazil, over two million settled there and vice versa, there are over a quarter of a million people with Brazilian ancestry living in Japan. The Manaus disaster was going to hit both countries hard, at least it would if it were the sole tragedy to befall the world that week.

Elaine was the first to break the silence and she reflected the others' thoughts to a tee. "Is this the beginning of the end?" she spoke quietly and deliberately. "Or is it a random, one in a billion sinkhole that has nothing to do with Pete's theory?" Elaine felt it needed to be said, although none of them were in any doubt the answer lay firmly in between these options.

"I suspect Louis Charles will be able to help with that when you guys see him later." Jeff suggested. "Once they reprogrammed their systems with the Masai Theory," he nodded, smiling at his friend Peter, "they may even have been able to predict the whole Brazilian…" he was struggling for the right word, "well, hole." He wasn't trying to make a joke, far from it. It was just difficult to know how to refer to something as geologically unprecedented as an entire region collapsing in on itself. "Although I suspect it'll be a bit like earthquakes and volcanoes, the data they provide in hindsight is a perfect indication of what was happening, problem is you need them to happen before you can use the data to predict them."

"So, you're saying Louis Charles will be able to tell us that a massive hole has appeared in Brazil, but really accurately?" Jane quizzed him, unsure yet of his point.

"Yep, that's my bet. But what it may do is provide new and much needed data and geological, seismic, God knows what other kinds of readings that can be cross-referenced with other global information which could pinpoint future epicentres."

"Good summary Jeff, we might make a scientist out of you yet," smiled Pete across the back seats of the car. "We've got so little to go on until we get the full picture from Charles or elsewhere. But it could, and I say 'could' lightly, explain what's been going on under the sea when we all thought it was the tectonic boundaries the water was seeping through. The whole tectonic make-up may have become fractured for all we know, like sea ice as it melts. But we can throw conjecture around as much as we like, and believe me, that's my speciality, but for the purposes of the next few hours I'll be listening and answering whatever questions are thrown at me."

"You'll do great Pete, you both will." Elaine spoke genuinely from the heart and head. "If I were a world leader looking for great people to guide me, I'd be pretty happy if you and Jane walked into the room." Jane was thankful for the lack of light in the car as she knew she was blushing. She had worried that Elaine's arrival might alienate her as a female but she scolded herself of that thought with Elaine's refreshing passionate support for her and Pete. Any further deep reflections would have to wait as the car pulled up in front of their hotel. Jeff instinctively tried to open the door but found it locked.

"They know enough about you to use the child lock," laughed Jane, breaking the previously mounting tension.

Once the group were freed from the back of the car by the taller of the men who had escorted them from the izakaya, they entered the lobby, in which there were already a number of local police present. As they approached the lift, a member of the hotel reception team scampered across, clearly recognising their guests and hastily bowed before announcing, "Sir, madam, your delivery was taken up to your rooms, thank you sir, madam, have a good evening." The two security men tensed up noticeably and spoke urgently in Japanese to the receptionist. The fact the receptionist looked at her watch led the group to assume she'd been asked when the delivery was made. Plus, all of them were wondering what the delivery was, and judging from the security guard's reaction, they guessed it wasn't flowers and chocolates.

"When we exit the elevator, stay behind us." There was a commanding and imposing directive from the thicker set Japanese guard with totally unnecessary shades on as if he were auditioning for a Tokyo remake of The Matrix, but if he was going to protect them, Jeff conceded the fact he was wearing sunglasses might be a small price to pay for his safety and got over himself. Second, third, fourth, fifth floor, the elevator doors opened, the tall guy motioned to his mate to step out. Rather alarmingly for the group, they had their handguns out now. *This has escalated fast,* thought Jane, *but better safe than sorry.* The bigger guard held the door open with his foot as his colleague confirmed the corridor to be clear, so they all headed out onto the carpeted floor. Pete's room was first, he passed his key card to the agent who raised his finger to his lips, as far as Pete was concerned, entirely unnecessarily. Faced with a couple of gun-wielding security men provided by a high-ranking Senator to protect you from a power-crazy president-seeking wannabee who wouldn't blink twice at the thought of removing a blockage whatever the cost, Pete's first and only thought was to be quiet and follow instructions so he was very willingly compliant. The key slid into the door slot, a knowing click telling them it was unlocked and a slow push as the door swung open into the hotel room, which Pete was momentarily happy he'd kept tidy, contrary to his normal scattergun approach to clothes arranging. That tidy illusion was very quickly shattered as once the door was fully open, the security guard lowered his gun in a 'we got here too late' kind of motion, his shoulders visibly slumped. As they all stepped forward to peer into Pete's room, it became obvious it had been fully and mercilessly trashed.

Jane reacted first, with more clarity than even she expected. "Was there anything here that whoever did this could have got hold of?"

Pete replied, equally calmly. "We're in no doubt this is on the orders of Johnson, right?" he asked rhetorically. "No thankfully not, do any of us have anything left in our rooms which may be of material use to the Senator?" It then dawned on each of them that most likely their rooms would be in a similar state too.

DROUGHT

"No." they all chimed in unison.

"Jane, best let Harpinder know to be extra vigilant."

"Already on it, message delivered but not yet read."

"OK, let us know when you hear from her."

Jeff was already heading out of Pete's room, anxious to see if his own room had been given similar treatment. Ten minutes later they were all back in Pete's room, each of them fully packed having had their personal items upturned and strewn across the floor indiscriminately yet ultimately frustratingly for the perpetrator.

"I assume they were after this," Pete declared, holding his laptop tight to his chest. "Glad I didn't leave my passport in the safe too." he chuckled jokingly, and all eyes directed towards the broken wardrobe and remains of the casing that previously housed the hotel room safe. "They'll be bitterly disappointed when they break into it. I was planning to use it so I set a code, promptly forgot the code and just shut the door."

"OK, you have everything?" Direct but not aggressive from the taller of two Japanese security guards. "You two," pointing at Elaine and Jeff, "your car is waiting out front, Ishihashi-san will take you," indicating his partner who beckoned them both to follow him out.

"Good luck this evening," Elaine spoke for them both. "Let us know how you get on with, well you know, and let us know Harpinder is OK, maybe she'll be at wherever we're going to now."

"Thank you, Elaine, yeah I hope so, I've not heard from her yet and she's not obviously read my message and she didn't pick up when I called." Jane sounded worried, and she was. If they'd known about the hotel room invasion, she would never have let Harpinder go on her own.

As if reminding Jane she had somewhere pretty important to be, the tall security man focused her again. "Now we go."

As they snaked through the busy streets of Shinjuku, it felt to Pete like being in an arcade game, high rises on both sides, wall-to-wall neon, even in the tinted windowed car it was an attack on the senses. He was doing his best to gather himself before this unprecedented meeting and couldn't help playing back that conversation with his mother that maybe he should focus on something more positive than the end of the world. *Oh, the irony*, he smiled wryly to himself, wondering whether she had seen the Brazil land collapse and linked it to her son's theory. There's one thing predicting the physical crumbling of the Earth, quite another being there when it actually happens. He couldn't get his head around what noise and collateral damage several square kilometres of land would cause as it folded in on itself, taking every single non-flying entity down with it. He also wished he had a god to pray to that this would be an isolated occurrence, that maybe he was wrong, and Louis Charles would confirm that in a few minutes' time.

He was brought back to focus by a shrill gasp from Jane whose face froze in shock. No words were needed. She just passed her phone to Pete, who could see there was a video ready to play. It was Harpinder, her mouth gagged shut, arms and legs tied to a wooden chair on which she was perched. A plain background gave little away as to her location. There was no sound on the video, just a caption which appeared across the bottom which chillingly read: *When Professor Masai fails to show at the IGA conference, she will be freed.* Jane was in bits. She felt responsible.

"You weren't to know Jane, this is not on you, if anything, it's on me." Pete tried to comfort her, knowing little could help. Even less so given the fact the car had pulled up at the Park Hyatt, where they assumed the UK Prime Minister was staying. Pete didn't know Harpinder well at all so naturally found it easier to detach himself from the enormity of the hostage situation. "We'll make Senator Gordon aware of this immediately Jane, he's more likely to know what to do, or at least know who to call."

"Yes, Pete I agree." Jane's voice was shaky at best. "But I'm out of my depth here Peter, I'm about to meet the fucking Prime Minister of Britain, my hotel room's been trashed, my friend's being held hostage and I feel weirdly responsible for the deaths of two million Brazilians."

"Jane, in the short time I've known you, I've been so impressed with the way you carry yourself and deal with all this craziness, if anyone can find a way through this, I think it's you." Pete meant every word; he could see why Jeff was so equally fond and respectful of Jane but now it was his turn to step up and shoulder some of the burden whilst she processed the horror of Harpinder's situation. "Give me your phone, I'll take the lead with Gordon, you take your time, if you want to wait here, I'm sure that'll be well understood." He suspected the offer of backing out might spur her into action and he was right, she was having none of it. With a deep breath she gathered herself, sat bolt upright and almost leapt from the car with such purpose, Pete was almost left behind.

48

Senator Gordon was in the lobby waiting for them with a solemn look on his face. "Perhaps he already knows about Harpinder," whispered Jane as they approached him.

"Jane, Professor."

"Senator." It was a very formal interaction; it was clear something was troubling the statesman.

"Please walk with me, we'll have company but please try to ignore them," he nodded towards a couple of miked-up, armed security escorts who looked ready for action if anyone so much as coughed in the general direction of the Senator. He directed them to a corridor to the left of the marble reception desk which seemingly led to the main conference rooms. Once through the first set of doors, Pete reached for Jane's phone to share the video of poor Harpinder, but the Senator spoke first. "I heard about your rooms, I'm sorry this situation has taken a turn for the worse. Rose and Kelly have been kidnapped I'm afraid and are being held in an undisclosed and unknown location against their will."

"Oh my god," Jane couldn't hold it in. "Them too." Gordon gave her a quizzical look, to which Peter responded by passing him the video of Harpinder tied and gagged.

"I see." Gordon was processing fast and silently. "I'm so sorry Jane, I know you two are close. This has become a very unsavoury episode and it would appear our mutual friend Senator Johnson has elevated self-preservation to a whole new level." That was enough confirmation for Jane and Pete that Johnson was behind the kidnapping, now kidnappings, not that they suspected anyone else but at least it produced a clear enemy with a widely understood motive.

"Professor," Gordon turned to Pete, "give the phone to Agent Peralta, I can assure you he and his team are the best there is."

Jane found her voice again, "Senator thank you. I, we, are equally sorry to hear about Rose and Kelly, they are such brilliant people, they don't deserve to be caught up in this."

"Jane," Gordon's face was tight and serious, "no one deserves this. The world is literally collapsing and Senator Johnson, and it pains me to say it aloud, the president of the United States, are only bothered about power and money, and they're so blinkered they'll use innocent US citizens as a bargaining chip. I'm afraid I don't have the vocabulary to describe my incandescent rage and the words I want to use are not appropriate for you or the UK Prime Minister to hear but I can assure you he will not get away with this. The reality is there is absolutely nothing we three can do right now to help Harpinder, Rose or Kelly, or indeed whoever else they got their grubby hands on."

Senator Gordon visibly shook himself down as if trying to rid himself of all his current burdens. He placed his hand on the doorknob to a suite called the Hyatt Room. "Louis Charles and Penny Norton are through here, Prime Minister Keeble will be with us shortly, I believe she's been speaking with her counterparts in Brazil."

As they entered the room, both Pete and Jane were taken aback by the level of technology confronting them. Rather naively, they'd both just assumed they'd be chatting across a table with the others, forgetting this was for all intents and purposes the nerve centre for the counter offensive against Senator Johnson and his behemoth political allies. Pete felt he was on the deck of the Starship Enterprise mixed with a Saturday afternoon sports roundup show, screens everywhere, some with stats and graphs on, some with live feeds from around the world, with Louis Charles seemingly controlling them all like a high-tech orchestral conductor, although in reality his NASA team were ten thousand miles away managing the outputs. Penny Norton strode over purposefully and introduced herself to Peter but there was no time for niceties.

"Senator, there's been another land collapse, this time in Australia."

"Add Siberia to that sir," added Charles hastily.

"Louis talk to me." Gordon was back, fully switched on, straining for information.

"Well, it's only fitting the professor is here, good evening, Peter, and Jane of course." Louis Charles was unfeasibly calm, almost indifferent to the magnitude of what he was sharing. "The Manaus event measured eighteen kilometres across, give or take it was a circle. Six hundred feet deep at its shallowest point, five kilometres at its deepest, although more data is coming in on that one. Within an hour of each other, similar events have occurred in outback Australia, up towards Katherine in the Northern Territories and in the middle of Siberia. Both are bigger than in Brazil by a factor of three by diameter so a serious amount of crust displacement. You'll have to forgive me when I go into this mode, but I need to be entirely dispassionate and believe me, the reality of this makes me sick to my core, but the locations of these new two incidents have diminished human impact in the thousands, not millions." At this moment, they all locked into Louis Charles' professional mode where loss of life is positive when it's 'only' thousands.

"What does this mean Louis?" the UK Ambassador to the US Penny Norton's urgency was twofold. Her boss was about to walk in wanting to know what to tell not just the UK but, given where the other global superpowers were at geologically and environmentally speaking, the world and secondly, for herself and her own family. She was in Tokyo, was Japan next to collapse? Her husband was at a conference in Bilbao, Spain and both her daughters were travelling separately after finishing their A-level and degree courses respectively. She quickly resolved to compartmentalise this high-level worry as she looked around and realised everyone had their own loved ones to worry about. There wasn't a negotiation to be had to curb these land collapses, Mother Nature was certainly in charge here. Penny did wonder momentarily if this was simply karma for human interference in billions of years of nature's ups and downs being spoiled by two hundred years of myopic industrialisation. *Is it God punishing us all?* she thought to herself. A deep thought punctured by Louis Charles answering her question.

"Well Penny, apologies, Ms Ambassador."

"Don't you dare, Penny is my name."

"Yes, sorry Penny, not everyone in these circles is quite as humble as you. Best case scenario, these are isolated events as the tectonic makeup of the planet adjusts to recent subterranean movements. Kind of the opposite to how earthquakes happen. Instead of the land slippage at the edge of the plates, the way the plates have been behaving in the past geological era means there is increased tension towards the centre of each plate and that's where we think the instability has manifested. I know you want to know what will happen next and believe me, we are working furiously on it," Charles was referring to his NASA colleagues back in Texas, "and I can promise you, Tanya and I will not rest until we have a clearer picture of the situation and how we can manage of influence it."

None of them had noticed Tanya James, Charles' research colleague, who was beavering away on one of the button-heavy consoles at the far end of the Hyatt Suite. Tanya didn't register she was being talked about and carried on her business which pleased Louis, the last thing he needed was for her to get distracted too. He was all too aware that every minute he spent explaining what was, or what he thought might be going on, was a minute less he could spend on actually finding out the answer to all the questions he would have thrown at him. Although he'd probably never come out and say it and certainly not to Senator Gordon, he was quite the supporter of having political leaders who had the gift of the gab, orators not thinkers. He didn't want the top guys to be the experts, he wanted experts to be the rung below but felt all too often people got promoted to either a place where their expertise was wasted, or even worse, great orators were given status as experts. He was reminded of the poet Matthew Prior who is quoted as saying, 'he who talks the most, often has the least to say' or words to that effect. Either way, Charles knew his role right now was that of expert and explainer, so he'd better make the best of it. And he did this by bringing a severe dose of realism to the room.

"Worst case, as you can probably guess, is the total collapse of the world's inhabitable land mass, superseding even the drought apocalypse we've been working to up until now. At this stage, we're unable to make predictions, as awful as it sounds, we need more events than the three we've had." Charles paused as he looked at his iPad intently. "Make that four events. The team are reporting that Paris has fallen."

"Fallen, what do you mean fallen?" Penny spoke for all of them.

"Look." Louis Charles was struggling to contain his own emotions and with a flick of his finger on his iPad, he shared his screen with them all. A satellite image of the

French capital appeared on the massive wall screen behind him. It was hard to make anything out as all they could really see was a cloud of dust but as the image panned across the city it became clear that huge areas were gone and a murky, almost non-descript darkness had replaced where they'd expected to have seen southern Paris and its suburbs. Tellingly, and chillingly, the land destruction had left central Paris untouched, and it became clear that the Arc de Triomphe and Tour Eiffel remained, as if looking over the carnage wrought over the rest of the city.

"I won't lie," Louis Charles had lost his previously personality-defining surfer characteristics and suddenly looked sombre. "I think we might be fucked".

"Is that a NASA-endorsed synopsis?" a crystal-clear female English accent made everyone look up at the two women entering the suite with Senator Gordon. Louis Charles went red, mildly embarrassed by his crass summary, despite its accuracy, but doubly so as he immediately recognised both visitors.

49

"Madame Prime Minister, apologies for my rudeness and Nancy Rastik..." Charles was momentarily lost for words, sharing disbelief with Pete and Jane telepathically. *What on earth is she doing here* was what he was thinking and exactly what his face was saying. "...I won't lie, we weren't expecting you Ms Rastik." Senator Gordon stepped in, recognising the awkwardness, knowing Rastik was essentially the enemy as far as his team were concerned and, until a few minutes ago, she ranked only a tiny bit above his disdain for her partner in crime, Senator Johnson.

"I know we have a very real-time human and geological disaster unfolding now in Paris as well as Brazil and Siberia and goodness knows where else or where next, but we need to establish some sort of position on this, and Nancy Rastik, with the support from Prime Minister Keeble, might well be key to navigating this situation."

Pre-empting the potentially visceral reaction her mere presence might have on Senator Gordon's team in front of her, Nancy Rastik took the initiative before someone said something they'd be unable to retract. "I sense I'm enemy number one here," she began, sparking an instant reaction from Jane.

"Joint number one I think you'll find." Jane stared at Rastik, baiting a response. Jeff looked over at his American friend and colleague, simultaneously impressed she was going after Rastik in front of the UK Prime Minister no less, so out of character for someone with such compliant self-control, but also he felt pity that Jane was struggling to cope with the magnitude of recent events, like they all were to some extent, looking for a fall guy, someone to blame. And when your common enemy strolls in unexpectedly, tempers are going to rise.

"Yes, I got that. Jane, is it?" It was surprising to Jane that she knew her name. She simply nodded in reply. Prime Minister Ruth Keeble motioned to speak but Rastik ushered her to keep her silence.

"Prime Minister, I think it's only right for me to explain to these good people what brings me here."

"We're all ears." It was Jeff's turn to chip in, wanting to make sure Jane knew she had an ally in there, as if she needed reminding.

"I know there is likely little I can say which will change your minds about me and believe me, I'm not trying to side swipe you here. But we have to acknowledge our shared adversary right now is not our difference in beliefs or policies, but the rage of Mother Nature and it is in our common interests to understand what's going on and what's going to happen next. Once, and indeed, if that happens, I know there is a massive question hanging over us on what then happens." Rastik could see from the stern and entirely unmoved faces of everyone in the suite that sweeping the elephant in the room under the carpet was not an option here. She was well aware she couldn't just waltz into the room, declare that because there are a few, admittedly significant global disasters going on, all will be forgiven and she'd be welcomed on to the team. She knew a bond had grown between those in front of her and despite the fact they all knew full well their emotions would have no bearing on the geology of the situation, human nature dictated that they sort out the palpable tension Rastik's unexpected appearance had generated.

"I'm not here asking for your forgiveness or pity." Jeff scoffed at the very thought of feeling pity for someone who appears to be more than comfortable destroying the planet's climate. But he did acknowledge that it was a curious choice of emotion to call out. "Peter," the whole room turned towards the professor, whose face remain unchanged, just the hint of a raised eyebrow. "It may come as some surprise that I am a big fan of your work, a Masai disciple if you can believe it?"

"I do not," replied Pete flatly.

"I too studied Geology in Manchester." Now she really had their attention. "But a couple of years after you guys and only on a study exchange from Harvard." She made eyes towards Jeff and Elaine, noting their surprise, feeling she needed to fill in the gaps before proceeding. "Which is why I don't register as Manchester alumni and this is no doubt new news to you but might go some way to explain this unfortunate and awkward situation." She then reverted to addressing Pete. "You had quite the legacy in the department Peter, a number of your pieces were used as discussion case studies, pushing the narrow minds of the textbook junkies which was, and still is, the pervading characteristic of Western students. But you Peter, you saw beyond that and introduced me to big thinking geopolitics. I was captured by your Everest theory and have been an avid follower of your mantle disintegration theory for the past decade, long before anyone else threw some data at it to stress-test it, which I'm led to believe the NASA team have now done to a fairly conclusive level?" She glanced over to Louis Charles and Tanya James, who both instinctively nodded silently, intrigued as to where this was leading. "I had access to similar levels of data years ago when my PhD was sponsored, in part, by the Environmental Agency. They gave universal access to their students, so I figured I'd test your theory Peter, and it led me to conclude, and I'd love to compare Mr Charles if we had the time or the motivation, that Planet Earth was heading in one direction and fast. As I rose through the ranks in the following years, I refined the output from my original analysis and sadly what we are seeing around the world is ahead even of my own worst-case scenarios. My team's forecast was for two or three significant tectonic events by 2150, with large-scale topographical disintegration making Planet Earth uninhabitable for ninety per cent of the population by 2230. I know you hate me, and I understand, but there really are no upsides to having this level of certainty about the fate of the world. I swore my team to secrecy by investing in their trust." Rastik rubbed her fingers together signalling she'd paid them to be quiet.

"It's a damaging thing, certainty," Rastik continued. "I fear, at least feared, for humanity with recent advances in medical diagnoses inevitably leading to a predicted death date for individuals. I am a case in point for what happens when you have been shown a fixed future when really the future should be ever-changing, and changeable. It's what keeps the human race going. The unknown. Hope. Having a future. A feeling of destiny. Preparing a future for our children. And their children."

"With all due respect Ms Rastik, the stench of bullshit in here is overwhelming." Jeff didn't hold back. "You and that psychopath Johnson have been working on a plan to royally fuck up Mother Earth and my guess is that partnership has gone sour, so you've jumped ship, trying to cozy up to the good guys." Jeff was straight to the point as ever.

"Thank you for your input and I suspect you do indeed speak for a great many of us in the room."

Senator Gordon felt the need the step in as he could feel the animosity could boil over. "If I may offer a view from a relative outsider here."

The UK Prime Minister, who had entered the room with Nancy Rastik in tow, reminded everyone that this was not a college departmental row over who gets to write their theory or who has access to the most data. This was epoch-defining geopolitics and if it dawned on Jeff, then it had definitely dawned on everyone else, that this was not the time for a bitch fight. Gordon was a pro at this, and Prime Minister Keeble was equally adept at managing her emotions.

"There may be an opportunity for you to sit around a table and process all of whatever this is." Keeble managed to sound both respectful and irritated at the same time. "But as it stands, millions of lives have been lost, our closest neighbour has lost large parts of its capital city, one of our Commonwealth nations has witnessed an event, and goodness knows where is next, so can I suggest you give this two more minutes, decide if you are willing to work together or not so we can get on with the job of managing this frankly terrifying situation? For the record, and Ms Rastik knows my views, up until a couple of hours ago I felt very much the same as you appear to, disgust and contempt at an apparent agenda putting not only the Paris Accord at risk but also the long-term health of our planet. But things are rarely as they initially appear on the surface so let's listen to, not just hear, what Nancy has to say, then you'll have context with which to decide your next steps."

"The floor is yours." Jane simply said on behalf of the group.

Rastik picked up once more. "My alliance with Senator Johnson, taken at face value, does appear misguided. He is power-hungry, egotistical, privileged and short-termist in the extreme but if you want something done and Johnson believes it will benefit him in some way, then chances are he'll find a way to get it done. I too fell victim to a similar short-term outlook, but I know, and it's a big but, you can choose whether to believe me or not." Rastik paused briefly, no one interjected. "I felt there was no long-term. Everything I'd seen until that point, and indeed beyond, told me we had limited time on this earth, so why not give everyone a chance of wealth?" There were still no interruptions, which Nancy found surprising, although everyone listening was currently speechless, sensing where this might be heading. "The world we were, indeed are living in, is fragmented, bleak, fractious with a poor standard of living across the globe, even for those who are educated with stable jobs, life is hard. But people are toiling or struggling to make ends meet for some kind of future, either for themselves or the next generation. What I found, what you foresaw Professor, that NASA have validated, as have these awful events around the world, was that there was no future and without a future there is no room nor need for hope. A futility pervades, stripping back the fragile purpose of living." *Fuck me she's dramatic,* thought Jeff impatiently.

"So, I turned my focus towards trying to give the people of the world one final chance for a present, rather than a future. It's a simple, and I admit rather crass plan, but the industrial revolution brought prosperity to those who experienced it."

"But at what cost?" Peter challenged.

Nancy Rastik didn't expect an easy ride here, she knew how ridiculous this may sound to them but perhaps they could find a solution she had been unable to unearth. "Irreversible climate change professor indeed is the true cost of progress, so humankind is on an inextricably slippery slope to its own destruction but at least it was in our gift to change it, although we couldn't or wouldn't. Greed is a stronger emotion than selflessness. Once it became clear that global politicians were never going to fully commit to green economic policy and the cessation of carbon emissions, despite all the rhetoric - and fact, I might add - what we're left with, current situation outstanding, is an even more frustrating decline, not only in climate but global living standards. I'm unashamedly a laissez-faire capitalist at threat and picked up on our mutual friend Johnson's drive to bring a renewed industrialisation to generate wealth, in his world for himself but as a consequence for a great many people around the world. The thing holding him back?"

Rastik hadn't planned on this being an answered question, but Elaine was right on the money. "The green agenda. He needed a way around that and you gave him something to obliterate it with. The sea level data."

"Exactly," Rastik gestured towards her to check her name, "Elaine."

"Yes, Elaine."

"I showed Johnson and his team enough data that meant they got what they wanted; they weren't going to challenge it. I honestly thought his plan, once he got Franks, President Zarkov and Supreme Leader Guo aligned, could at least bring some level of wealth and dignity to the world, as well as making these self-serving men stupidly rich in the process. I figured it didn't really matter what it would do to the environment given the predicted demise of the planet anyway."

Prime Minister Keeble spoke up again, she had a calm authority that made everyone pay that little more attention. "At first hearing I must admit that the idea of the Director of the Environment Bureau disregarding the planet's climate so defiantly is wholly incongruous. But with a gentle tailwind, I personally have been able to make sense of it. It's not uncommon for outlandish scientific theories to pass the nose of a national leader, be it apocalyptic or miracle and I know for a fact that Ms Rastik had an audience with the office of the president of the United States to present the exact scenarios we are witnessing with alarming severity and apparent randomness, although it goes without saying I do hope we are able to bring some clarity to future potential events."

The immediate reaction from almost all parties in the room had been one which no one would have been proud of with both the UK Prime Minister and Senator Gordon in attendance. Their presence had undoubtedly allowed them to process Nancy Rastik's story more rationally than their initial instincts. Jane looked over at Jeff, Elaine caught Pete's eye, Tanya James had taken her eyes from the many screens she was managing, Senator Gordon and Louis Charles remained passive. It is a very difficult emotional situation to potentially have to admit that your sworn enemy might not be quite so evil, like when a player for your most hated team leaves and joins the team you support. There is almost always a transition that the things they were hated for are now cherished and feted. Nancy Rastik was neither a spokesperson not likely to be celebrated by anyone present in the Hyatt Suite but that was a glimmer of acceptance driven by the very believable and respected Ruth Keeble.

"Why now though?" Pete was intrigued by her timing. On the one hand, he accepted Rastik might just be owning her mistakes and coming clean but there was a serious element of doubt as to her sincerity that he needed to flesh out. "I can only imagine that the leader of the free world and self-proclaimed climate change sceptic and capitalist would be more receptive to a scientist telling him what he wants to hear vs the world ending, or starting to end, on his watch. So, I'll run with it, you have yourself a classic Hobson's Choice. Or maybe it's a Morton's Fork. Either way, a dilemma."

Jeff gave Pete a puzzled look, partly because his friend appeared to be publicly grappling with the English language in an attempt to sound wise, but mainly because said grappling confused Jeff to the extent he was convinced Pete just said 'Nobson's Choice' and he found it inappropriately amusing. He managed to gather himself and resolved to check later, maybe when things weren't so apocalypsy with a world leader in the room. *Priorities Jeff, priorities.*

"Professor, you are on the money as ever. At the time I thought I was making a decision which might ultimately make people's lives better, given my certainty of our shared inevitable outcome."

"Well, it certainly hasn't made Harpinder, Rose nor Kelly's lives better." Jane was getting impatient beyond her capability to remain calm. "If anything happens to them, it's on you Nancy." Prime Minister Keeble motioned to step in again, but Nancy Rastik was not looking for protection.

"Look, I know I'm in the wrong here but in answer to both you and Professor Masai's questions, as soon as I realised Senator Johnson had gone rogue, I severed ties. As with many power-hungry egotists, Johnson is apple pie and smiles when things are going his way but as soon as he saw what a threat you guys were shaping up to be to his world domination plan, he flipped. I have given the Prime Minister and her UK security detail all the information I have, and I am in doubt the close links they have with local security forces will see to their freedoms in no time. I am so humbly sorry they were caught up in all this.

"Before you ask, I have also requested the Prime Minister to arrange safe housing for both Marco Hernandez and his PR Manager Chester Rogers. I am genuinely worried about the mental wellbeing of the Senator. In his myopic world he is king, and he doesn't know how to lose. I told him about the tectonic destruction that is happening now and how my, and your professor, forecast looks for the world but he wasn't having it. It's almost as if he couldn't acknowledge that Manaus had happened because it's not in his plan. I really think he's expecting to stand on that stage with Marco and his triumvirate of global leaders and tell the world to enjoy his new industrial revolution, whilst the world literally falls apart. He's a fucking lunatic truth be told." A knowing glance between Prime Minister Keeble and the Director, which despite its subtlety, was the most reassuring sign that, in all likelihood, Rastik was genuine.

"I suspect Johnson's lunacy is set to go nuclear, not militarily thankfully, when he discovers Guo, Zarkov and Franks will be sitting with us." Rastik demonstrably shuffled closer to Keeble. "With the good Senator's support and connections," she gave a nod to Gordon, impassive as ever, "I was able to reach out to POTUS and this time directly explain the existential threat to the planet. To be fair to the man, it's quite some U-turn but it's hard to deny when actual parts of the Earth are collapsing in on themselves. He didn't want a lengthy conversation on your theory professor, we're past that now, what he wants and what we all want is a solution. Or at the very least some foresight. It didn't need explicitly calling out, but President Franks wants to know if and when the USA will be impacted, and he made it pretty clear that his counterparts would be in the same boat. We're not operating in a vacuum here people, the president of the world's largest country is demanding answers as to why part of his landmass is no longer there and we, more accurately you, are well ahead in the race to provide these answers, like it or not."

"But we're simply not," Jane replied calmly.

Pete jumped in, "Rastik is right, trust her or not, the rest of the world will be so focused on trying to understand why this is happening they won't be able to work on any useful solutions until it's potentially too late. Remember you can't truly solve a problem without knowing what the problem is in the first place, that's been a universal issue for politicians and people in general since the dawn of time. We've been through all that questioning and understanding, it won't take up valuable working memory or precious time for us so yes Jane, like it or not, you, and the rest of us here, are likely the world's best chance of survival. Which is pretty depressing as Director Rastik has already touched on the grim view that this is an unstoppable geological phenomenon."

"Ladies and gentlemen." Senator Gordon addressed the room with a force that told everyone the time for talking had ended and it was time for action, "We need to be crystal clear now that the solution we're working towards may manifest in several ways. Option one: we stop the Earth from crumbling – in reality that's a non-starter. Option two: and this is where Peter, Nancy, Louis, we need you and your teams to mobilise and tell us whatever you need to forecast imminent or future locations of destabilisation. Peter, I know I don't have to tell you this but for the sake of clarity, think big. If you need every living soul with a PhD working on this, we'll make it happen. Option 3: this will be the domain of Prime Minister Keeble and myself. Obviously, we are planning for success, but we need to be ruthless in our honesty here and need some kind of plan B for the human race, the movie script version where a selection of people fly off to the moon to colonise but we will worry about that if and when it comes to it." The vision flashed through Jeff's mind of Senator Gordon and Prime Minister Keeble making a list of people in the world to save and how ridiculously impossible that would actually be, a train of thought pierced by Gordon addressing a message on his phone. "Harpinder, Kelly and Rose are free and on their way back."

"Oh, thank goodness," exclaimed Jane, accompanied by huge smiles from the rest, Louis Charles in particular.

"We'll also ensure the Senator is dealt with swiftly and decisively, do excuse me for a moment."

As Gordon left the suite, Elaine idly remarked, "Off to call the president," whereas she just assumed he'd be calling his security detail.

"Elaine, I suspect that's exactly who he's calling." Prime Minister Keeble replied with a straight face. "Now what's the latest Mr Charles?" she added as Tanya James handed Louis a note with a few scribbles on.

"Not good I'm afraid. Key global readings tell us sea levels have gone down by over a foot in the past forty-eight hours, that is an incomprehensible amount of water loss into the Earth."

Tanya took over. "That's not all folks, we have a satellite feed about to show us the Great Lakes." A crackly image slowly cleared on the large plasma behind the analyst showing a very un-lake image.

"When will it be in range?" Keeble asked anxiously, unsure what to expect.

Tanya responded coldly, "It is in place ma'am. The Great Lakes are dry."

49

Poor Marco Hernandez struggled to comprehend everything Chester Rogers had just told him on the doorstep of his Tokyo hotel room. Five minutes ago, he was enjoying room service and a tacky teen comedy, comfortable in his mind that he was ready for the single most important day of his life tomorrow. He simply stood there, ashen faced, silently imploring Rogers to tell him all of this was a lie, some elaborate prank. Rogers did not relent, and a single tear filled Marco's left eye. And like his dreams, it rolled down his cheek and fell to the floor. Nothing could replace this sudden feeling of emptiness creeping through his body. Rogers sympathised on a personal level with Marco. It wasn't hard to like the guy in a plucky, underdog kind of way, having just had his big break shattered.

On another level, Rogers acknowledged that he'd need to get over it pretty quickly. Given the grave events happening around the world, and the fact that Hernandez might actually be able to help, but he needed a few more minutes to come to terms with the developments, just as Rodgers had to just half an hour prior. He too had been holed up in his room, working his way through a double portion of wings and dips, watching a different but similarly lowbrow movie, entirely switched off from the world. A world that was brought back to the fore by an impatient and forceful knock on his door. Assuming it would be housekeeping for an entirely unneeded turn-down service, Rogers rolled off his bed expecting to simply usher the staff member along the corridor. Wasn't he surprised to see a couple of seriously well-built suited gentlemen standing at his door in a very un-turned down service manner. One of the men handed Rodgers a note which he took in his hand and instantly left grubby wing sauce prints on it. He then realised what his face must look like, because he'd made no effort to wipe it before answering the door and was suddenly grateful and embarrassed in equal measure that the two mighty specimens in front of him pretended not to notice. Unfolding the note written on Hyatt Hotel headed paper, he read, 'Call me. Now. Nancy.' *Punchy*, he thought, *and quite foreboding*. Before he had a chance to question if this was from, as he assumed, Nancy Rastik. Although he was hard pressed to think of an alternative Nancy that for one he knew, and for second would send two burly men to his hotel room with a demand he called her. It also dawned on him that he didn't actually have her number, but that momentary worry was quashed as big man number two handed him a phone with a number already on the screen.

"Just press call." For a man whose craft was words, this was an object lesson in 'less is more'.

Rastik answered, and for the next few minutes, all Rogers could muster with the occasional grunt. "Yes." "I understand." "OK." And "of course." Chester Rogers was well used to last-minute changes and managing challenging circumstances, but what the director just told him took that to another level.

"Now, get some stuff together and go get Hernandez. You'll be brought back to the Hyatt and Rogers," she paused. "Don't call anyone, especially not the Senator." Chester did not need advising against calling Senator Johnson. If he was annoyed earlier, God knows what kind of mood he'd be in now. It was only then that it hit him, Rastik was removing him and Marco out of Johnson's reach, a feeling that heightened his senses and quickened his step back into his room. A quick glance at the hallway full-length mirror confirmed he looked like a toddler at dinner time. So, as he grabbed his toiletries, he gave himself a vigorous face wash. Now at least he looked a bit more professional. His mind was awash with worry. Was he a target? Was his life in danger? Was the Earth really imploding, as Rastik had said? Could he trust her? He closed the bathroom door so he could be out of sight of the two men who, if they so desired, could probably snap him in half without breaking sweat. Clearly compliance was his best option. He powered up his phone. An avalanche of messages and notifications rolled across his screen. He brought up his Twitter feed.

"Christ almighty," he muttered to himself.

50

Back in the Hyatt Suite, there was a buzz of frenzied activity. The hotel manager had had a long conversation with Senator Gordon and Prime Minister Keeble. And he was busy corralling his many eager staff members to open the suite next door and turn it into a makeshift television studio. Earlier that day, which seemed an immeasurably long time ago for the hotel manager Higashi, he'd had a local communications and marketing agency in to update the Hyatt Hotel corporate video. Those same agency workers were now busy arranging for a global broadcast to be made. And they had under two hours to manage it. Keeble had put the producer in touch with the BBC to talk them through what they needed to do to go live. This was a far cry from promo videos, but the team, in true Japanese spirit, didn't complain. They just got on with the job in hand. When Rastik asked the Senator why they didn't just get the local BBC, or any international TV station in to do the job, the answer was simple; "they can't get here, Nancy." And then it clicked. Whilst she and the rest of them in the Hyatt suite were heads down, trying to figure out what should happen next and where events could lead in a calm and structured manner, the rest of the world were out there, exposed to wild social media streams wall-to-wall news feeds and, in a nutshell, total anarchy.

Initially, the reports had been sketchy and centred around landslides in remote parts of Brazil, Russia and Australia, barely making news bulletins, aside from on the dedicated news channels. But as more and more eyewitness accounts poured in and the Paris collapse hit the airwaves, minor intrigue turned to media panic on a global scale, like a tsunami of hysteria fuelled by claims of new disasters and mass deaths. Some verified, some fake news. Given the obvious major incident in Paris yet uncertainty about the scale, most European networks abandoned their schedules and switched to public broadcast mode, activating the plans only ever devised and simulated for a nuclear war. Such protocols had never been expected to see the light of day, and some networks managed it better than others. Twitter was awash with news feeds showing journalists and broadcasters in front of nuclear mushroom clouds or with rolling texts beneath claiming nuclear war had broken out. Hastily enacted emergency protocols were projected without the time or discipline to remove or correct the visuals. People everywhere were jittery. In the US, memories of 9/11 were revived, for many, it was too fresh in the memory. Newsrooms struggled to articulate that the Great Lakes, long since an American symbol of nature and purity were no more. Bearded and occasionally clean-shaven geologists, geographers and seismologists were being piped in from their dark rooms in university basements or directly from their field work. Conflicting stories abound these were 'isolated incidents and things would settle' all the way 'to this is the end', and everything in between. The broadcast which was getting most airtime was from a Kenyan reporter who happened to be on a job with a bunch of geology undergraduates from the University of Nairobi out in the Masai Mara on expedition. She was interviewing a couple of the students about the global events, speculating on the why and wherefores, when in the distance an enormous dust cloud appeared. Not uncommon in the remote plains of Africa, but what the camera picked up way before the operator or reporter or interviewers did was the ground in front of the moving cloud appearing to be unzipping towards them. A few of the students out of shot of the camera could be heard screaming and shouting and the reporter stopped talking as they all turned towards the oncoming wall of dust. To her credit, the camera operator held her ground and nerve against all natural expectations to turn and run as the Earth opened up in front of them, getting closer by the second.

"Oh my God, what is that?" The reporter was the only one who could get any words out. And a few seconds later, the image was engulfed within the orange cloud. A deafening roar. The screams of those nearby. Then nothing. A terrifying end for those poor souls, which in part fuelled a change of mindset for the watching billions from bewildering intrigue to mortal panic.

"Look out of the window, Nancy," the Senator ushered the Director to the far side of the room which overlooked central Shinjuku.

"I understand sir," Rastik whispered calmly. The streets were full of people as if attending a parade but turning up on the wrong day.

"It's mostly under control," Gordon commented, "but other countries are not as orderly as Tokyo. We've had several reports from all over the world about large scale civil unrest. People don't know what to do and who can blame them? I tuned in to a few news feeds from what I would call capable broadcasters like CNN, Sky News, Al Jazeera and ZDF and to be honest, it made me feel pretty anarchic myself. They don't know what to tell people Nancy aside from 'stay in your homes' and we all know what happens when you tell them to do something like that." He peeled back the curtains once again, "And this is the most compliant population on Earth. We can only imagine the carnage happening elsewhere…" his voice trailed off as he held the thick curtain open for a few seconds trying to take in the scene in front of him, playing out in his mind what must be happening in towns and cities across the world. He snapped out of his momentary daydream and brought his ruthless focus back to the fore. Such was his attention elsewhere, he hadn't noticed that Kelly Chan, Rose Carmichael and Harpinder Tarkovski had all returned safely from their brief but terrifying kidnap experience at the behest of the rogue Senator Johnson. Nancy Rastik had decided not to interrupt the Senator, given the amount he was already dealing with, but it gave him a renewed boost of energy to know that at least the three of them were safe from harm. The irony was not lost in him that, despite the millions of lives being lost around the world, his natural human emotions put greater emphasis on three individuals he barely knew. He made a conscious decision not to feel guilty, but to celebrate any small sense of victory or positivity.

51

Not long after Prime Minister Keeble had raised the alarm about Senator Johnson and the three kidnap victims they knew about, there was a very real concern about more, but thankfully that turned out to be unproven. Shortly before the return of Rose, Kelly and Harpinder, a team of US and Japanese Secret Service agents arrived at the door of the Senator's Hotel. Nick Johnson was unaccustomed to being told what to do at the best of times. But in his current mood, he was particularly belligerent. He took one look at the burly armed guards at his door and promptly told them where they could go and what they could do to themselves, and slammed the door shut. A handful of seconds later, the same door flew off its hinges and across the hotel room entrance hall in a shower of wood chips and busted screws. The Senator's defiance turned to anger, and even the pointing of four loaded military-grade semi-automatic guns in his direction wasn't enough of a hint for him to manage his emotions more carefully.

"Senator," the lead Japanese agent spoke first, "you need to tell us the whereabouts of Kelly Chan, Rose Carmichael and Harpinder Tarkovski." With the parting of the ways with Rastik the all but mortal implosion of his Industrial Revolution plan, given world events and the very abnormal feeling of being totally out of control, he dismissed the highly illegal and immoral kidnapping of the three ladies as if they were human-less characters.

"A fat lot of use they were to anything and anyone." He spat out the words aggressively, his mind wildly trying to process his obvious predicament and come up with a Plan B.

"Sir, their location." A second prompt, which, again, fell on deaf ears. Such was Senator Johnson's superiority complex, even a weapon trained solely on his torso was not enough to shake him from his self-absorbed power craze. A loud Texan accent cut into his whirring thoughts, the second armed security agent spoke with such commanding authority, even Johnson paid attention.

"Senator Johnson, one last time. Where are the captives?"

"Oh really. As if they matter now?" responded Johnson contemptuously.

"Right now, sir. In your world, telling us is the only thing that matters." He moved his weapon closer to the Senator to reinforce the message.

"Do you have any idea who you're dealing with? This will be the very last time you wear that uniform. I can tell you that." The agent cocked his gun. He was a trained professional and a privileged douchebag like Johnson wasn't going to distract him. Not one bit.

"Location now!" Johnson carried on muttering to himself, seemingly entirely unaffected by the guns trained on his every motion.

"Waste of bloody time they were. A couple of little earthquakes and the world's gone mad. They'll all be sorry. Those three dollies in the basement sure ain't gonna change anything. It'll only be a matter of time before the president makes sure you're on traffic duty for the rest of your career. Same for the rest of you chimps." It was a curious scene in the hotel room. The security forces guns trained on the Senator, waiting for imminent news of the captives, while the Johnson himself appeared to be preparing himself for the next part of his ambitious plans.

"It'll all blow over soon, and they'll all come running back. You'll see. I'll find someone more reliable than that snake Rastik." A voice crackled over the radio of the gunman just outside the room.

"We have secured the release of the three captives. All unharmed and evacuating the premises." This was the news they were waiting for to increase the pressure on the Senator.

"Senator Johnson, you need to stop what you're doing right now and come with us. This ends now." The agent took a step closer to Johnson. "Put your hands on your head Senator and stand completely still." Again, the Senator acted as if these heavily armed men were as much able to give him instruction as would a child.

"Hands on your head Senator." He may have just asked him to do a dance and sing a song such was the ineffectiveness of the command. Johnson was getting even more riled up by the agents. Not only were they getting in his way, and he needed to get stuff done and quickly if he were to save his plan and keep his allies on side, but they were also trying to tell him, the future president of the United States, what to do. And this made him even more determined to show them who the real boss was here. He once again turned his back on the agents and their guns and headed straight for the top drawer in the hotel room bureau.

"I'm going to call the president directly myself and have you removed from duty with immediate effect." He reached into his jacket pocket, which instantly made all the agents tense up and refocus their aims. Chances are, if he wasn't a high-ranking government official, just this level of defiance would have led to a swifter escalation, but US Special Forces Agent Bean and Japanese Delta Force Commander Mame were experienced enough to read the situation. However, Johnson's actions were erratic and the fact he so quickly produced the phone saved him for now.

"OK you Neanderthals, you do not have the power here. We all know I'm untouchable. And we're going to even things up a little bit in this room." Johnson's confidence and sense of his own immortality were astonishing and about to be put to the ultimate test.

"Sir, you will stop right there." Agent Bean had also lost patience with this altercation and the Senator's behaviour meant he was on heightened alert.

"Just stop telling me what to do, for fuck's sake." In the anthology of last words, these were never likely to make it as a permanent entry. Again, Johnson did not heed the warning from Agent Bean and opened the top drawer with aggressive impatience and with his free hand rummaged loudly until he clasped his fingers around his own weapon. A 9mm Smith and Wesson, a compact handgun that Johnson had only used once before, and then covered up, following a heated disagreement with a green lobbyist who had trailed him to his home and confronted him on his own lawn about his association with big energy conglomerates and the motor industry. The protester was everything Johnson despised, so ridding the world of him made the Senator feel he was doing the public a favour. Whilst others may have felt long term guilt about ending the life of a fellow human just for having a different opinion, it only hardened Johnson's self-righteous feeling of entitlement in evidence in droves in hotel room 437 of the Tokyo Hilton.

The key difference here, which Senator Johnson had inexplicably failed to take into account, was the confrontation was not between himself and an unarmed, mostly harmless, yet passionate lobbyist, but a group of military trained assassins armed to the teeth with loaded weapons pointed directly at him, warning him to stop what he was doing. So, when Johnson's hand left the drawer and the agents caught sight of the metallic pistol, the cry of "gun" from both of the agents was only going to end in one outcome. Amidst the deafening crackle of the semi-automatics unleashing a devastating burst of bullets into the

Senator, and despite the searing heat rushing through his body as he crumpled to the floor with only seconds left to live, Nick Johnson still had absolutely no doubt in his mind that one day he'd be president and the world would be universally at his beck and call. As he lay on the thick rug by the large wooden drawers, his body convulsing, reacting to the flurry of bullets which had loaded themselves into several of his major organs, he could see the boots of the men who had fired the guns. And it was only when he heard Agent Bean call for a body bag that it dawned on him that it was for him. And this really was the end. Then everything went dark and silent.

52

Prime Minister Keeble approached Gordon and Rastik at the window and calmly informed them that, "Senator Johnson has been neutralised." They both knew what she meant by that but to fill in any gaps, Keeble added, "He decided to draw a gun when faced with the finest marksman in the US and Japanese Secret Services. You've got to hand it to him, confident to the end. But we have bigger things to deal with now. We have the mother of all press conferences to give right here in about ninety minutes, once the three leaders arrive by helicopter. For the past few hours, Penny Norton, UK Ambassador to the US and Klaus Jurgensen, Germany's Environment Minister, have been working their many back channels to bring both Presidents Franks and Zarkov up to speed on the reality of the events unfolding. Both had been easy to access and needed little convincing, given the evidence and constant news feeds hitting them every few minutes." Keeble had anticipated that the shaky global relationship with the Chinese might make Chairman Guo harder to convince of their much-needed alignment.

But Louis Charles provided the material should it be needed. "Multiple events across the Chinese mainland, including the entire metropolitan area of Shenyang in the northeast of the country, going under with hundreds of miles of the iconic Great Wall also gone... should be an open-door ma'am." Keeble need not to have worried about securing global consensus. Even she was unaware how close the three men had become in their allegiances with the now very ex-Senator Johnson. Incredibly the only one in the room who could have told them was the recently arrived PR man, Chester Rogers, whose primary role now was to manage the local marketing agency into becoming a global TV network in under two hours.

Senator Gordon looked at his watch. He knew every second counted and did not want to take everyone's time up with unnecessary detail. But there were a lot of people in the suite now and with more global leaders about to arrive, he sensed this was a good moment just to bring the group together to ensure they were maximising resource and brain power. He cleared his throat and gained the attention of the room, one of his defining skills.

"Ladies and gentlemen, please be ready to update the group in five minutes. We are going live to the world at 2200 hours local time and will need to brief the leaders of the USA, China and Russia beforehand and have a coherent message scripted out and have it available in at least three languages."

Michelle Grant, Jane's former boss at the Bureau was the only member of the extended team who had not flown out to Tokyo for the IGA conference. Little did she or anyone know at that time, that the IGA would be cut so dramatically short for precisely the manifestation of one of its key presenters' outlandish theories, Peter Masai. She had flown back to the UK at the request of Senator Gordon to tie in with the geology department at Manchester University. Gordon hadn't notified the three alumni Elaine, Peter and Jeff on the basis that they'd already had enough to manage without another trip down memory lane, and also the reason it was Manchester specifically was a member of Louis Charles' NASA research team and professional acquaintance of the Senator himself was completing a year's PhD sabbatical to work with and mentor the tectonics specialists on campus.

Monty Symonds wasn't quite the spitting image of a surfer-cum-boffin Louis Charles, but one could be forgiven for thinking they could be related. Of all the people in the entrance hall for the Department of Earth and Environmental Sciences, Michelle Grant would have picked Monty Symonds out in a heartbeat to spend time with. She may be in town on purely professional duties, but she's only human, she told herself as she shook off the rather inappropriate images which were racing around her head as the broad shouldered, casually dressed, sculpted body of the American scientist strode towards her, hand outstretched at the end of a supremely toned arm, accompanied by a genuinely warm smile, greeting her and welcoming her to the Williamson Building.

"It's an honour to meet you, Ms Grant. You come very highly recommended by some fairly impressive people. I do hope I don't disappoint." Michelle blushed bright pink but managed not to slur her words. *God, he is even better up close,* she thought.

Managing to get hold of her entirely inappropriate emotions, Michelle responded in kind and banished her lack of focus on the job in hand. "Please, do call me Michelle, and likewise to be promoted by Louis Charles and the Senator puts you in pretty sparse company."

"Monty," he assisted her, "I only make the undergrads call me Mr Symonds." They both laughed, which helped Michelle relax and progress to more relevant topics than her brain was previously conjuring in her mind. Symonds had been well briefed by Charles on everything but the politics of the situation. He felt that would only pollute, not enhance the scientific process. Which meant he and Michelle talked freely about the lowering of the water levels, the shifting of the planet beneath the surface, the potential of climatic mega shifts from a drought of fresh water combined with humidity and rainfall from subterranean evaporation.

"Seems incongruous that the ICCS are spinning this into some kind of win for humanity, doesn't it?" Unsurprisingly, Monty Symonds had done his homework, and once his mate, Louis, had so clearly and deliberately steered clear of politics, it didn't take long to find out how the so-called International Council for Climate Stability were going to capitalise on it.

"Indeed, Monty, a very sad state of affairs, which is why it's critical we work out what's going on."

"True dat," replied Monty, which really brought home the generation gap between the two of them thought Michelle ruefully. "You need bad guys if you want to be the good guys," Monty grinned like Louis Charles. He seemed to take everything in his stride. He had such a positive aura, eye candy aside. Michelle thought the next few days in his company would be very productive and insightful. Indeed, little that they both know at the time how quickly the tectonic events would unfold and how extensive and widespread they would become.

"OK, people, it's time," Gordon rallied the team. "We have almost everyone here now. We applaud your stoicism and defiance, and I'm pleased to say Senator Johnson is totally out of the picture now." Humbly, the three ladies, merely smiled and intimated the Senator should continue. Only Harpinder dwelled on Gordon's phrasing around Senator Johnson being "totally out of the picture", to her it could only mean one thing, or surely he'd have simply said he'd been arrested or detained. *Good riddance*, she thought and much deserved.

Gordon continued, "I'm sure you've all heard or worked out by now, this is the global nerve centre for, and sincerest apologies professor, managing what has become known as the Masai Events." Entirely inappropriately, given the global devastation and unfathomable loss of life and livelihoods, Jeff sniggered uncomfortably loudly. This wasn't quite the outcome Peter had envisaged from his trip to Tokyo as his mind's eye watched helplessly as his dream New Scientist front cover now read 'Rock Bottom' (not Star). And, instead of 'it's gonna happen', now it read 'it's happened early, sorry folks', and it evaporated in a puff of smoke. Senator Gordon overlooked Jeff's lapse in maturity and continued around the room.

"Peter, Chester, we need you to work with Prime Minister Keeble to turn this into a script fit for the world." *A nice, easy brief,* thought Chester Rogers to himself, but in reality, he was chuffed to bits to be involved. This was as big as it gets, although he was still curious why Nancy Rastik appeared to be part of this team too and resolved to find out when things calmed down a little. Louis Charles updated on behalf of NASA with Tanya Kelly and Rose in support. He also piped in Monty Symonds and Michelle Grant from Manchester. Rather fittingly, the room they were using to video call from, had photos all around it with notable alumni. Louis wondered entirely correctly, if they'd positioned themselves with this in mind, because over one shoulder was a very young-looking Peter Masai, with the caption, "eminent professor" beneath his grinning face. And on the other side, the unmistakable visage of Nancy Rastik, bespectacled and holding her diploma, conspicuously a Harvard certification. The Manchester University Geology Department clearly had no qualms about cashing in on her brief stay with them all those years ago.

"OK," said Louis Charles, shaking off the rather comical image of the pair of them in Manchester, "we've got mostly bad news, but a glimmer of a thought," he continued, trying to sound positive. "We can't establish any kind of pattern yet, at least not one we've got any real confidence in." Rose clicked a couple of buttons, and a world map appeared on the huge screen. All eyes fixed upon it. "The red dots are events, Masai Events, I understand that we refer to them as, sorry Peter, that we know of based on credible sources. You'll notice there's a running total down the side. This reflects three major estimates. And believe me, they are just that. One: a basic count of events. We're up to twenty now. The team in Houston are feeding the model. Oh, now Twenty-one. Nope, twenty-two." Louis paused, hoping on a number of levels that the number wouldn't change for at least as long as he was talking. "Two: the estimated land mass impacted, frighteningly it's in square kilometres," a hush followed by a collective breathing out in concern at the scale of the devastation. The count read 247,948.

Prime Minister Keeble made it even more real for everyone. "That's the size of the United Kingdom."

Louis continued, "And sadly we don't think it'll stop there. I suspect you've all worked out what the third count is?" A few grim nods as eyes focused in on the red number in the bottom right of the screen which was ticking up like a population counter at a museum and it just went over four million. "Given some estimates which hold up to certain scrutiny, put global deaths per year at the door of climate change at around five million, this really brings home the impact our unstable planet can wreak. I don't know where this will take us but, if and when we do come out the other side, we have to quash immediately any ambition of the like Johnson showed." He took a fleeting glance at Nancy Rastik, whose head bowed slightly as if trying to avoid any gazes in her direction. Louis had made his point and moved on to summarising their hypothesis. "Best estimates from everything we can see is given the elliptical nature of the Earth is that the concentrations of these Masai Events will be, and we're talking eighty to ninety per cent, between the

Tropic of Capricorn and the Arctic Circle, and in all likelihood, it'll be further South than Capricorn. Let's say to the Antarctic circle. We just don't have as much topical landmass with sensors in."

"So basically, the world?" Jeff checking to ensure he'd not missed any nuances.

"Yes, certainly in terms of the population, Jeff, rather unfortunately, we need probably another twenty to thirty events to really pick up a predictable pattern. But, stating the bleeding obvious, we may not even be around ourselves if Japan is hit or such may be the severity of subsequent events that it may end up being a futile exercise. The real conundrum and pick your evil here, folks, is whether the world's available fresh water will be around long enough, or will the majority of Earth's inhabitable land be subterranean? If we thought rising sea levels were bad, try no sea levels at all. And the impact that would have."

Jeff flashed back to his dream of a few days ago and painfully accepted he may have been seeing the future of sorts.

"But it's not quite the drought you think it may be," Peter took over, and everyone was keen to hear the professor's take. "Disappearing water doesn't itself mean drought. It'll still be in the Earth's atmosphere to continue the water cycle, just not the one we all learned about at school. Main issue, it'll either be under our feet or over our heads. So, whatever is left of the planet and people on it, we, I hope it's we, will need to radically and quickly think about water capture. But that's a bit further down the line I guess, along with agriculture and general housing and sanitation." Professor Masai knew there was a lot more thinking to do about life after this if they were lucky enough to escape Earth's fury. But his mind zoned in on how he'd script a coherent message to go out to the world. Louis motioned to the video screen, taken up mostly by Michelle Grant and Monty Symonds, although not entirely, with the youthful mug shots of Nancy Rastik and Peter Masai adding some very apt back story to these already unprecedented proceedings. Monty took charge after citing Michelle Grant's contribution to their update, starting with an acknowledgement of Louis Charles' rather sombre and, on the surface unsurprising, hypothesis that most of the world will be impacted at some point.

"What we are seeing quite strongly is sensor data and on-the-ground reports of instability just as Louis outlined and I suspect you're all thinking so what? Well, and this is a work in progress hypothesis, at this stage we have so far - touch wood," he tapped his head accordingly, although it was obvious to some who bothered to think about such things that a man of science either should refrain from such malapropos phrasing or at the very least touch something actually made of wood like the very table he was sitting at. Monty continued, head well and truly tapped.

"We have measured activity from pretty much everywhere except for the Antarctic plate." He let this hang in the air for a moment to allow the room of very intelligent people in Tokyo draw their own mini conclusions. "We've been in touch with the team at the UK research base in Antarctica, Halley VI, and their readings are totally normal, not just on the ice shelf on which they reside, but across the continent. Compare that to the information coming in from Cape Froward Patagonia, Cape Agulhas, South Africa and Jacquemart Island, the southernmost points on their continents, and not a million miles away from Antarctica; we are seeing significant seismic activity through those regions. And we are yet to prove this, but all signs point towards stronger activity, meaning higher probability of large scale Masai Events." The professor was both shamed and proud how quickly his name had become attached to this apparent apocalypse. Would his mother be proud, or just remind him again that she thought he could have focused his efforts on something less end of the worldy? Bit late for that, he resolved.

"In addition, in the Arctic, we're not seeing the same levels of subterranean activity versus the tip of Alaska, Siberia and Norway. However, the team at the UK Arctic Research Station in Ny-Ålesund have reported ground movements, all be it very minor ones, and are making plans to restrict incomings and outgoings as a precaution. If nothing else, what we're wanting to note here is big decisions like access restriction are being taken with very little information to support them. We need to offer some clarity where I appreciate there is little, and even more hope which might again be hollow and scientifically unfounded."

Michelle Grant, still within shot of the video link, had been slightly distracted by someone or something off camera and jumped into the conversation, taking it back to the scale of destruction.

"Not sure if you guys have seen, I suspect it's coming to you, maybe even before us."

Tanya James nodded grimly, "The news from Florida and Malaysia?"

"Indeed," Michelle replied. And all eyes in the Hyatt Suite flicked back to the flashing world map again, which noticeably had two more flashing red dots, more obvious now given Michelle and Tanya's brief exchange, in northern Florida and southern Peninsula Malaysia. Suddenly, the very real personal tragedy of the situation hit Elaine as she instinctively cried out a gasp of horror filled with exasperation. Only Jeff, Jane and Peter were aware southern Malaysia, Johor Bahru to be precise, was Elaine's home. At least it was prior to her self-proclaimed one-way ticket out of there. Nevertheless, it was clear to everyone that at some point individual circumstances would start to cloud judgement and impact them on a deeply emotional level. Elaine, it seemed, was the first either to let it show or be impacted directly.

"Oh my God, my house, my friends." It didn't go unnoticed by Jeff that she didn't mention her husband. Or was it ex- or estranged husband now, Mark? Maybe she just didn't care, or perhaps she simply knew he wasn't in Malaysia. Either way, her reaction made him realise how deep his feelings for her were and how quickly they resurfaced even at a time like this.

"Apologies," Elaine hurriedly addressed the room. "I know I won't be the only one who is watching this human-less screen and thinking of our loved ones and acquaintances being those horrible numbers at the bottom there." She managed to hold back tears, but her voice gave away so much sadness.

Prime Minister Keeble spoke first. "Elaine dear, you are allowed to feel all the pain you need to. We all process grief and fear in different ways, and there's no guidebook. We all need to do our best to channel our collective strengths and find a way through this. But if anyone needs time to themselves, it's only right and human for us to support that." There were nods around the room. It felt important that it had been addressed and they were not going through this ordeal in a vacuum. None of them would be saved from losing precious family and friends. Not with the devastating scale of these events.

Michelle took the pause after Keeble's address to pick up again, sadly no time for sentiment, however brutal that felt. No one was judging her for carrying on.

"We must expect many more of these and let's be honest, we might get caught up in an event ourselves given our current inability to pinpoint locations. One positive that has surprised us, and it's more the absence of a negative, is dust clouds. We'd expect the immense level of lithospheric collapse to create vast amounts of dust and debris to be released into our atmosphere, both suffocating life and obscuring the sun. In fact, we'd might as well pack up and go home now, given what enormous areas have collapsed inwards, which tells us Professor Masai was potentially right in that there are stronger forces below that are effectively keeping the lighter particles from releasing into our air."

Pete's face contorted quizzically for a moment at the suggestion his core expansion theory might only be 'potentially' right. But to be fair, he'd not discussed dust clouds formation or lack of them in his paper and was grateful his name wouldn't be used for some kind of global asphyxiation or solar blackout as well.

Grant continued, "So that's one major issue we're not faced with at least."

"Thanks Michelle, Monty. Stay online, stay safe."

53

Louis signed them off and motioned towards Jane Henderson who, with Elaine, had been diligently working through the hordes of data provided by Louis Charles' NASA colleagues and had further comment on Grant and Symonds' Antarctic anomalies.

"Elaine and I concur with the working hypothesis that the South Pole is the best bet for stability for the foreseeable future. We are assuming the ice sheet is contributing to the stability, but appreciate that doesn't explain the Arctic disturbances, although they are less aggressive. What we do see globally as you will know…" in the corner of the room Chester Rogers was pretty sure he would not know but didn't flinch. He was engrossed in the discussion "…is that oceanic levels are inconsistent across the planet given currents, winds, temperature and indeed gravity. All global readings tell us the sea is vanishing deep underground. Hundreds of thousands of cubic miles and counting. But again, the zone where we're seeing less impact is around Antarctica."

Senator Gordon had received word that the world leaders were now on site and that gave them ninety minutes until their shared broadcast. He gestured to the room to pause and focus on him. Everyone was looking for leadership. Being told what to do, even for the highly intelligent people in the Hyatt Suite, was an attractive option given the impossible decisions facing them all.

"There are no favourites here. No preferential roles. You may not always agree, and I truly value your support and commitment to find a way through this awful, unimaginable crisis. Louis, Professor, Prime Minister, Nancy, we need to brief our distinguished guests. Harpinder, Chester, please make this broadcast as far-reaching as you can. The target is every screen, in front of every pair of eyes on the planet. Jane you'll be proof-reading the broadcast script for validity, credibility and accessibility. Dame Norton will be the de facto leader in here in my absence as much to give a focal point for any decisions." Penny nodded in acknowledgement. Gordon beckoned Jeff across to speak to him before heading out.

"Jeff, this group needs you now. They are tired, scared and working on an almost insoluble problem. It won't be long until cracks appear. It's only natural with a burden this great but you are a people person Jeff and a fine geologist. I need you to work the room talk to them, gee them up. I'm not asking you to be a clown, just be you, be present and we'll all regroup after the broadcast."

"What's the end game here Senator?" Jeff wasn't totally sure he understood his role, but he felt honoured to be singled out by Gordon.

"Jeff," the Senator smiled, "perfect, you get it. That's exactly the type of question we're not asking right now. So, let's just keep everyone focused until we can work that out."

"Roger that sir," Jeff was uncharacteristically speechless, but it didn't take long for the pennies to drop. Gordon had no idea himself where this was going. He just carried himself as if he did.

"Good luck with broadcast, sir. We're here if you need anything," Gordon looked Jeff in the eye with an air of respect.

"Thank you, Jeff, that's why I asked you to do this," and with a firm slap on Jeff's upper arm, Gordon turned and headed out of the suite with Nancy Rastik, Prime Minister Keeble, Louis Charles and Jane Henderson.

Jane exited the suite with NASA scientist Louis Charles and took a huge gulp of air to steady herself for her audience with the three most powerful politicians on the planet.

"How are you so calm and in control Jane?" was an entirely unexpected question.

"Louis, what are you talking about? I'm freaking out. And coming from you. You're like the most composed guy I've ever seen."

Louis smiled. "I guess for both of us, appearances can be deceiving. I'm way out of my depth here. Jane. I'm not even the best scientist in that room. Never mind being the one to brief global leaders."

"Are you kidding me right now? You ooze confidence. I'm the odd one out here," Jane was taken aback by Louis' sudden vulnerability.

"You, Jane, have the knowledge, the intellect and the skill to do this. I'm very much in awe of how you conduct yourself. I'm a mouthpiece for my team They're the experts and they're in there and I'm exposed, and I don't want to let the Senator down. Not now, not ever." Jane was surprised herself at how far she'd come in terms of her self-confidence that seeing such an apparently assured character like Louis Charles expressing such self-doubt spurred her on even more.

"I guess we're all gonna have our wobbles. I suspect Senator Gordon is a bag of nerves under that calm demeanour and think about it, if we think we're scientific frauds, what must he or Prime Minister Keeble be thinking? They trust us. Maybe we should trust ourselves too Louis."

"You see Jane. That's why you're here. Thank you. I needed to say it. Feels better to get it out there."

"I hear you. Louis, maybe let's leave it with the fact I trust you, you trust me, the Senator trusts us both, even if we don't trust ourselves."

Both Jane and Louis felt they'd established an important bond in their short and devastatingly honest exchange, priming themselves for their audience with Frank, Zarkov and Guo. Spotting them together in the corridor, Chester Rogers sidled up next to them, sensing they were establishing some kind of relationship ahead of the big meeting.

"I just thought you'd want to know, and I'm working on the basis you don't hang out with world leaders very often, that I saw these guys together the other day."

"Rogers, do we need the Senator here for this?"

"No, he's aware," Chester continued and shared with Jane and Louis his near encounter with the three leaders at Marco's dress rehearsal for the IGA conference, which now felt like an eternity ago. "Just thought it'd be worth mentioning that these dudes are well able to work together to destroy the world's climate with very little credible scientific evidence. I only hope they can do the same to try and save it, even if there's not a billion dollars on the table for each of them," *Bit cynical,* he thought. But important they knew there was already collusion between these oft-sparring nations.

"Thanks, Chester, appreciate the heads up." Louis was the first to react. "What do you reckon is gonna happen here? You've seen stuff like this, or maybe not exactly like this, obviously, but you know what I mean. Political stuff. Your job is to piece it together and make it into a public sound bite."

"In a nutshell, yes." Chester decided this wasn't the time to discuss the intricacies of public relations work. And Louis was broadly right in truth. "Honestly, from what I've seen so far and understood about what's going on around and under the world, we've got a classic illusion of choice. I'm pretty sure you guys, sorry to be so blunt, haven't the faintest idea how to stop this planet from imploding. So, you either tell people that and watch them go crazy, or you lie and tell them you have a plan, which they'll see through pretty fast and go crazy. The latter buys time, and in areas where land and water remain, you are telling the truth. And in areas which collapse, brutally, really brutally, it doesn't matter you're lying as they'll all be dead. So, my counsel is to get those men into a place where they think they can save the world. If they're not getting a shit ton of climate killing cash, then at least write them a legacy they'll bite your arms off for." Jane was impressed at Chester Rogers' succinct precis of their dilemma, and she could tell Louis Charles shared that view.

"Now," Chester was on a roll, and this is why he'd risen to the top of his field, "you two will be the smartest people in the room." He raised his hand, preventing them from interjecting and disagreeing and repeated himself. "You will be the smartest people in the room so use that to your advantage, they have no option, but listen to you. So, if it's going in a direction you feel uncomfortable with, you can step in. Remember, they only know what you, or scientists like you, have told them so you have the real power in the room." Jane and Louis, despite their combined brain power, wouldn't ever be as perceptive as this. And were grateful to Rogers for catching them before heading in.

"Should you not be in there with us, Chester?"

"Ah, no. Remember you know stuff. Actual stuff. Then I get to tell the story. Sadly, unless someone comes out of that Hyatt Suite with an idiot's guide to controlling Mother Nature, we will be telling the world to have hope that the best scientists on the planet are working on a plan." Rogers was leading more and more. "Now you go in there and make sure that triumvirate don't get cold feet. We need to say something to the good people of the world, and I'm about to go and make sure they all get to see it." Roger's voice tailed off somewhat as his bravado seeped away, "Although I'm not exactly sure how yet. Harpinder," he called out down the corridor, "let's do this. Good luck chaps. See you before the broadcast. Remember, all we're selling is hope. No promises."

54

Senator Gordon wondered if there had ever been a summit of world leaders with the lack of security available in the Tokyo Hyatt. The three men had clearly formed a bond over Senator Johnson's new Industrial Revolution. So, Gordon was intrigued to find out if they were equally accepting of this new turn of events. He was sure of one thing though, which was to avoid pointing to any of the seemingly obvious fallacies on which Johnson's plan had been based. His strategy was to lean into their combined buy-in to sea levels lowering and take it from there. He assumed correctly that each principal had been briefed to some degree, he knew they were not the only collection of scientists and geologists trying to work this thing out and figured none of those had clearly offered anything tangible. Which is why all three had arrived together to hear what Gordon and his team had to say. It was President Franks who was first to arrive at the makeshift briefing room, which had been hastily rearranged from hosting some local accounting firm annual conference. Incongruously, a couple of the freestanding banners were still in place as Frank entered the room.

"Well, this is some welcome Committee Gordon, you gonna blind me with science like that dirtbag Johnson?" Franks was faced by Peter, Louis, Jane, Keeble, Gordon and Nancy Rastik. He addressed Rastik directly, smiling sarcastically, "I see you came to your senses, Ms Rastik."

"Sir," was her sensible and simple response.

Jane had worked in and around politicians, at least politically minded people, for years in the Bureau. And it wasn't the first time she'd seen a U-turn in someone's views. Forty-eight hours ago, she mused the US president was about to embark on a massive fossil fuel investment drive based on the same scientific principles he was now almost mocking Nancy Rastik for supporting. *The ultimate jumping ship,* she thought, back a new horse and make it clear you never believed in the first one anyway. Gordon quickly got to the point and briefly introduced Jane and Louis to the president. Louis was oblivious, but Jane noticed the president lingering on each of them as if consciously storing their identities using some kind of memory technique.

In an instant, Franks moved on having effectively assumed control of the room from Gordon. "Prime Minister Keeble, always an honour." She gently nodded in the president's direction. *No love lost there,* thought Jane.

"So to brass tacks. We're fucked aren't we Senator?" *The clash of styles between the leaders of the US and UK was marked,* thought Jane, and really played into the national stereotypes. Keeble; thoughtful and understated with a calm, assured intelligence. Franks; outspoken, charismatic, opinionated, and right on the money, with a sharpness to cut through unnecessary discussion. Although it made her annoyed to admit it, what they all needed right now was a dose of Franks' honest, challenging pace.

He hadn't always been brash and seemingly impulsive in the way Senator Johnson had conducted his business. Nelson Franks, was a fine scholar in his day, graduating first in his class at Princeton, where he read political science and rose through the political ranks largely on performance and intellect rather than relying on pulling strings or using Daddy's influence. He developed his style over the years, largely as a result of frustration that the people around him, and crucially above him, did not share his intelligence. He grew tired of endless political waffle and reinvented himself as a no-nonsense, get things out there, do it now, kind of all-American hero. His academic background and superior mental agility didn't mean he was in any way altruistic. He was comfortable making deals where all parties took a slice of pie and he enjoyed being at the top, which is why Senator Johnson's plan was so attractive to him. He knew deep down that, in all likelihood, the world's climate was in long term decline, but figured profoundly selfishly that the glimmer of hope Johnson had dug up could put his beloved America back on the global map. Like all political leaders, President Franks knew that it was impossible to simply 'do the right thing', because that is predicated as he had said in many a speech on 'which of the 330 million US citizens you are', never mind being the leader of the free world, therefore having several billion opinions to satisfy. And today, he was certainly not going to entertain the idea he'd flipflopped from one position on climate change to the other, and he made that clear to those in the room with him. He had let his simple, yet dramatic synopsis of their current situation hang in the air to see what response would come, essentially fishing for the solution he, and all of them, craved. Inevitably, he figured one wouldn't immediately materialise.

"Sir. We've been trying to avoid such finality in our language,"

A wry grin formed on President Frank's face. "So, I'm right? We're fucked."

It was Prime Minister Keeble who attempted to defuse the tension. "We don't know that for a fact, Nelson." Everyone, including the president himself, noticed how Keeble used his first name tactically, avoiding the usual formality. She was a strong, astute lady, more than willing to openly disagree with a fellow national statesman. "But yes, all indications are that this situation is going to get worse before it gets better."

"Or, as I read it," Franks took over again, "the situation only gets worse. That appears to be the most likely outcome from what I can glean. Professor Masai?" Franks turned to Pete, who had been intently watching the shifting dynamic in the room, but now refocused on the president.

"Sir."

"If you had come to my office with your theory, your paper, the one I believe you were going to present at this geology conference we're all here for, there's a fair chance you'd have not made it through the outer gates, never mind come into the Oval Office. We all know it. And from everything I have read and heard, and this does not apply to you, professor, but there are myriads of wannabe apocalyptic predators who want an audience with the president. My advisers, and I dare say yours too Prime Minister." Keeble nodded in agreement, knowing where this was going. "We are constantly filtering out the rumblings and doom sayings of scientists and non-scientists alike," he paused and took a deep gulp of air and exhaled wearily. "Turns out one of you, that's you professor, were right. I've read up on your mantle disintegration prophecy and how the planet is effectively going to implode. But the one thing this has in common with the other apocalyptic scenarios that bubble up time and again," Pete felt he was back in school now, about to have his homework, which he was proud of, torn to shreds by the teacher, "that all we got are problems. Disaster, end of the world stuff. Correct me if I'm wrong, Professor, but I suspect I didn't miss the part in your paper where it details what we do when the world fundamentally collapses in on itself, and all the water and most inhabitable land masses disappear?"

"That's correct, sir," Pete said.

"This is the ultimate example people of why we always got told to bring solutions, not problems."

"Respectfully, Mr President," Pete felt compelled to stick up, not only for himself, but his fellow scientific community, who, by choice, experimented with theory to test the boundaries of reality to enable closer-in models to be created and executed. A little like designing a Formula One car, the technology eventually feeds down the chain to power granny's hatchback. Except Formula One only kills people occasionally, rather than threatening the very existence of mankind.

"The concept of core expansion and mantle disintegration isn't a million monkeys with a million typewriters territory, I haven't forcibly made this happen and collectively, we're in a better place to manage it simply because we believe we know what's happening. This is not just a lot of earthquakes that nobody saw coming but I bet that's the default position of the global media, am I right? A chain reaction that is forecast to rumble itself out in the next few days or so." Pete was passionate in his defence but not rude, he also wasn't stupid enough not to have checked out what the world's media were actually saying.

"Professor, you are right of course." President Franks humbly replied in a change of demeanour. "Please forgive how I sometimes come across. I think we all just wish you were wrong and there is a way to stop this. I'm not missing something am I? We can't stop the land collapse or plug the water up?"

"Not that we can establish sir, no." Gordon interjected, feeling it was a good time to take Pete out of the firing line.

"Then you'd better fill in the gaps I have before Chairman Guo and President Zarkov arrive in about twenty minutes, and don't sugarcoat it." He looked at his phone and grimaced. "Since I've been in this room, there has been destruction in North Africa and Ukraine that we know of."

Then his face fell as his phone buzzed again. "You can add Texas to that list." President Franks drifted off momentarily, muttering to himself, "Oh Jesus, what in God's name are we going to tell people?" A question they'd all been wondering how to answer. The team shared in as much detail as they could with President Franks, including Nancy Rastik's apparent change of position, something Gordon insisted on to ensure they were taken seriously. Franks openly admitted it wasn't whether the team needed to be taken seriously, it was whether they were correct or not. And he decided to withhold that opinion until his fellow leaders had received the similar briefing.

"I suspect my good friends Guo and Andrei will have many more questions, and I'd be astonished if they turn up without their own scientific advisers, hell, they might have their own version of events to share with us. Their research budgets are eye-watering, sorry Nancy." Rather myopically, since Louis Charles confirmed on behalf of NASA that his theory was indeed being played out in real time, Pete hadn't entertained there might be another viewpoint. Could he be mistaken? He hated his own reaction to that, given being wrong could mean millions, maybe billions of lives might not be lost. But he kind of hoped he was right for pride's sake. Jane caught his eye with a similar look of doubt, but the answer came pretty much as soon as the Russian and Chinese supremos entered the room together.

55

It was Chairman Guo who spoke first, flanked by two identically dressed, serious-looking women.

"Professor Masai," Pete was taken aback based by the fact his name was the first thing the supreme leader said but mainly because he seemed to know exactly who he was.

"Yes sir." Guo's English was impeccable, which made it clear to everyone his sturdy companions were unlikely to be translators.

Guo continued, "Our countries," he moved a step closer to Zarkov, presenting a united front, "entirely concur with your theory and our shared data corroborates recent unfortunate events and we humbly admit to misplaced loyalties based on convincing, yet inadequate, scientific evidence." Like Franks, the Chinese president readily acknowledged without specifically referring to the Johnson plan and Zarkov backed him up as if they were issuing a kind of apology which, when President Franks had referred to it, felt a little hollow but now the two global behemoths had rejected their Johnson alliance, it was developing a rather genuine feel to it.

"We make decisions based on information and the quality of that information. We wanted to believe the world had a positive future and my fellow leaders and I have worked together to overcome our political differences to forge a partnership to make the world a better place." Sadly, for President Zarkov, it became immediately clear that he was the weak link in the three leaders, making it sound more like their greed had been revealed, and he was frantically making stuff up to sound genuine, whereas Franks and Guo had hit it straight on. Even though there was more power in the room than one could ever imagine, Louis Charles looked across at Jane and made a face as if to sniff the air. She also thought it was bullshit but certainly wasn't going to make that known. Senator Gordon spotted their interaction and used his body language as best he could to reprimand Louis, who instantly corrected himself, cursing his own lack of discipline. He wasn't a political player and prided himself on his integrity rather than just saying what people wanted to hear. But he did inwardly acknowledge that Franks, Guo and Zarkov had taken quite the step down from their new industrial revolution plan to admit firstly, it was based on a fallacy and secondly, their admission predicated trust in the room so he told himself to grow up and deal with it.

Prime Minister Keeble, assertive in her own calm, assured way, saw the opportunity to move things on given there seemed to be a broad agreement on the cause of the events.

"With all of our nations and friends affected by this, we need to show a united front in how we're going to deal with it." Before anyone could point out they didn't have a practical solution, she continued, raising her voice initially to ensure the room knew she was in control. "This is not about solving the problem, this is about hope, giving the people the idea that it may stop without telling them that. No lies. But let's be honest, the truth as we see it is not broadcastable. I was inclined to recommend the professor to join the transmission." Pete gulped: he liked an audience, but this was a step up even in his world. "But I'm not sanctioning the idea of us live on air telling everyone on Earth that the world literally is imploding in on itself." There were supportive nods and grunts of agreement all round.

"It's a recipe for total anarchy, but I wouldn't rule it out further down the line if indeed we get that far. So, to business. Senator, I'll hand back to you to coordinate the response."

Gordon was grateful Keeble was in the room. Her demeanour was exactly the tone they all needed; especially given the egos she was dealing with. He momentarily thought to himself how far the world had come in such a short time that a woman and a black man would be coordinating the three most powerful leaders on the planet. But that they did. And within half an hour of focus, they thrashed out a plan of attack.

56

Back in the Hyatt Suite was a continuing coffee-fuelled hive of activity. As requested by Senator Gordon, Jeff had been circling the room. There was no shortage of effort, motivation, or passion. But the pervading sense of futility was suffocating. The moment Prime Minister Keeble returned, Jeff made a beeline for her to update on progress, but crucially, to suggest they turn off the screen detailing the global loss of surface and life.

"Prime Minister, I wish I had good news, but the reality is the team are starting to take ownership of this. And there is a creeping guilt. We've got to at least turn that doom-mongering tally chart off the wall. It's not doing anyone any favours. And I'm not saying anyone has their head in the sand, but it just tipped over fifty million." Acutely aware he needed to avoid coming across like they'd thrown in the towel, he made a practical suggestion to Keeble. "There's only so much reassuring I can give them, but you they are all in a bit of awe of you, Madame Prime Minister. And what they need is a reminder that their priority is pattern sniffing and somehow, and I know what this means in reality, but we have to say it, that every new geological event gives us fresh data so fresh optimism, as ridiculous as it sounds."

Keeble understood, although in her mind, it seemed ludicrous that anyone would ever be in awe of her. But she often forgot she herself was a global leader of some repute, rather than plain old Ruth from Northampton, which is how her old school friends gently ribbed her about on the rare occasions when they could get together. Right now, standing in the Hyatt Suite in central Tokyo, Northampton felt an awfully long way away, which indeed it was. She smiled to herself mournfully, quietly reflecting that perhaps her hometown was no more, like so many inconsequential towns and cities across the world, vanishing catastrophically into the lithosphere. But as she glanced around the room at the mix of people who were giving their all to find some glimmer of hope to save the planet, she realised everyone came from inconsequential towns and cities, birthplaces are a level playing field that shouldn't define someone. If only that were true. She rued the global inequality she had been working so hard to correct through the lens of economics and education. Geography and climate had already been pretty significant obstacles, but now she wasn't sure if there would be a future generation. But she did know already that Mother Nature didn't seem to have favourites in terms of money and power. She was, it seems, arbitrarily destroying the world with scant regard for wealth or privilege. This was very much an equal opportunities Armageddon. She chastised herself for ever thinking of the situation as a sound bite, but that's the life of a politician especially in the modern world of nano attention spans.

She allowed herself a moment to reminisce about her life, as she figured in all likelihood it would be over quite soon, given where the world was heading. Music was one of her escapes, and she took a deep breath, closed her eyes and reached deep into her memories of a simpler time of endless summers and teenage immortality, listening to 45s with her then-boyfriend Herbie in her bedroom in her parents' end of terrace in Hunsbury Meadows. They used to go down to Abington Street on a Monday after the charts were published and get a couple of records to play on repeat. Sadly for Herbie, his life didn't quite pan out the same way as his girlfriend's. After they broke up, she buried her head in GCSE textbooks, fuelling a pathway to university and politics. He buried his head in questionable substances and spent the majority of his adult life living at Her Majesty's Pleasure in Bath, where he moved to, as he said, 'to find himself'. She knew she'd dodged a bullet with that one, but ironically, she thought he'd probably survive all of this, and she'd be the one swallowed into oblivion.

"Ruth!" She audibly said out loud, realising she need to be present and get back to supporting this room of exhausted but relentlessly committed scientists. *Game face,* she thought to herself as she called everyone to attention. All eyes looked towards her. Tired, almost desolate eyes, yearning for some kind of relief. She gave them what she could.

"The future of our planet is not your responsibility. The fact that each and every one of you feels that is a testament to your courage, professionalism and sense of true purpose. We have always been at the mercy of geological events, pre-dating human existence of course, so perhaps this will lead to a totally new beginning for Earth with no human life. But there may be survivors. And if there's one thing that has defined the human race, it's that we have a knack of surviving. Yes, we may be fighting a losing battle. But what if we're not? What if what you do here in this room gives humanity the chance to survive even if we do not? What a legacy. What a justification for all your sacrifices now and for your whole lives, giving generations to come a platform from which to rebuild society. My God, what a fresh start would do for this world. In different circumstances, this would be amazing. I'm not pretending this is anything other than a tragedy but just think what if the solution you find in here, the safe havens across the world, a tiny slice of certainty perhaps, or you never know, a way to stop or at least predict these terrible events could lead to a new beginning. One where every living soul has the same chance of not only survival but flourishing wherever they are or whatever land they inhabit. This is now what we're working on. So, I won't patronise you by thanking you. I have no right to assume a position of authority over you, but you have a unique chance to identify the future path for billions of terrified and helpless individuals, families and loved ones across the world. Stay strong and who knows what may come of this. All I can say to you is that a few metres away in another room, global leaders are trying their darn hardest to come up with a way to talk to the world before we lose the ability to communicate. They believe in you. You need to believe in you. I'll let you get back to your workstations. Godspeed." Keeble followed up her passionate rally cry by walking the room and checking in on everyone individually on an emotional level, while Jeff collated and summarised the team's latest modelling data and headed down the corridor to pass it to the Senator, Peter and Jane.

57

"We're on air in twenty minutes Jeff, any miracles from the Hyatt Suite?" Jane probed optimistically.

"Sadly not and their heads are going down. Prime Minister Keeble probably pumped a couple more hours of any energy into them, but the data doesn't change. We simply don't have probes in the ground able to feedback on the kind of information that would allow us to make predictions and manage large-scale evacuations ahead of time. It feels like the world is sitting on a million trapdoors with each one set to go off randomly."

"Nothing is random," Pete interjected. "We all know that Jeff, it just feels like it when we don't get to see the patterns. Either the gravitational force is equal and there are inconsistencies in the structural strength of the lithosphere, or the forces are pulsing based on deeper geological factors or a mix of everything which is most likely. My primary source of hope, which I shared with the leaders, is the current events and surface collapse are down to intolerable geological pressures deep inside the Earth, and that somehow these fissures through which the water is seeping and into which our land messes are folding is alleviating the pressure either temporarily, or maybe even permanently. Or as permanent as geological time allowance, say a million years."

"But you don't actually believe that do you Pete?" Jeff senses his college buddy was sugarcoating this whole scenario.

"I do not," Pete replied succinctly. "But it doesn't mean they shouldn't." He motioned towards the room-cum-studio housing the political galacticos. "I'm not spreading lies, but it's tough to sell hope when you don't have any yourself. So yes, maybe the Earth will feel relieved to have released some gravitational tension, seal itself back up, recycle the water back into the atmosphere and revert to stability. Ironically, this is exactly what will happen, of course. The land and water aren't going to leave the planet, so at a point in time, there will be stability, just without human life. Unless somehow, we can tough it out in the poles. They look like the only zones which could be escaping the worst of this. Closer to the core, less pressure, ice sheets acting as shock absorbers. If only we weren't actually destroying them with our wanton disregard for natural resources. Anyhow, for the time being, we need to get through the next hour without spooking President Franks and his buddies. They're about to talk to whoever is left able to access the internet."

Towards the end of the corridor of meeting rooms and suites, there was a hubbub of activity from the attending hotel staff and a flurry of bowing suggesting one or more of the leaders had exited. It was President Franks and Chairman Guo who emerged from the throng of Japanese who had been busy preparing the makeshift TV studio from which the impending broadcast would take place. Jane, Peter and Jeff stepped aside to allow the two men to pass by, but it was the Chinese leader who motioned them to gather together.

"We would value your opinion Professor and that of your colleagues." Guo handed each of them a single A4 piece of Hyatt Hotel headed paper with one side of text with the headline 'Global Disaster Announcement'.

Franks took over, "Come and see us in ten minutes, then we have ten more minutes to make any amends and translate it. So, you know we're each going to read the statement in our own tongue. Then we're planning on piping in the Spanish president and French Prime Minister thanks to, I think you know him Jane, Klaus Jurgensen's help. We'll then post it across multiple platforms in several other languages, but the PR chap Rogers and the journalist Harpinder are working on that. I must say it's some team the Senator has assembled." Guo nodded in agreement.

"Please do take a look, we need to get back to President Zarkov." Jane was dying to ask where the Russian was but felt it better not to pry and Franks answered it anyway.

"Sadly, St Petersburg has gone under so the president is dealing with that."

Such was the intensity of the situation and frequency of such devastating news it was becoming matter of fact to talk about whole metropolises being decimated. Peter took the sheets from the US president and said they look over them right away and with that, the two men turned and returned to their meeting room to prepare for the announcement. Five minutes later, Jane knocked on the door leading to the leader's room and was surprised when Guo himself opened it.

"Sir, we have no changes." It was straight to the point and largely true. They had discussed re-wording certain elements but ultimately decided the message would be the same. And in reality, they had arguably been the main contributors to the announcement anyway.

"Higashi-san we're ready," Frank called out to the Hyatt Hotel manager, who had been rushed off his feet more than ever before preparing his business centre to become a global media hub without an experienced team to facilitate it. But with a local crew and aided by Harpinder Tarkovski and Chester Rogers, they were set. Rogers had been given unprecedented access to the world's foremost leaders to coordinate the global announcement, liaising with Prime Minister Ito in Japan, Wahyani in Indonesia, Kapoor in India, Klaus for the EU, Argentinian President Santos, and Deri Koont of the African Union. Harpinder had worked her media contacts to coordinate between themselves to effectively blackout other streams to essentially jam the airwaves with the Tokyo announcement. The majority of nations had the ability to message every internet-enabled device in their jurisdiction and planned to forcibly stream the announcement without prior warning. The general consensus was that, despite the potential legal ramifications of privacy being invaded, such was the significance of the situation that everyone, except the Brazilian president, signed up to the plan. Brazil, argued President Firmino, would have their own announcement. Despite Manaus being one of the worst hit and earliest affected area, Firmino claimed it was a local anomaly and not a global disaster anywhere near the scale his counterparts were talking about. What it boiled down to was he was so involved in Senator Johnson's new Industrial Revolution plan that his stubbornness wouldn't let him acknowledge that the plan was not only dead in the water, but it had been superseded by Mother Nature's own plan for his country. Rogers also suspected he was smarting that Portuguese had not been selected as one of the announcement languages despite his protestations, correctly Rogers had to concede given it was the most widely spoken language in the southern hemisphere.

    Proof that the media coordination plan was taking effect was the fact that everyone's phone in the business centre and presumably across Tokyo and beyond, had a message pop up on their screen in kanji. Everyone in the Hyatt Suite stopped whatever they were doing, eyes glued to the large screen, showing three chairs behind a large wooden table that was but fifty feet from where they were all sitting down the corridor. There was a sense of palpable tension as the three leaders had a token application of make-up from the local Tokyo TV crew, mainly it was assumed, to take the shine from their faces rather than for any cosmetic narcissism.

Jeff, Peter, and Jane beckoned Elaine to come and join them in the broadcast suite. She felt better to be around them as she was still reeling from the shock of seeing her expat hometown, Johor Bahru, be impacted by this geographical wrath meaning almost certainly that all her friends there had perished without a chance, possibly her estranged husband too.

President Franks led his Russian and Chinese counterparts into the room, and they all took their seats. Franks on the right, Zarkov on the left with Guo central, decided moments ago by drawn lots to save any petty arguments. They had also drawn lots as to which order to speak in with Guo up first, then Franks, then Zarkov, with the Spanish and French leaders to follow remotely. Guo was a confident orator, although pretty much no one knew what he was saying so they assumed he had followed the script. What was clear was his mention of President Franks, who took it as his cue to speak. He cleared his throat, took a deep breath and looked visibly emotional. As he prepared to read his auto-text on the camera facing him, in a spontaneous act of sensing the occasion, he removed his tie and undid his top button, feeling this was a moment to seem less of a distant, stuffy, out of touch politician and more of a regular man on the street talking one-to-one rather than from some official functional podium. He looked straight in the camera and began to read.

58

"Good day to you Planet Earth. We are broadcasting live from the heart of Tokyo, Japan and in other circumstances, we would be announcing to you a far-reaching economic renewal programme as part of a new global alliance. Instead, we draw on the close bonds between global partners, turning our backs on historical differences and focusing together on securing a future for you and generations to come. Humankind has walked the Earth for only a fraction of our great planet's existence. And, in this relatively short time, we have directly experienced some of Mother Nature's majestic, yet devastating forces. From volcanoes to earthquakes, tidal waves to droughts, many of us around the world already live at her mercy. But now we all do. Unimaginable destruction of areas of landmass leading to large scale loss of life in immeasurable quantities means the world is on red alert and we are working with a world class team of geologists, scientists and climatologists using the finest minds at NASA and equivalent centres across the globe, a number of whom are with us here in Tokyo, to establish a predictable pattern for these events, should they continue to occur. We must stress that although these events are not earthquakes, in that they do not depend on the coming together of tectonic plates which impact only certain global regions, geological anomalies like the ones we are witnessing within the Earth are notoriously challenging to predict. So, I'm genuinely heartbroken to say we need to be preparing ourselves for more of these destructive events to occur across the globe. We will work tirelessly, and I can personally attest to the dedication of those working on a solution, but in the meantime, we all need to take some personal responsibility. Now," the president took a deep breath, removed his glasses and momentarily put his head in his hands as he deviated from the script, clasping his hands almost in prayer under his chin in an act of genuine humility, although inevitably it wouldn't be seen as such by many. "When I talk about personal responsibility, this is not about me, the US president telling you how to live your life. I know, as do my fellow leaders sitting alongside me, that our lives are nothing like yours. But what we do know is that your actions in the next period of time will potentially be more impactful and important than ours in our collective battle to survive these terrible, unearthly events. More information will be available for you following this broadcast so please do what you can." Franks went back to the script, "We ask you to be sensible with water. If you live near the sea or inland bodies of water, you won't fail to notice the levels are dropping as the Earth opens up and drains our precious lifeblood deep inside. We're going to have some shortages." He veered off script again in a blur of emotion. "My childhood holiday destination, North America's Great Lakes, are dry. It seems extraordinary to say it out loud. But if it helps bring clarity, then let's be real about this. Save water, whatever that means for you." Franks went back and finished the rest of the script without further adlibbing. Much to the relief of President Guo and Zarkov, who were less inclined to emotion and neither had a population with the freedoms to protest and disagree like the US leader. Franks quickly listed some potential strategies to cope with the events along the tried and tested lines of staying in homes, welcoming in displaced neighbours, being practical with food and water supplies. But he stopped short of saying what he was intimating that 'if it happens where you live, you will certainly die' and more along the lines of 'stay where you are and pray to God it's not you'.

"In the next forty-eight hours," Franks was at the final stage of the announcement before handing over to President Zarkov, "we," he motioned towards the Russian and Chinese alongside him, "will return to our countries, as I suspect all global leaders will, to be with our countrymen and women in this time of turmoil. There is no secret bunker or safe house. We don't know yet how this is going to end, but our team here in Tokyo will disband and spread itself across the globe, joined internationally by many networks of scientists and great minds alike, all working indefatigably to forge a path to global stability. Please play your part by continuing to be good citizens and helping your neighbours. At times like these, we need each other more than ever. Stay safe everyone and Godspeed. President Zarkov, the floor is yours dear comrade."

Once Zarkov had finished, the live feed cut off from the Hyatt Hotel as the French and Spanish broadcasts were beamed around the world. And the three world leaders emerged from behind the makeshift press conference desk, Prime Minister Keeble was waiting to greet them.

59

"Well?" President Franks was always keen to know his impact. Years of politicking had conditioned him to be mindful of ratings after every decision rally or public event.

"Nelson, you're damned if you do, damned if you don't."

"That doesn't sound good. Did we miss the mark?"

"The mark isn't the issue here. Quite simply we've just told the world about its intending collapse and advised they stay calm and consume less water whilst around them, it's literally disappearing. Or even worse their neighbourhood is disappearing. So yes, there has been some reaction to it. But in every country, not just the English-speaking ones you targeted, people are scared. Hell, I'm scared. And, once you talk to Louis, I suspect you'll be in the same place. But remember, there was rioting and disorder before this announcement and the amount of insanity on social, and conventional media I might add, needed addressing. I hope in the long run we are proved right but come and speak to Louis and his team. You might want to bring Zarkov and Guo too."

During the broadcasts, Tanya James, Rose Carmichael, and Kelly Chan had been in deep discussion with NASA research lead Louis Charles. They had been joined by one of Chairman Guo's trusted scientific advisers, a thick-set middle-aged man called Penn. President Franks hadn't been far off when he joked about China's spending on research. Penn had told them very matter of factly that their monthly budget was roughly the same as the US and EU annual spending on scientific research combined. He did admit that the investment meant more about manpower and technology power rather than brain power, and that thinkers on the level of Peter Masai, or indeed his present company, are rare in China.

He explained, "In China we have an over-reliance on supercomputers, however sophisticated, and this had made our science graduates less reliant on their own cognitive powers. We have a generation of programmers, whereas you in the West are still producing thinkers."

"Who'd have thought global collaboration could be a positive thing? Bringing a mix of skills together for the greater good." Louis chuckled as he said it.

"Indeed," although Penn didn't quite have the gallows humour of the free-spirited American.

"We have the data. We have the processing power. Which is why we aligned with Professor Masai and your president. So, what we can now offer is what the future likely holds for Planet Earth. Sadly, what we are missing is a timeline and the confidence to predict locations of upcoming Masai Events, as I believe they are now called. But what we do believe, is that by 2200 the Earth will look more like this."

Louis Charles took one look at the rotating range of the world and without hesitation called out across the room, "Prime Minister Keeble you need to take a look at this."

In a surprising democratisation of power, at least to her, Elaine had been asked by Keeble to recommend geographical locations for the Tokyo team to disperse to, following the broadcasts and mop-up afterwards. She wasn't sure if it was just something to take her attention away from her grief around Malaysia being hit, and she chastised herself for her own self-doubt. Yes, she was upset but she wasn't alone in that, and everyone was being asked to do things which a month ago would have seemed ludicrous. So, she accepted the task confidently and without fuss, although she assumed whatever she came up with would not simply be imposed on the team. There must be some kind of opt out or negotiation, she assumed. Either way, she figured names and places needed listing, so she started with what she thought were the easiest, and this was before they announced their travel plans to the world, which were the global leaders. They simply needed to go home to be with their people. There were others similarly straightforward to place. Michelle Grant and Monty Symonds were already in Manchester. Marco Hernandez might appreciate being repatriated to Mexico after his date with destiny was dramatically snatched away. Keeble and Norton would head back to London. Klaus Jurgensen would go to Europe and base himself in the EU somewhere. She didn't feel the need to stipulate where exactly. Louis Charles and Tanya James would be best operating out of NASA HQ in Houston. Harpinder and Peter could go back to Berlin. She understood Nancy Rastik had family in Australia, and somewhere out of the way felt quite appropriate for her. Rose and Kelly had already told Elaine how much they loved Tokyo and wanted to stay. Prime Minister Keeble and Senator Gordon had direct lines to Deri Koont, chair of the African Union, so he could coordinate the African response. She knew little about Chester Rogers, so pencilled him down for South America, to which his response was, "if I can go to Santiago, I'm in" so that proved easier than expected. That left Senator Gordon, who was likely to go to New York or somewhere other than Washington or Houston, and apart from Jeff, Jane and herself. Would Jeff and Jane just want to go back to the Bureau in DC? She suspected Jane would want to be in the thick of things. But Jeff, she wasn't sure about. And what about herself? It felt so much more straightforward placing other people, she wasn't quite ready to think about where she should head next, so she added their three names to the bottom of the page with 'TBC' next to them and passed it to Prime Minister Keeble, who took one look, said, "Excellent work. Elaine," and continued almost without breaking stride down the corridor.

President Franks invited Zarkov Guo to join him at Prime Minister Keeble's behest back in the Hyatt Suite.

"Professor," Franks called over to Peter, who was with Jane and Elaine, digesting the announcement and discussing their views on ramifications which they immediately stopped and followed the leaders down the brightly lit corridor.

"It sounds like we'd all better be present for this. Let's hope it's good news." His tone confirmed this was indeed in hope, not expectation. Prime Minister Keeble once again took the lead. She had quietly but assuredly filled the gap left by the otherwise occupied Senator Gordon and he did not feel any need to wrestle back control. That was not his modus operandi.

"This may be the last time in the foreseeable future, or even ever, that we're able to be in the same room together as we head out across the globe to continue our work. I have posted a list of destinations for us all." She glanced over and nodded to Elaine a silent acknowledgement of thanks. "Let me or the Senator know if there are issues with your placement location." Elaine could see the list on the opposite wall and spotted straight away that the TBC for her, Jeff and Jane had been crossed through, but she couldn't quite make out what it said. She quietly and slowly moved around the back of the group and sidled up to Jeff who was intently reading the post too. Jane had been allocated Berlin to work with Peter, that made sense. And Michelle Grant had been posted to the Arctic instead of Manchester. Elaine assumed correctly, that was the result of a conversation. *Maybe it coincided with her work at the Bee*

Foundation? Either way, it immediately sparked Elaine into realising where her name would be, they needed representation at both poles. It had become clear to everyone that she no longer had family or geographical ties in Malaysia so, as her eyes darted to the bottom of the list, the surprise wasn't that her name was against Antarctica, but there was another name next to hers, one which made her heart skip a beat and face go bright red.

60

"I see we've been banished together," Jeff smiled warmly at Elaine, "and from what I've seen we may end up being Adam and Eve 2.0, we might be the only ones left. I'll bring an apple if you've got a snake." Before Elaine got the chance to really process what all this would mean for her and Jeff, and the idea of her and Jeff together, Keeble cut off her thoughts.

"Louis please update us." Louis ran his fingers through his thick blond hair, and it didn't go unnoticed how the UK Prime Minister blushed which brought a tiny slice of light relief to a morbid situation.

"Thank you, Prime Minister, but the work is primarily Penn and his team's, I'm just a mouthpiece on this." Penn nodded generously. He had grown up being told Americans were selfish, useless oafs but his recent experience had corrected him. The collaboration was more than he'd ever imagined possible. Such a pity it had an air of futility about it.

Louis Charles continued. "Reminder, as if we need it. Professor Masai's hypothesis is that subterranean forces in the Earth's core are leading to a weakness of the outer surface structure of the planet, a) resulting in large-scale lithospheric collapse and we know the impact this is having in the populated areas. And b) causing fissures, allowing surface water, fresh and ocean, depending on location, to escape into the Earth, how deep and permanent we're yet to establish. Predictability is the cornerstone of any response and sadly, we're not in that place yet. But what Penn's model is showing us, is a long-term realignment of the Earth's crust between the polar circles, coupled with a near complete deletion of surface water. Our blue planet, ladies and gentlemen, is turning brown." The image of Earth's future appeared on the big screen to audible gasps. The current continental outlines were still visible, but instead of oceanic blue surrounding them, there was an orangey brown with sporadic patches of water dotted across the planet.

"Aside from the very real possibility of widespread inhabited land collapse, which we'll address second, the absence of surface water and consequently apocalyptic drought will cause arguably the greatest threat to humankind since the last Ice Age, notwithstanding the man-made climatic destruction we've allowed ourselves to permit in the last fifty years or so. Maybe Mother Nature wants to wipe out humanity on her terms instead of watching us do it to ourselves," Louis said bleakly. "At current rates of depletion, the model tells us we'll be in this drought phase you see on the screen here within five years. It doesn't take a climatologist to tell you this is bad news. It's going to get hot, possibly unsurvivably hot, partly due to what will happen to weather patterns, but also because oceans sequester so much carbon that without them greenhouse gases will go crazy, that's the technical term folks. Vegetation will struggle to cope and is a vicious circle and race to the bottom. What the model also tells us, and we had an advanced hypothesis on this, is that the polar regions might be less impacted by the crust collapses we've seen around the world. The ice acts as a geological shock absorber, so we think as the surface water floods the mantle, it too will mitigate the impact of these massive events. So, we may, and I say this with all fingers and toes crossed, we may have seen the worst of the land destruction, although it will continue as weaknesses become apparent, deep beneath us. Just to be clear, as I'd hate to mislead you and don't want to encourage undue optimism," that was a word far from everyone's lips right now. "This supposes by 2200 about twenty-five per cent of the world's landmass will experience some kind of topographical realignment, which is still quite a significant portion. For context, the European Commission's joint research centre estimated in 2009 that ninety-five per cent of the world's population is concentrated in just ten per cent of the land surface." Everyone in the Hyatt Suite was promptly mentally juggling numbers before Louis continued.

"The likelihood is most population hubs will be unaffected, but not necessarily. It would be impossible to know until it happens. Sadly, the Professor and I spoke briefly about this before, and at this point, it remains our only hope, and I appreciate hope is a word I'm over-using right now, given the absence of certainties, it is the very disintegration of the Earth's insides which has caused surface water dissipation, causes enough shuggling, for want of a better word, of the lithosphere that the fissures are closed by default, and we don't lose as much water as this suggests." A new image appeared which had 'best case' in emboldened yellow.

"We need time to establish the climate impact of fifty per cent water preservation. But this would likely facilitate the survival of the human race in some form, in some locations. But folks, unless there is anything anyone wants to add at this point, I suggest we take fifteen minutes if that's OK with you, Prime Minister?" Keeble nodded silently, allowing Louis to close out, "And consider our options both as a group but also as individuals because, and I'm not going to sugarcoat this, most of us, if not all, are unlikely to see in the next decade."

"Senator, Professor, Charles." President Franks called across the three men to join him and Prime Minister Keeble in one corner of the suite. "I won't lie. I'm kinda glad we didn't have this information when we went on air.

Although I suspect there will be total anarchy anyway. I envy Guo. He's pretty much got a compliant population already. I reckon I'll have to roll out martial law to keep society from destroying itself back in the US."

"Sir," Gordon interrupted Franks, sensing his desperation. "You don't have to have all the answers. None of us do. As you said yourself, all we're getting are problems because solutions are hard, and in this situation, damn near impossible, all we can do is get home and surround ourselves physically or more likely remotely with some very bright people who can offer practical strategies to deal with this, all the while praying the ground stays beneath our feet."

Keeble added, "I entirely concur Senator. The enormity of the task ahead is not for one person to consider their own. Every action you take will be one of many options, but I know, we know, you'll make the best choice available to you at each moment. We all will. That's all we can do. I'm sure the professor will attest to the fact we're up against unstoppable forces here, not political or economic barriers. We'd be better putting Louis and Peter in charge in many ways." She took a quick glance at the two scientists, "We probably won't, don't worry chaps." Instantly dashing Pete's wild imagination running riot with visions of him being Prime Minister of the United Kingdom. *I'd be on more than the front cover of New Scientist if that's what happened,* he mused. *What would his mother say?* He suddenly realised he should call her.

"Professor!" Keeble snapped Peter's attention back.

"Entirely sir. I'm afraid we are dinosaurs watching the asteroid come hurtling down towards us, the only real difference is we are sentient beings, and we know what that asteroid means to us."

"But how are you seemingly so okay about all this Professor? It's as if it hasn't affected you and to a certain degree you too Louis."

"Simple," Pete replied on behalf of them both without needing to confer. "I've spent most of my adult life prophesising the end of the world. I don't have children and I'm not a leader of millions of citizens. Aside from the very annoying downside that I'll inevitably die early along with the rest of the human race, I'll get to see one of, if not the greatest, geological event in history unfold in real-time."

"Professor I hear you," Louis added, "and it's kind of exciting, the finality of it all, but there's still jeopardy and things might just work out in our favour and I, we, get to be part of that. Although, whilst we're being a bit macabre and self-obsessed, Peter you have the extraordinary honour, I know that's the wrong word, of this whole Armageddon being named after you." For the second time in as many minutes, Peter's 'rock star' front cover flashed into his mind.

Charles continued, "We know this is different for you guys and I'm pretty sure neither of us would swap places with you, but you've proven to a group of very judgmental and discerning scientists that you have the guts, values and personalities to support your countries and beyond whatever course this takes."

Gordon and Keeble exchanged knowing glances and the Senator wrapped things up requesting the attention of everyone in the room.

"Is this our time?" He consciously decided to go big. "Quite possibly our generation will be the last to represent the human race but, and it's an important but, we all know how robust Planet Earth is, how strong the human survival instinct is and most importantly, if science is going to be the key to navigating this most heinous of chapters in our history, then it will be you, the brave and dedicated people in this room who will guide us to a new era. In the coming forty-eight hours we will scatter ourselves across the globe, taking our chances in geographical roulette but, despite the imminent threat of destruction, in spite of the thousands of miles between us, we stand shoulder to shoulder. We will work smart and leave no stone unturned to discover a pattern so we can predict these terrible land collapses and water releases. But also, so we may uncover a real and practical solution. I believe it can be done; you have to believe too. Therefore, let's part with a plan for success and agree…" he paused for effect "…we will meet again." Although for the most part a serious man, the Senator was himself wondering if he'd gone a bit overboard with his 'this is our Independence Day' speech rip-off. So, he quickly decided to temper his largely over-positive rally cry with a more humbling message.

With his voice slightly lowered, he spoke. "Look guys, now even I'm spinning this, and it seems easy when you're locked in a room like this, working like you are to find a way through. I'm not pretending millions of people haven't died or our very evolutionary lifeblood isn't disappearing beneath our feet and in all likelihood, some, maybe all of us, might go too, but as I prepare to return home I know if I could choose a bunch of people to find a way out of this, it's you. Good luck everyone."

It felt like the room was about to release its emotion in a round of applause. But Chairman Guo raised his hand as if to pre-emptively stop the clapping.

"Please, please do not feel this is a Western problem. I know our countries and regions have often failed to work together, although some of you know President Franks, Zarkov and I were keen to join forces to reinvigorate the global economy, albeit on shaky foundations I admit. But now our focus is on survival and rebuilding. I would like to invite Louis Charles and his exceptional colleague, Miss James, to join Dr Penn in Shanghai at our Science Institute so they can work together. It's a risk that I am personally willing to take." He looked over at Franks, who nodded enthusiastically. Louis and Tanya seemed pretty unnerved by this so everyone assumed they already knew. They also know the risk Guo was talking about wasn't the threat of professional disagreements, but the risk if Shanghai went down, then they'd lose all three experts in one go.

President Franks called the group's likely final session together to a close by rather macabrely drawing their attention back to the main screen, which was once again showing the global status board complete the flashing red zones and death toll, which had now topped two hundred million. Franks himself winced when he saw this, partly at the incredible number, but also that it was someone's job, probably back in Louis' team in Houston, to be inputting this data. It was impossible to comprehend the scale, so it made Franks and the others home in on individual circumstances to try and make sense of it. He had wanted the team to see their allocated or chosen location was still in existence, literally. And he could see their eyes frantically scanning to check relevant places around the world either they themselves were headed or were more likely where their family or friends resided. There was a visible mix of relief, pain, and overarching dread, so Franks sped up the exit.

"Folks; arrangements have been made, or are being made, for your travel in the coming day or two and you will all be recompensed for your hard work and commitments from your relevant governments. Not quite a blank cheque or credit card, but we recognise this isn't a time to be worrying about money, so be respectful, make good choices, don't be strangers and be lucky."

61

In the taxi on their way back to their hotel Peter, Jane, Elaine and Jeff sat mostly in exhausted brain-drain silence as their car weaved its way through crowds of people lining the streets. They weren't rioting, weren't quite protesting, it just seemed like being out and about was the right thing to be doing. A contrast to the many other countries, most in fact, where law and order weren't quite as upheld as in Japan and news of the widespread disorder and looting was leading many nations, just as President Franks had predicted for the US, to implement martial law.

It was Elaine who broke the stillness. "Franks' telling us to be lucky. This is really what this boils down to, isn't it?"

"Depends on what he or you mean by lucky." Pete had seen nothing in the past twenty-four hours to convince him of anything other than total human annihilation. "Lucky to be caught up in these land collapses, please don't make me call them Masai Events, or lucky to avoid them and be on a planet with no viable infrastructure governance or way to sustainably feed its remaining population? All assuming whoever does survive can exist in what will be a vastly different climate. You can shove your 1.5-degree Celsius rise up your wherever compared to the combined threat of water loss and greenhouse gas release. Although we talked about the increased gravitational pull, however slight, holding down dust clouds from the land collapses, but it won't stop it all. That'll start to impact sunlight, rain purity and surface temperature."

"OK, Mr Positive, we all get it," Jeff interjected, "at least we'll be inland." Although he wasn't totally sure where the Antarctic base, which would be his and Elaine's in the coming days was. But he assumed, incorrectly as it turned out, it was pretty central. He was referring to, which the others recognised, the mid-ocean land collapses which were causing mega tsunamis, two at least they knew of. One in the Indian Ocean had caused devastation in southern Africa, taking out much of South Africa's East Coast north of Durban right up to the Bazaruto Archipelago in Mozambique and wiped out much of the southern tip of Madagascar the other side. Halfway round the world off the coast of Columbia, a similar displacement of the sea floor had sent a three hundred metre wave crashing into Panama, with initial reports suggesting most of the country's low-lying areas had been destroyed.

"Does Antarctica count as inland?" Jane wanted to steer the conversation away from anything which might raise tensions, given how tired they all were. And she also wanted to find out what the story was with Jeff and Elaine going to the pole together. Pete was delighted at the change of subject and dived straight in, no filters.

"Given Antarctica is the most likely region to escape all this apocalyptic destruction, you guys might be part of a select few around to rebirth the human race Jeff, you'd better start eating more veg and drinking eight glasses of water a day." Luckily for Elaine, the darkness in the taxi hid her rose red blushing cheeks.

"Jeff and I haven't had a proper chance to talk about it, but I, for one, I'm looking forward to spending some quality time with him." She looked over and smiled at her former college flame, and he returned a warm smile, the exchange just discernible in the fading light.

"But what about eternity?" laughed Pete.

"Could be worse, Pete," Jeff matched the laugh and gently nudged Jane. "Could be stuck with you for eternity instead. I know where I'd rather be and that's with the penguins." The rest of the journey passed in silence, each of them lost in their own thoughts thinking of these near and far, each one wondering what fate had installed for them. The adrenaline which had powered them through the night in the Hyatt Hotel drained away as heads finally hit pillows back at the Cherry Blossom Hotel, Shibuya.

62

Pete woke around midday, showered, dressed, and headed out into the city for some air. He was used to spending days on end inside but he was convinced that he would likely never visit Tokyo again based on a number of fairly depressing factors that he decided to block out of his mind as he wandered the immaculate streets of Shinjuku, despite the many locals still bustling aimlessly around, stopping for some green tea and chilli ramen from a street vendor, seemingly going about his daily business as if he had no cares in the world. *Potentially*, thought Pete, *he may be entirely oblivious to the impending end of the world as they knew it.* Or perhaps a little like Pete himself, he was sanguine about the whole scenario and would simply carry on as long as he was able. He was soon joined by Jeff, who had been the second to rise and pick up Pete's message about his stroll and location. After a few loud, taste-enhancing slurps and inspired by the old man serving them, Pete posed a question.

"When do people stop living their daily lives? At what point will futility surpass hope?" Jeff stayed silent, not because he didn't want to engage but he knew from experience, Pete liked to do his thinking out loud, so he kept the floor clear for him to explore his thoughts.

"Take this chap here. He'll be here, or somewhere not far away, for as long as there are people to feed who can pay, and he's able to do it physically. I'd wager no amount of apocalyptic media will stop him. What might stop him, though, is lack of supply ingredients or water, power, et cetera. But even then, he will find something else to make and sell that he can source. Necessity is the mother of invention remember. But what about his customers? This dude here, the banker." Jeff clocked the thirty-something man sitting at the table next to them had an HSBC lanyard.

Pete continued, "At what point will the global banking system fail, and the extrinsic value of money and investments become worthless? City infrastructure becomes unsustainable with no means of payment. Utility companies cease trading and governments are powerless to keep them going, aside from dictating it. With a non-monetised Internet, global national and local communications will grind to a halt. Within years, maybe even months, we're back in the Dark Ages where tradable commodities such as clean water, non-perishable food shelter and clothing will be the new Bitcoin, and people will be burning cash instead of spending it. And who carries on in this situation? Not the first fresh-faced banker we have here with his shiny shoes and slick hair. No, it's the wily, old, wrinkly man with the most precious of resources; endeavour."

"I think it's a great question Pete, that of when the turning point is and I guess it'll vary by location as events happen around people, or collectively society realises the current way of life is just no more. It'll be fascinating to watch. Well for you guys in Berlin, not sure our base in Antarctica will see quite the same changes. When will parents stop sending their children to school, when will people simply stop paying bills or paying for anything in fact? I'm no sociologist, but I wonder if humanity might turn on itself before Mother Nature even gets the chance to do it for us?"

"I think you're right to a certain extent Jeff. We can already see pockets of anarchy breaking out across the world, but I can guarantee there will be more examples of kindness, kinship, and coming together of communities That's just not a social media worthy. The world loves a tragedy, so my bet is over time new communities will develop based on coincidence of wants and bartering becoming the norm between these communities."

"OK Pete, you're going glass half full, I'm going for total anarchy. Let's see who's right. Come and visit us in twenty years on our floating island paradise when you're the only land-based savage who's survived, or in your world, ride your flying unicorn of peace to our community of love." They both laughed. It was a rare moment of joy amongst the bewildering reality of their situation. Hours away from inevitable permanent separation.

"We see you've really been affected by all this chaps." Jane grinned at the still chuckling two men whose laughing was infectious, even making the incredibly uptight Jane relax for a few moments.

"We've ditched geology for sociology. I'm backing total Wild West bedlam and Professor Pete, against all the odds, is going for collective peace and love. Where are you guys on the spectrum?"

Jane jumped straight in, "I reckon anarchy leading to community. Humans need to be together. So, I'm going for a terrible few years then the rise of a new philosophy of living."

"Bingpot!" exclaimed Pete, "That's why the dream team are heading for Berlin."

"And you Elaine?" Jeff asked. "Are you with Professor Peace or Jeff's world of carnage?"

"A few months ago, I'd have been a classic fence sitter, but new improved end-of-the-world-Elaine is a decisive beast and a bleak one at that. I think I'm in your world of carnage, Jeff. We'll be better off in our snow cave. But I hope you guys are right. I also think the fact you're going back to Germany is making your subconscious minds give your state of reality some hope."

"Now, who's the psychologist?" Jeff was impressed as Elaine continued, pretty much telling Pete and Jane they were kidding themselves into feeling positive.

"If I were, we were," a glance at Jeff as if they were a couple, "going back to let's say Washington or Manchester, instead of Antarctica, I'd want to believe people wouldn't be forever trying to hunt me down or attack me, but with the promise of geographical isolation from almost all other souls, my general disdain for what humans do to each other and the planet makes me entirely devoid of hope that any good will come from this. The most likely outcome is the selfish, aggressive, and emotionless will survive and they're not, in my book anyway, the best blueprint for restarting the human race. Albeit one that'll need to tough out some pretty challenging environments. So having said all that, you're probably right to an extent but it won't be a colony of hippies that emerge but a battle-hardened bunch of out-for-mes." They all looked at Elaine waiting for the penny to drop for her too.

"Bugger!" she exclaimed. "I'm back on that fucking fence again, aren't I?" More raucous laughter rolled around the four or so wooden tables, drawing smiles from both the other patrons and concession owner himself. Normally he catered for solo diners, mainly Tokyo's salarymen, grabbing a quick bite. Few of them had either time or facilities at home for cooking meals. They worked long hours, invariably lived way out of town, given the cost of housing, so a few minutes of fresh air and some nutritious noodle broth was just the tonic to get them through their tough days. So, a lively group of gaijans, foreigners, made a refreshing change to the introverted ambiance of solo eaters.

The laughing came to an abrupt halt as the ground beneath them began to vibrate, a little like a subway train was passing right beneath them.

"Oh, you're kidding me!" Jeff blurted out, fearing the worst, that this was Tokyo's turn to implode, taking them all down with it. Everyone else at the stall remained silent with bated breath, physically frozen in place, waiting to see if the vibrations would increase. Locals, of course, had been waiting for X-day for their whole lives, the expected Big One, an earthquake to end all urban earthquakes. So, every tremor they feel puts the Tokyo population on red alert. Their relentless training kicks in, hoping to whichever God is theirs, that the public address system doesn't sound signifying that this is it.

Therefore, if any city is prepared for large scale destruction, it is Tokyo. As everyone at the stall held their chair tightly, the vibrations slowed instead of increasing and in a matter of seconds, all was still once again. Without a word or signal, the Tokyoites carried on their business as if they just been playing musical statues. They were used to the occasional tremor, living as they did, above two very active tectonic plates. So, once it had passed, they just got on with it. The concession owner lit some incense by an offering and muttered some words as a thank you for sparing them this time and went back to his huge pan of chilli ramen as if nothing had happened. Unbeknownst to the Japanese on the street corner, it was anything but nothing which had just happened, as Peter Masai was about to tell his friends, given his phone just lit up with a message from NASA researcher Louis Charles.

"That wasn't an earthquake, folks. We just dodged a bullet. That was Louis, just checking up on us. Japan's had its first major collapse, and it's a biggie." They all looked at Pete imploring him to spill the beans. "Niigata and surrounds have gone."

Elaine was first to react. "Niigata?" she exclaimed. "That's over three hundred kilometres away."

"Christ, this thing is really happening." Jeff pretty much just said it to himself but all four of them suddenly felt this was very real. Watching something happen on a screen through data points is markedly different than actually feeling the ground beneath you shake when all you've been thinking about was the ground giving way. The mood instantly changed for the four Westerners, and Pete wondered how soon the news would filter through to the other patrons at the store and of course to the thirty-odd million people who lived in this most densely populated of cities. *They may be preparing for X-day*, thought Peter to himself, *but if the Earth opens up and swallows you, nothing can prepare you for that.*

A number of phones started pinging both in the kiosk area and with passers-by. Every glance at the phone was followed by the owner gasping, then standing or sitting open mouthed in disbelief. Jane, Jeff and Elaine were no different. The most widely circulating video had appeared almost instantly, presumably because it was already being uploaded when the drone camera caught the collapse. The drone operator was clearly on unaffected ground high up overlooking the city when the earth visibly started moving and in a matter of seconds all buildings in view disappeared downwards as far as the drone's eye could see. A huge cloud of dust and dirt started to emerge from the affected area, but the vast majority stopped rising and started to follow the buildings, cars, roads and inevitably people downwards.

As Pete watched it, he voluntarily exclaimed, "It's not gravity that stopping the dust clouds. It's pressure. The planet is directly sucking the stuff back inside."

"Does that make a difference to anything Pete?" Jeff asked hopefully.

"Nope not one jot, but it has scratched an itch for me if nothing else. And also, we need to get out of Japan before we get grounded. Let's head back and pack."

64

By the time they got back to their hotel Senator Gordon had messaged them explaining, as per Pete's initial reaction, that Japanese civilian airspace had been shut down with immediate effect. A sure sign that life in the country would never be the same again. A military cargo plane had been arranged for several of the team to fly to Shanghai and from there, Chairman Guo had committed to arrange onward transportation for them across the globe, whilst Primate Minister Ito was to facilitate direct travel from Tokyo for others. As if the previous night's multi-presidential address wasn't enough to spark a nationwide panic, the rapidly spreading news of Niigata's event sent some into total meltdown. And in this country, with arguably the calmest, most rational of people, despite a hastily released plea from the Japanese Prime Minister for her citizens to stay at home, inevitably thousands took that as a reason to flee, starting a mass self-evacuation. Even the most carefully planned large scale evacuation means traffic carnage, but when a city of thirty million people decides with no evidence other than fear of the unknown to empty itself, total and absolute gridlock is guaranteed. Something which was not lost on Jeff as they walked with a slightly anxious purpose back to their hotel.

"There's absolutely no way we're getting to the airport. Narita's well out of the centre. Unless we're walking and I'm not walking." He suddenly thought that walking was inevitable. "We're not walking, are we?"

"We're not walking, Jeff, no." Jane put his worst fear, but not his mind, to rest.

"Not the subway. Surely that'll a) be carnage and b) be closed. See point A."

"Also correct Jeff. I got word from the Senator. The Japanese Air Force are sending a helicopter to collect us from the Shangri-La a couple of blocks away. We've got an hour. So, let's get our stuff together and meet in our lobby in thirty-five minutes. OK? Gordon told me the PM and military chiefs want eyes in the sky, so we'll be up for a while before heading Northwest to Narita."

The Chinook was huge, two sets of enormous blades and room inside for a platoon. Not just the four scientists plus the six Japanese crew who were running surveillance on the city. The shell of the aircraft may have been pretty antiquated, but it had been kitted out inside with some mighty high-tech equipment. Jeff was impressed.

"I feel like I'm in Airwolf," he exclaimed. A cultural reference which just hung in the air, lost on the others. As if it would help, he started singing, at least loud humming, the theme tune and got pretty animated.

"Ah Airwolf, very good," one of the Air Force crew at a monitor raised his head with a big smile at Jeff much to his and everyone else's surprise. That was the only light moment of their air tour of Tokyo's central districts. The helicopter's cameras were able to zoom in to street level and the low windows offered a perfect bird's eye view of a city gone rogue. Both offered a perspective of what was usually organised chaos, but now was disorganised carnage. The streets were gridlocked with cars facing all directions and people were everywhere. Some cars had been set on fire. In a disturbing juxtaposition, the camera zoomed in on looters ramming a department store window whilst nearby, a group of elderly locals were just kneeling on the roadside, presumably praying.

"God knows what it must be like anywhere else," Elaine remarked directly in Jeff's right ear. "I'm glad we're going to Antarctica."

And with that, placed her trembling hand on his and as he put his other hand on hers, encompassing it, he replied, "I'm glad we're going too. Really, really glad," and almost instantly her nervous shake stopped, and she felt at peace. The two of them spent the rest of the airborne journey with their hands clasped together. No talking, just enjoying the touch of a long-lost lover. All the while, looking out helplessly at the commotion below.

65

When they reached Narita, there was a brief reunion with some of their colleagues from the Hyatt Suite and beyond. Harpinder and Marco were there. She was heading Germany-bound with Jane and Peter, Marco was indeed heading back to Mexico City. They'd been working directly with the president, making sure there was historical documentation of what was happening. Both for posterity, and as Franks put it, "in case we get through this, and anyone accuses me of bailing on the US of A."

Chester Rogers looked like a man who needed a deep tissue massage and a long sleep. Sadly for him, neither of those things had happened. But he was committed to the former once he arrived in Santiago, Chile's bustling and fascinating capital, given the latter on the flight there. Although he'd checked out Auckland's departure lounge and saw there was a mini spa for his layover. He felt he might deserve it, as President Franks had asked him to arrange another live-streamed address with only two hours' notice. But Rogers, however tired he felt, knew the hard yards were ahead of the president rather himself, for obvious reasons. And the idea of another address was his anyway, so he'd created his own workload. Franks had really warmed to the PR man, and they talked for a good while on a communication strategy that would be less about telling people – US citizens – to be precise, other nationalities were welcome to tune in, but this was a plan for Americans wherever they may be in the world, what to do and more about a constant. President Franks, in Chester Rogers' plan, would be a figurehead more than a politician, giving frequent brief updates every forty-eight hours. Rogers suggested he needed to stay visible and essentially be an emotional anchor. Franks had questioned whether the frequency was too much, and people would be cynical and bored with him. But Rogers was a big-picture thinker, developed through years of media experience and counselled the president as if he were one of his clients rather than the leader of the free world. No one can be prepared for this kind of scenario, so Roger's worked with, or rather on Franks, to ensure he was the one to guide the country through the difficult times because, as Roger succinctly put it to the president, "If you don't stand up, then someone else will fill that void and you'll lose your power." Rogers explained to Franks that 'power' in the coming period would not be defined by politics, but by humility and empathy and above all, the simple concept of presence and consistency. The president was initially concerned that he'd be too much of a try hard attempting to be the face of the disaster, but Rogers convinced him to stop thinking like a vote winner and that the rules of the game were over, and this was no longer about polls, but about simple leadership. So, not to overthink what to say, but to simply talk from the heart and not through the lens of parties and politics. Their broadcast was to go out before Chester's plane took off for the first leg of his long journey to Chile and his final advice to the president, once he'd had his science, geology and general gruesome fact update from Louis Charles and Tanya James was, "Be yourself and talk to them as individuals." Franks' message focused on community and kinship in the face of nature's wrath, imploring people to help each other, whilst promising as much federal support as he was able to arrange remotely, before heading back to DC. He had set in motion the mobilisation of the near two-hundred thousand strong US Army Reserve to be available to support communities impacted by existing or future surface collapses. He had also instructed, in consultation with several other global leaders, the food and drink industry to exponentially increase their output of long-life produce and, in particular, bottled and canned water.

Citizens around the world were already panic buying their way through pretty much all household essentials and local law enforcement and military personnel had been deployed to manage supermarket disputes of stockpiling customers who were creating shortages and tensions were growing. It was made all the worse by the agonising uncertainty of whether they should stay put or relocate to another area like a massive game of geographical game of chance. In summary, and Franks knew it, there was total bedlam, not just in the US, but pretty much everywhere. So, he hoped he might just take some of the edge off the situation by calling for responsibility and calm. At least, that's what he told himself as he addressed who knew how many people from the airport in Tokyo, hoping the promise of him returning might make them a little more trusting and positive that if the president is happy to be on US soil, maybe this isn't so bad after all. Of course. Franks neglected to share researcher Penn's grim prediction of what was likely to happen in the coming months and years.

Once Franks had signed off his broadcast, Harpinder Tarkovski, freelance journalist now alongside Chester Rogers as one of Franks' newly appointed communication and media advisers, sent a few messages from her tablet and hurried over to see her long-time friend Jane.

"Well, this has turned out to be quite the global shit-show, hasn't it?" Harpinder said with a sarcastic tone and grimace. "I kind of wish we were back just trying to uncover the original deceit of climate change reversal. Then your new mate Pete goes and maps out these crazy events and now we've got Armageddon to deal with and the president has gone from greedy world-ending enemy #1 to social media agony Aunt and emotional counsellor."

"There's quite a lot to unpick in it all that H." Jane felt guilty for laughing, *but how else could they cope with this*, she thought. "I'm not sure Pete wanted his professional legacy to be quite this devastating. a) Because being the name associated with the extinction of most living organisms is suboptimal at best and b), to have a proper legacy you really need people to be alive to know about it. And yeah, I agree with you on the president with so much having happened in Tokyo, I kind of forgot he and the other leaders had. Pretty much signed up to killing the planet anyway."

"Karma's a bitch huh?" Harpinder hit the nail squarely on the head.

"How are you feeling about working for him now then Harpinder?" Jane asked her former college buddy.

"Well Jane, despite the absolute insanity and assholery, I think he's genuinely trying to do the right thing now whatever that really means and given we all seem to be pretty much fucked anyway, I think I'll compromise my former values and ride this out with some State protection. If nothing else, this has been the most remarkable part of my professional career. And God willing, if we come out of this, I will have some pretty impressive memoirs to write. Don't you think?"

"Do you know Harpinder; I've pretty much stopped all thoughts of the future. It's too uncertain. And you can probably guess that's an untidy place for me to be. So, I'm taking each day, really, each hour at a time, and working my way through this like that. I'm so glad we're both going back to Berlin. Maybe some of your devil may care attitude will rub off on me." Harpinder laughed. She was trying hard to detach herself from reality.

"Given it's the end of humanity, are you going to let Professor Masai rub off on you? You're both single, aren't you? I'm guessing the dating scene in Berlin won't quite be what it was with all this going on. Just thought I'd throw it out there." Harpinder had been half joking, but as she said it, the two of them paused for a couple of seconds, considering it. Admittedly, from different perspectives. Harpinder just wanted her old friend to make the most of her life and have someone in it as she had with her husband, Jakub. Jane, on the other hand, had no one, especially not in Berlin, and had spent most of the last few years focusing on her career, rather than men. She'd had a few one-night stands and did have a short but unsuccessful attempt at a relationship with the guy she'd met at a seminar that he had turned out to be less interesting to her than her job so, although it was almost a throwaway comment by Harpinder, it had really hit her quite hard. She did admire Peter Masai and for her, respect and intelligence outweighed physical attractiveness. But she didn't look at him and think *yuck*, so perhaps this wasn't the craziest thing in the world.

She glanced across the terminal building to where Pete was standing, chatting to Jeff and Elaine. *Did he sense my stare?* He did break off his conversation, looked over and smiled. Jane chastised herself, and Harpinder too.

"Harpinder, stop it. You're making me feel like a high schooler again."

"Ha, made you think about it, though, didn't I? Look, Jane, I'm only teasing, but you never know, we're all going to need someone."

"Yes, who knows?" Jane closed off this conversation. With a blush in her face and a strange buzz in her body at the thought of intimacy with Peter, luckily for her, the airport Tannoy interrupted her daydreaming. It was the recognisable tones of President Franks.

66

"Ladies and gentlemen, please make your way to departure zone B for a final briefing. Departure zone B please. Briefing in ten minutes." At the same time, the airport display screen changed to flash up the same message, encouraging the few people who were in Narita Airport to head to the shared location. Whilst the airport concourses were vacuously empty, there was a semi-controlled pandemonium in front of the terminals as people, despite the nationally declared no flying zone, had made their way to Narita in the hope of escaping the country. Oblivious to the fact that almost all other destinations would have a similar uncertain future, a lot of those outside were foreign nationals who just wanted to get home to family and loved ones. Wrongly assuming the flight ban would only be temporary, and they'd be at the front of the queue for the first restart out flights, little did they know Narita had already said farewell to his final charter flight and once the airlift of the world leaders and team of scientists and associated entourage had been completed later that day, the airport would close to commercial operators. It would, however, remain open to military and emergency cargo and would soon become one of Tokyo's major storage depots to house and ultimately distribute the increased production of long-life food and bottled water. The Japanese military had already commandeered the conference centre at the Hilton Tokyo Narita Airport, much to the dismay of Panasonic who had been forced to be removed from their AGM, whose chief executive, in an act of extraordinary denial, pronounced their removal as a "constitutional war crime," a view shared by almost none of the thousand delegates and Panasonic colleagues, some of whom were mourning the loss of loved ones in the recent catastrophe in Niigata. They were simply desperate to leave Tokyo and make their way, by whatever means possible, home. In a matter of hours, the very same CEO announced on Twitter, "a partnership built on trust and respect," between the electronics giant and Japanese military and that his earlier comments, although when repeated verbatim were pretty exacting, were in fact misconstrued and were essentially fake news.

"Panasonic," he tweeted, "had always been and would always be sacrificial in the Japanese national interest and the military were welcome to take their space in the conference centre." What he didn't tweet was the potentially multi-billion-yen deal with the government to sign over drone and remote access vehicular technology. Prime Minister Ito was under no illusions that without pace and decisiveness, the window of opportunity to acquire or sequester critical technology might be lost if there were to be further imminent land losses in Japan. So, she had instructed her government to essentially part-nationalise any corporation they felt could offer some protection against, and navigation through, the tumultuous time to come. She brought into effect a decree not used as the Second World War, legally permitting the state to control any Japanese assets deemed to be in the 'national interest'.

Therefore, in the space of the day, the government essentially took control of key industries: food and drink production, communications, weaponry, aviation technology, tantamount to Panasonic's non-entertainment arm, and key utility and energy providers. Japan's ability to organise itself was unparalleled. A mix of calm intelligence and nationalistic compliance primed it for such large scale and swift change, ironic for a country which had built its reputation on such progressive thinking. But in recent decades, it had seemingly lost its way in terms of international innovation and growth to the likes of China and even the US outgrowing Japan. But Japan's island mentality, much like the British, meant it had always been on high alert since the dawn of civilization to defend itself from sea-faring or other attacks, so switching into defence-mode came easier to them. Coupled with the cultural vulnerability and national humiliation which came from World War Two, meant the country and its people, consciously or not, were always ready to act as one to protect its sovereignty.

As the military police formed barriers across Narita's entrances and exits, holding the desperate outside, the soon to be airlifted group made their way through the eerily quiet terminal to departure zone B where a small familiar crowd was gathering, some with luggage, some who had been picked up with so little warning they only had a few essentials with them. There was an uncomfortable feeling of finality about them as President Franks once again addressed them. He had little intention of dragging this out but paused briefly to beckon both Chairman Guo and President Zarkov to join him incongruously in front of the check-in desk where they'd gathered.

"Although right now we are predicting these Masai Events, sorry, Professor," he nodded slightly awkwardly at Peter, "they will continue to near destruction of our inhabitable planet. We will continue to work as long as we can to understand their path timings, impact and even on a preventative solution. We..." and this time he motioned to Guo and Zarkov, "...and our allies across the globe have mobilised, as best we can at this stage, military peacekeeping interventions, public communication strategies and increased levels of non-perishable food and drink production and mass storage. We anticipate wireless communication to remain functional via terrestrial and satellite technology until, and we all know better than to put a time frame on this, until we lose the ability either to generate power or more likely the infrastructure to deliver it. So, until that point, we will maintain contact initially every forty-eight hours and will vary the time given where we will be in the world, but should you discover anything, or have a geological epiphany…" again he looked at Professor Masai imploringly as if Peter might magic up a solution, "…don't wait. Speed of response and sharing data information is critical with an emphasis on sharing. We all know the likelihood of losing one another given the sweeping nature of these land collapses so we must stay open, agile and most importantly, full of hope. God willing, whatever our faith system, we may still have a future. Which means, in the spirit of hope and eternal optimism, I, and we, wish you good journeys and not goodbye. My esteemed colleagues and friends…" indicating to the Russian and Chinese leaders, "…would like to personally thank you for your commitment and sacrifices throughout this ordeal before we all head off on our flights to places far and wide." He held his hand out to both Gou and Zarkov intimating this was going to be a round robin of handshaking and back-patting. What could have been a clumsy wedding line up exchange, turned into a poignant few minutes as they said their adieus to one another calmly and respectfully. Even Nancy Rastik was receiving warm handshakes, having extricated herself from being villain of the piece with some humble backtracking, as had President Franks. But most interactions, hers and the leaders' aside, were marked by heartfelt, lingering hugs, kisses and tenderness. Bonds had been made within the team, united against the common fury of Mother Nature, each individual mindful of their own mortality and the importance of the group being greater than the sum of its parts.

Perhaps the most heartfelt and emotional farewells were between Jane and Jeff, who briefly reminisced about their late-night drinking sessions in DC, speculating about the disappearance of oceanic water, knowing nothing about what was to come. This was a friendship built on laughter, respect and experience and a tear formed in Jeff's eye wiped away by Jane.

She smiled, "Jeff, you're going to outlive all this, you know that, look after yourself, and Elaine," referencing their Antarctic destination potentially being out of the destruction zone in this current wave of land distortion.

"Berlin will never fall, Jane. It's been through so much that this won't phase it," Jeff replied. Although they both knew the city had no defence against the powers of the Earth, aside from luck. He managed one final quip. "Just try to control Pete. Make sure he doesn't come up with another way to end the world!"

Pete overheard and shot him a wink. "I heard Everest was inching up faster these past few weeks, Jeff." They all laughed, picked up their bags and trudged off towards their gates to board the military aircraft waiting to transport them across the globe.

The majority of the aircraft taking the team across the world were either state run, like Air Force One and Air Force 3701, China's presidential aircraft or military planes of various sizes belonging to the Japanese Air Force. President Ito had offered use of these in a quid pro quo agreement with fellow leaders to use the return flights to repatriate Japanese nationals, where invited, from international locations. Ito had sanctioned the principle that bringing even a small number of Japanese nationals home, however arbitrary the rapid selection process, was the right thing to do. She was uncomfortable with the idea of empty planes returning and had contacted the ambassadors in the countries of destination; UK, Chile Germany, Mexico, USA, and Australia to offer non-residential government officials the option to make their way, if appropriate and accessible, to the airports within forty-eight hours.

Ito knew this would lead to high emotion of those either left behind or unable to access the locations, but she made it clear to the ambassadors that they had the option to select individuals by choice or randomly, but permanent staff should remain in post. What this meant for those leaving Tokyo, was they pretty much had massive planes all to themselves, given the pervasive geographical and seemingly arbitrary nature of the destruction, there was little point in sending any army or rescue forces from Japan with no current way to predict what level of support countries and cities might need. So, during that day, a number of almost empty aircraft lifted off, climbing high over the Pacific Ocean, each one turning and heading off to destinations far and wide.

67

Whilst Peter and Jane had found themselves in a fairly drab Airbus A400 military carrier for their flight back to Berlin, Jeff, Elaine and Chester Rogers had the domesticated comforts of being transported in a Nippon Airways commercial aircraft. With Rogers connecting to head to Chile and Jeff and Elaine routing to Antarctica, Auckland was their hub destination, but also happened to be the location of a trade conference attended by a couple of hundred Japanese government employees. Therefore, with all other routes back to Japan impossible, the ambassador in Wellington had agreed to transport them all on the soon-to-be-arriving plane from Tokyo. Nippon Airways senior executives had signed off on the plan in return for repatriating fifty of its staff based in New Zealand. As a result, the upside for the three weary travellers was a first-class travel experience. And for Rogers, the first of many massages he had planned to ease the growing tension in his shoulders. Whilst he was enjoying the bliss of his knots being hammered out of him in a first-class cabin, Jeff and Elaine shared a chilled bottle of Bollinger and pored over the hastily drafted dossier that researchers Penn and Louis Charles' wider teams had pulled together. The text made for grim reading and the bubbly acted as a suppressant to the destruction and loss of life detailed within the first few pages which summarised the situation, date coded to the nearest hour never mind day, implying that the scientific viewpoint was a rapidly moving feast. Jeff flicked past the bleak reading neither he nor Elaine needed or wanted to revisit, with the cabin isolation offering emotional and mental protection from reality and although they had nothing real to celebrate, the champagne offered comfort and respite. The second part of the dossier was bespoke to them, and they assumed, correctly, that Rogers had his own personalised version too. Neither of them knew a great deal about Antarctica aside from what they'd picked up either at school or through their careers.

"I know Antarctica it is the only land that has ever been truly 'discovered'." Elaine said, accentuating the word discovered.

"How so?"

"It's the only continent on Earth with no indigenous population, which also makes it one of the least polluted places on the planet."

"Sounds good. Does it say where we're actually going?"

Elaine flicked through the pages, mostly maps and key information that were basically printouts from Wikipedia. She made a mental note to keep hold of them in case the internet ever went down and assumed this was why there was so much web-accessible information in hard copy. At the back, on a page headed 'Jeff Williamson and Elaine Brennan: destination Antarctica', she read the first couple of lines to Jeff.

"You will be accommodated until further notice at the US Antarctic research post 'McMurdo Station', located in the South of Ross Island (see map) and plans have been arranged for the evacuation of approximately six hundred research and support staff by land and sea in the coming days. This will leave in the region of three hundred of you on the whole of Antarctica. Due to the possibility of short to medium or even long-term isolation, cargo will be stockpiling McMurdo to cater for thirty years without further shipment." Elaine stumbled over the last few words, "They're sending us to die Jeff."

Jeff was much less despondent and as he often did, saw this through his rose-tinted specs. "I see it as the opposite. If we were being sent there to die, then no additional provision would be necessary. Why go to all these logistical challenges and cost of stockpiling so much food, fuel I assume, clothing, you name it? This is a sign, for me at least, that if the world becomes habitable again once the worst of this is over, we're going to be one of the few groups who can live through it and come out the other side. I wonder if those being evacuated know much about what's going on?" he mused to himself rhetorically.

"They must be moving people out to make space for the stockpiling. Jeff, hear this," Elaine turned the page and felt slightly more at ease with their part in the plan.

"In 2016, the G20 signed off on a plan to isolate and secure Antarctica in the face of global catastrophe be it man-made or from natural forces. This has always been in the public domain but was never highly publicised as is one of many large-scale contingency plans drawn up by the group. As a result, ever since the agreement was made, at any given time, Dunedin in New Zealand and Concón, Chile, which is a US military base, there are stockpiles of food, beverage, medical, fuel, and basic survival kits available for immediate transportation, not just to Antarctica but anywhere in the southern hemisphere. There are also two northern hemisphere hubs in Newfoundland and southern India."

"So, they've been preparing for this all along." Jeff sounded upbeat, but that was also impacted by the fact that his second flute of Champagne was now empty. "Does it say what we're expected to do once were there and everything's been delivered for our isolation?"

"No Jeff, nothing more than we're already being told. I guess we just join the call and make the most of whatever processing power and web access they have. From what I understand, there's no mobile phone reception there and the internet speeds are glacially, no pun intended, slow."

"So, we're going back in time. It'll be like being back in college, just without Pete and a stable planet Earth."

"Jeff," Elaine looked across the first-class bar at her former, and potentially soon to be again beau, "what do you think's going to happen to us?" Jeff moved his glass to one side and reached for Elaine's hand.

"All I know Elaine, is ever since you came back into my life, and I'm indebted for Pete for making it happen, I feel I can deal with whatever is going to unfold in the next few days, months, even years. So, let's get, as ridiculous as it sounds, to Antarctica and make the best of it, whatever happens." Then the Bollinger-induced romantic in Jeff popped out. "Even if all the food runs out and the station collapses into the ice, I will build an igloo and hunt penguins for us to eat. However, our focus will be to help the team however we can, to find a way through this catastrophe and maybe we'll make it to the other side, God knows, but if we don't there's no one I'd rather be stuck with."

"I'll drink to that Jeff," and Elaine leant forward and the two exchanged their first kiss since their days at college.

"I will too." A beaming Chester Rogers had emerged from his massage and earwigged the back end of Jeff and Elaine's conversation. The three of them sat there at the first-class bar in the empty airliner, silently contemplating their futures. Once the bottle had been emptied, their tiredness caught up with them and they separated and slept for the remainder of the journey to Auckland. On landing, Chester Rogers bade them farewell as he headed off to his next flight to Santiago, whilst Jeff and Elaine headed to the terminal to await further instructions on their next leg to the South Pole. They were informed by a very young-looking officer of the New Zealand Army that the Antarctic Flyer, the affectionate name given to the aircraft mostly used for that journey south, was on its way from its base in Christchurch to collect them. Thirty minutes later, just as promised, they watched the gun-metal Globemaster C-17 land effortlessly on the single runway at Auckland Airport.

"Well, this is it, Elaine, terra firma for the final time," as they headed off through the departure gate and into the fresh air of the North Island, Jeff pulled out his phone and held it in front of the two of them, with the plane in the background.

"One final selfie for Pete and Jane, they'll be landing soon I reckon." As they climbed the steps into the massive body of the strategic transport aircraft, Jeff's phone buzzed with a message.

"Turns out they have arrived back in Berlin, look." Jeff laughed, as did Elaine, when they saw the image of Pete and Jane on the tarmac at Schönefeld Airport, all goofy looking and smiles, totally at odds with the situation they were heading back into.

Stay safe, look after Jane and see you later on Planet Earth 2.0, Jeff messaged back with a few smiley-face emojis. Pete responded with a globe, heart, and strong arm. And with that, Jeff switched his phone, off unsure when he'd be using it again.

68

Aukland, New Zealand

The C-17 wasn't quite as luxuriously kitted out as the Nippon Airways first-class cabin but was comfortable enough for the six-and-a-half-hour flight to the Phoenix Runway at McMurdo Station. As the huge military plane taxied across Auckland's mostly deserted airport, Elaine could see a hundred or more suited Japanese officials heading out to the commercial airliner they'd flown in on, destined to return to Tokyo, on what was planned to be the last civilian flight from the country for the foreseeable future. And that future was much shorter lived than anyone could have ever wished. As the Globemaster hurtled south-westerly down the runway, the plane began to shake, which immediately caused Elaine to feel panic, not because of the shaking, she just assumed planes like this were naturally bumpier than commercial jets, but because of the reaction of the military personnel who were alongside her and Jeff. There were ten of them in the front section of the plane in a civilian style cabin area located behind the cockpit. Elaine and Jeff, plus a selection of men and women who hadn't had the time for introductions so early this was in the flight. All eight of them sat bolt upright, clinging on to their seats with a look of undiluted terror on their faces.

Over the plane's speaker system, a voice bellowed, Elaine assumed it was the pilot or copilot, "Hold tight folks." Elaine grabbed Jeff and squeezed him so hard he yelped, having no idea anything was up. He wasn't a nervous flyer, so a bit of rumbling at take-off didn't raise his concerns at all, but having Elaine's nails digging into his arm certainly did. Everything seemed to happen in slow motion, but the whole episode was less than thirty seconds long. As Elaine looked to her left, about to shout to Jeff to hold on to her, she could see straight out of the window and across the grassy zone alongside the runway, out to the car park and across to the freeway. But what she saw stopped her shout before it even got close to leaving her throat. An elevated section of freeway disappeared from view as if the pillars holding it up had all been removed at the same time. A wall of dusty cloud was rolling towards the airport around a hundred feet high, although Elaine realised the dust itself wasn't moving, it was coming up from below, engulfing where the freeway had been almost like a wave. In a flash, the entire car park vanished from view.

"Jeff..." she managed to call out feebly. He turned and looked out of the window and instantly realised why the plane was juddering and why the pilot had told them all to hold on. In a matter of seconds, the vibrations stopped as the aircraft's wheels left the runway and the Globemaster ascended into the relative safety of the New Zealand sky.

"Oh my God, Jeff." Elaine was still gripping his arm to the extent that blood was starting to flow from the scratch marks. But Jeff couldn't feel that. He was entirely consumed with the events unfolding on the ground, thankfully for them, an ever-increasing distance away. As the plane climbed, the pilot made a tight turn back towards the city.

"Folks, we're going to take a detour. We've lost all communication with the ground team, and if you're seeing what I'm seeing down there, then something crazy is going on. I've activated belly cam; it should be coming up on the screens in just a second." Elaine saw Jeff also knew exactly what had happened and didn't need video footage of the ground to tell them. But what it did show was a crumpled mess where Auckland City once stood. Jeff instinctively thought of his family, not that they lived in New Zealand, and what it would be like to be in a building brutally sucked into the Earth with zero chance of survival. He glanced across at the others who were sharing this flight south and hoped upon hope that none of them had anyone close living in Auckland. But he knew that was very unlikely and it made him feel physically sick. As they cruised so calmly over what only minutes ago was central Auckland, a bustling hive of life and activity, but now was a wasteland, a city folded into Earth's crust, the odd skyscraper poking out of a chasm like a piece of discarded Lego. Elaine had finally let go of Jeff's forearm but was too shocked to speak. She had seen countless images of earthquake zones and the carnage and destruction wrought by tectonic disturbances, but this was on a different level. Earthquakes essentially knock stuff down and on the fault line itself there can be losses into the earth but, by and large, its surface damage. But this, as she looked down at New Zealand's biggest city by some distance, was akin to sieving everything man-made and more and losing it into the open Earth. The city had gone and, as the plane continued over land, it became clear that this was a Masai Event, not isolated in Auckland, but far reaching across the North Island. The pilot had clearly opted not to fly at standard altitude but remain under the cloud cover in order to keep visual on the catastrophic situation developing below.

"Jeff, it might be worth going and talking to the pilots. They might not know much about what's going on, and this will be freaking them out. Because it's freaking me out."

After a few minutes in the cockpit bringing the flight crew fully up to speed on the situation, joining the dots for them and critically, giving them precious moments to try and grasp what this would mean for family and friends on the ground, their military training kicked in, and they courageously carried on professionally. Jeff was keen to understand the scale of the events unfolding across New Zealand and figured this might be his and the wider team's only chance to see first-hand the Earth's self-destruction.

"How much fuel have we got sir?" he asked the captain.

"We could get to Antarctica and back and still put some back in the tanker if you want, Jeff. What are you thinking?"

By the time he returned to Elaine, she had similarly brought the ten other passengers, a split of military personnel and researchers, who'd also be stationed at McMurdo, up to speed with the reality of the activity below them. She beckoned Jeff to share with them all the plan, as it hadn't gone unnoticed that the plane had banked in a U-turn, and they all assumed a detour was in play.

"We're heading north to assess the damage and get a first-hand view to share with the team. All we've had so far is satellite imagery and the odd drone shot. The cameras on this thing have been recording all the time, it's like being in a flying Google Maps car." When he motioned to Elaine to join him in private, the others largely ignored them as they pressed their faces against the windows.

"There's not been a peep from ground control in Auckland. No surprise there, but they haven't been able to contact anyone or anything on the North Island at all. Radar and comms are all down. Not even Wellington and that's seven hundred kilometres away."

"Well, I guess we'll be able to see more of what's happened when we get back on land again," said Elaine, trying to sound positive as she glanced up at the monitor showing the watery scene directly below them.

"That's the point Elaine," Jeff could barely believe what he was saying. "We are above land or should be. From what we can establish, vast swathes, maybe even the whole of the North Island, has been taken by the ocean. As the plane banked and headed back in a southerly direction again, the captain's voice came over the speakers.

"Jeff, can we borrow you again, please? Over."

"Come," he grabbed Elaine's hand affectionately. "We need you in there too. I need you in there."

"Look, I only know what you only just told us about how serious this thing is. But if I'm honest and I think I speak for these guys too," the captain indicated he was talking about his two copilots, "we didn't grasp or believe the magnitude. We were assuming a few earthquakes, land slips, that kind of thing." Jeff almost interrupted because he'd been brutally honest with them about Pete's theory and how it was playing out across the globe, but he could see the captain hadn't finished.

"But we just weren't listening. We should be flying directly above a town called Dargaville right now, and nothing but ocean. It's like we're off course. And yes, local radar might be out, but satellites are still functioning, and the land has literally gone under."

For a few moments, the quiet humming of the jet engines was the only sound in the cockpit as the five of them stared impassively out front at the vast expanse of sea, where an hour or so ago there had been land. Not only land, but inhabited land, people going about their daily business, driving to see friends, meeting business associates, playing golf, just being normal. Animals roaming free in the forests, colonies of insects scurrying around. Just life, a teaming entwined cacophony of life, extinguished and replaced by the blue-green vastness of the ocean, as if land were never there. Given the cloudless skies now, they had climbed higher to afford a greater view, but Elaine asked if they could descend as she wanted proof, if that were the right word, because, like the pilots, she was struggling to square off the fact that half of New Zealand had been claimed by the high seas. She wondered to herself if perhaps all the subterranean activity could be affecting Earth's magnetism, and thus throwing off navigation devices. But deep down, she knew the C-17 Globe Master was not relying on iron filings to find a path and that satellites had replaced the humble compass many moons ago, although if there was to be a blackout coming their way, she'd be looking for one soon enough. What she was searching for, and it didn't take the plane much time to make visible, was debris, tell-tale signs of life sucked under the ocean.

"Oh man!" blurted Jeff instinctively. A reaction shared by them all, enormous amounts of detritus was clearly visible bobbing in the choppy waters beneath them, like a town had thrown itself into the sea. Prefab houses, cars, lorries, trees, sheep, so many sheep, and the unmistakable outlines of human bodies, scores of them. They'd all seen the devastation flooding and tidal waves caused and the scene below was reminiscent of what they'd seen in those pictures.

"And this is from a town of about five thousand people." The captain pre-empted what they were all thinking. "We'll be over Auckland, or what's left of it in about thirty minutes."

As they flew south over what was now ocean covered land, Wing Commander Clements was hunched over a selection of technology, frantically attempting to communicate with any available ground controls, whilst simultaneously scanning the multiple blasts coming from the global emergency's news feed, a rather depressing ticker tape of live events the G20 had developed following the 2001 tsunami across Southeast Asia. Clements motioned to speak and the contemplatory silence in the cockpit allowed her to share the update. She was precise and spoke with brevity, the professional in her taking over, her manner totally at odds with the words she was speaking.

"North Island has gone under in entirety. South Island remains intact. Christchurch is online and secure. Sydney air-traffic-control reporting mega tsunami-caused by subsistence heading to East Coast Australia. Speed six hundred mph, height two thousand metres, likely wiping out the whole of the eastern seaboard. Elsewhere, million plus hot spots, zones where loss of life exceeds one million," Clements added for macabre clarity. "Europe: Paris, St Petersburg, now Marseille, Munich, Athens, Milan, the whole of Gran Canaria, Stockholm. Africa: Lagos, Dakar, Kampala, Lusaka, Dar es Salaam, Johannesburg. South America: Bogota, Caracas, Manaus we know about, Cordoba, Callao." Clements' voice was breaking as she read out the destroyed cities, a tear rolled down her cheek followed by another as she continued stoically, but Captain Shaskins intervened, much to the relief of everyone.

"Thank you, Wing Commander. Please duplicate the information for us to access separately. I think we are now all bought into the severity of the local," he motioned towards the ocean below, "and global conditions. Let us pray and spare a thought for those impacted, especially our cousins in Australia who are about to be hit by a merciless tsunami but given our powerlessness, we have no option but to remain professional as you have demonstrated so far and detach ourselves from the havoc and set course for Antarctica," he was looking towards Jeff for tacit agreement and greeted by an imperceptible but acknowledged nod. "Then we regroup and establish base and report for duty on arrival."

69

Berlin

A week after leaving the flat overlooking Tiergarten with Jeff and Elaine, Pete and Jane returned to the Berlin apartment with one overriding thought dominating their already manic thoughts. Had their friends managed to get out of Auckland before its disappearance? They had both been issued with high-tech laptops before leaving Tokyo, as had the others not heading to military or research bases. Pete fired it up, initially ignoring the messages detailing the same global carnage Wing Commander Clements had just conveyed those aboard the C-17 and focused on flight tracking software. He didn't know the exact details of the flight Jeff and Elaine had taken, or how many other planes had managed to depart Auckland before the event. He called Jane across who looked visibly worried. She was sick at the idea that Jeff and Elaine might have been caught up in the North Island disaster.

"See here," Pete pointed at a single flight path over the clear outline of New Zealand as it was before it was reduced to one significant body of land, "it looks like a single plane managed to get airborne before…" He didn't know how to finish the sentence but figured out he'd not need to. "It started south then headed north before coming back and heading out across the Southern Ocean. Now, we're assuming Chester Rogers' flight to Santiago is separate to Jeff and Elaine going to Antarctica, but they may be together with Rogers as just a stopover. Or Rogers' plane is travelling directly over Antarctica instead of via Easter Island. Or third option; it is carrying neither of them."

There had been so much jeopardy and bad news to deal with that the uncertainty about their friend's survival didn't derail them as much as it would have done a couple of weeks ago. This didn't make Pete or Jane selfish humans; they were just conforming to Maslow's base needs of survival mode. Although there was little control over the external environment, it is human nature, and indeed, the cornerstone of life on Earth to protect one's own existence when faced with no influence on the survival of others.

Jane allowed herself to wonder whether Maslow was an oversimplification, and, in reality, one's own physiological needs didn't need to be met to embrace the more emotional elements to the theory. She was all in on the idea that being safe, secure, housed and fed was a good building block on which to forge strong relationships with others, freeing headspace to tend to the non-physical. And, as she pondered deeper in those few moments, as they considered the fate of Jeff and Elaine and the fact they might not know for hours, until their flight did or did not reach Antarctica with them on it or not, that she was only able to fully contemplate it because she indeed had shelter, safety, at least for now, and access to food and water, again at least for now. Satisfied she'd come full circle on Maslow and her own sense of self, she felt able to compartmentalise Jeff and Elaine's flight uncertainty and open up some bandwidth to the others in the hope of confirmation that all reached their destinations.

She and Pete had travelled back with journalist-cum-presidential advisor Harpinder, who would remain in Berlin with her husband Jakub at his family home in the Mitte district of the city, not far from Pete's apartment in fact. His family had moved from Poland in the sixties, one of many Polish settlers in the old east of the city, following the war. Her role, as long as communication channels remained open, was to draft and/or tweak President Franks' bi-nightly addresses. Her blend of US politics, keen journalistic integrity and Euro-Asian background placed her well against Franks' self-styled old-white American through-and-through persona. Even Harpinder, usually pretty sceptical about politicians, was impressed at the turnaround in the president's morals and conscientiousness after the Industrial Revolution pact with Senator Johnson collapsed. His former partner in crime in that episode, Nancy Rastik, had made contact, confirming safe landing in Sydney over twelve hours ago. She had been one of the first to leave Tokyo which was so fortunate too. It was highly likely air travel to the region, even military would be cut short given the terrifying and impending mega tsunami about to engulf the East Coast. Nancy's extended family were former opal miners in the remote South Australian town of Coober Pedy, now famous on the Red Centre tourist trail for the fact that most residents live underground, given the intensity of the heat. Her uncle now ran stargazing tours, whilst Nancy's cousin stayed in the opal industry, more on the business and logistics side, rather than drilling. On landing in Sydney, Rastik had connected straight out to Adelaide and headed north via Coober Pedy for a brief reconnection with her friends and family, en route to Pine Gap, a satellite surveillance base operated jointly by the US and Australia, located pretty much dead centre in the country. Seven hundred kilometres north of Coober Pedy and about twenty kilometres from Alice Springs. She was certainly far enough away from the sea to be unaffected, but simply knowing such a devastating wave was about to hit was unbearable. Advance warning systems on the whole were still functioning globally. The networked power of the internet and satellite contact meant there was no shortage of communication to the seven or so million at-risk inhabitants of the vast stretch of the coastline towards which an unimaginable wall of water was hurtling.

"Although I'm still wary of Nancy, I'm glad she's safe, but watching the satellite of that wave makes me feel sick." Jane had pulled up a line of feed tracking the mega tsunami by one of the military grade channels Louis Charles and Penn had installed on their laptops, with a morbid countdown to impact, which was now under two hours.

"God, it must be mayhem down there," said Jane ruefully, trying not to think about it too much. "There's one thing one of the events happening when you don't really expect it, but this; there's going to be no escape. It'll destroy everything for miles inland."

Pete had CNN streaming not long after they arrived back in the apartment as he wanted to get a feel for how everything was playing out in the traditional media channels. He'd pretty much ditched Twitter, given the incendiary inaccuracies of the posts, even from academics he probably respected on a good day. He assumed the rest were no better, although had no profile on any other mass social media sites. He had always avidly followed, avidly being an overstatement, he really only looked now and again, at the New Scientist online feed and made a mental note to check it once he'd scanned the TV news. CNN was a mix of grim global reports of Masai Events.

"Oh my God, they're using my name on CNN to describe these things. I thought that was an internal term." The egotist in him was spectacularly proud his name was finally in light but the realist in him wasn't overly keen with his moniker being given to such ruinous proceedings. BBC World was the same. 'New Masai Event reported in Spain' was the text below an image of what he assumed was Seville, but could have been Madrid or anywhere there, his Spanish geography was not great. The reporter confirmed it was indeed Seville and went on to matter of factly explain this historic city had been wiped out, like so many others.

He left the TV running on Al Jazeera and replays of the Great Pyramid of a Giza being swallowed up into the sand along with a large swathe of populous Cairo. The feed along the bottom of the screen flashed with breaking news: 'Australia braces for mother of all tsunamis, evacuations under way'.

"The authorities must know that any attempted evacuation is largely token, they'll never be able to get them far enough away."

"But at least some people may escape Pete. That's got to be a good thing," Jane challenged.

"True Jane. I've just become so anaesthetised to multiple deaths, as in millions of casualties, that I forget how precious a single life can be for that person and their loved ones. Instinctively, he pulled out his phone and scrolled through the many messages that he'd simply not had the time to acknowledge. A sudden jolt of guilt engulfed him as he saw a message from his mother from a couple of days ago.

Guess you were right then! Are you OK? We are for now. When will this be over, Peter? Love mum.

Immediately he replied, *so sorry, one for being slow responding, Tokyo was crazy and two, for being right. Not sure this is a quick thing so get food and water in and sit tight. We can't predict where next, so I'll call in the next day or so. Pete xx.* He closed messages and opened up his browser and clicked on New Scientist from his favourites tab, the only other choices being Nat Geo and YouTube Shorts. He often wanted some light relief and couldn't face downloading TikTok. His heart skipped a beat when, on the landing page of New Scientist Online, he saw his own face staring back at him. This was not the eulogy he'd spent his formative academic years dreaming of, he was not holding the earth in one hand and the rock star headline was very much not in evidence; 'Masai Hits Rock Bottom' was in large bold text.

"It doesn't even make sense!" He called out to no one.

Jane looked across and asked sensibly, "What doesn't Peter?" He was entirely lost in his own world now, so he didn't even acknowledge her. Under the photo it read; 'Peter Professor Masai gives his name to Mother Nature's wrath after predicting such events could signal the end of life as we know it.'

"It wouldn't have taken much to have talked to me." Again, Jane enquired if Pete needed any kind of response. Again, he didn't hear her. He scrolled speedily through the article which paraphrased his mantle disintegration theory quite accurately he felt and included a link to his actual paper. The article then discussed the geological implications given what had happened to date, rather than the human cost. Pete found himself nodding in agreement as he read the article's standpoint that the most significant future barrier to sustained life on Earth would be drought and the resulting temperature rise rather than the ground instability. According to NS, ten per cent of the world's water had already vanished deep in the Earth's mantle. Not just fractionally under the surface, but deep, deep within. The author, one Pete held in high regard and was a scientist of some repute in academic circles, referenced Peter as having 'given global governments and decision makers a vital head start in the response to these eponymous events that would mean a rather questionable but notable legacy or Professor Masai himself '. He couldn't resist forwarding the link on to his mother. He just wished he was able to predict where the events might strike next but that was something that evidently was beyond anyone's grasp right now. This time he did call out intentionally to Jane.

"What if Jane, we could actually forecast these land collapses? Do you think the governments could risk going public? It would cause even more chaos than telling people to stay home." Jane had considered this herself as part of what might unfold if the data presented a predictable pattern.

"I agree Peter. Could they risk not going public though? Or would they mobilise critical infrastructure to be in place first, then go for it? I think it's something for us to worry about if we ever get to that point Peter, my view right now is to settle back in here, ensure we have access to food, drink, power, and communications and see if Louis and Penn have anything further we can access when we're online with them in forty-five minutes."

70

With the only members of the core team unaccounted for being Jeff, Elaine and Chester Rogers, Louis Charles was now housed in the Chinese research facility in Shanghai and sent a blast out for those in position, and with secure access, to join a briefing online primarily to share the data available to them all, especially considering the fact an event could strike at any moment. Louis wanted them all to be able to access the info should Shanghai go down, either physically or virtually.

Despite the unfolding tragedies dominating the news and pretty much everyone's media feeds, life was surprisingly normal in Berlin. The tipping point hadn't been reached yet when society, Berlin society at least, it was certainly not true for other cities across the world, decided to turn its back on convention and hit survival mode. Sure, there were long queues at supermarkets and empty shelves for long-life goods and water, but anarchy hadn't yet won out. Schools, incredibly, were still open and businesses were trading. Even the news that Munich had fallen didn't seem to derail the Berlin spirit. As cities go, Berlin had experienced turmoil more than most, so the small matter of Earth's destruction was going to have to work pretty hard to knock Berliners from their stride. All of which had meant Pete's regular cleaner had continued working and not only kept his apartment tidy and dust-free, but he had also stocked the kitchen cupboards and fridge with enough food to keep Pete and Jane going for over a week.

"Perishables first," as if Pete needed to tell Jane, who had offered to prepare their food before the check-in call with their new globally spread team. This gave Pete a chance to open up the many boxes he'd had delivered in preparation for what he saw as a journey back to the Middle

Ages. He'd figured, correctly, that as it becomes clear to everyone that life is about to change fundamentally, taking out most technological advances in the past hundred years, making them redundant with no power, internet or batteries, even that the run on the kind of things Peter ordered would render it a bun fight. He was so grateful to Manu, his cleaner and had tipped him generously. *Thank you, President Franks,* he smiled to himself, given the door to the second bedroom could barely open given the number of boxes piled up in there. He'd given his new corporate credit card a proper workout, to the extent Jane had suggested he might have it removed soon for being frivolous.

"Au contraire Madame Doubter. They, whoever the hell 'they' are, are using my order as a survival pack kit list for others to follow." Pete laughed at his own cheery disposition, making Jane break out into a rare smile too.

"I was going to suggest I get a cut of the orders but thought better of it. An infinite credit card is probably enough even for my ambitions."

"Pete," Jane was super curious now putting down her chopping knife. "What have you actually bought?"

"Just a few apocalypse-ready knickknacks. Solar battery packs and charging equipment, clockwork radio for when we lose internet, a couple of generators, compass, sextant, weapons, flashlights, wind-up clock, flares, tranquillisers, military grade first aid kit, SLR film and camera, water purification hardware and tablets, mini desalinator, toiletries, and a lot of cash. Small denominations Euro and US dollars. I thought it might get vetoed but again makes sense that whilst currency has value it will be cash that returns to the throne. Our bottled water delivery is tomorrow, that'll be currency once we need things of intrinsic value as money loses its meaning."

"Well Pete," Jane was, as ever, impressed with Pete's bigger picture view of life. "I'm impressed. I think I'll hang around a bit longer then." She smiled warmly at the professor, allowing herself to imagine a very real possibility about spending the rest of her days with him. "You look like a man with a plan. I'm just not sure what it is yet, other than becoming some kind of end-of-days vigilante with all your toys."

"Haha. Not vigilante Jane, survivor. I'm still working on the premise that Mother Nature is not a crazed yet sentient being, hellbent on destroying us all with random attacks on our surface. There must be a pattern. There's always a pattern. We've just got to know where to look for it, and crucially know when we've found it. I would imagine there's enough data from the current events now to go back through it and establish a model. If it were linear, then Louis, Penn and their teams would have cracked it by now but they've not, so we might need to take a leap of faith and join some dots that are pretty far apart. That's what I'm good at and I'm pretty sure you're good at everything you set your mind to, so together we're going to be something else Jane." Jane felt a sudden rush of confidence. She found Pete's positivity and enthusiasm intoxicating, doubly so because he had the scientific acumen to back it up.

"If Berlin stays standing long enough Jane, we're going to survive this thing by remaining where we are because we'll be unaffected, or by getting to wherever will still be around." And with that he marched off into the bedroom to sift through his new equipment, whilst Jane returned to chopping up the veg with renewed vigour.

The check-in with Louis, Penn, Franks, and the rest of the team went smoothly. All were in situ and there was little discussion about death and destruction, just facts and next steps, which meant a sharing of all data backup codes and plans in case of a lost connection or station. Everyone knew that was code for an event taking someone out, but they had strategically decided not to address it so blatantly. With global cooperation being at an all-time high, previously covert satellite and monitor activity could be redeployed in a shared attempt to decipher what would happen next and when. President Franks shared his communications to go out the following night eastern US time. With no Chester Rogers available and whereabouts still unknown, Harpinder had been the sole proofreader and, given she was happy with it, the others were too. Louis addressed the elephant in the room, the obvious absence of Rogers, Jeff, and Elaine.

"I'm not one for speculation but what we do know is there were three scheduled flights out of Auckland that we know of, with only one currently being detected as airborne. Flight radar and satellites clearly show the C-17 Globemaster heading for Antarctica. It is highly likely that the Santiago route would have traversed the Pacific, but it's not inconceivable that it would go over the South Pole. But folks, even the C-17 trajectory is not one that would make aviation sense if the destination was central Chile." They all knew what Louis was implying and it was Nancy Rastik who provided the conclusive proof.

"Hi everyone. The team at the research base here have taken over Australasian air traffic control with Auckland going down and the East Coast about to get hit hard. They've had verbal confirmation from Captain Shaskins on the C-17 that Jeff Henderson and Elaine Brennan are the only civilian passengers, and they were the only aircraft to make it airborne before the North Island event. They have first-hand video accounts of the land implosion and will upload once grounded in McMurdo within four hours. Spare a thought for Chester, may God rest his soul." A poignant moment, juxtaposed with the elation felt by Pete and Jane knowing their good friends were alive, not yet knowing how they were only seconds away from suffering the same gruesome fate as PR man Rogers and almost four million North Islanders.

71

McMurdo Station, Antarctica

In a cruel twist of fate, which had not been shared with the group, although Nancy Rastik had been informed, was that the C-17 carrying Jeff and Elaine was actually scheduled to continue on from Antarctica to none other than Santiago. Although this wasn't known at take-off, and the crew had not been yet informed, the largest share of researchers currently at the McMurdo Research Station were Chilean nationals. All the station staff had been given the option to stay on site with the potential long-term implications outlined in a very honest briefing session explaining the Masai Events, or alternatively return home to, or via, Santiago. Such was the affirmative response that Chilean government immediately charted a plane to head south to repatriate their nationals all 375 of them. The C-17 would then carry the 150 non-Chilean research and support staff.

As this news filtered through to the cockpit of the Globemaster via Wing Commander Clements, Elaine immediately blurted out as much to herself than in need of an answer. "Are we going to be there all alone?"

Captain Shaskins was familiar with the base having been stationed there many years ago. "No Elaine don't worry. There'll be around a hundred of you. At this stage we obviously can't be clear of the split of research and support staff but given the circumstances, I'd imagine everyone will have to do their bit. And you've got the guys through there, of course," he said, pointing back through the cockpit door.

Ever the pragmatist, Jeff chimed in. "Well, it'll mean the stores will last longer, I guess. We don't know how long we'll be there for."

Captain Shaskins nodded. "True Jeff, true. Once the cargo ship arrives from Concón, you'll be set for life. No need to go penguin hunting." Jeff threw a mocking sad face at Elaine. But really, he had very little desire to either eat a penguin or hunt one down and kill it for food. He was more than happy with eating canned goods for the remainder of his existence.

The ice runway at Williamsfield is the principal airfield in Antarctica and serves both McMurdo station and New Zealand's Scott base. The latter was closing, with all personnel either relocating to McMurdo or leaving for Santiago. Captain Shaskins was a frequent flyer to the pole and usually and understandably frequently fielded questions about the condition of the icy runway versus a tarmac one. Jeff and Elaine did not bother him with such queries. They understood it was not their area of expertise to worry about. And with good reason, the eight metres of heavy, compacted snow made landing on it feel much like landing on concrete. And the Globemaster touched ground with minimal bounce or disturbance. Both Captain Shaskins and Wing Commander Clements wished Jeff and Elaine the best as they alighted the giant aircraft. Their journeys were only part-complete and the following day they'd be evacuating to Chile those who had chosen not to stay put on the ice.

73

Jeff and Elaine were met on the ground by the researcher assigned to integrate them, a very youthful looking Japanese lady, who introduced herself as Scarlet Haku.

"Very pleased to welcome you to McMurdo Station. I'm sorry your visit here is due to such unpleasant circumstances."

"I think we can all agree to that Scarlet, lovely to meet you. Our aim, with your help I'm sure, is to find a way through and fingers crossed we're in the best place on the planet from which to do this." Elaine replied with a warm smile. She felt relieved to have her feet on solid ground, despite the fact it was ice, after the trauma of what they'd witnessed on their flight. A specially adapted 4x4 was waiting for Jeff and Elaine, the rest of the crew would follow later. Scarlet saw them both looking at their phones expecting messages to come flooding through as per usual after a long flight.

"No mobile data here I'm afraid. Once we get on base, we have reasonable Wi-Fi for you to contact people." The first few of the fifteen or so kilometres to the research station was taken in silence with Jeff and Elaine marvelling at the sheer white expanse of the ice sheet. Independently, both wondered how long they'd be isolated here for and, given the sparsity in every direction, equally pondered what they do to keep themselves from going insane. They'd heard about the explorer Ken Blaiklock, who reportedly spent fourteen years on Antarctica in the early 1900s and there were accounts that some of the children born at the Argentinian and Chilean bases were still living there. But pretty much if you weren't a penguin, then the longest you'd expect to be there for is about eighteen months, or two summers and a winter.

It was Elaine who broke the silence, "Is Scarlet a popular name in Japan?" She wondered if the young researcher had adopted a western moniker as so many Asians did to assimilate with the lazy, xenophobic ignorance that is predominant in white, western expat cultures.

"I'm the only one I know, but I bet there are many more. My parents were huge fans of the film 'Lost in Translation' which featured Scarlett Johansson, so much so they named me after her, but dropped a T to make it slightly different."

"Don't tell me your middle name is Bill or Murray?" Jeff chimed in. He was also a fan of Scarlett Johansson, but for reasons aside her filmography.

"You guessed it," replied Scarlet.

"No way?" Jeff replied disbelievingly.

"No, you're right, my middle name is Chinatsu. It means 'a thousand summers', but I'm pretty sure if I were a boy or had younger brother, one of us would be called Bill, they really were obsessed with the film."

"It was a great film," added Jeff, "and it's nice to have a story about your name. I'll never know what led my parents to call me Jeffrey. It's just about OK now I'm middle aged, but at school, Jeff was not considered cool, which I'm sure surprises you, Elaine."

"Well, I'm living in the wrong century for my name, Jeff, should we just change them now? No one here knows us. What do you reckon? I quite fancy being called Aurora or Luna."

"Oh, can I be Blade? No Chase. No Jet. No Hunter. No Audi. No Horse. No Stallion. No Hawk."

"Let's stick to Elaine and Jeff for now. Maybe if we live through this, we can celebrate by changing our names."

"Good plan," Jeff agreed, and Scarlet thought better than to offer an opinion. She just kept her eyes on the road but was clearly giggling to herself.

Bringing the conversation back to a version of normality, Elaine questioned Scarlet, given that she was at most twenty years of age.

"What brings you to Antarctica, Scarlet? I'm assuming you were already stationed here before we arrived?"

"Yes, Elaine, I have been here for five months now, I am part of a project run by the United States Antarctica Programme, they sponsor two annual placements at the Department of Aquatic Bioscience at the University of Tokyo."

"Wow, congratulations Scarlet, that sounds very impressive, what's the focus of your placement here?"

"I don't spend a great deal of time in the field, I'm a bit of a, how do you say, nerd? A computer geek."

"That sounds more negative than it should Scarlet, we are both scientists at heart, and that is not geeky in our eyes."

"I understand, sorry for my English, I do love what I do, looking for patterns in the weekly marine centres to establish sustainability thresholds for the penguins and mammals which inhabit Antarctica. One day, I hope to write all about it, but for now, I must work on the data processing." Scarlet was not used to being asked about herself, it was very un-Japanese, and she wasn't sure how to deal with it, but Elaine was genuinely interested, so probed further, she'd taken quite a shine to this young, smart researcher from Tokyo. Plus, it was a nice distraction from thinking about what else was going on across the world.

"You're a writer too Scarlet?"

"Oh no," the Japanese blushed and looked away shyly. "One day, maybe, but for now, I have my focus."

Elaine gave her space to continue, feeling there was more in it. She was right, Scarlet continued, "At high school. I always either had my nose in a book, I think that's how you say it, or my fingers on a piano but I had the most inspirational Mathematics teacher who changed my view on the world and, from that point on, I've been focused on using the skills and thinking techniques he taught me to change the world for the better. Sorry, I know how crazy that sounds, but he was like a sensei to me, a mentor you guys would say, he gave me a path to follow, and Maths, then science led me to here."

"Scarlet, he sounds like an amazing influence, I'm sure he'd be proud you've been selected to be part of this programme."

"Thank you. Elaine, I hope so, once I have fulfilled this destiny and we get out of here, I shall move to the south of France and become a journalist."

"Scarlet, I love it, good for you." Elaine was taken back vividly to the moment she chose what she thought was love for Mark over her love for science. She'd barely given him a moment's thought once she packed her bags and left Johor Bahru to join Pete in Berlin. Even the news that the Southern Malay Peninsula was one of the first land masses to collapse, did not drag up even an ounce of regret, at least not for him. And she was trying her damnedest not to dwell on the lost years when she effectively turned her back on a promising career in the sciences. Or any career for that matter. In that moment, as they quietly traversed through the bleak majesty of the polar ice, she glanced at the young, impressionable Japanese researcher and vicariously felt the world of possibility Scarlet had in front of her. She was snapped out of her daydream, not by the obscene reality of their current predicament, but by the braking of the jeep in front of the army barrack style buildings of McMurdo Station.

Given the impending exodus from the remote station, accommodation for Jeff and Elaine was more homely than either had been expecting. Although the support staff preparing for their, and others' arrival, had advanced informal notice that the two appeared to be entering an intimate relationship, their quarters did not reflect this, and their two-bedroom lodgings were essentially self-contained with separate kitchen and living spaces. And it certainly impressed Elaine, who feared a life of bunk beds and shared bathrooms. As they entered the apartment, Scarlet told them to take an hour or so to make themselves at home and passed them the Wi-Fi code and what was essentially a welcome pack, detailing the amenities and activities on the base. Scarlet informed them, as opposed to asking them, to brief the remaining researchers and site staff in the mess room.

So, as Scarlet succinctly put it, "we kill the rumours of misinformation."

"Sounds good," Elaine responded. "See you in an hour."

Before she left them, Scarlet explained that in the coming days, they would be fully kitted out with clothes, toiletries, and furnishings. The two had travelled light and understood there was a great deal of upheaval at the station as resource was redeployed following the mass departure of a whole range of staff.

"There are clothes in the wardrobe and some basics in the bathroom, I'm sure that will keep you going for a while until we get settled again." No hint of an apology from Scarlet. She was polite but this was not a hotel and Jeff and Elaine had no airs or graces to that extent.

"Thank you, Scarlet, and to whomever has organised this so quickly. We really appreciate it," said Jeff humbly and genuinely as he closed the door and turned to Elaine.

"You want first choice on bedrooms roomie?"

"Jeff, I was kind of hoping we'd be sharing," replied Elaine, half embarrassed, half provocative.

"I was also hoping you'd say that," he grinned and gave her a long lingering kiss which made her heart flutter and be thankful that, despite the circumstances, she'd been given a second chance of happiness. She half expected Jeff to take her straight to the bedroom and was a little frustrated he didn't, instead he went into action mode, which she admitted to herself was probably a better use of their time. Especially if they were to be talking to the whole corps in an hour.

74

As soon as their phones locked onto the McMurdo Wi-Fi, a slew of messages and mails arrived, the most pressing of which were from their friends in Berlin, awaiting an update on their very survival. Under other contexts, Jeff would have sent a selfie of proof, but given the implication that theirs was the only plane to have left Auckland, it was clear that Chester Rogers, along with millions of other unknowns, had perished. As Pete and Jane's phones alerted simultaneously to the messages from Jeff, their relief was palpable. They'd known pretty much for sure they were safely on board the flight from Auckland, but the confirmation they'd arrived at the South Pole permitted a rare moment of joy and precipitated an unexpected embrace between them in the Berlin flat. Both Pete and Jane allowed the hug to linger slightly longer than the spontaneity suggested, each enjoying the comfort and security of physical touch, hands loitering, chests exchanging the calmness of the other's breathing, cheeks brushing tenderly. Much like the solidarity Elaine and Jeff were feeling ten thousand miles away, in that moment of joyous relief, Pete and Jane exchanged unspoken commitments to each other in a way words can only clumsily confuse.

Jeff and Elaine finally checked and responded to their key personal messages, painfully aware of their inaccessibility, geographically and virtually, meaning they could not offer meaningful help to friends nor family, aside from wishing them luck and advising to prepare for the worst. Easy to say when you're isolated from bordering on all humanity with plentiful supplies and secure lodgings, plus, if the models were accurate, security under foot too.

Just glimpsing at the rolling news on the sitting room TV gave Jeff and Elaine a reality check on the mayhem spreading across the world. After quick, refreshing hot showers, and clothing themselves in the army style fatigues left for them until they could be more appropriately kitted out, Jeff and Elaine focused on bulleting the information they needed to share with the station personnel. They were far from in command of them, but clearly someone had given them leadership status and, given all the turmoil and panic evacuations, Jeff could understand why they'd been asked to bring everyone left up to speed. He expected there to be a lot of intelligent, progressive, but ultimately frightened scientists, biologists and non-specialist support staff looking for some kind of clarity to steady their nerves. Thankfully, Louis Charles had issued a briefing statement after the check-in call that took place whilst the C-17 was mid-flight. And, amidst the utter decimation of large areas of the lithosphere, there were titbits of positivity to share with the McMurdo remainers.

75

The Shanghai Research Centre was China's foremost centre for the development and application of artificial intelligence software and Chairman Guo had decreed that all non-essential AI projects be cancelled, and full processing power was to be dedicated to establishing a discernible and conclusive predictability of the events ravaging Earth. In this new spirit of openness, the Chinese had given access to the AI software to the core team, including Louis Charles' colleagues back in Houston, now led by Tanya James, given Louis' relocation to Shanghai, and Kelly Chan and Rose Carmichael, who remained in Tokyo. Plus, it gave Pete, Jane, Elaine, and Jeff additional resource to plug in their own hypotheses, as and when they developed them. Albeit mightily unfair and unfounded, there was a Hail Mary hope that Professor Masai might pluck some form of solution out of the madness, something which he also backed himself privately to achieve. The main slice of good news for Team McMurdo was there had been no further evidence to suggest the South Pole would not escape the events. No murmurings or tremors from ground activated sensors had been detected, which meant it was the planet's only region to have reported no material disturbance in the past month or so. As Jeff explained to the gathering in the mess hall, this didn't mean complacency about their survival, as ultimately it could lead them to being cut off indefinitely, but it did potentially mean they could plan longer term than those in more precarious regions of the world, namely anywhere except Antarctica.

Following Jeff's briefing to the hundred or so remaining McMurdians, as long-term residents were inclined to call themselves, he and Elaine had to field a great many and varied questions from the floor as expected. Some accused him directly and indirectly as being a conspiracy theorist, to which Jeff responded by uploading his phone camera data to the nearest laptop and connecting it to the giant TV-cum-projector screen. Unless he had somehow doctored footage and added a fake timestamp on it in the past few hours, which some still believed, the recording showed the North Island collapse in all its brutal horror, to the gasps of the audience. One researcher asked about the end game geologically, something Pete had discussed with them back in Tokyo when it became clear water levels were going down dramatically.

"Great question." He paused to elicit her name.

"Ellie," replied the petite blonde lady who'd posed the question.

"Bear with, as this is clearly a work-in-progress answer, as we don't yet know when, or if, the lithospheric events will cease. But an attempt to answer is this; we know water is disappearing beneath the Earth's surface, which is going to lead to significant climate distress on a number of levels. One; ocean currents are currently a key determinant of climate and weather, two; there will be catastrophic droughts in regions where fresh water just isn't available, or rainfall can no longer be captured and contained, and three; it's important to recognise that sea levels can only go down so much, unless we either enter another ice age or water physically leaves our atmosphere, we don't know the impact these events will have on global climate in terms of temperature, but it could lead to extremes, correction, it is likely, extremely likely, to lead to extremes, but where and what we can only speculate. Also, despite the vast volume of our planet, we think it is highly improbable that it could absorb all the world's water, given we're essentially a giant rock, rather than a balloon. But a combination of seepage underground, coupled with, albeit unexpected, extremely low temperatures could lead to water being captured in the form of ice. From a topographical perspective, as we've seen thus far, Ellie, and everyone, we could see a fundamentally different version of our planet, assuming there is indeed a period of sustained geological calm. Coupled with lower sea levels, we will literally have to redraw the map of the world. The long and short of it is, we just don't know. And, to answer a question I was asked before I stood up here to talk to you all, what I'm worried about is the not knowing. The certainty is life can be unpredictable, I get that, but most things are actually relatively certain, even in our previously changing world. With all this, these cataclysmic, epoch-defining events, we're entering a period with a 'when will it happen?' mentality. And sure, we feel safer than most down here, but being here forever, waiting for an event, is that it? Sadly, we can only prove something like this when it happens. So, gloves off, that's my worry, uncertainty and isolation. You guys are smart people, and I'm not here to tell you everything's going to be okay, but I'll do my damnedest to make sure it is. It may not be long until we're cut off from the outside world, as the Earth's surface caves in, undersea cables, terrestrial fibre optic lines, basically the physical infrastructure which underpins internet and hence global connectivity, could all lead to us being thrown back a couple of hundred years." Elaine threw a look at Jeff to imply he needed to end on a more positive note. "But of course, on the flip side, which is equally likely at this stage, is that the Earth stabilises, and we get the chance to rebuild, maybe even redefine humanity. If this is what it takes for reset, then we'd better make the most of it. I say."

"Better," whispered Elaine.

After a further half hour of general milling around meeting and greeting a mix of McMurdians, Scarlet escorted them out of the hall and gave them a tour of their new home. They passed a couple of huge empty storage facilities, which Scarlet explained had been cleared, ready for the arrival of the supplies vessel due any day now.

"We're still consuming juice powder that's ten years expired," Scarlet exclaimed proudly. "Nothing is wasted down here on the ice."

"My mantra every meal Scarlet," joked Jeff.

Unsure if it was just a coincidence or the young Japanese researcher's sense of humour peeking through, but she seamlessly pointed out where the station gym was located, much to Elaine's amusement and Jeff's chagrin. Their chat was interrupted by a short sharp high-pitched alarm that rang around the station buildings, bringing a look of concern to Jeff and Elaine's faces, fearing it to be an advance warning of some kind of impending problem. Scarlet looked less concerned and calmly told them for the past six months, whenever internet connectivity went down, the alarm would ring to notify everyone.

"Sometimes, speeds can get very slow so they use the alarm, more of a notification than alarm, so we can tell what is merely online congestion and what's just not going to work." That didn't make Jeff feel any better and Elaine picked up on his tension.

"Doesn't the satellite feed for communications get relayed via Sydney?" Elaine instantly realised what Jeff was intimating. "We need to get back inside right away to the comms centre."

75

They scuttled to another nondescript, grey shed-like building about one hundred metres away and entered the cold porch, essentially a double door airlock protecting the building from the icy conditions. They quickly removed their boots, jackets and gloves and made their way purposefully to what was the nerve centre of the base. NASA it was not, but to Jeff and Elaine's untrained eyes, it seemed pretty well kitted out and, as the brilliantly named comms officer Dave Dobbin proudly announced, ironically given the evolving state of affairs, that his core team had opted to stay on base. The predicament, as Jeff and Elaine had feared, was the mega tsunami having made land on the Australian East Coast, pictures of which were broadcasting on the several screens in the room. It didn't take an expert in any field to know what they were witnessing was going to wipe out pretty much everything for several kilometres inland, up and down, approximately one thousand kilometres of heavily populated coastline. Critically, for McMurdo, what it did mean was the obliteration of the communications network feeding the base, and the subsequent online status of the whole site. Elaine and Jeff were becoming emotionally immune to the horrors of the Masai Events by necessity, rather than callousness and, as their pained eyes linked, there was a tacit feeling of solidarity, as if this were the moment their isolation would begin. They both felt it, and it was much sooner than either had predicted, even amidst the uncertainties around them.

It was Scarlet who spoke first. "Dave, haven't we got back up for this, surely there's another route or satellite feed?"

"You'd be right in normal circumstances, Scarlet, but these are far from fucking normal circumstances." Dave

DROUGHT

Dobbin was angry, he was powerless, and he knew everyone would be, at him, constantly asking him how to get online again. And he had nothing. At that moment, he wished he'd left on that flight to Santiago, not yet knowing that moments after landing, a massive event would take down the Chilean capital and airport with it. But that's the thing with the regrets, you never really get to know what might have happened. And that can be tough to deal with, especially for a proud man like comms officer Dobbin. His professional raison d'etre was moments from being washed away by the tsunami.

Gathering himself to address Scarlet, Jeff and Elaine properly and professionally he filled in the gaps. "We closed the Starlink affiliation earlier on this year, and the voice communications hub in Colorado has been wiped out too. We also believe, make that know, sorry, that whatever global communication links were still active are now massively impacted by deep ocean disturbances cause. Irreparable ruptures in the transatlantic and transpacific cables and a whole host of intercontinental fibre optics have been destroyed. I'm afraid Jeff, you may have been pretty close to nailing it earlier in the mess hall, we are all alone down here now, we've got to pray that container ship gets here unscathed, or we're in a world of trouble."

"Hope you've got a load of DVDs down here then." Jeff gambled on trying to lighten the mood; it failed.

"Got ourselves a comedian, have we?" remarked Dobbins snidely. Jeff made a mental note to keep well away from the comms officer.

Elaine intervened, very aware emotions were running high in the room and suggested they all head back to their quarters to reflect on what had happened and what it might mean. Scarlet agreed, but only after getting new worst-of-friends comms officer Dobbin and Jeff to jointly address the site community after evening supper.

"They will only find you and your team and keep asking questions about Wi-Fi Dave, so let's get it out there for people to deal with and support them because I think they'll find it hard to get their heads around. A lot of the guys, like me, have grown up with the internet being part of their life, a human right to be connected to the world, so the implications of it going out of their lives could lead to some significant mental health and grieving issues." Elaine was so impressed by the maturity and wisdom of the young Japanese researcher, she was strong and clearly developing into quite the leader, and leadership is exactly what McMurdo Station was going to need.

76

Jeff and Elaine walked back to their apartment in silence, their thick gloves linked together giving them both a much-needed emotional boost as they contemplated not just the next few hours, but the rest of their lives. Without the container ship, they'd be out of food within three years and suddenly that felt like a short deadline, but as both Scarlet and Dobbin had said, the likelihood of the cargo pilot turning back to a country that had just experienced a traumatic event was slim, so chances are, unless the ocean claimed her, the vessel would be docking as scheduled within forty-eight hours.

The situation they were facing was by no means fatal, but there was the feeling of last rites about their predicament in that the finality of human contact that was now upon them. They would not want for food, at least sustenance, but they'd for sure missed out on a final communication to loved ones and colleagues, both the same in some cases. It's a morbid thought, pondering what you'd say if you had one last call, text, or email to share. Who would it be with? How could you decide the person with whom you'd share your very last remote communication? The Blackout, as it was to be referred to on base, had materialised sooner than expected, 'expected' being the key word so on reflection, it was sooner than Elaine, Jeff, or any of them had really planned for.

Jeff wondered if it was a blessing in disguise, as it precipitated a sense of togetherness, a siege mentality that the lingering and probably intermittent contact from around the world would prevent. The painful quandary that absence of contact from a loved one could be due to infrastructure issues or simply death would be emotionally impossible to deal with. Now that uncertainty had been taken away and replaced by a certainty of not knowing, meant hope could override fear. But it didn't change the missed opportunity and, for some, abiding regret that the sudden loss of comms meant no final goodbyes, good lucks and I love yous. The silence was palpable, but as Jeff and Elaine discovered when they got back to their phones, it wasn't total oblivion. Thankfully they'd both left their phones on charge and, crucially, connected whilst on walkabout and this meant the messages sent in that time were fully downloaded on there for eternity. Much to their relief and excitement, there was a typically forward thinking, extensive email from Pete in Berlin, accompanied by a photo of the two of them, grinning inanely with a sun-drenched Tiergarten in the background. Even Jeff welled up, knowing this would be the last time he'd hear from his friend of twenty years. Elaine simply burst into tears. They both needed a good cry to let out the emotions of the past few weeks, embracing passionately, sealing their union, and steeling themselves for their impending seclusion. Once the emotion pared back, the two were able to digest the contents of Pete's unexpectedly long email. The tears still rolled down both their cheeks, but this time they were accompanied by broad smiles, much like those beaming in the final photo from Berlin.

"Of course, he knew this was going to happen," Jeff semi-spoke, still choked up with emotion. "That's our Pete for you, one step ahead of the rest of us." They both fell silent as they read through the text, which Peter had sent to them both allowing them to digest it at their own speed.

77

 Dearest Elaine and the Mighty Jeff, this may be sent from me, but it really is from the both of us all the way up here in sunny, and currently stable, Berlin. Jane, being Jane, the amazing mind that she is, did a little background research on your icy home from home, and with Colorado in ruins and this dreadful mega tsunami on its way to poor defenceless Australia, we struggled to see how we'll be able to contact you in a matter of days but maybe even hours. I'm sure the comms team on base are fully aware global communications infrastructure is on its knees but, as you'll have read, or will read from Louis, the mantle disintegration has caused some form of atmospheric distortion that has disabled satellite internet connectivity too. Just like we spoke about together, get your horses and candles out, we're going back in time folks. As Jeff read it, he was reminded how even the bleakest circumstances can be addressed with such a glass half full mentality, this was classic Pete. If Wally was a glimmer of hope hiding in a mass of misery and pain, Pete would find him straight away.

 So now we have no phones, no internet, no TV and, such is our reliance on technology, core global infrastructure will quickly collapse. Utility companies will cease output, fuel stations will run dry, supermarkets and general retail will simply grind to a halt, unable to acquire supply or charge for goods. The LSE, NASDAQ, NYSE, Frankfurt, Hong Kong, Shanghai, and Tokyo Stock Exchanges are winding up, banks have closed their doors, as much for the safety of their employees as due to the inevitable run for cash. I'm told by Jane, the wise sage, that the technical term for what's happening up here is, verbatim et literatim: "total fucking anarchy". We're a bit jealous of your igloo, it would be a lie to say otherwise. Before we get on to the plan, might as well unload the rest of the bad tidings. Forgive me if you've got all this already, it feels a lot has happened in the last few dark hours, quicker than we'd imagined. As if it needed clarifying, we're not hoping for the world's demise, just if it's going to happen, a little forewarning would be appreciated, and I'll come on to this. Santiago has gone, almost all the way across to Mendoza in Argentina, the scale of the land collapses is mind-boggling, I refuse to call them Masai Events. Colorado you know, Washington DC an hour ago, RIP Senator, RIP President Franks, Georgia, RIP Augusta National (you know I love the Masters), a huge swathe of Africa is now underwater. Interestingly, coastal regions are most affected across that majestic continent, have made a note to look into that, Australia and NZ you clearly know about and thank you for uploading the North Island footage, harrowing yet fascinating.

"You reading this Jeff? How does he switch between cracking deeply dark jokes to being so matter of fact?" Elaine was blown away by Pete's news and realised how desensitised he, and Jane, must feel to be in the eye of the storm, knowing that at any moment their world might suddenly collapse.

"Same answer as ever, Elaine. That's Pete." They read on, reverting to silence as if simultaneously reading the final chapter of a novel.

The biggest news I'm afraid, although with the likely lack of means to communicate it, I guess it's largely irrelevant from some perspectives, is the loss of the Shanghai research facility in China's worst scale disturbance to date. Poor Louis and Penn went downward with twenty-five million others. Although it feels crass to single out two in such a monstrous loss of life, I wonder if Stalin had a point, however misguided, that the death of a man, in this case two men is a tragedy, the death of a million, make that twenty-five million, is a statistic. And we've been building up quite a bank of statistics, all of which means unimaginable tragedy. Whether Stalin said it or not, Jane has told me to add that disclaimer, (side note, I think we'll get on just fine here), we have taken a moment to remember our fallen colleagues. I'm sure you'll find time to do the same. Chester Rogers, Louis Charles, Dr Penn, President Franks, and the legend of Senator Gordon. I acknowledge we're unlikely to reconvene again but so far, the UK and North Germany are unaffected, as is Tokyo still we believe. So, for us, Harpinder, Penny, Michelle, Monty, Tanya, Prime Minister Keeble, Rose, Kelly, even Nancy in the Outback, we are all still head above water, so to speak. We're not certain if Guo was in Shanghai and we assume Zarkov is safe for now in Moscow, especially after St Petersburg went under. And we mustn't forget poor Marco, if anyone deserves to survive this, it's him bless his naïve cotton socks. As far as we know, Mexico City is still standing firm and long may it remain so.

Now, Jeff, Elaine, I'm assuming you're reading this together, If, you're not you should do. Jeff and Elaine exchanged glances, confirming they were reading at the same pace. *If we're right, and as you well know, we have a track record of being right, check out exhibit a) the almost total destruction of planet Earth, then you guys are in the safest place of all. Cherish it, you could be there a while. And cherish each other, isolation will be a strange bedfellow, and soon you'll be plunged into actual as well as virtual blackness, so look after each other and those who aren't as strong as you on the base. Never, and we mean it, never give up hope. Humans saw out the Ice Age, mammoths and sabre tooth tigers did not, we always find a way, and you can bet your bottom dollar, we will throw ourselves into finding a way out of this mess. I went over our historical Everest notes in search of geoscientific inspiration on the flight home, and there were some potential clues in that theory which are surprisingly appropriate to apply to this current geological turmoil. I'm kicking myself for not having thought about this before. Jane gets to enjoy all this for the first time, but you guys are well versed in my dabbles in asthenospheric flows. Jeff will no doubt say again, it's too far down to have an impact on the lithosphere. But think about it, the molten, semi-fluid rock would have been hyper-agitated by the* core's expansion and the very, I previously thought theoretical, collection of this highly pressurised rock mixture under the Himalayas would accelerate Everest's already speedy growth but apply that to what we have happening right here right now. We know tectonic plates move on the asthenosphere's convection currents and yet we have largely dismissed classic tectonic disturbances as being the primary cause for all these land collapses, and I still subscribe to that. But think about it, guys.* Pete wrote in such a conversational style it was easy to get carried along with the flow given their familiarity with Pete's early Everest work, however fantastical, both Jeff and Elaine were in little doubt there'd be some truth in this new theory. Elaine put her own phone down and scooched next to Jeff on the bed, and they read the rest together.

We already have a hundred or so sites where the crust has given way and over half are not within hundred miles of a tectonic border. So, what Jane and I will be focusing on is deep diving into everything we've got on both the thickness of the crust in the critical hot spots, but also stable areas like the UK, northern Germany/Poland and the like and overlay the subterranean volume, depth, and speed of asthenosphere rock flows. At least that's our current plan, and Jane is busy downloading and storing as much of the Shanghai and Houston data as she can for when we all go offline. With a fair wind behind us, and a sprinkling of fortune from our scorned Mother Nature, I hope this is not as final as it feels, but within a very short time frame we're facing the abyss and you know very well we are abyss people. That's where we thrive. So, Jeff, Elaine, keep warm, be kind to each other and the penguins, stay positive, procreate, live life, be patient and most importantly keep a bottle or two beers aside for you and me Jeff. Jane is right here with me now and tells me to say "hi, not bye and I love you both". I'm all over that. This is not done yet.

And with that, Jeff put the phone on the bed and breathed out a huge sigh, half processing the enormity of

Pete's words but half steadying himself for what was to come. He grasped Elaine's shaking hand, she turned to him, tears forming again in her already red eyes.

78

"Do you really think that's it now Jeff? That's the last we'll see or hear from them? It feels so final, I'm so scared for them Jeff, what do you think really, honestly?" Jeff paused for a moment in consideration and delicately kissed his college sweetheart on her cheek, tasting her tears which continue to roll down the sides of Elaine's face.

"Never in my wildest dreams did I think we'd end up together again so for one, I'm so happy whatever the circumstances that you are here with me now and if there's one thing I also know, is in that both of our wildest dreams, we'd be crazy to doubt the resourcefulness and sheer mad genius of Peter Masai."

Elaine broke out into a smile but couldn't stop the tears, but this time they felt like tears of a renewed optimism, and she resolved in that moment to look forward not backward.

"I do hope you're right Jeff." They embraced in a long, emotional hug, silently enjoying each other's love and companionship, neither wanting to let go, as if they could cocoon themselves as one for eternity. A bold knock at their door brought them both back to reality and, with a dry of the eyes and a couple of deep breaths, they rose together.

"That'll be Scarlet to take us to the mess all for the second briefing." Jeff was first to speak.

"OK, Jeff, let's do this. This is our home now, I'm accepting of that, let's make the most of it whilst we can." She managed another smile.

"To use a great man's words, I'm all over that." Jeff sounded similarly upbeat. "This is not done yet."

Epilogue

Antarctica - many years later……

"Dad, who is The Senator Gordon?" the young blond boy asked.

"Well, that's a name we've not mentioned for a long time hey, Elaine?"

"No, indeed, Jeff."

"So, Dad, Mum, who is it, is he real?" This time the question came from an even younger girl, with rose red cheeks and long, but slightly matted, strawberry blonde hair.

"Let's get you two properly inside with a hot drink. You always stay out for too long with those penguins, don't you?" Elaine's scolding was only mild, she loved how their children would go out and almost play with the penguins on the colony, which had moved only a few hundred metres from the base, given the receding ice.

"Well kids," Jeff said proudly, "before the Blackout we were in a team of great scientists and geologists."

"Geologists study the materials, processes, products, physical nature and history of the Earth," the girl said enthusiastically.

"That's my girl!" Jeff beamed as his son rolled his eyes, although he too was a budding scientist in the making.

"And the man who brought us all together was a very kind, very intelligent, and very honourable man called Edward Gordon and he was a Senator, which meant he was a high-ranking politician in the United States."

"So, a bit like Scarlet is here at McMurdo?"

"A little bit I guess yes darling, in that she's kind of in charge here."

Elaine jumped in, "Why do you ask Son?"

Jeff and Elaine had made a conscious decision to be selective about the events leading up to their isolation in Antarctica eighteen years ago, waiting until their children were old enough, at least mature enough, to deal with the significance of the catastrophe. They knew of course from all the books and videos on base what the world was like before they were born, but so far they had only been told a sanitised version of events, given their boy was eleven and his sister nine. Jeff simply assumed one of the guys on base had mentioned Gordon's name.

"The big boat on the other side of the penguins Dad," the boy said casually.

"What?" Jeff asked bluntly, as if he'd misheard.

"The boat. I saw it too." His daughter added.

"Do you mean a picture of a boat you've seen somewhere on their base?" Jeff pressed his kids.

"No Daddy, the big boat in the sea by the penguins. It says 'The Senator Gordon' in big gold writing on it. A lovely wooden boat, like the ones in the Spanish armadillo book." Elaine suppressed her instinct to correct her young, precocious daughter because, like Jeff, she was mentally scrambling to make sense of what their children were saying.

"Will you take us out and show us?" Elaine asked calmly, simply assuming their imagination had taken over so them all going out on the ice would bring it to a close and they could all laugh about it. Although, she did concede to herself it was a pretty specific thing to be making up. Despite his ageing years, Jeff sprang up and helped the kids get back into their ice-protecting outdoor gear they'd only just removed, and speedily put on his own jacket, boots, and gloves and prized open the cold porch airlock door to the freezing outside. They headed out west from the main base, passing the mess hall where they still attended weekly gatherings, which started with Jeff's announcement all those years ago, around the gym complex, to which Jeff was now a frequent and willing visitor and out beyond the storage sheds, one of which had been emptied, having been stocked full to the brim by the Chilean cargo ship which indeed arrived as planned a couple of days after the full Blackout began. They had had about four hundred metres to walk to get to the penguin colony. The birds had made a base on a raised area of compacted snow from an abandoned lookout mound the McMurdians made about ten years prior, to give them a better vantage point to search the horizon for potential visitors or rescuers. When none came, they left it to nature and, given the encroaching ice shelf due to accelerated climate change, the penguins had claimed it, much to the delight of all the children born on base in the intervening years. Taking a circuitous route to avoid disturbing the penguins, despite their rush to get to the edge of the ice, it took only around ten minutes to get to a place where their now very animated young lad started pointing and shouting.

"There it is Daddy, I told you so, we weren't lying." Jeff had been so focused on the penguin colony he wasn't looking ahead of him and, if he were honest, thought this whole escapade was going to be fun but ultimately a total waste of time.

"OK Son, show me," and he crouched down by his boy and followed his outstretched arm. "Oh my goodness Son, Elaine look."

"I'm seeing it, Jeff. I'm seeing it," Elaine screeched. She almost couldn't breathe with anticipation. There, in front of them, a few hundred feet off the coast, glinting in the Antarctic sunshine was, as their daughter had so accurately described, a galleon with huge billowing white sails attached to a thick wooden mast atop a majestic oak constructed keel, emblazoned with the crystal-clear gilded wording 'THE SENATOR GORDON.'

"Mummy, why are you crying? Daddy are you okay?" Jeff and Elaine knew this could only mean one thing.

"He bloody did it!" Jeff bellowed. The ship was close enough to the shore that Jeff could make out there were crew members aboard, looking out and back towards them. There were at least ten people that Jeff and Elaine could see but their eyes were drawn to two unmistakable faces they'd resigned themselves to never seeing again.

Thirty minutes later, the galleon's clearly very competent skipper had pulled the vessel alongside the ice shelf and secured it enough for the crew to disembark. First off was a beaming yet weather-beaten Peter Masai, white beard tangled across his face looking every part the sixty-year-old explorer he was. Behind him, holding his hand was Jane, whose tears masked her overwhelming delight at finally finding their long-lost friends.

Jeff played it cool, but he was delirious. "Pete, glad you could make it. Jane lovely to see you again." They all embraced in a manic, passionate four-way hug. As they broke away, further passengers disembarked, most entirely unknown to Jeff and Jane but then a few faces, despite the twenty-odd years of ageing, who were familiar to them.

"Oh yeah, we stopped off in London and collected some old friends. And before you say it, she's not Prime Minister anymore. Simply Ruth." Former UK PM Ruth Keeble was followed off the ship by Penny Norton, Michelle Grant and Monty Symonds.

"What took you so long Pete, last I heard you had some plan around floating tectonics, please tell me Everest is a hundred miles high now?"

"Ha probably," Pete laughed a laugh he'd been looking forward to for years. "Well, we needed to wait for these guys to be old enough to travel." Jane beckoned over two almost identical looking children, mainly due to the amount of clothes they were wearing but also because they were clearly twins.

"Oh my God, you, you know, wow!" Elaine couldn't quite get the words out.

"This is Jeffrey Junior, and this is our beautiful daughter Elaine."

"Well kids, it's amazing to meet you and we are so happy to see your mum and dad again. Welcome to Antarctica, don't worry, we have lovely snuggly beds, heating, and plenty of food." The twins grinned at the very thought of some home comforts.

Jeff looked over his shoulder and beckoned his own children to his side. "I can't believe I'm saying this guys," he addressed his kids, "but here are the awesome people who you've been named after. Pete and Jane, meet Peter and Jane."

"No way!" exclaimed Peter in comedy delight.

Jane senior was the first to talk. "Did I hear you mention proper beds and heating, please tell me that includes a hot shower?"

"Sure does, let's go and show you the base and get you warm, dry and full of canned food." Jeff signalled for everyone to follow them back around the penguins and back towards the base.

The thirty or so of them trudged across the ice in an orderly line, headed by reunited friends Jeff and Pete.

"I, we, have so many questions. I would say I can't believe you're here, but we always kept a part of our minds open to the idea that you are mad enough to pull off something like this."

Pete just smiled, he figured he had time to tell Jeff, Elaine, and whoever else, their incredible story of solving the riddle of mapping the events and plotting a course through what was left of the oceans in a resurrected galleon from Hamburg, across Europe and down past what used to be Africa, and on to find his best mate on a diminishing block of ice at the South Pole.

"Told you geologists are the new rock stars," was all he said. The two men walked side by side back through the McMurdo buildings toward the main living quarters. As everyone squeezed into the cold porch to disrobe before entering the relative luxury of a static, non-floating, heated building, Jeff told Pete to wait a moment. He headed across to the window of his and Elaine's apartment, knelt down in front of the outer wall and started scraping the snow away until he found what he was looking for. Pete looked on, intrigued, at least momentarily distracted from the enticing warmth he was about to enjoy. Jeff came back over carrying a shoe box sized metal case and handed it to Pete.

"Open it." It was a bit fiddly with his thick gloves, but Pete managed to unhinge the clasp and lift the lid, revealing another box inside on which Jeff had written 'Pete and Jeff's beers'.

"I've been looking forward to these for twenty years, Pete."

"Jeff my friend, so have I," and they both stepped into the now empty cold porch and closed the heavy door behind them with a loud and satisfying clunk. Ten minutes later, with their children mesmerised at their first ever sight of a television and Elaine and Jane catching up on pretty much everything, Jeff and Pete enjoyed the satisfying whoosh of the long buried, and now almost defrosted beers opening. They clashed bottles, saluted each other and took long satisfying sips.

"So then, Professor Masai, whilst I've been making snowmen, watching penguins move in down the road and reaping the benefits of physical exercise, tell me what on Earth you've been up to."

"Well Jeff, it's been one heck of a journey, get me a couple more of these and I'll tell you all about it. And if dinner's as good as I've dreamt, I'll tell you where we're all going next."

THE END

DROUGHT

DROUGHT

Printed in Great Britain
by Amazon

adc64391-c0a9-486f-b6c5-e9cb93779778R01